PRAISE FOR THE REPAIRMAN JACK
BOOKS BY F. PAUL WILSON

"*The Tomb* is one of the best all-out adventure stories I've read in years."

—Stephen King (President of the Repairman Jack fan club)

"The plot FIC WIL ue is
salty and w o ele-
vate them Wilson, F. Paul (Francis Paul) an 20
years ago, Infernal :a Repairman Jack novel *ernal*

"If you dor er but
better ong ence,
proving that Mr. Wilson is quite a storyteller."

—*The Midwest Book Review* on *Hosts*

"F. Paul Wilson is a hot writer, and his hottest, and my favorite creation, is Repairman Jack. No one does this kind of weird-meets-crime better than Wilson. Gripping, fascinating, one of a kind. That's F. Paul Wilson and Repairman Jack."

—Joe R. Lansdale

"Wilson deftly contrasts the self-imposed isolation of his vigilante hero with the forced exile of society's outcasts. . . . Wilson is unsurpassed in depicting his characters' feelings of alienation as they attempt to comprehend the cosmic forces that have misshapen their lives. . . . This one will appeal to horror aficionados and to fans of Carl Hiassen and James Lee Burke."

—*Publishers Weekly* on *Gateways*

"The latest Repairman Jack novel by F. Paul Wilson, *Infernal,* blasts into action with a (literally) shocking bang that thuds into your chest like a high-caliber bullet."

—*Atlas Magazine* on *Infernal*

"Call a plumber when the sink is clogged, the cops when you've been robbed, but he fan, it's time to call Repairm es, rat-tles, and rolls." —*Ne* *ed Air*

ALSO BY F. PAUL WILSON

REPAIRMAN JACK NOVELS

The Tomb	*Hosts*
Legacies	*The Haunted Air*
Conspiracies	*Gateways*
All the Rage	*Crisscross*

THE ADVERSARY CYCLE

The Keep	*Reborn*
The Tomb	*Reprisal*
The Touch	*Nightworld*

OTHER NOVELS

Healer	*Mirage* (with Matthew J. Costello)
Wheels Within Wheels	*Nightkill* (with Steven Spruill)
An Enemy of the State	
Black Wind	*Masque* (with Matthew J. Costello)
Dydeetown World	
The Tery	*The Christmas Thingy*
Sibs	*Sims*
The Select	*The Fifth Harmonic*
Implant	*Midnight Mass*
Deep as the Marrow	

SHORT FICTION
Soft and Others
The Barrens and Others

EDITOR
Freak Show
Diagnosis: Terminal

F. PAUL WILSON

INFERNAL

A Repairman Jack Novel

TOR®

A TOM DOHERTY ASSOCIATES BOOK
NEW YORK

This is a work of fiction. All the characters and events portrayed in this book are either products of the author's imagination or are used fictitiously.

INFERNAL

Edited by David G. Hartwell

A Tor Book
Published by Tom Doherty Associates, LLC
175 Fifth Avenue
New York, NY 10010

www.tor.com

Tor® is a registered trademark of Tom Doherty Associates, LLC.

ISBN 978-1-250-16391-2

First edition: November 2005
First mass market edition: September 2006

Printed in the United States of America

P1

for

Ethan
Hannah
Quinn
Daniel
Tess

the future

ACKNOWLEDGMENTS

Thanks to the usual crew for their editorial help on the manuscript: my wife, Mary; my editor, David Hartwell; Elizabeth Monteleone; Steven Spruill (especially Steve); and my agent, Albert Zuckerman.

Thanks, too, to all the gunnies on the repairmanjack.com Forum for their spirited and informed debate about Jack's new backup pistol. As usual, I did a little improvising along the way, so any errors in the weaponry department are mine.

Thank you, Bob Massey, for finding the Hinkley T40. It's perfect.

Additional thanks to Peter Wilson, Douglas E. Winter, and Paul Stanko for insights on legal and judicial matters, and to Ken Valentine for his tip on disabling a revolver.

MONDAY

1

Jack checked his watch: *2:30*. Dad's plane would be touching down in an hour.

"I should hit the road."

He and Gia sat in the antiquated kitchen of number eight Sutton Square, in one of the most select neighborhoods in Manhattan. The low December sun kept the room bright despite the dark cabinets and paneling.

Jack drained his Yuengling lager. He'd rediscovered the oldest working brewery in the country a few weeks ago. The name had triggered memories of summer afternoons in his backyard, his father sipping from a Yuengling between tossing him pop flies. So he'd tried it and liked it so much he'd made it his official house brew. And Gia's house brew as well, since he made sure to keep her fridge stocked with at least a six-pack.

Gia glanced at the Regulator clock from her seat across the round oak table where she sipped her tea.

"He's not due in for an hour. You've got a little time." She smiled at him. "Are you looking forward to seeing your father or not? You're hard to read on this."

He gazed at the love of his life, the mother of his unborn child. Gia seemed to thrive on her pregnancy. Jack had always thought the old saw about the "glow" of mothers-to-be was a sentimental fiction, but lately he'd had to revise that: No question, Gia glowed. Her short blond hair seemed glossier, her eyes brighter and bluer, her smiles more dazzling than ever. She was still in the warm-up she wore for her daily walks. Though nearing the end of her sixth month, she looked like other women do ending their third. The loose-fitting top hid the bulge of her abdomen, still barely noticeable even in more form-fitting outfits.

"I'm definitely looking forward to it. And to introducing him to you and Vicky."

Gia smiled. "I'm dying to meet him. You've talked so much about him since your Florida trip. Before that, it was as if you were an orphan."

Yeah, the Florida fiasco had changed things. He and Dad had been close during his childhood, but estranged—not completely, but mostly—during the past fifteen years. The goings-on in South Florida had forged a new bond between them. And Jack had learned that he wasn't the only one in the family with secrets.

"Glad as I'll be to see him, I'd prefer going to him instead of him coming to me. No lodging problems that way."

Wide-eyed, Gia said, "Did he think he was staying with you?"

Jack nodded. "Uh-huh."

She stifled a laugh. "How did you tell him that *nobody* stays with his son?"

"Nobody except you." And only when Vicky was sleeping over somewhere.

"How did you break it to him?"

"Told him my place is too small and too crowded." He shrugged. "Best I could come up with on such short notice."

His father's holiday jaunt had been sprung on Jack. Dad had planned to be moved back to the northeast by now. He'd found a buyer for his Florida house and had had a signed contract in hand. Then, a week before closing, the buyer dropped dead. Talk about inconsiderate.

So Dad had had to put the place back on the market. He found another buyer, but the new closing wasn't until mid-January.

He'd planned to be settled in time to spend Christmas with his sons and grandkids. Since that wasn't happening, he'd decided on the spur of the moment to come north just for the holidays. Spend a couple of weeks up here, then head back to finish packing for the move.

Great, Jack had thought, until Dad had announced that his first leg involved a stay in New York City.

Yikes.

"But didn't you tell me you think he has a pretty good idea of what you do?"

Jack nodded. "Yes. An *idea*. But he doesn't *know*. And I'd like to leave it like that. It's one thing for him to suspect what I hire out for; it's another entirely for him to get involved in the day-to-day workings of my life." He had to laugh. "He'll be giving me all sorts of advice and maybe even trying to set up a pension plan for me. He's very big on pension plans."

"Well, he's an accountant, isn't he?"

"Was. And once an accountant, always an accountant, I guess. But that's not the only reason I'm putting him up in a hotel. I—"

Gia shook her head. "I think that's awful. Here's this old man—"

"He's a very spry seventy-one."

"—coming here for the first time in ages to visit his son, and he gets stuck in a hotel. It's not right."

"Gia, we were together in his place down there maybe three or four days and he was making me crazy, always asking me where I was going or where I'd been, worrying about me if I was out late . . . like I was a teenager again. I can't handle that."

"Even for a few days?"

He could hear Dad's voice in his head now. He'd meet Gia, his future daughter-in-law, and be enchanted by her and Vicky, but when they were alone he'd start in on how they did things differently in his day: First they got married, *then* started a family. Jack didn't want to hear it.

A tough old bird, Dad, and traditional to the core.

"You're making me sound like a Blue Meanie. I can't have him nosing around my place while I'm out. He might pull open the wrong drawer. You know how that is."

Gia nodded. She knew.

Jack remembered the time, early in their relationship, when she'd wanted to surprise him by cleaning his apartment. She'd happened upon a stash of guns and phony ID and he'd almost lost her.

"Well, did he buy your too-small story?"

"I doubt it—not completely. It was awkward, and it's going to remain awkward the whole time he's here."

"It's going to be *really* awkward when he sees your place and notices the daybed in the TV room."

"I'll think of something."

"You don't have to. He'll stay here."

Not this again.

"Gia, we've been through—"

She held up her hand. "Too late. I've taken it into my own hands. It's a fait accompli."

"As much as I love when you speak French, what are you talking about?"

"I canceled your father's hotel reservation."

"You *what*?"

"I'm the one who made it, remember? So I figure I have a right to cancel it."

"Do you know how hard it is to find a hotel room this time of year?"

She smiled. "Virtually impossible. Which means he'll have to stay here." She reached across the table and took his hand. "Come on, Jack. Lighten up. He's going to be Vicky's adoptive grandfather. Shouldn't she get to know him, and he her?"

Jack couldn't argue. It would take his father ten minutes—probably less—to fall in love with Vicky.

"I just don't like the burden it'll put on you, being pregnant and all. The extra work—"

"What extra work? I'll bet he makes his own bed. That leaves me with the burden of putting out an extra coffee cup and toasting extra bread in the morning." She gave a dramatic sigh and pressed the back of her wrist against her forehead. "It's going to be rough but I think I'll be able to muddle through."

"Okay, okay. He stays here." He stared at her. "Have I told you lately that you're wonderful?"

She smiled that smile. "No. At least not in recent memory."

He gently squeezed her fingers. "You're wonderful."

2

Tom quelled a ripple of anxiety as he started down to the baggage claim area. The flight had been perfect, the attendants beautiful, the food . . . edible. If this were Miami International he'd feel fine; he could make his way through there blindfolded. But he'd never been to La Guardia.

He supposed it was part of aging: You come to depend on things being comfortable and familiar, and get rattled by the new and different. But a big part was Jack's damned secretiveness. He'd said he'd meet him in the baggage area, but what if he forgot? Or what if he got tied up in traffic or delayed by something? Tom wasn't averse to taking a cab, but to where? He didn't know Jack's address. Oh, he had a mailing address, but Jack didn't live there.

Relax, he told himself. You're borrowing trouble. You have a cell phone and you know his number.

A gaggle of bearded men in black hats or yarmulkes and women in wigs and long-sleeved dresses descended ahead of him. These fifty or so Orthodox Jews—he'd heard someone mention that they were Hasidic—had occupied the rear half of the plane. Tom wondered what they'd all been doing in Miami. Not one of them looked tan.

He reached the bottom of the stairs and followed the crowd along a short corridor that opened into the baggage claim. He found a lake of expectant faces spread out in a thick semicircle. Dozens of black-suited, white-shirted limo drivers milled about, some holding up handwritten signs with the names of their fares, others simply killing time until a given plane arrived. Behind them stood relatives and friends waiting for loved ones. Jack would—should—be somewhere in the throng.

But where?

He scanned the faces, looking for his son's familiar features. There—a brown-haired man waving at him. Jack. Good thing he was waving or Tom would have missed him. He could have been anybody in his hooded blue sweatshirt, plaid flannel shirt, jeans, and sneakers. Virtually invisible.

Tom felt a flood of love tinged with relief. He didn't understand his younger son—didn't much understand the older one either, for that matter—but his time with Jack back in September had been an eye-opener. The affable, laid-back man he'd come to think of as rudderless, perhaps even something of a loser, had metamorphosed into a grim warrior, intensely focused, who'd wrought a terrible vengeance on a murderous crew.

Tom had participated in the killing and afterward had expected fits of guilt and remorse. They never came. Strangely, the killing didn't bother him: The dead in this case deserved it. And taking the long view, hell, he'd killed more and probably better men during his tour in Korea.

But though he'd learned to respect Jack that night, he still didn't understand him. Which was why he'd decided to come here. He wanted time with his son in his own environment.

Jack's excuse about his apartment being too small . . . it didn't ring true. He'd been disappointed and even tempted to call him on it, but decided to go along. Just more of his number-two son's obsessive secretiveness. He guessed he'd have to accept that as part of the package.

Tom locked on to Jack's deceptively mild brown eyes as they worked toward each other through the crowd. Jack waited as the line of Hasidim passed, and then he was reaching for Tom's hand. What started as a shake turned into a brief embrace.

"Hey, Dad, you made it."

For a reason he could not explain, Tom filled up. His throat constricted and it took him a few seconds to find his voice.

"Hi, Jack. Damn, it's good to see you again."

They broke apart and Jack grabbed Tom's carry-on.

"I can handle that," Tom said.

"What a coincidence. So can I." He nodded toward the small horde of Hasidim. "What'd you do, come in on El Al?"

"I remember reading about some gathering in Miami."

On the way to the baggage carousel Jack pinched a fold of fabric on Tom's green-and-white jacket.

"Look at you—puffy starter coat. Very cool. Eagles colors, no less."

Tom nodded. He'd been a lifelong Eagles fan.

"Bought it last week. Figured I'd need something to protect me from the cold."

As they joined the passengers and waited for their luggage, he studied his son. Hard to believe that this regular-looking Joe had led them into a firefight in the Everglades and saved him from being sucked into a tornado.

He owed Jack his life.

"Well, Dad, anything special you want to do while you're here?"

"Spend time with you."

Jack blinked. The remark—the bold-faced truth as far as Tom was concerned—seemed to take him by surprise.

"That's a given. I'm just putting the finishing touches on a job, and after that, I've cleared the deck."

"What sort of job?"

A shrug. "Just fixing something for somebody."

. . . *fixing something for somebody* . . . not big with the details, his son.

"But other than hanging out," Jack went on, "is there any play you want to see, restaurant you want to try?"

"I'd like to go to the top of the Empire State Building."

Jack grinned. "Really?"

"I've never been. Lived less than two hours outside this city most of my life and never once made it there. So, before I die—"

Jack rolled his eyes. "Oh man!"

"No, seriously. I've decided to make a list of certain things I've always wanted to do, and the Empire State Building is one of them. Have *you* ever been to the top, Mr. New Yorker?"

"Lots of times. I always bring flowers and leave them there."

"What? I'd never take you for a fan of *An Affair to Remember.*"

He laughed. "No, I bring them for Kong."

"Kong?"

"King Kong. That's where he was killed."

Tom stared. "You were always a weird kid, Jack. Now you're a weird adult."

He shook his head. "Uh-uh. Still a kid."

But not acting like one now, Tom thought as he noticed the way Jack's eyes darted back and forth, constantly on the move. Watching for what? Terrorists?

No . . . his gaze seemed to linger more on the security personnel than on the Arabic-looking members of the crowd. Why? What about them concerned him?

He realized Jack looked edgy. He suspected that whatever it was Jack did for a living, it probably wasn't on the right side of the law. Tom hoped that was only a sometime thing.

After what Tom had seen of Jack's capabilities back in

Florida, he'd make one formidable foe, no matter which side of the law he was on.

But from what Tom had seen during Jack's visit he knew that his son was involved in something else, something beyond legal systems. Perhaps even beyond normal reality.

A girl who could control swamp creatures . . . a hole in the earth that went God knew where . . . a man who could walk on water, who Jack had called by name. They seemed to be enemies.

And that was all Tom knew. He hadn't been able to squeeze much explanation from Jack beyond cryptic statements about having had a "peek behind the curtain."

His stated purpose now was to spend the holidays with his sons and grandchildren, and that was true to an extent. But Tom was determined to use the time to learn more about the man his son had become. Which wouldn't be easy. He knew Jack saw him as a bedrock traditionalist, and to some extent he was. He made no excuses about hewing to traditional values. He sensed Jack had no quarrel with those, but held to a looser, more flexible view as to how to uphold them.

Still, no way to deny that Jack was on guard here. Not that he had to worry about the two blue-uniformed security people in sight—a skinny guy and a big-butted woman standing together near the exit. They seemed more interested in each other than in what was going on around them.

Still, Tom looked for a way to ease Jack's discomfort.

"Where's the car?"

Jack jerked a thumb over his shoulder. "In the big garage across the way."

"Much of a trip?"

"Not bad. We go upstairs, take the skywalk across. That'll put us on level four. I'm parked on level two, so we take an elevator down and go from there."

That seemed like too much time. If being here bothered Jack, this could be a way to get him out more quickly.

"Why don't you go get the car? By the time you come back, I'll be waiting at the curb with my luggage."

"How many bags?"

"One big one. And don't give me that can-the-old-guy-handle-it? look. I handled it in Miami and I can handle it here. It's got wheels."

Jack hesitated, then said, "Not a bad idea. The sooner we get on and off the BQE, the better. Rush hour starts early around here. Meet you outside."

His relief at getting out of the terminal was obvious.

3

As Tom watched Jack thread the crowd toward the stairs, trailing his carry-on, someone opened an exit door. A gust of cold December air sneaked through and wrapped around him. He shivered. Now he knew why he'd moved to Florida.

He returned his attention to the still and empty baggage carousel. A moment or two later a Klaxon sounded as an orange light began blinking; the carousel shuddered into motion.

As luggage started to slide down a chute to the revolving surface Tom edged forward with everyone else, looking for his bag. It was black, like ninety percent of the rest, but he'd wrapped the handle in Day-Glo orange tape to make it easier to spot.

One of the Hasidic women stood in front of him, carrying a one-year-old. A little girl, bundled head to toe against winter. Her large brown eyes fixed on Tom and he gave her a little wave. She smiled and covered her face. A shy one.

From the corner of his eye he saw a door swing open on the far side of the carousel. Two figures emerged but he paid them no mind until he heard the unmistakable ratchet of a breech bolt. He froze, then spun toward the doorway in time to see two figures in gray coveralls, ski-masked under black-and-white *kufiyas*, raising assault pistols.

Instinct and training took over as Tom dove for the floor, carrying the mother and her little girl with him. The woman cried out, and as the three of them fell, her fat, bearded husband in his long black coat and sealskin hat whirled toward them, his face a mask of shock and outrage.

Then the shooting began and the man dove floorward along with everybody else.

Tom heard shattering glass and a scream of pain behind him. He turned in time to see the two security guards go down, caught in a spray of bullets that shattered the glass doors behind them. The woman's legs folded under her and she hit the floor not six feet from him. A pulsating crimson fountain arced from her throat. He saw more shock than pain in her eyes. She'd never had a chance to draw her pistol.

The shooters seemed to have made a point of taking down the guards first. More would be coming, but for the moment the killers were unopposed. They mowed down anyone trying to run, and then began a systematic slaughter of the rest.

Tom watched in horror as the two faceless gunmen split, each taking a side of the carousel, tearing up the helpless, cowering passengers with a succession of short bursts from their stubby, odd-looking assault pistols. They worked quickly and methodically, pausing only to change magazines or cut down those who tried to flee.

Tom's gut writhed and his bladder clenched with the

realization that he was going to die here. He'd been shot in Korea, he'd survived the firefight of his life and Hurricane Elvis just a few months ago, only to be exterminated here like a roach trapped on the floor. If only he had a gun—even a .22 pistol—he could stop these arrogant murderous shits. They knew no one could fight back.

Tom turned. The dead guard's pistol beckoned to him from its holster.

Just then a man leaped up and tried to dive into the baggage chute, but an extended burst cut him nearly in half, leaving his body wedged in the opening.

That long burst emptied the killer's magazine. As he switched to a fresh one, a brawny Hasid leaped to his feet and charged, roaring like the bear he resembled. The killer, caught off guard, backpedaled and slipped on the bloody floor. The Hasid was almost upon him when the other killer turned and ripped him up with a burst to the chest and abdomen that sent him spinning to the floor.

Now! Tom thought, not giving himself time to think as he pushed himself up to a crouch and started a high-assed scramble. *Now!*

He heard shooting behind him, saw pieces chip out of the floor as bullets hit it, felt something tear into his thigh. It knocked him flat, but pushed him forward as it did, putting the gun within reach. He heard the hollow *clink!* of an empty chamber and knew with a sudden burst of hope that the shooter's magazine had run dry. Bolts of agony shot through his leg when he tried to move it, but he'd been hurt worse than this. All that mattered was the pistol. He had a tiny window of opportunity here and had to make the most of it.

His fingers were closing around the grip when he began to shake. Not just his hand and arms, his whole body. He tried again for the pistol but his arm seized up. He couldn't breathe. He felt his body begin to flop around like a beached fish. His pulse pounded in his ears, slowing.

What was happening? He'd only been hit in the leg. Had he taken another slug somewhere else? What . . . ?

Tom's light, his air, his questions, his time . . . faded to nothingness.

4

Jack had to take a circular route to reach the pickup area, a reluctant mini-tour of the airport. La Guardia was small as major airports went, and appeared to be the victim of some weird temporal dislocation. The dingy, Quonset hut–style hangars looked to be of 1930s vintage, while the green-glassed terminal itself was strictly fifties in design. The massive, six-story, bare concrete parking garage could have been built yesterday.

As he nosed his Crown Vic along the pickup lane outside the Central Terminal, he saw people running—not toward the doors, like late travelers, but from them. Screaming people, faces masks of terror, fleeing for their lives.

Jack's heart double-clutched. They were pouring from the baggage area . . . fleeing the far section . . . the section where he'd left Dad.

No . . . it can't . . .

He gunned the engine and sped toward the far section, narrowly missing a panicked man and a screaming woman. He jerked to a halt when he saw the shattered doors and broken glass glittering on the sidewalk, the bullet holes in the still-intact panes.

Oh, Christ . . . oh no-no-no!

He jumped out and dashed across the sidewalk, almost slipping on the shards of glass, and skidded to a halt inside the baggage area.

Blood . . . blood everywhere . . . lakes of red on the floor . . . even the carousel was red . . . a man's feet and legs hung out of the baggage chute . . . the bloody rag-doll body of a baby girl sprawled among the endlessly circling luggage.

No other movement, no crying, no screams or wails of the wounded. Just silence. Not one of the victims so much as stirred.

Jack stood frozen and stared, numb, paralyzed . . .

Dad . . . ?

Where was his father? He'd left him standing right over there by the—

There! Shit! A body, a gray-haired man in a green-and-white coat.

No-no-no-no!

As Jack forced himself forward a voice shouted from somewhere to his left.

"Freeze!"

Jack heard the word but it didn't register. Stiff and slow, he kept moving, a living zombie.

"Freeze, goddammit, or I'll drop you where you stand!"

Jack kept moving, forcing himself forward a few more steps until he reached the corpse. He dropped to his knees in a pool of still-warm blood, grabbed one of the shoulders, and rolled him over.

The face—his lips were pulled back in a horrific, agonized grimace, but his glazed eyes left no doubt about it.

Dad.

Dead.

Jack felt as if his chest might explode. He let out a sound that was equal parts moan and sob.

He shook his father. It couldn't be. They'd been talking just a few minutes ago. He couldn't be dead!

"Dad! Dad, it's me, Jack! Can you hear me?"

The voice said, "Are you fuckin' deaf? I told you to freeze!"

Jack looked up into the muzzle of a pistol held by a mustached security guard.

"This . . . this is my father."

"I don't give a fuck, I told you to—"

"That will be enough!"

An older man had come up behind the guard. He looked to be about fifty and wore a blue NYPD uniform with sergeant stripes. His nameplate read DRISCOLL.

The guard backed off a step. "I found this guy wandering around. He could be—"

Sergeant Driscoll's voice dripped scorn. "He wasn't wandering around. I saw him come in. He was looking for someone." His eyes dropped to Jack's father's inert form. "And he found him."

"But—"

"But nothing." He shoved the guard away. "Get over by the door in case anyone else tries to wander in."

The guard moved off.

Driscoll muttered, "Asshole," then squatted beside Jack. "Look, I'm sorry about your dad, but you've got to go outside."

"What happened?" His own voice sounded far away. "I left him here just a few minutes ago . . . we were talking about going to the Empire State Build—"

"I'm really sorry, but you're going to have to wait outside. This whole area is a crime scene and you're contaminating it, so you've got to leave."

"But—"

He pointed to the floor beneath Jack. "Look at what you're kneeling in. If we're gonna catch these guys, we need every scrap of evidence we can get." He slipped a hand into Jack's armpit and lifted. "Come on. If you want to help us catch the fucks who did this to your dad, wait outside."

The cop's touch lit a flicker of rage that flashed through the dead, dumb grayness that filled Jack, but he quickly doused it. Lashing out at this man who was trying to do the decent thing would solve nothing. He could walk away or be carried away; either way, he'd be leaving his dad behind. And if he was carried away, they'd find his ankle holster and the unregistered AMT .380 it held.

So he let the cop help him to his feet and shuffled toward the shattered doorway where the security guard stood.

He watched Jack's approach.

"Hey, sorry about back there. Case like this, you don't know who's friend or foe."

Jack nodded without making eye contact.

Outside—chaos. EMS trucks screeching to a halt, shuttles trying to get out of the way, limos inching out from the curb, hundreds of people milling about, some weeping, some hysterical, some in slack-faced shock.

He saw a harried-looking cop standing by the Vic, shouting, "One last time: Who owns this?"

Jack hesitated, unsure of what he might be getting himself into, then decided that stepping forward would be less complicated, especially since his fingerprints were all over the car and it was registered in someone else's name—someone unaware of that.

Jack waved and hurried toward the cop. "Me! It's mine!"

"Then move it! You're blocking the—hey, you hurt?"

"What?"

He pointed to Jack's legs. "You're bleeding."

Jack looked down and saw the wet red splotches on his knees. For a few seconds, he didn't understand. Then—

"No . . ." His voice caught. "No, that's my father's."

"Jesus. He all right?"

Jack wanted to tell him what a stupid fucking question that was but bit it back. He simply shook his head.

"Listen, I'm sorry." The cop pointed to the Vic. "But ya still gotta move it. Just drive it into the garage. Then you can come back and wait with the rest."

"Wait for what?" Dad was dead.

The cop shrugged. "I dunno. News about survivors, I

guess. Not like you gotta choice. Airport's locked down. Nobody out, nobody in."

Jack said nothing as he slipped behind the wheel and pulled away.

5

Dad . . . gone . . .

The words registered but his mind couldn't get a grip on it, the . . . finality.

He'd returned to the garage, found a spot on the perimeter of an upper level, and parked facing west. The falling December sun gleamed through the crystalline sky and stabbed his eyes. The sky had no right being so bright. It should be dark, with wind and hail and lightning.

Numb, he lowered the visor and . . . just . . . sat.

Gone . . . one minute alive and full of plans and enthusiasm, the next a cooling lump of meat in a pool of blood. Part of Jack insisted it was all a bad dream, but the rest of him knew he wouldn't wake up from this.

Knowing nothing made it worse. Who? Why? Some al-Qaeda strike? Or maybe al-Qaeda wannabes massacring a crowd of Orthodox Jews? Was that what this was all about? Made a sick sort of sense. But what made no sense was why, with all the flights from Miami to New York, his father had to wind up on *that* one.

Jack had a blood-red urge to gun up and shoot down every Arab he could find. He knew that insanity would pass, but he reveled in the fantasy until it reminded him of the backup piece strapped to his ankle.

He glanced around, saw no one about, so he reached down and pulled the little AMT .380 from its holster.

When the FBI and CIA and NYPD and Homeland Security and whoever else would be involved began allowing people to leave the airport, he'd bet the ranch they'd be searching every person, every car. He wasn't sure his tried-and-true John Tyleski ID would hold up—Ernie was painstakingly thorough when he created an identity, but no fake was perfect.

And even if it did pass, he couldn't risk carrying. Had to dump the pistol.

He turned the little backup over in his hands. He'd bought it from Abe six months ago after his trusty old Semmerling had been connected to the subway massacre. Hadn't had to pull it once since. Now he was going to have to toss it away unused.

Unused . . . he wondered if it could have made a difference in there. The shooter—probably more than one—must have used an automatic, machine pistol, most likely. He couldn't have killed so many in so little time with a single-shot weapon.

I should've been there, goddamn it.

He didn't know what use his little six-shot .380 would have been against Mac-10s or HK-5s. Not much, probably, but you never knew.

Another fantasy . . . taking down a single shooter with a couple of .380s into his face . . . or, if there'd been two or three, taking one down, tossing his AMT to Dad, then grabbing the downed shooter's weapon and the two of them taking on the others . . . just as they'd taken on Semelee's clan in the Everglades.

More likely he'd now be lying dead beside his dad.

At least they'd have put up a fight, kept whoever it was from getting clean away.

And maybe being dead wouldn't be as bad as dealing with this blistering guilt for not being there when his father needed him most.

Jack forced himself out of the fantasy to deal with the reality of the moment: The gun had to go.

He popped out the magazine, removed the chambered cartridge, then pulled out the old, oil-stained rag he kept in the glove compartment. He emptied the magazine, wiped it down, then did the same with each casing. He removed the leather ankle holster and wiped that down. Then he removed the slide assembly from the pistol frame and wiped each part.

He opened the car door. A look around showed no one in sight, so he got out and leaned over the edge of the parapet. No one below. He dropped the slide onto the pavement six stories down.

He began walking the perimeter of the level, tossing a cartridge every hundred feet or so, then finally the frame and the holster.

When he returned to his car he moved it to a more centrally located slot.

Then he crossed the skyway back toward the terminal. At the end he turned the corner and found himself in the middle of a crowd. Security personnel were blocking the escalators down to the ticketing and baggage levels.

Jack tapped a heavyset woman on her arm.

"What's going on?"

She looked at him—bloodshot eyes, blotchy face, tear-smeared mascara.

"They won't let us down! My daughter was due in! I— I don't know if she's alive or dead!"

At least you still have hope, Jack thought.

6

He'd been standing on the glass-walled skyway for two hours. Dark now—the sun had set around four thirty. He'd called Gia to tell her he was okay. She said she'd heard the news and had been worried sick. When he told her about his father she broke down. Listening to her sob, he'd almost lost it himself.

Two hours with the crowd of mourners and stranded passengers watching a seemingly endless parade of stretchers wheeled back and forth from the terminal to the ambulances below. All carried bagged bodies. He saw no wounded and wondered why.

No matter. Dad wouldn't be among them. It ate at Jack that he hadn't known which bag contained his father.

And finally the stretchers stopped rolling, and the last of the ambulances pulled away.

"Where are the survivors?" said a forty-something woman nearby. "Aren't there any survivors?"

"Maybe they were taken out another way."

"No way," she said with an emphatic shake of her head. "I know this airport, everything at this end has to funnel through directly below us. I've watched the ambulances coming and going, and right down there was the only spot they stopped."

"There *have* to be *some* survivors," said a man in a herringbone overcoat. "I mean, they couldn't have killed *everybody*."

Seemed logical, but Jack couldn't remember seeing anyone stirring amid the bloodbath.

He kept that to himself, however. He was concerned

with where they'd taken his father . . . and how he was going to claim the body when he didn't own a single piece of ID under his real name.

He wandered back to the escalators. Still blocked, but he spotted a familiar-looking cop—the older one from inside—giving instructions to the security men.

"Sergeant?" he called. "Hey, sergeant?"

The cop didn't turn.

What was his name? He'd seen the nameplate but had been in shock—wait. Driscoll. Yeah.

"Sergeant Driscoll?"

When he turned Jack waved to him. He looked as if he couldn't place Jack's face.

"We met inside. Where can I claim my father's body?"

As Jack's question was echoed by other voices, Driscoll stepped closer.

"Call the one-one-five—"

"Precinct?" someone said.

"Right. They'll have a procedure in place."

"What about the wounded?" a woman asked. "What hospital were—?"

Driscoll shook his head. His grim expression became grimmer.

"We have no wounded."

"No wounded!" the woman cried, her voice edging into a wail. "They can't *all* be dead!"

"We have survivors who saw what happened, and they're being debriefed, but we have no wounded."

"How can that *be*?"

"We're working on that, ma'am."

"What happened?" someone else said as horrified cries rose all around. "Who did this? Who's responsible?"

He shook his head. "I can't answer that. The mayor and the commissioner will be holding a press conference at City Hall soon. You'll have to wait till then."

"But—"

He held up his hand. "I've told you all I can."

"When can we leave?" someone shouted as he turned.

"The checkpoints are in place now. You can start to head out."

And then his back was to them and he was walking away. If he heard any of the questions called out after him, he gave no sign.

Jack too barely heard them. The word "checkpoints" was blaring though his mind.

His earlier misgivings about his Tyleski ID withstanding full-bore scrutiny had became full-blown doubt. But even if it did pass muster, his car was another story. A check of the registration would raise a horde of questions. Like why was he driving a car registered to someone else? And to Vinny "the Donut" Donato, of all people? If someone checked with the owner they'd learn that the black Crown Vic in question was sitting in his garage in Brooklyn.

Then even more shit would hit the fan.

Bad enough to be bagged for false ID, but to be suspected of being connected to the terrorists who'd killed his own father . . . a father he couldn't officially claim as his own . . .

Had to find another way out.

7

Jack fought the numbness his mind yearned to yield to and forced it to focus. He shuttled between the garage and the skyway, getting the lay of the land and not finding much in the way of potential escape routes.

To the north lay the runways, the East River, and Rikers

Island. If he didn't get out of here soon, Rikers might be his new home.

To the south, past Ditmars Boulevard and Grand Central Parkway, the glowing house windows of Jackson Heights beckoned.

East offered only dark expanses of marsh and more of the East River. The west had possibilities, but involved long stretches of exposure.

He had to get down to the highway.

Jack fell in with a group heading from the skyway to the garage. No one spoke. Shock was the order of the day.

As they entered the fourth level and scattered toward their respective cars, Jack took the elevator down to the ground floor. Crossed to the outer rim and hopped over the wall. Cut across an access lane to a low concrete wall. Hopped that, landing on a patch of bare ground. Directly ahead, across a scraggly winter lawn, lay Grand Central Parkway.

All that stood between Jack and freedom was an eight-foot, chain-link fence with a barbed-wire crown.

Blue-and-white police units and sinister black SUVs kept roaring in and out along the airport access roads.

That fence . . . that damn fence . . .

Couldn't go over it. No big deal physically—he could easily climb the links and throw his sweatshirt over the barbed wire—but he'd be spotted for sure.

Had to find another way.

Jack lay flat and began to belly crawl through the cold, dead grass. When he reached the fence he turned and crept along its base, feeling his way, searching for—

His hand slipped into a depression in the dirt. Knew he'd find one somewhere along the line. Inevitable that some dog at some time would want to get past the fence. To do that it would dig. And one had dug here.

Not deep enough to allow Jack through, but okay. The dog trough gave him a head start. All he had to do was make it a little deeper, strip down to his underwear, and slip through.

He pulled out his knife and flipped it open. A sin to use a Spyderco Endura as a digging tool, but . . .

At least the ground was still soft. Though cold, winter was a couple weeks off, and the ground hadn't frozen yet.

He began to dig, loosening the dirt with the knife blade and scooping it out with his free hand . . .

8

Jack crouched in the shadows under an overpass. He punched Abe's number into his phone and prayed he was still at the store. He released a breath when he heard him pick up.

"Abe? It's me."

"Hello, Me. I don't recall ever meeting a Me. I should know you?"

"Hold the jokes, okay. I need a favor."

"Always with the favors."

"This is serious."

Abe must have picked up on his tone. "Serious how?"

"I need a ride."

"You call that serious?"

"Abe, I'm stranded on the Grand Central. Can you pick me up?"

"I should drive all the way out to Queens when you can take a cab?"

"I can't take a cab."

"Why? Someone pick your pock—hey, wait. Are you out near the airport?"

"Very."

"Are you okay?"

"No."

"Wait—your father was coming in today. Was he—?"

"Yeah."

"*Gevalt!* He's not . . . ?"

"Yeah, Abe. He's gone."

"What?"

"Gone."

Silence on the other end. Finally Abe spoke, his voice thick.

"Jack . . . Jack, I'm so sorry. What can I do? Anything. Just tell me."

"Come get me, Abe. Check the underpasses near the airport exit ramp. I'm under one of them. Wish I could tell you which one but . . ."

"I'll take the truck."

"Hurry."

9

Hours later Jack sat slumped in a funk on Gia's couch while she huddled against him. Vicky was upstairs doing her homework. Gia had told her that Jack's father had died and left it at that. Knowing that he'd been slaughtered in what the media were now calling the "Flight 715 Massacre" would only frighten her. Better for now to let her think he was an old man who'd died of natural causes—whatever those were.

They stared at the old TV, watching the same shots of La Guardia's Central Terminal, hearing the same clips of the mayor, the police commissioner, the head of Homeland Security, and the president himself. No new news, just repetitions of what little had been gleaned from witnesses who had been close enough to see the massacre, but far enough away to stay clear:

Two gunmen wearing airport coveralls, ski masks, and Arab headdress—described as "the kind of thing Arafat wore"—had entered baggage claim through an employees-only doorway and opened up on the passengers of American Airlines flight 715. The result was one hundred and fifty-two dead—men, women, children, passengers, relatives, limo drivers, security guards—everyone who'd been anywhere near the carousel.

Among the dead were forty-seven members of the ultraorthodox Satmar Hasidic sect returning to Crown Heights from a gathering in Miami. Since the killers did not attack any of the other nearby carousels, the news heads speculated that the presence of such a sizable group of Hasidim might have been why that particular flight was targeted.

After finishing their bloody work, the killers had fled through the same doorway. In the hallway beyond they'd discarded their coveralls, their masks and *kufiyas,* as well as their assault pistols. Word had leaked that both pistols were Tavor-2 models, manufactured in Israel. That started speculation that the choice of weapon might have been a way of adding insult to injury: Jews slaughtered by Israeli-made weapons.

But the question most asked by the news heads to their endless parade of experts on terrorism and Arabs and Islam, singly or on panels, was why there were no wounded. How could every wound be fatal? Finally someone offered the possibility that the terrorists might have used cyanide-filled hollow-point rounds.

"Oh, my God!" Gia said. "How could they?" Then she shook her head. "Sorry. Stupid question."

"I figured it might be something like that."

"Why? How?"

As he'd knelt next to his dead father, Jack's reeling mind hadn't been able to process all the surrounding sights and sounds. But as he'd waited in the cold darkness for Abe, he'd slowed and corralled his chaotic thoughts, and painstakingly pieced together what he had seen.

Dad hadn't been lying in a pool of blood—he'd been lying *next* to one that seemed to have come from the uniformed woman beside him. His body wasn't bullet riddled; in fact Jack had seen only one wound, a bloody hole near the left buttock, but not much bleeding from that.

"My father's wound—at least the one I could see—seemed to be a flesh wound. Of course the bullet could have ricocheted off a bone and cut through a major artery. But after I heard there were no wounded, that everyone who'd been shot was dead, I began to suspect cyanide."

None of this had been confirmed, but Jack was pretty sure it would turn out to be something along those lines.

Gia shivered against him. "I've never heard of—I mean, what hideous sort of mind dreams up these things?"

"Cyanide bullets aren't new. They're a terrorist favorite, but usually when they're out to assassinate a specific target. The poison guarantees that an otherwise nonlethal wound will be fatal. First I ever heard of them was back when we were kids—when those Symbionese Liberation Army nuts used cyanide-tipped bullets to kill that school superintendent. But for mass murder? Never heard of them being used for that. At least until now."

Gia closed her eyes as a tear slid from each. "So if they'd used regular bullets your father could have lived . . . if he'd laid still and played dead, he might have survived, and we'd be standing around his hospital bed now talking about how lucky he was."

Thinking about what could have been and might have been never worked for Jack. Seemed like self-torture, and he felt tortured enough right now.

"I doubt it."

Gia opened her eyes. "What do you mean?"

"I saw a smear of blood about the length of his leg on the floor beside him. His hand was on the holster of a dead security guard. I think—no, I'm sure he was going after her gun. Dad wasn't the type to sit and wait to be killed. He was an excellent shot. If he'd reached the gun . . . who knows? I doubt he could have taken down both of them, but maybe he could have hit one of them, and that might have scared off the other."

Could have . . . might have . . .

Useless.

Just as useless as the rerun of his fantasy of teaming up with Dad to take out the killers.

Gia said, "He would have been a hero."

"Most likely they'd have cut him to ribbons as soon as he fired his first shot."

"At least you got to see him again. If this had happened down in Miami, you, well . . . you're now the last one to see him alive."

Jack knew he couldn't claim that blessing for himself.

"No, the killers were."

"I mean in his family—oh, God! Family! Did you call your brother?"

Shit!

"No. I didn't even think . . ."

Truth was, thoughts of his brother rarely if ever crossed Jack's mind. He'd never considered Tom a real brother, just someone who shared some of his genes and, for the first eight years of Jack's life, the same house. Ten years older than Jack, Tom hadn't been a presence even before he'd gone off to college, and after that he'd faded to a wraith who'd float in and out over the holidays and breaks.

Jack had his number somewhere. He'd had to call him a few times last September to update him on Dad's coma, but not often enough to remember.

"You've got to call him."

Yeah, he did. But how much would Tom care?

Jack caught himself. Not fair. Maybe Tom hadn't gone to visit Dad in Florida when he'd been hurt, but that didn't mean he wouldn't be devastated to learn he was a victim of the flight 715 massacre. Back then he'd said he was tied up with "judicial matters," whatever that meant. Yeah, he was a judge in Philadelphia and maybe he couldn't leave in the middle of hearing a case, but still ... if your father's in a coma and no one knows whether or not he's going to come out of it, hell, you find a way.

"Tom's number is back at my apartment. So's Ron's."

His sister's kids needed to know about their grandfather.

He kissed Gia on the top of her head. "Got to get home and make those calls."

Gia looked up at him. "Can't you call information?"

"For Ron, yeah, I suppose. But I know Tom's is unlisted, him being a judge and all."

She grabbed his hand. "You're going to come back, aren't you?"

"Sure, I guess."

"Jack, you shouldn't be alone tonight. This is something that needs to be shared. Vicky and I can help you through this, but you've got to let us. I know you, Jack. You're like an injured wolf that goes off to lick its wounds alone. You can't keep this bottled up. You've got to let it out. I'm— *we're* here for you, Jack. Please don't shut us out."

"I won't. I'll make my calls and then come back."

As Jack left, he hoped he'd be able to keep that promise.

10

Jack sat in the cluttered front room of his apartment. Still numb, he hadn't turned on the lights. He sat in the dark with the glowing touchpad of his phone providing the only illumination. He started his calls.

The one-hundred-and-fifteenth precinct came first. A woman there told him they didn't have any information yet on how relatives could claim the bodies of the deceased. The victims were being IDed and examined, and then they'd be released.

"Was your loved one with the Hasidic group?" she said.

"No. Why?"

"Well, there's a lot of religious concerns on their part."

"Like what?"

"Like burying the body before sundown and—"

"That's long past."

"I know, but there are issues about icing the bodies down and—well, it's been very trying to say the least."

"I'll bet."

"We've got assemblymen and congressmen and city council members calling, pushing to expedite matters and—"

"What? Their dead are more important than my father?" Jack could feel a quick burn accelerating. His rage wanted a target—any target. "Like hell!"

"I'm sorry, sir. Please call tomorrow morning. The post mortems should be completed and we'll have a procedure in place by then. Thank you. Good-bye."

Jack found himself holding a dead phone.

After taking a few moments to cool, he called Kate's ex, praying Ron would answer instead of one of the kids. Jack had never met his niece and nephew, never even spoken to them, and didn't want to start now. Kevin and Lizzie had lost their mother earlier this year; he hated being the one to tell them their grandfather was gone too.

Jack freely copped to cowardice in this.

Ron answered. It took Jack's ex-brother-in-law a moment to figure out who he was. He took it hard, asking over and over how he was going to tell Lizzie. Jack promised to get back to him with the funeral arrangements.

"Oh?" his brother-in-law said in an acid-etched tone. "You're going to show up this time?"

Jack hadn't been able to attend his sister Kate's funeral. Forced to stay away for reasons he couldn't explain to them.

"Ron," Jack said, feeling a lead weight in his chest, "you don't know me, so I'll let that pass. But if you had any idea of how much I loved Kate, you'd know that I would have been there if at all possible. Talk to you soon."

And then he'd hung up.

God. Two tough calls. And now the last and possibly least: big brother Tom.

After half a dozen rings and no pickup or answering machine, Jack was about to hang up when a slurred voice came on.

"Tom?"

"Yeah. Who's this?"

"Your brother Jack."

"Oh-ho! Jackie, the prodigal brother. And to what do I owe this honor?"

"You been drinking?"

"What business of it is yours?"

Yep, he'd been drinking. Probably not a bad thing, considering what he was about to hear.

"None. You sitting down?"

"I'm lying down—you woke me up. I hope this is fucking important."

"Dad's dead."

A good ten, fifteen seconds of silence, then, "You're not bullshitting me?"

"You know better than to ask that."

"Jesus, when? What? Heart attack? Hit by another car? *What?*"

When Jack told him, the ensuing silence stretched even longer.

"Holy Christ. I knew he was swinging by to see you but I didn't know when . . . never dreamed he was on that flight. This is unbelievable!"

"Tell me about it. I was there and I still don't believe it. When can you get here? We need to claim the body."

"Can't you do that?"

"No."

"Why the hell not?"

Because I can't even prove I'm related, let alone his son.

"Can't explain. Just get here. I don't want him on a slab in the morgue any longer than necessary."

"Shit-shit-shit! Goddamn it! All right, I'll come up. But the earliest I can get there is tomorrow afternoon, if then."

"Christ, Tom—"

His voice jumped in volume. "That's it, okay? I've got things coming at me from all sides here, and it's going to take me a while to cut myself free. Tomorrow afternoon's the best I can do. And since you, for God knows whatever reason, can't seem to handle this on your own, you're just going to have to wait!"

He was nearly shouting by the time he finished.

"Fine," Jack said softly. "I'll give you my number. Call me before you get here and I'll meet you."

He gave Tom his Tracfone number and hung up.

He leaned back and rubbed his eyes.

What was up with Tom? His brother had always been self-centered. No matter what happened, good or bad, his first reaction had always been, How does this affect me? But this seemed to go beyond that.

Jack sensed it was more than just the pressure of being a judge in a city like Philly. Another divorce? That would make three. Or was it something more serious?

Whatever it was, this was more important. He had to put everything else aside for a few days and tend to this.

Jack so wished he could handle this, but that was impossible. He needed Tom.

And he hated needing Tom.

11

"Don't wait up for me," he told Gia.

"You're not coming back?"

"I don't think so."

"Oh, Jack . . ."

The hurt and worry in her voice scalded him.

"I'm sorry. It's just—"

"But we discussed this. You shouldn't be alone tonight."

"Yeah, I should."

"Jack—"

"Really, Gia, I'm okay. I'm just better off alone with this. I'm edgy and the truth is, I don't think I can sit still. I need to be up and about . . . need to move around."

"Move around how?"

"Take a walk, maybe a jog. Something to burn off this . . ."

He didn't have a name for it.

"Don't shut me out, Jack."

"I'm not. I swear I'm not. I'll be there early tomorrow. I'll spend the whole day with you. But tonight . . . I need to move."

"All right. I don't think it's a good idea, but I can tell I'm not going to change your mind. Be careful. Please?"

"I will. I promise."

"I love you, Jack."

"Love you too, Gi."

12

Jack ambled in a slow jog along the most poorly lit paths in Central Park. He made a point of cutting through dark groves of naked trees as he moved between paths, hoping—*praying*—someone would make a move on him.

God, he needed to let loose on somebody. It would feel sooo good to fire his rage laser and crisp some asshole.

But something about him must have sent out warning signals, because no one bothered him. No one even spoke to him.

Figured. You could never find a dirtbag when you needed one.

TUESDAY

1

As Jack pushed through the front door of the Isher Sports Shop he realized he was arriving empty-handed. He always brought something to eat. Today he'd forgotten.

So be it. Abe would survive.

He walked toward the rear.

If Set, the Egyptian God of Chaos, had been a sports nut, his temples would have resembled Abe's shop. Every size and shape ball imaginable plus the various instruments used to strike them, every wheeled contraption that could be sat or stood upon, plus a wide array of cocooning safety gear necessary to protect the users from grievous bodily harm during their pursuit of "fun," all tossed with utter disregard for coherence or continuity onto rows of eight-foot shelves teetering over narrow winding aisles laid out in a pattern to rival the Wiltshire hedge maze.

The man responsible, Jack's best and oldest friend, sat in his usual spot behind the scarred wooden counter near the rear. A few years shy of sixty, Abe Grossman had a Humpty-Dumpty shape and a balding crown. He was dressed in the Abe uniform of white—except for the food stains—half-sleeve shirt and black pants. And as usual, the morning editions of every daily newspaper in the city lay spread out on his counter.

He looked up, saw Jack coming, and quickly began shuffling the papers into a pile. He was shoving them under the counter when Jack arrived.

"It's okay, Abe. I've seen them—the front pages at least."

How could he have missed them? Every newsstand

he'd passed on the walk over from his apartment had the screaming headlines on display. The radio and TV weren't talking about anything else. He'd listened briefly this morning for new developments, but heard only the same old speculations. If the cops and FBI had learned anything new, they weren't sharing it.

Abe stashed them out of sight anyway.

"A terrible, terrible thing, Jack. I feel so bad for you. I feel worse for your father, of course, but you . . . how are you doing?"

"Still in shock . . . in rage. But no grief. Kind of worries me. Think there's something wrong with me?"

"With you? Something wrong? Not a chance."

He knew Abe was trying to lighten his mood, but Jack wasn't looking for that. And he hadn't been kidding about being worried. He'd broken down and cried when Kate died. Why hadn't he cried for Dad?

"I'm serious, Abe. I don't feel like moping or crying, I just want to break things. Or people."

"Grief will come in its time. We all have our own way of living through something like this." He shook his head. "Listen to me. Like a living, breathing cliché."

Jack reached across the counter and patted Abe's beefy arm.

"It's okay. At least you didn't say he's in a better place. I swear I'll do some damage if someone tells me that."

"That's not an 'if,' it's a 'when.' You know it is."

"The thing is, we'd just found each other. After all these years, we'd made real contact and discovered we liked each other. And then . . ."

There—a lump in his throat, cutting off his voice. It felt . . . good.

Parabellum, Abe's little blue parakeet, hopped over and stopped between Jack and Abe. He cocked his head and looked up at Jack as if to say, Where's my food? He usually served as the cleanup crew, policing the counter-top for spilled bits of whatever Jack had brought. With the way his master ate, crumbs were never in short supply. But today he'd have to settle for birdseed.

"At least you reconnected. Think how you should feel if you hadn't."

Jack opened his mouth to speak, then closed it as a realization hit him like a runaway train.

"Oh, hell . . ."

"What?"

"I'd be feeling fine right now—because he'd still be alive."

Abe rubbed his partially denuded scalp. "This you'll have to explain."

"He was coming to visit me, Abe. If we were still on the outs he'd have stayed in Florida, or would have been flying into Philly to see his grandkids for Christmas. Either way, he wouldn't have been at La Guardia yesterday. My dad's dead *because* we connected."

"You're holding yourself responsible? This is not my Jack."

"The ones I'm holding responsible are the two shits with the guns. But goddamn!" He slammed his fist on the counter, sending Parabellum fluttering toward the ceiling. "If only he'd taken another flight . . ."

"You can if-only yourself into a straitjacket."

"Yeah, I know. I'm halfway there."

"More like three quarters. How much sleep did you get last night?"

"Zilch."

Hadn't even tried. After he'd crapped out in the park, he'd wandered around until predawn. When he'd finally put himself to bed he just lay there, staring at the ceiling in the growing light. Finally he'd given up.

He was running on caffeine and adrenaline.

"Can I get you something to eat?" Abe said. "Some leftover Entenmann's, I'm sure."

Jack had to smile. Food was Abe's answer to everything. He shook his head.

"Thanks, but my appetite hasn't come back yet."

"You've got to eat."

"I've got to get a new backup is what I've got to do."

"Something's wrong with the AMT?"

"Yeah. It's scattered in pieces around one of the airport parking lots."

"You want another?"

Jack had been thinking about that. His Glock was a 9mm model, but the little AMT had been a .380. Dealing with two kinds of ammo wasn't a major chore, but he liked to keep things as simple as possible. And he hadn't been crazy about the AMT's trigger.

"Got anything in a nine?"

Abe thought a moment, then held up a pudgy finger.

"Just the thing. Lock the door and I'll show you."

2

After hanging up the BACK IN A FEW MINUTES sign, Jack joined Abe in a rear closet. He closed the door behind him as Abe pushed on the closet wall. It swung open. Abe hit a light switch, revealing the worn stone stairway down to the basement. Ahead a neon sign buzzed to life.

Fine Weapons
The Right to Buy   eapons is the
Right to Be Free

"You lost a *W*," Jack said.

"I know, but I'm not having it fixed."

Abe hit another switch at the bottom, lighting up the

basement to reveal the lethal stock of his true trade: bludgeons, knives, pistols, rifles, and sundry weapons of every size and configuration. Even a bazooka. In contrast to the mess upstairs, everything here was neatly arranged and arrayed in rows of display racks.

"Got a Tavor-two?" Jack said.

Abe looked at him. "The model that kill—that was used at the airport? Why for?"

Jack wasn't sure he had an answer to that.

"Just want to see one."

Abe shook his head. "Never carried them."

"What? You carry everything."

"It only seems that way. The Micro Uzi, Tec-nine, and Mac-eleven are much more popular. Not that the Tavor is any *bohmer* in firepower—spits five-fifty-six NATOs at something like nine hundred per minute—but no one's ever even asked about one. I should stock something no one wants?"

"Somebody wanted them."

"For reasons other than firepower, I suspect."

"The Israel connection."

"So it seems."

Silence hung between them.

Finally Jack said, "What about that backup?"

Abe stepped over to a rack and returned holding a small, sleek-looking semiautomatic with a dull gray finish.

"You want a small nine? Smaller and lighter you don't get than this Kel-Tec P-eleven. Double-action only with a ten-round double-column magazine."

Jack took it and hefted it. Light—a little under a pound; lighter even than his AMT. That would change when the magazine was in place—ten would double the number of rounds the AMT held—but still . . .

"It looks a little longer . . ."

"Only half an inch more than the AMT. This one's used, but that's good. You need to go through about fifty rounds to smooth out the action. For you that's been done already. And note the parkerized finish. What's not to like?"

Jack couldn't think of a thing. Ten backup rounds . . . his primary-carry Glock 19 with the extended magazine held seventeen. Keep a round in the breech of each and he'd have almost thirty shots.

He retracted the slide, checked to make sure the breech was empty, then pulled the trigger. He guesstimated the pull at somewhere in the neighborhood of ten pounds, maybe a tad less. Just the way he liked it.

If only he'd been there yesterday with one of these . . .

"Sold. How much?"

"It's a gift."

"Abe—"

"Considering the circumstances surrounding the loss of its predecessor, I should charge you? Your money's no good today."

"It must have cost you at least a—"

"Never mind what it cost me. Allow me a mitzvah, already, will you?"

Jack wasn't in a gift-getting mood, but felt obliged to let Abe do his good deed.

"Thanks, Abe."

"May you never have to use it."

As they headed back upstairs, Abe said, "When are they releasing your father's, you know, remains?"

Remains . . . jeez.

"Not until tomorrow."

Earlier this morning he'd made another call to the one-fifteenth, and this time he was referred to some city office downtown. The woman there told him that half of the bodies were being released today and the rest tomorrow. What was the deceased's name?

Jack told her and was informed that his father's remains could be picked up at the city morgue after ten tomorrow morning.

"The schmucks."

"Yeah. Another day, damn it. Tom left a message that he'll be arriving on the Metroliner and I couldn't get hold of him to tell him to wait till tomorrow. Which means he's on his way."

They exited the closet and returned to the legal portion of Abe's shop.

"So? That's bad?"

"I was planning on meeting him, taking him over to the morgue to claim Dad's body, getting it shipped to Johnson—"

"Johnson?" Abe said as he reinstalled himself on his stool behind the counter. "Never heard of it. Jersey?"

Jack nodded. "Our home town. Burlington County. Our mother's buried there."

Mom . . . the man he was today could be traced back to her murder.

"Damn." Jack felt like hitting the counter again but didn't want to put another scare into Parabellum. "This means he'll have to stay over. Where am I going to put him?"

"Well, he could stay with you."

Jack gave him a look.

Abe waved his hands. "Never mind. Forget I said that. Oy, what was I thinking?"

Jack showed his sweetest smile. "How about your place, ol' buddy, ol' pal?"

"Never! Barely room for me."

"Which means I have to find him a hotel room."

"This week? One in Yonkers, maybe. Maybe not."

"And he'll probably expect me to entertain him—which is not going to happen."

"Why not?"

"Business."

"You can't let it slide?"

Jack shook his head. "I'd love to, but there's only a small window of opportunity. And even if there weren't, I want it off my plate before I start going to wakes and the funeral." And facing his nieces and nephews. "Besides, I made a promise."

"Better get calling. Such an earache you'll have."

"Yeah, thanks. Where's your phone book?"

3

Jack had to look twice and then a third time before he was sure this was his brother coming up the steps.

Entering the main floor of Penn Station had triggered an almost unnerving sense of déjà vu. Yes, it was a train station instead of an airport, but the crowd of waiting travelers and expectant friends and family drew his thoughts kicking and screaming back to the baggage claim at La Guardia.

He was glad Tom had decided on Amtrak instead of a plane. Jack had never liked airports, and after yesterday's massacre . . .

Lots of people were steering clear of airports now. But flying from Philly to New York had never made much sense anyway. Not only was the train cheaper, but when you added up all the delays and wasted time in and around the airports, it was faster. Cheaper even than driving, considering what it cost to park in Manhattan.

He spotted a number of armed soldiers in black berets, camo suits, and combat boots patrolling the station.

Sure, he thought with a surge of anger. Now you're out in force. Where the hell were you yesterday?

He shook it off.

He'd finally found Tom a hotel room—managed to book him one right across the street from the station—but only because he'd once done a little fix-it for someone in the back office. He'd secured the room with a credit card under one of his aliases.

He'd arrived a little early, so he killed time wandering the marble floor of the main level. He browsed the Book Corner where he saw a new Stephen Hunter book; he made a note to pick it up for some future time when he could focus on something longer than a train schedule.

Speaking of which . . . he wandered toward the big arrival-departure board overhanging the main waiting area. A crowd clustered below, staring up at it like rapt worshippers before a shrine. He joined the congregation. Tom had taken the Metroliner and was due in at 1:59. The board said it was on time and ten minutes away.

He spent the remaining time people watching.

Folks in Penn Station looked tense, skittish. Jack figured he probably looked a little the same. What could happen at an airport could happen at a train station.

He wondered how many of them were armed. He had the new backup strapped around his ankle and his Glock in a nylon holster tucked in the small of his back under the waistband of his jeans.

Anyone started shooting around here was going to find someone shooting back.

Finally the Metroliner arrived. And here was this lardy, mid-forties guy in a dark gray suit, red faced and puffing as he lugged an overnight suitcase up the stairs.

Tom already had started putting on weight before Jack split to become nameless in Manhattan. But he'd really packed on the pounds in the fifteen years since Jack had last seen him. Looked like the "before" guy on an Overeaters Anonymous poster. But he had the same brown hair and eyes as the brother Tom he'd known, and the features in the puffy expanse of his face looked vaguely familiar.

"Tom?"

The guy looked up, blinked, then frowned. "Jackie?"

"That's me." He extended his hand. "Even though I haven't been 'Jackie' for a long, long time."

Tom's palm was moist as they shook. His lips curved into a half smile.

"Yeah, I should've figured that." He shook his head and puffed out his cheeks. "Hell of a thing, isn't it? One fucking hell of a thing."

Jack couldn't argue with that.

Tom looked around. "I'm going to need a drink before we head for the morgue."

Jack explained about the delayed release of the body.

"Christ, why didn't you tell me?"

"I left you a message."

Tom shook his head. "I still need a drink. Anyplace around here we can grab one?"

Jack shrugged. "You kidding? This is New York. Bars everywhere. Or, if you're really thirsty and can't wait . . ." He turned toward the string of shops and eateries framing the main floor and pointed to the glowing yellow sign over Houlihan's entrance. "We can stop there."

"Looks as good as any. Let's go."

4

Tom guzzled Grey Goose on the rocks. Jack had watched him pound back two and order a third during their first ten minutes at the bar. He was still working on the first half of his Brooklyn Lager pint. The light was low but Jack thought he could make out a fine network of dilated capillaries on Tom's nose. Drinker's tats?

"You were always his favorite, you know."

Jack forced a laugh. "Are we going to start a Smothers Brothers routine? 'Mom always liked you best'? That sort of thing?"

"It's true." Tom stared morosely into his third vodka. He was nursing this one. "I don't think Dad particularly cared for me. I'm not saying he didn't love me—I'm sure he did in the paternal sense—but I never had the feeling he liked me."

Jack didn't want to go there.

"Tom . . ."

"Hey, don't get me wrong. I'm not feeling sorry for myself. I know I can be an egotistic jerk at times. Ask the Skanks from Hell."

"Who?"

"My exes."

"How many are there?" Jack asked, though he knew the answer.

"Two. And number three's not so crazy about me at the moment. Anyway, they're not important. It's Dad who's dead."

Jack didn't respond. He was trying to get a grip on this virtual stranger who was his brother. He sensed a deep melancholy. He seemed almost . . . dispirited.

Tom sighed. "Maybe I should have done what you did."

"Meaning?"

"Disappear. All Dad did was talk about you and how he was going to track you down and bring you back. I was there but all he cared about was you."

"Cut me a break," Jack said. "He had Kate and Kevin and Lizzie, and . . . and your kids."

Tom looked at him. "You don't even know their names, do you. They're your nieces and nephews and you don't know a thing about them."

True. He didn't. Hadn't met any of his family's next generation.

"Yeah, well, maybe it's time for me to start remedying that."

"Don't do us any favors."

Jack fought a flare of anger.

"Christ, Tom, you're here, what, fifteen minutes, and listen to you. That why you came? To start a fight? That's not what this is about."

Tom sighed again. "Yeah, you're right. It's not." He drained his drink. "Sorry."

Jack did the same with his ale.

"Let's get you to your hotel room."

His head snapped toward Jack. "Hotel? I sort of figured I'd be staying with you."

"Nobody stays with me, Tom."

"Really?" He took on a pugnacious look. "How about Dad? Where was he going to stay?"

"Not with me."

Tom shook his head. "You're a weird one, Jackie—"

"Jack."

"Okay: Jack. I talked to Dad last week about the Philly leg of his trip—during which he was going to stay at *my* place, by the way—and he said some strange things about you."

Uh-oh.

"Like what?"

"Well, I mean besides all the hagiographic blather about how you'd turned out and how good it was to get to know you again and all, he said something like, 'If you ever need someone to watch your back, call Jack.' Now what did he mean by that?"

"Couldn't say."

"What went on down in Florida that made the two of you so buddy-buddy?"

"I guess you could say we bonded."

Bonded . . . the lump reformed in Jack's throat, smaller this time, but definitely there. If he'd only known how little time they had left.

"Yeah? How? I saw him a lot more than you did over the past fifteen years and we never 'bonded.' What happened?"

"We took care of a problem together."

"What sort of problem?"

"Not important."

"Shit. You're as oblique as he was."

Jack shrugged. He was glad Dad hadn't discussed it with Tom. Jack didn't want to.

Since Tom was making no move to pay for the drinks, Jack reached for his wallet.

"I've got it," Tom said. He pulled out a roll of bills, peeled off a twenty, and passed it to Jack. "How's that look to you?"

Jack recognized the workmanship—the same crew that had made the C-notes he'd passed to a pair of psychics last summer.

"Queer."

"Damn it! You can tell?"

"Stuff's been all over town. Question is, what's a judge, an officer of the court, doing with bogus bills?"

Tom shrugged. "Evidence in a case. They looked fairly genuine so I pocketed a sample."

"Why? You haven't been passing them, have you?"

Another shrug. "It's kind of a hobby. You know, to see if I can get away with it."

"Jesus, if you get caught—"

"Hey, I'm a judge. I had no idea. Someone passed it to me and I innocently passed it on." He smiled and put a hand over his heart. "I shall adopt the plaint of victimhood."

That might work for Tom, but Jack couldn't risk being pulled in as an accomplice. Someone might ask him questions he couldn't answer.

"Well, don't try it here." Jack pointed to a twenty and a C-note taped to the mirror next to the cash register. "Everybody's on the lookout for them."

Tom's smile held. "No problem. I'll bet I can work out a way around that."

This time he took out his wallet and removed a fifty. He waved to the barmaid and handed it to her along with the tab. Seconds later she was back with the change.

As she turned away, Jack watched Tom pocket the real twenty and hold up the queer.

"Oh, excuse me, miss. Can I have two tens for this?"

She said, "Sure," and went to the cash register and pushed in the twenty without checking it. Why would she? She thought it was the same bill she'd just given him. She returned and handed Tom the tens.

When she was out of earshot, he grinned at Jack. "How about that for slick?"

It took Jack about half a minute to recover. He'd seen a lot—a *lot*—of off-the-wall things, but his brother the judge pulling a two-bit bill switch . . .

"You've gotta be kidding me, Tom. Are you crazy?"

"Maybe. So what?"

"Get that bill back."

"Relax. It's a game. And it's only twenty bucks."

"It's not 'only' to her, and she'll get docked for accepting it."

Tom shook his head and stared at him. "No need to get all touchy-feely on me, Jack. I got the impression from Dad that you were some sort of tough guy. I guess I got it wrong."

"If I'm tough, it's not with working stiffs trying to earn a living."

My brother the judge, Jack thought.

Wasn't that about as high as you could go in the legal profession? The arbiter of right and wrong, of admissible and inadmissible, the guy in charge of the blind lady's scales . . . and he was acting like a lowlife. A bottom-feeding lowlife.

Jack knew loads of people on the wrong side of the law, and could think of a few who'd be only too happy to knock over Houlihan's and clean the cash registers of every last dime. But none of those guys would stoop to stiffing the barmaid. Okay, maybe he knew one or two who'd shortchange their blind, deaf, crippled mother, but they left a telltale trail of slime wherever they went and topped Jack's AVOID list.

"Well?" he said, giving Tom a hard stare. "You gonna get it back?"

Tom looked at him as if he'd just told him Dad was a space alien.

"Hell no."

Jack resisted the impulse to punch his brother's doughy face. Instead he took out his wallet, found a ten and two fives, and flagged down the barmaid.

"Could you give me a twenty for these?"

She glanced at Jack, then at Tom, then back again.

"Is this some kind of game?"

"No. I just need a twenty."

She shrugged and retrieved the bogus bill. Jack took it, then snatched a five from Tom's change and handed it to her.

"For your troubles."

She smiled. "Thanks."

Tom shot him a venomous look.

Screw him.

Jack started toward the elevators up to street level.

"Let's get you set up in your room."

5

"The Pennsylvania Hotel?" Tom said as he followed Jack across Seventh Avenue. "Never heard of it."

He was feeling the vodka percolating through his bloodstream now, dulling the pervasive shock of being the son of a man murdered by terrorists. He and Dad had

never been close—hell, who have I ever been close to?—
but still . . . he was his father and he'd been scheduled for
a stayover next week. Tom didn't kid himself—Dad's pri-
mary reason for coming had been to see his grandkids.

But still . . .

Vodka usually made the world look a little friendlier, a
little easier to handle. Not today.

This city was partly to blame. He'd never liked New
York. Always struck him as more toxic landfill than city.
Too big, too coarse, completely lacking the élan of
Philadelphia. Philly . . . now *there* was a city.

But here . . .

He eyed the passing parade of New York's *lumpenpro-
letariat*: the glaborous, the rugose, the nodose, the
labrose. An endless procession of elves, spriggins, gob-
lins, trolls, fakirs, shellycoats, gorgons, Quasimodos, and
Merricks.

He watched his brother walking ahead of him. The
Jackie—oops, he wants to be called Jack now—Tom remembered used to be a klutzy younker. A skinny little
pain in the ass who was always underfoot.

He was still a pain in the ass—an *uptight* pain in the
ass. Look at how he'd reacted to switching that twenty.
Like some sort of Miss Priss. Where'd he pick up his
holier-than-thou?

Yeah, still a pain in the ass, but no longer skinny. His
shoulders filled out his sweatshirt; he'd pushed his sleeves
up to his elbows revealing forearms that rippled with sleek
muscles just below the skin. Not much fat on Little Brother.

But that's okay, Tom thought. I've got enough for two.

"Used to be the Statler," Jack said. "Look, you're right
across the street from Madison Square Garden, and just
crosstown from the morgue."

Tom shook his head. "Yeah. The morgue." He looked
up at the tall ionic columns of the entrance. "*This* could
be a morgue."

"It's old, but it's been completely renovated."

Tom had a feeling Jack didn't give a good goddamn if he liked it or not.

Too bad they'd got off on the wrong foot, but that was Jack's fault, not his. And anyway, who cared what a college dropout loser thought of him?

Jack led him across the wide, retro lobby toward the registration desk.

Blast. He'd been sort of counting on staying with Jack. He didn't feel like ponying up for a hotel, especially on a completely unnecessary trip like this. Why Jack couldn't have simply signed for the body and shipped it back to Johnson was beyond him.

Well, at least it had got him out of Philly. That counted for something. As much as he revered the place, he wished he could find a way to be a former Philadelphian for good.

"I reserved it in your name," Jack said, pulling out his cell phone. "Go ahead. I've got a call to make."

Tom gave his name to the check-in clerk, an attractive twenty-something with curly black hair, pretty despite the fact she looked like a mix of every race on earth, and waited while she checked her computer.

"Ah, here it is," she said with a dazzling smile. "You're staying only one night, correct?"

She put down the card and began tapping on her keyboard. Tom noticed his own name on the form; a credit card slip with a handwritten name and number was attached. He edged forward for a closer look.

John L. Tyleski . . . who was that? Jack would have had to give a credit card number to hold the room, but this obviously wasn't his. The hotel must have screwed it up.

Tom hid a smile. This presented an interesting opportunity. Could he pull it off?

Well, never look a gift horse . . .

The clerk looked up and smiled at him. "Which credit card will you be using, sir?"

"Mr. Tyleski is covering the room."

"Really?" She studied the reservation card. "It doesn't say so here."

Tom gave a perturbed sniff. "Well, he is. He *always* covers my accommodations when I'm in town. Whoever took the reservation must have forgotten to write it down."

She was shaking her head. "I don't know . . ."

Tom sighed. "This *never* happens at the Plaza. He *always* puts me up at the Plaza, but this consultation was a last-minute thing and they're full. More the pity."

"I'm sorry, sir, but—"

"On the other hand, the Plaza is used to our arrangement. I suppose John simply could have forgotten to mention it." He waved his hand in bored annoyance. "Call him if you must."

He watched her hesitate, then pick up the phone.

Oh, shit. His bluff hadn't worked.

Well, it had been fun while it lasted.

He glanced over at his brother the wet blanket, still talking on the phone. Tom would have to come up with an explanation for the clerk as to why John Tyleski had never heard of him, and bring it off without Jack knowing. He didn't need another of those appalled looks. What a ninny.

"Mr. Tyleski, this is the Pennsylvania Hotel calling. We'd like to confirm the payment arrangement on the room you reserved today. Please call us back at . . ."

She was leaving voice mail! Tom almost let out a whoop.

Now, if this Tyleski character didn't check his messages until tomorrow . . .

The clerk hung up and turned to him.

"We'll leave it on Mr. Tyleski's card for now. If you speak to him, please ask him to confirm with us."

"Of course. I'm scheduled for a dinner meeting with him tonight at the Plaza."

She gave him a card to fill out with his address and telephone number, both of which he fabricated out of thin air. The less the Pennsylvania Hotel knew, the better.

Jack finished his call and walked over just as she handed him the key.

"All set?"

Tom nodded. "Room six-twenty-seven. Is there a restaurant here?"

"Joe O's. Never been but it's supposed to be pretty good."

"Great. What time do you want to meet for dinner?"

"Sorry. Can't."

"Come on. We'll eat at this Joe O's—my treat."

Actually, John Tyleski's treat. Tom would charge it to the room.

Jack shook his head. "Got some loose ends I've got to tie up tonight."

"Okay." He feigned a sad look. "I guess I'll have to eat alone."

Jack appeared unmoved.

Tom gave him a wink. "I suppose I could always rent some company."

"Jesus, Tom. Don't get rolled. I need you in one piece tomorrow."

The implication was not lost on him: no concern for Tom himself, just his presence to claim Dad's body. Talk about getting off on the wrong foot . . .

He'd been kidding about the rented company. He'd seen plenty of hookers during his years at the bar and on the bench. Some were knockouts and some were harridans, and some weren't even women. Trouble was, you never knew who their last john was or what you might catch.

Not that he'd ever needed them—plenty of legal secretaries around the courthouse happy to give it up for a judge.

"Don't worry, Jack. I'll be here, intact and ready to

roll. And maybe on the way over to the morgue you can explain why you couldn't take care of this yourself."

"Maybe," Jack said. "And maybe not. Pick you up at nine thirty tomorrow morning."

He watched Jack exit through the glass doors. Just as well. The thought of spending a couple of hours over dinner with that guy, trying to make conversation . . . Jesus, what could they talk about besides Dad? Not as if they had a store of fond memories to revisit.

Nope. Looked like dinner for one tonight.

At least that would give him time to gather his thoughts as to what he should do with the money he'd inherit. Tom had helped Dad change his will after Kate's death and in the process had got a peek into the old guy's finances. Still couldn't believe it—seven figures and growing. Dad had practically invented day trading and was damn good at it.

A third to Tom, a third to Jack, and a third to Kate's kids. His share would help loosen *some* of his financial straits, but not all. Especially if he couldn't keep it.

Had to find a way to hide it. He was executor, after all. He was sure he could find a way.

What a fucking mess he'd got himself into.

But no point in more self-excoriation. He'd done plenty already, and it hadn't changed a thing.

6

Here you are, Jack thought.

He crouched in a tiny, dark, stuffy Bronx apartment. The neighbor directly above was playing one of Polio's thrashing aural assaults at subway-train volume. The pounding bass sounded ready to peel the paint from the walls. If it was that loud down here, what was it like up there?

In Jack's hand sat a baseball—pardon, an "Official National League" baseball—encased in a clear plastic sphere on a round, gold-plated base. For something more than fifty years old, it appeared to be in damn good shape. Then again, why not? It had never been in a game.

He flashed his penlight on it again to double-check the inscription, directly below the Spalding logo:

To Danny Finder
Batter up!
Duke Snider
1955

The scribbled "Duke" looked like "Dude" but, yeah, this was the one. And Danny Finder Jr. was paying Jack a pretty penny to get it back.

Seems it belonged to his father who was way on in years and not thinking too clearly. His mind had regressed to childhood when he'd been a rabid Dodgers fan. His favorite had been the cleanup hitter, Duke Snider. Danny Sr. had been at Ebbet's Field for one of the World Series games in 1955 when the Bums beat the Yanks, and he'd snagged a signature from his hero.

That signed baseball loomed large in what was left of the old man's mind, and when it disappeared from his nursing home room, he went into a tailspin. The man-child was inconsolable, refusing to leave his bed or even eat.

His son had gone to the police but the NYPD had no time for a stolen baseball, even one worth a couple-three thousand because it was signed and dated by Duke Snider in a World Series year.

And so he'd come to Jack.

Money was no object—he seemed to have plenty—if he could get back that ball.

Strange what ends a man will go to for a sick father. Fathers and sons . . .

Here came that lump again.

So Jack had put out feelers but got nary a nibble. For the hell of it he'd checked eBay and whattaya know—there it was. Jack had started bidding. The price topped out at $2,983. Jack simply could have bought it and ended the job then and there. But the thief would have walked off with nearly three grand. Yeah, he'd have retrieved the ball but he wouldn't have worked a fix. And that was a big part of what it was all about. Jack liked to leave his stamp on his work.

So he'd e-mailed the guy asking where to send the check and received the address of this rat hole.

Tonight he'd come to collect.

Leaving the ball in its display globe, Jack placed it in the flimsy plastic grocery bag he'd brought along, then looked around for a few other small items to take. He wanted this to look like a simple B and E—nothing personal.

A lot of . . . merchandise littered the floor and tables: DVD decks, iPods and other MP3 players, X-Boxes and PlayStations, video games. This guy had to be a small-time fence.

He opened the room's only closet and let out a yelp as someone leaped toward him. He had his Glock in hand and snapping up before he realized it wasn't human: But it looked human. Well, as much as a blow-up sex doll could look human. Its wide eyes and mouth fixed in a perfect *O* lent it a perpetually surprised look.

Jack backed away and watched it make a slow-motion descent to the floor, where it bounced once and lay still.

Nothing much else in the closet but some ratty-looking clothes.

Jack reholstered the Glock and stuffed a couple of iPods and some video games—he'd heard good things about the new *Metal Gear*—into the bag. He stepped to the door and pressed his ear to the wood. All quiet in the hallway. He turned the knob—

—and felt the door slam into him, knocking him back. He was reaching for the Glock when he saw the pistol in the skinny white guy's hand.

"Hold it right there, fucker! Don't you fuckin' move!"

"You need help, Scotty?" said a black guy in the hall.

"Nah, I'm cool. Thanks for the call, though."

"Want me get the cops?"

"I'm cool, Chuck, I'm cool. Let me handle this."

Of course he didn't want anyone calling the cops—not with all this hot stuff in his pad.

With his free hand Scotty flipped on the overhead light, then kicked the door closed.

"Well, well, well," he said, swaggering closer. "What have we here?"

Jack put on a sheepish grin—damn well should be sheepish. He'd screwed up. One of Jack's rules was never go out on a fix if you're not one hundred percent. And he hadn't been near a hundred percent since yesterday afternoon. His concentration had been way off.

Jack could see how it went down: Someone spotted him picking Scotty's lock. The spotter called Scotty and the fence had been waiting in the hall for Jack to open the door. Good strategy, especially with Polio's delicate musicianship to mask any sounds that might have given him away.

"Heh-heh. Kind of funny, isn't it," Jack said. "I mean, you with all this stolen stuff and me stealing some of it."

"Do you see me laughing, fuck face?"

Jack flicked his gaze between Scotty's mean dark eyes and the .32-caliber pistol—a Saturday night special if he'd ever seen one—pointed at his midsection. A revolver—good. Hammer down—even better.

Guy was an amateur.

"Well, no, but—"

"But nothin'. Drop the bag."

Jack complied and raised his hands to upper-chest level. He was waiting for Scotty either to check the contents of the bag or try to pistol whip him. That was when Jack would make his move.

"Wh-what are you gonna do?"

"Know what Dumpster divin' is?"

"Sure. I had to do it now and then when I was hungry and tapped out. Why?"

"Because you're gonna do it again. Long distance. From the roof."

Jack added a quaver to his voice. "N-no, wait. W-we can—"

"We can nothin', fuck face!" He sidled in an arc to Jack's right and cocked his head toward the door. "Move. We got us some stairs to climb."

Jack shook his head. "N-no. I ain't goin'."

"Fuck you ain't!" He stepped closer, extending the pistol toward Jack's midsection. "Shoot you right here an' be done with it!"

A little closer . . . just a little closer . . .

"What are you so mad about?" He jutted his chin toward the love doll on the floor. "Not like I raped your girl or nothin'!"

Scotty's gaze flicked toward the doll. His face reddened, then whitened.

"That does it!"

The muzzle pushed forward. Jack's hand darted out and grabbed the top of the pistol. Wrapped his fingers around the cylinder. Clutched it in a death grip.

"Hey!"

Scotty pulled on the trigger. But the cylinder had to rotate before the hammer could fall. Jack had the cylinder locked in place.

Yanked on the gun, bringing Scotty closer. The fence's eyes wild with shock, confusion. Kept yanking on the trigger but getting no result. When Jack had him close enough, he let loose a vicious head butt, crushing Scotty's nose. The sound of collapsing bone and cartilage echoed through Jack's skull.

Music.

Scotty's head snapped back. Blood flowed from his flattened nose. But he didn't let go of the gun. So Jack reeled him back in for another butt. Scotty tried to use his free hand to fend him off. Jack slapped it aside and butted him again. Harder this time.

That did it. Scotty's knees buckled, his grip loosened, and Jack had the pistol all to himself.

But Scotty wasn't finished. With the loss of his weapon he became a wobbly, panicked, fist-swinging dynamo. Must have thought Jack was going to shoot him. Not the plan. Too much noise.

Ducked or blocked the fence's wild swings until he had an opening, then slammed the pistol against the side of his skull. Opened a gash but he didn't go down. Guy must have an iron skull. Leaped at Jack, slammed into him and got his arms around him. They went down, landing on the love doll. It popped and deflated with a loud hiss.

Scotty took a wild swing at Jack. This one connected. The flash of pain through Jack's chin released something within him. Dropped the gun. Grabbed one of the doll's deflated legs. Wrapped it around Scotty's throat and pulled. Felt a fierce joy, building toward exaltation, then rapture, finally exploding into a black consuming ecstasy as he tightened the plastic noose further and further—

Until he heard a small, weak, strangled voice whimper, "Please . . . you're killin' me . . . please . . . killin' . . ."

Jack stopped and saw Scotty's face. Felt the dark joy boil away. Let go and backed off, scrabbling away on palms and heels. And sat and stared at what he'd done.

A pressure built in his chest, then released. He heard a sound like a sob. And realized it had come from him.

Jesus, what's wrong with me?

The fence opened his left eye—the right was swollen shut—and looked at Jack.

"You crying?" he croaked. "You beat the shit outta me and almost choke me t'death and then you cry about it? Motherfuck, what's wrong with you?"

Jack wished he knew. He closed his eyes and felt tears squeeze between the lids.

He opened them to find the fence sneaking a hand toward the pistol lying on the floor between them. Jack stomped on the hand with the heel of his boot and heard a bone snap. The fenced wailed as he snatched it back and cradled it on his chest.

Jack sobbed again.

WEDNESDAY

1

The New York City Morgue . . . in the basement of Bellevue Hospital . . .

I'm seeing far too much of this place, Jack thought.

Just six weeks or so ago he'd walked this same hallway. The tiled walls and floor drains looked too familiar.

He'd picked up Tom at the hotel and they cabbed over. Jack would have preferred walking. It would take longer. He wasn't in any hurry to see his father's corpse. Again.

"That's one hell of a welcome sign they've got back there," Tom whispered as they followed an attendant. Something about this place made you whisper.

"Welcome sign? Where?"

Tom jerked a thumb over his shoulder. "Back there. It says *Hic locus est ubi mors gaudet succurrere vitae.*"

"Which means?"

"It's Latin. 'Here is where death delights to teach the living.'"

"You know Latin?"

"I've picked up some. Unavoidable in my profession. A dead language comes in handy when you want to confound and confuse the hoi polloi. Hence its use by lawyers and doctors."

Jack noticed that Tom's ruddy complexion of yesterday and earlier this morning had faded to gray. His skin glistened with a sheen of sweat that reflected the harsh overhead fluorescents.

"You all right?"

Tom nodded. "Yeah. Fine." A heartbeat later he shook his head. "No. Not really. This has all been abstract until now. Surreal. Like a fever dream. Ever since you called I could almost pretend it hadn't really happened. But after filling out those papers . . ."

"Now it all becomes real."

It was already real for Jack. He'd seen Dad lying on the air terminal floor, seen the blood, his slack face, his dead eyes . . . all without a grace period to brace himself.

Tom swallowed. "I'll be okay. I've seen dead bodies before. It's just that none of them was my father."

Just then Jack spotted a painfully thin guy with pale, shoulder-length hair and a goatee coming their way. He wore green scrubs.

Oh, hell. Ron Clarkson. One of the attendants. Maybe he wouldn't see—

"Jack?" Ron smiled. "What're you doing here, man? You're getting to be a regular."

Jack kept walking. "Here to pick up somebody."

"One of our boarders?"

"Yeah."

Ron fell into step with him. "Which one? Maybe I can—"

"Thanks, Ron." He pointed to the other attendant walking two steps ahead of him. "It's all taken care of."

"Yeah, but—"

"Ron . . . this is a private thing. I appreciate your concern, but everything is arranged, okay?"

"Okay, man. But you need anything, you let me know, okay?"

"Right."

If paid enough, Ron would do just about anything. And on those rare occasions when Jack needed a body part for a fix-it, Ron supplied it. For cash.

Ron turned and continued on in his original direction.

Tom glanced over his shoulder at the retreating figure. "You *know* people here?"

"Just him."

"What was that crack about being a regular?"

"I had to . . . identify someone last month."

"Really? Who?"

"Just somebody."

"You were a bit rough on him, don't you think?"

"He's a nosy busybody."

Jack hadn't wanted Ron to know that the "boarder" he was picking up was his father. Ron would then know Jack's real last name. That used to matter a lot—he hadn't wanted anyone from his past to find his present, and no one in his present to know his past—not for his sake but for his family's. Now, with his past encroaching on the present, he didn't know if it mattered much. Still, better to keep things the way they were, especially where a weasel like Ron Clarkson was concerned.

Up ahead the attendant pushed through a pair of swinging doors and held one open for them. Jack propelled his brother ahead of him. Tom had completed all the paperwork upstairs. All that remained now was the official identification of the body and a final signature—Tom's.

As he stepped into the room, Jack heard a voice to his left.

"Jack? That you?"

Who now?

He turned and saw Joey Castles standing by a gurney as an attendant zipped up a black body bag. He was short, maybe five-five, Jack's age, with black hair and dark eyes; the surname on his birth certificate had not been "Castles." He wore a black sport coat, gray slacks, and a black polo shirt. His hair, usually blow-dry perfect and sprayed granite hard, was in disarray today. His eyes looked red and puffy.

Jack stepped closer and extended his hand.

"Joey. Jeez, what happened? Who—?"

His Adam's apple worked, his voice sounded choked. "Frankie . . . the La Guardia thing."

Jack gave his hand an extra squeeze.

"Oh, no. Christ, I'm sorry."

Joey and his brother Frankie came from a long line of

scammers, most prominent among them their father, Frank Castellano Sr.

"He was coming back from visiting Dad—he's got this big place in the Keys—and I was supposed to pick him up but I was late and . . ."

The words choked off.

"How's your dad taking it?"

Joey shook his head. "You ever hear a grown man cry? Especially your father. It's . . ." He shook his head again. "A son shouldn't have to hear that. And a father shouldn't have to hear that his oldest son was shot down like a dog on his way home from visiting him. *Merda!* You know what kind of guilt he's going through?"

"Yeah, I know," Jack said.

Joey looked at him. "You in the same boat? Who?"

Jack hesitated, then decided he could trust Joey with the truth. Joey wasn't a nosy sort, and didn't know or care enough about Jack to check it out.

"My dad."

"Oh, shit, Jack. Fucking shit. I'm sorry."

"Yeah."

Joey's features hardened. "You know that story going 'round about cyanide bullets? True."

Jack felt his gut tighten. "How do you know?"

"Got a connection who got a little look-see at some reports and says it was cyanide-filled hollow-points." His features tightened, his lips drew into a tight line. "Frankie got clipped in the shoulder, Jack. That's all. He might've lived through that whole mess he hadn't been poisoned too." Joey bared his teeth. "Wrath of Allah can kiss my ass. Like to show them where they can stick their—"

"Whoa. Wrath of Allah? What's that?"

"Didn't you hear? Some group of stronzos called the *Times* and the three networks this morning saying they did it and that's only the beginning. They're gonna keep it up till the enemies of God and helpers of Satan are cleansed from the face of the earth. Or some such shit."

Jack hadn't turned on the TV this morning. He'd figured they'd only be talking about today being a national day of mourning and he'd heard all he wanted to about that.

He squeezed his eyes shut. So it *was* an Arab thing after all . . .

"Jeez."

He felt a bloom of rage, but Joey was way ahead of him.

"Dirty, rat-fucking—"

"Hey, Jack?" Tom's voice behind him.

Jack turned and saw his brother, face whiter than ever, lips almost blue, motioning him over.

"They're bringing him out and I don't want to do this alone."

As Jack stepped away, Joey gave his upper arm a squeeze. "Hang in there, Jack. And don't take off right away. Got a little something I want to talk to you about."

Jack nodded and moved toward Tom, thinking about cyanide bullets. Dad had caught one in his thigh, a flesh wound that under normal circumstances would—

Listen to me . . . "normal circumstances" . . . shit, what was normal about being shot while waiting for your baggage?

He had little doubt that Dad, like Frankie Castles, would have survived a wound like that from a normal bullet.

Jack's jaw muscles ached from clenching his teeth as he stood next to Tom and watched them wheel out a body bag on a gurney. The attendant, a black guy with short spiky dreads, looked bored. Jack wanted to punch him.

He steeled himself as the guy grabbed the zipper tab and pulled. When he'd opened an eighteen-inch gap, he spread the sides to reveal someone's head.

For an awful instant Jack thought it might not be Dad, that somehow his body had been misidentified or gone missing or been spirited away. But no, there he was. He looked better than yesterday, his eyes closed, his mouth shut, his features more composed.

But still very dead.

Jack heard the air whoosh out of Tom.

"Oh, shit," he croaked. "Oh, shit, it's him. It's really him."

Jack said nothing. He couldn't.

2

When they stepped outside, the sky was as clear and blue as Gia's eyes, but the wind flowing down First Avenue had developed a cold, sharp edge.

"What next?" Tom said.

"I have to call the Knight Funeral Home. Soon as I confirm the body's been released, they'll send a car to pick him up and take him back to Johnson."

Tom sighed. "I guess that's the best course. Bury him next to Mom."

Jack looked at him. "Was there ever a question in your mind?"

"Until now there's never been a reason for the question to *be* in my mind."

"Yeah. I hear you."

He looked around and saw Joey Castles waiting down on the sidewalk. Despite the wind he looked comfortable inside a full-length black leather coat.

Jack turned to Tom as they reached the bottom of the steps. "Wait here. I need to talk to someone."

Tom made a face. "Can't it wait? It's cold out here."

Jack pointed across the sidewalk to a pushcart by the curb. A plastic banner proclaiming HOT COFFEE & BAGLES waved in the breeze.

"Maybe his coffee is better than his spelling. Give it a try while I see what this guy wants."

"Jack," Joey said when he came up to him. He lowered his voice as he hooked Jack's arm and drew him closer. "You gonna do anything about this?"

Jack stiffened. "What do you mean?"

"I need payback. Need it real bad."

Jack knew the feeling. "Don't we all."

"You don't have to play cute with me. I don't know exactly what you're into, but I can make guesses. Word gets around and word is you ain't no guy to mess with."

Jack kept his underworld contacts and acquaintances in the dark as to the details of how he made his living, but every so often he'd drop hints to leave the impression that he had his hand in some smuggling and fencing with a little grift thrown in just for fun.

He shrugged. "Can't believe everything you hear."

Joey's smile was tight. "Okay. Play it your way. Just let me know you hear anything. You decide to mix it up, I want in on the damage. Big time."

Jack slapped him on the upper arm. "You'll be the first guy I call."

"About what?"

Jack turned and saw Tom standing behind his right shoulder, sipping coffee from a paper cup.

Joey smiled. "This guy's got to be your brother, right?"

Jack felt as if he'd been slapped.

"What? Yeah. Joey, Tom. Tom, Joey Castles." As they shook hands Jack said, "How come he's 'got to be' my brother?"

Joey's eyebrows shot up. "You kidding? Like peas in a pod, man. Shit, you two could be identical twins except for, well, I mean, okay, Tom here is a little older and a little, um, bigger—"

A *lot* bigger, Jack wanted to say.

"—but no question you're brothers. Hey, what're you looking at me like that for? You can't see it?"

Jack shook his head and glanced at Tom who was shaking his head.

"I'm better looking," Tom said. "But what'll you be the first to know about?"

Joey stared at Tom. "You want in? You may look like Jack, but can you hack what he hacks?" He grinned. "Hey. I'm a poet."

" 'Hack'?"

Oh, shit. Jack knew the track this train was on and needed to stop it fast. Keeping his hand out of Tom's line of sight, he made a cutting motion, but Joey didn't see it.

"Oh, yeah. I'm sure you know this, but let me tell you as someone was there: Right from the start your little brother made it clear that he should not be messed with. Hit him with a hammer, he came back with a sledge, know what I mean?"

Jack felt Tom's eyes on him.

"Really."

"Yeah, so now nobody, I mean *no*body comes at Jack 'less they're some kinda *fessone*."

"Is that so? Doesn't sound like your typical appliance repairman."

Joey gave Tom a You-kidding-me? look. "Appliance repairman? Where'd you get that—?" Finally he spotted Jack's hand going cut-cut-cut. "Oh, yeah, well, I was speaking strictly in a business sense. You got something broke you want fixed, you call Jack. He, um, clobbers the competition. Yeah, that's it. Clobbers 'em. I'm speaking pricewise, of course."

Joey was starting to sound like Jon Lovitz. Any second now he'd be saying "Yeah, that's the ticket."

Just shut up, Joey. Shut. Up.

He could see that Tom, who'd probably heard every possible lie in his years on the bench, wasn't buying.

"I see. But just what is it that Jack is going to call you about?"

Joey looked uncomfortable. "Oh, nothing much. Just talking a little business. Probably not the right time or place." He turned and started off. "Nice meeting you. Stay in touch, Jack. I mean that."

They watched Joey Castles head downtown on First, then Tom turned to Jack.

"Mind telling me what that was all about?"

Very much, Jack thought.

"Just small talk."

"Well then, what was he talking about? Hit you with a hammer and you come back with a sledge. What's that mean?"

"Just running his mouth."

"Like hell. By the way, in case you didn't realize it, your friend Joey is a lousy liar."

"Actually he's pretty good—if he's got a script."

Tom gave him a baffled look. "Now you're doing it too—what the hell are *you* talking about?"

Jack repressed the reflex to stonewall his brother. Maybe if he started talking about Joey's line of work it would divert Tom from what Joey had said about him.

But he couldn't seem too agreeable.

He shook his head. "I don't know if I should talk about Joey's occupation. I mean, what with you being an officer of the court and all."

3

Tom wanted to hear about this Joey character. He didn't look like he belonged on *The Sopranos* exactly, but Tom had seen enough louche types to spot one a light year away.

"Don't worry about that. I'm not a judge up here. Not even licensed to practice. Just another plebeian. And let me tell you, I've already guessed your pal isn't a neurosurgeon. What's he do—sell stolen hubcaps or something?"

Jack hesitated, then, "He's a *bidonista.*"

"What's that mean?"

"Joey says it's Italian for grifter."

"He's a scam artist?"

Jack nodded. "Family tradition."

Tom treated himself to a pat on the back. But this raised a number of troubling questions. The big one: Jack had told this scam artist he'd be "the first to know." Know what?

Maybe things were starting to add up, disconnected pieces beginning to form a picture. Jack's leaving the family and hiding out in New York for fifteen years . . . everyone had wondered where he was and what he was doing. The word had come that he was an appliance repairman. Yeah, sure.

Tom had a growing conviction that his little brother was living, as they say, on the wrong side of the law.

It explained everything.

Jack pointed to the traffic lights on First Avenue. They'd turned red.

"Let's cross."

Tom held back. "We're walking?"

"I'd rather not talk about this in a cab."

Now *this* was interesting. Tom weighed which he wanted more: a warm cab or a peek into his brother's secret life.

No contest. He hunched his shoulders against the chill and stepped off the curb.

"Okay. Let's go. Start talking."

"Well, Joey's last name isn't Castles."

As if I didn't know, he thought.

"Let me guess: It's Castellano or something like that."

"Castellano—right. Very good. His older brother Frankie was killed along with Dad."

It shouldn't have come as something of a shock that other people had lost family members too, but Tom had been focused on Dad.

Not that that should surprise anyone, he thought.

He was always taking heat for being self-centered. Privately he agreed—nolo contendere—but made a point of blustering about the unfairness of the charge whenever one of his wives brought it up.

"Shit. Too bad. They were close, I bet. Not like us."

Jack gave him a long look. Was that regret in his eyes?

"No. Not like us."

Tom didn't want to get onto that subject.

"So what were these brothers into?"

"Their father, Frank Senior, used to run one of the original telephone booth scams out of Florida."

Florida . . .

Tom shivered as they started up 29th Street. A lessening of the wind here between the avenues made the air seem warmer, but not a whole hell of a lot. He could use a little Florida himself right now.

"Connected?"

"Yes and no. He wasn't in the outfit, but he paid them a piece of the action to, you know, avoid trouble."

"Telephone booths . . . I've had a lot of scams come through my court, but that's a new one."

"No, it's an old one. It's passé now. But back in the day Big Frank would take out ads in small town papers all over the South and in the Midwest offering to sell people phone booths."

"Phone booths? What would anyone want—?"

"Just hear me out and you'll know. The pitch was you could buy as many as you wanted; you could install them yourself or, for a small percentage, Big Frank's company would handle installation, maintenance, and collect all those coins. Once you were set up you'd have a steady stream of cash without lifting a finger. All you'd have to do was sit back and start counting your money. Everybody's dream, right?"

"And people fell for that?"

"Enough to make Frank Castellano rich."

"You mean people would see this ad, write out a check, and just send it to him?"

"Not with the price Frank was asking. No, the really interested ones would call the toll-free number, and if they sounded like live ones, Frank would buy them a plane ticket, fly them down, and show them around his telephone booth plant."

Tom was nodding. "I'm getting the picture. A Big Store."

He'd always found scams fascinating—the more elaborate, the better.

"Right." Jack gave him an appraising look. "So you know a Big Store when you hear it. Interesting."

"Everybody who's ever seen *The Sting* knows that."

"But they don't know it's called a Big Store. Anyway, Big Frank's first Big Store was a rented warehouse outside Fort Myers. He'd tour the people through, pass them by lab-coated technicians working on circuit boards, show them a sample booth and dozens of big wooden crates ready to be shipped, tell them how he's swamped with orders and having trouble keeping up with demand. He'd set the hook by telling them how the first people to place booths get the best locations; the johnny-come-latelys would have to take the leftovers."

"And so they started writing checks."

"Big ones. Thousands and thousands."

Tom had the picture now: "But the booths never showed up."

"Never. When folks started to complain, Frank put them off as long as he could. When they finally came looking for him, Frank was gone. He'd moved his operation to the other side of the state."

Tom shook his head. "Never ceases to amaze me how people never learn: If it sounds too good to be true, it almost certainly is."

"Yeah, well, so Joey and Frank Junior are—were carrying on the family tradition with an Internet booth variation. And they're cleaning up, though not as much as they did with cell phone licenses."

"There's another new one."

"Worked with the same come-on as the phone booth: Get a cell phone license for a given area and you can collect roaming fees from anyone making calls from your turf. Frankie and Joey charged folks eight, nine, ten thousand bucks for a mobile phone license."

"Which were worthless, right?"

"Nope. They delivered the real deal."

"The real thing?" Then Tom smiled. "Oh, I see. The victims could have got them on their own from the government for something like a hundred bucks, right?"

"Seven hundred, actually. All the marks would have had to do was fill out a form. They never needed Joey and Frankie."

Tom smiled. "Who says you can't cheat an honest man?" Then he shrugged. "At least those folks got something for their money. Better than a phone booth that never arrives."

"But not much. Seems the guys neglected to tell the marks that they'd have to spend well into six figures to build the cell tower that would allow them to collect. But how'd you guess about the government selling them for so much less?"

Tom shrugged again. "Not a guess really. A fair number of attorneys are doing very well with a variation on that."

Back when he was in private practice he used to work that sort of thing. Those were the days . . .

Tom sighed. Sometimes—many times, lately—he regretted leaving private practice. He'd wheeled and dealed and wheedled and angled for a judgeship. He'd heeded the siren song of the prestige, the opportunities it would afford him. But he'd have been better off now—*lots* better—if he'd stayed in the lawsuit game. Torts, wrongful deaths, and personal injuries had turned into such a gravy train. Guys he knew were making fortunes off plane crashes and even the 9/11 thing. Those kinds of claims almost never went to trial except maybe over the amount of money owed. Guys were collecting a third of the recovery for doing next to nothing.

"Why am I not surprised?" Jack said in a flat tone.

Tom waved his hands. "All perfectly legal."

"I can't wait to hear this."

"Here's how it works. All you need is a mass tort or a disaster that results in the creation of a fund. The breast implant settlement, for example. Or the Ramsey IUD settlement. Guys made tons by putting out ads indicating their 'expertise' in the Ramsey IUD case, then getting claimants to sign on to percentage agreements—some got pushed to as high as forty percent. But all the attorney had to do to earn it was show the claimants how to document their use of the product and their injuries, and then fill out the forms. All of which they could have done themselves in a written application to the fund."

"So instead of getting a hundred percent of the settlement, they wind up with sixty because forty goes into some shyster's pocket."

"Like I said: perfectly legal. *Lex scripta* is all that matters. But you have to take into account that a lot of those people wouldn't have wound up with a dime if the ads hadn't spurred them to action."

"Swell system. You sleep okay at night?"

Tom felt his jaw clench. "You're not going to do your Mr. Sanctimonious impersonation again, are you? What about your pal Joey?"

"Not my pal."

"You ever inculpate him about his cell phone scam?"

"That's different."

"Really? How? He bilks thousands. I want to play around with a bogus twenty and you get on your high horse. How come he gets a pass but not me?"

"I don't like what Joey does but, because of the way he was raised, he doesn't know any better. He thinks that's how life is. But that's only a side issue. Joey's not my brother. You are. And you and I were raised with the crazy notion that doing the right thing *mattered*—mattered more than just about anything else. And the right thing is the right thing, even if the law says otherwise. Remember?"

Tom tried to remember. But his boyhood days growing up in the tiny town of Johnson, New Jersey, were a blur. Echoes of Dad's voice flitted through his head, but he couldn't hear what he was saying. Probably because he hadn't been paying attention at the time.

All he'd wanted was out. He'd seen Philadelphia and Manhattan and Baltimore and D.C. on class trips and had known immediately that Johnson was not the place for him.

And then he remembered the night he'd almost been killed, and Dad shouting at him. First, because he was scared that Tom had almost killed himself, and then because of *how* he'd almost done it.

He'd come across this Trans Am with the keys in the ignition. Sixteen, no license, but he knew how to drive. So he'd taken it for a spin. Everything was going fine until he went into a curve a little too fast and wound up wrapping the car around a tree.

Just one of those teenage things.

"Oh, yeah. I forgot. Saint Jack. Daddy's boy. He never had to worry about you going for a joyride."

"No, he didn't."

Tom had been out of the house by then, but it irked him to think that his kid brother had spent his high school years as some kind of namby-pamby geek. A teenager, especially a boy, was supposed to shake things up, give his parents a few gray hairs. All part of the rite of passage.

"Didn't think so."

Jack grinned. "Even though I went for at least a dozen."

"Bullshit."

He raised his hand, palm out. "Truth."

"Dad never mentioned—"

"That's because he never knew. Nobody knew. After I learned to hot-wire a car—a lot easier in those days than now—I set a challenge for myself. The game was to borrow the ride, take it for a spin, then return it to the exact same spot with no one the wiser."

"And no one ever spotted you, no one ever looked out their window and noticed their car missing?"

Jack shrugged. "I did my homework."

Tom had to admit he was impressed. Maybe Jack hadn't been such a sissy boy after all.

4

As much as Jack liked to walk and enjoyed cooler weather, it felt good to step into the hotel lobby.

"When's check-out?"

Tom hesitated, a look of uncertainty flitting over his face.

"Wait here while I find out."

Jack didn't see why he shouldn't accompany him to the registration desk, but didn't argue. As he stood alone in the virtually deserted lobby, a wave of sadness swept over him.

Had things gone as planned, had the fucking Wrath of Allah stayed home, he and Dad would have been roaming the town, knee-deep in Jack's cool-building tour. They'd have seen the old Pythian Club and the Masons-built Level Club on West 70th by now, and would be heading toward 57th where he could show him the Hearst Magazine Building. Jack had a whole list of Manhattan buildings he loved. He'd looked forward to sharing them with his father. Now . . .

He felt his throat constrict.

Shit. Shit-shit-*shit!*

Tom's voice drew him back to the here and now.

"I'm going to stay another night."

"What?"

"I just checked to see if I could extend my stay and they said no problem. Seems the hotel's practically deserted. New York, it appears, has suddenly lost its cachet as a destination city."

"But why are you staying?"

Tom shrugged. "I don't know. Just feel I should. Then I can drive down to Johnson with you tomorrow."

Oh, hell.

"Why do you assume I have a car?"

Tom looked surprised. "The Phantom Joyrider doesn't own a set of wheels? I don't believe it."

"Lots of New Yorkers are wheelless. A car is more of a hassle—an expensive one—than a convenience in a city like this."

"But that doesn't answer the question: Do you own a car?"

"Yes."

Abe was going to drive him out to La Guardia this afternoon. They'd switch tickets and then drive out. As a recent arrival—he'd say he'd just dropped someone off—he'd be under less scrutiny.

"Are you driving down to make arrangements for the wake tomorrow?"

"Yes."

"Can I hitch a ride?"

How could he say no?

"Of course you can."

Tom gave him a tight smile. "There. Wasn't that easy?"

"But what about your wife—wives—and kids? Aren't they coming?"

"Sure. I'll hook up with them at the wake."

Jack couldn't see any way out of this. Even if Tom was his only living relative, an hour and a half cooped up with him in a car . . .

And then he had an awful thought. Gia and Vicky were planning on going—Gia was adamant about this—and that meant they'd be exposed to Tom.

"You should know that I'll have a couple of other people along."

Tom's eyebrows rose. "Is that so? Who, pray tell?"

"A woman I know and her daughter."

He grinned. "So, there's a woman in Jack's life. I can't wait to meet her." He snapped his fingers. "Hey! I've got an idea. Why don't I buy you two dinner tonight?"

"We've already got plans."

"Well, if they include dinner, I'm buying." He jerked his thumb over his shoulder at the hotel restaurant. "Right here."

He'd planned on it being just Gia and Jack tonight, but couldn't see a way out of this.

"Okay. But not here."

"Why not? It's excellent. I ate there last night and—"

"Sorry. We've got reservations at Lucille's tonight."

"So? Break them."

"Can't."

Jack didn't understand Tom's wistful look as he glanced toward the entrance of Joe O's.

"It'll be so easy. I'll just charge it to my room and—"

"Yeah, but the problem is I know the guy who's playing Lucille's tonight. He asked me to come down and listen, fill a couple of seats for him."

Actually the singer, Jesse Roy Bighead DuBois, had

told Jack he'd have a surprise for him if he showed. Wouldn't say what, but he'd piqued Jack's curiosity.

But with all that had happened, Jack had forgotten about Jesse and his gig. When Gia had reminded him this morning, telling him she'd call and cancel their reservation if he wanted, his first impulse had been to say yes. But when he considered his other options, sitting with Gia and listening to some blues while having dinner didn't seem like a bad thing. After all, it was the blues.

Tom frowned. "Playing what?"

"He fronts a blues band. Of course if you don't like blues—"

Hope-hope-hope.

"I'm a blues aficionado. Count me in."

Jack repressed a sigh.

But then, maybe it wasn't right to leave his only sib alone two nights in a row.

Or was it?

5

Jack sat at his computer in his apartment's cluttered front room. The blank eyes of his Daddy Warbucks lamp watched as he scanned through the newyorktimes.com story about the call from Wrath of Allah. It included an audio file of the call. He clicked it and heard an accented voice.

"We are the Wrath of Allah, fedayeen in the war against the Crusader-Jewish alliance. We have struck and we will strike again, until all the enemies of God and helpers of Satan are cleansed from the face of Allah's earth. This is but the beginning."

He slumped in the chair. The gloating, cold-blooded, matter-of-fact threats, the hatred in the tone stayed with him after the clip. How do people get to that point? Didn't they listen to themselves? If their god was so offended by western culture he could cleanse it from the face of the earth with a thought. Any self-respecting god would take offense at the notion that he needed a bunch of bearded crazies to defend him.

Jack listened twice more, then downloaded the file. He burned it onto a CD. He wasn't sure why. Maybe he simply needed to listen to it now and then to confirm that it was real. Maybe he'd need it as fuel should the fire of his simmering rage ever burn too low.

6

Gia leaned against him. "I can't believe I'm finally going to meet a member of your family."

"He's the only one left. And for all I know, he might not show."

Jack and Gia comprised two of half a dozen people at the bar in Lucille's Bar and Grill. Jack sipped a pint of Bass, Gia a club soda with a wedge of lime. He scanned the room. Beyond the barrier separating the bar from the rest of the space sat the stage and the front dining area. Beyond that lay a larger dining area two steps down toward the rear. Ceiling high and black, walls paneled in some sort of rich brown wood, carpet a half-abstract, half-surreal pattern of guitar shapes that had melted like Dali clocks.

The place looked deserted. It was early, of course, but

Jack couldn't help thinking that the La Guardia massacre had something to do with the low population density.

Lucille's was a casual place and they were dressed accordingly: Gia in black slacks and a loose, sapphire blue velour turtleneck that picked up her eyes and hid what little tummy she had; Jack in khakis, a plaid shirt, and a dark brown leather flight jacket. A nondescript couple out for a drink and a meal.

He glanced at his watch: *7:45.* Their reservation had been for seven thirty. Jesse went on at eight.

"We should be waiting for my dad instead of my brother."

Gia took his hand and gave a gentle squeeze. "I wish that too." Tears glistened on her lids. "God, I can't believe . . ."

"Yeah. I know." He looked around. Still no sign of Tom. "You know, if he doesn't show by the time we finish these, maybe we should take off."

"He's your brother, Jack."

Jack fiddled with the paper napkin that had come with the beer.

"Yeah, well, we never got along growing up and I don't see us getting along any better as adults."

"What did he do to get you so down on him?"

Jack thought of the first line of *The Cask of Amontillado.*

"If I may paraphrase Poe, 'The thousand injuries of Tom I had borne as I best could . . .' "

"Oh come on now, aren't we exaggerating just a little?"

He didn't want to tell her that Tom was the most self-centered human being he had ever known. Jack imagined him being pissed on 9/11 because the fall of the World Trade towers had preempted his favorite Tuesday night TV shows.

Okay. A little harsh. Tom would have been as aghast as everyone else.

He hoped.

"He was ten years older and when he wasn't ignoring me

he was hassling me. A little example. I was maybe eleven and I loved pistachios. As I remember, they were all red back then. Anyway, I didn't like to eat them one at a time. I liked a bunch at a time. So I'd shell a couple of dozen and then gobble them in one big bite. I remember it was summer, Tom was home from college, and I was sitting at the kitchen counter, doing the work of accumulating a pile of shelled nuts. Tom breezed along, grabbed them, shoved them into his face, and walked on. If he'd done it as a tease it would be one thing, but he acted as if he hadn't the slightest doubt about his right to them or that anyone would refuse him anything—as if I'd been shelling them for him."

"And what did you do?"

"Well, they were already in his mouth so I didn't want them back, and he was twice my size so I couldn't attack him. And I was too old to go whining to my folks. So I had to let it pass."

"Since when do you let things pass?"

"I was a kid, so I did. Then he did it again."

"Uh-oh."

"Yeah. Uh-oh. I was insane. Once was bad enough. Twice was intolerable. I decided to put a stop to it."

"Do I want to hear this?"

Jack smiled. "Of course you do. So I went to Mr. Canelli, this sweet old Italian guy up the street who had the town's best lawn in his front yard and a big vegetable garden in the back. I asked him if I could buy a couple of his hottest—*hottest* peppers."

Gia nodded. "I see where this is going."

"Need I say more?"

"Well, did it work?"

"Oh, it worked. Mr. Canelli could eat hot peppers like candy, but he said he had one tepin plant that produced peppers so hot he could only use a tiny bit at a time. Two or three times hotter than the red habañero. He gave me some—half a dozen tiny red things. I crushed them and coated about twenty shelled pistachios with the juice."

"Ouch."

"Ouch to the hundredth power." Jack laughed at the memory. "Tom came by, snatched them up, stuffed them into his mouth, and kept moving—for about five steps. Then it hit him."

"Did he turn red?"

"Red? Ever see someone washing out his mouth with a garden hose—for half an hour? It was two days before his tongue was something he wanted in his mouth."

Gia laughed. "Now I've *got* to meet him."

Jack sobered. "I don't know if you should. I'm still not sure we should even be here."

She frowned. "Where else should we be? Home? Doing what?"

Good question. The options were to go home alone or hang around Gia's house and be morose.

"Wallow?"

"You really want to do that?"

He shrugged. He didn't know what he wanted. "I guess not, but being here seems somehow disrespectful . . . almost sacrilegious."

Gia shook her head. "I didn't know your father, but from what you've told me I can't see him wanting you to do that."

"You're right. He wouldn't."

"And besides, you promised this fellow Jesse Bighead—"

"Jesse *Roy*—Jesse Roy Bighead DuBois."

She made a face. "He doesn't have hydrocephalus or anything like that, does he?"

"No. It's a bluesman thing to have a tag with your name. 'Blind' seems to be the most popular: Blind Boy Fuller, Blind Willie McTell, Blind Blake, and the guy with the double whammy, Blind Lemon Jefferson. Then there's Lightnin' Hopkins, Howlin' Wolf, Muddy Waters, Gatemouth Brown, T-Bone Walker, Pinetop Perkins—the list goes on and on."

"But how do you wind up being called 'Bighead'?"

"I asked him that once and he told me it was his mother's doing. He'd been a big baby and whenever anyone would mention childbirth, his mother would go on about what an awful time she had passing his head."

"Think I'm sorry I asked."

"He may have got the 'Bighead' from his mother, but not the rest. She named him William Sutton, and he grew up as Willie Sutton."

"Like the safecracker?" Gia shook her head. "That might be interesting, but Jesse Roy Bighead DuBois is definitely more picturesque." She nudged Jack with her elbow. "Still not going to tell me how you know him?"

"Told you: I did a fix-it for him a few years back."

It had been a simple fix, but Bighead had been impressed, and had never forgotten.

"Which tells me nothing. It's not as if you're a priest and he told you something in confession."

"Yes, it is."

Jack looked around again. Where the hell was Tom?

7

When will I learn to keep my big yap shut? Tom thought as he extracted himself from the cab. I should be back at Joe O's, feasting on John L. Tyleski's tab.

Instead he was going to get stuck with a three-meal bill in a midtown restaurant.

He slammed the cab door and looked around. Jack had given him a West 42nd Street address but nothing here looked like a restaurant. *The Lion King* . . . the biggest McDonald's he'd ever seen with a huge, Broadway-style flashing marquee . . . Madame Tussaud's Wax Museum . . . all so different from what he remembered.

Back in his late teens and early twenties, this block had been lined with grindhouse theaters showing grade-Z sleaze.

Then he spotted it: a marquee with B. B. KING scrawled across the top in big red letters. The place looked like a converted movie theater. Probably—no, most likely— one of those grindhouses from the earlier days. Even had a ticket booth out front.

But Jack had said this was the place. Lucille's—anyone who knew anything knew that B. B. King called his guitar Lucille—had to be inside.

If nothing else, the music should be good.

And he was dying to see what sort of floozy Jack had hooked up with. Maybe she had a friend . . .

Tom entered to the left of the ticket booth and found himself in a small souvenir shop. He asked the T-shirted girl behind the counter for the restaurant and followed her point down a wide circular staircase. He spotted "Lucille's Grill" in red neon over a doorway and walked through. Before the receptionist could ask about a reservation, he spotted Jack and a blonde at the bar.

He pointed. "I'm with them."

He approached from the rear. He couldn't see the woman's face, but he noticed that she dressed on the conservative side, and that her short blond hair did not appear to have originated in a bottle.

Surprise, surprise. Jack had latched onto a babe with a little class.

"Sorry, I'm late," he said.

Jack and the woman turned. Jack's expression remained neutral, but the woman smiled and Tom felt as if he'd run face first into an invisible wall.

That smile, those blue eyes, that face and the way her hair framed it and curved into feathery little wings . . . it seemed as if he'd stepped into some kind of cosmic shampoo commercial where everything dropped into slow motion as he approached her. He tingled, he flushed, he buzzed with an instantaneous chemical reaction.

A corny, old-hat question burned through his brain: *Where have you been all my life?*

He was blown away. Blown. A. Way.

Her lips moved. She was saying something. Had to come out of this, had to focus and hear that voice . . .

". . . *not* believe this!"

"Believe what?" Jack said.

"How much you two look alike. My God, it's incredible."

Her voice . . . like liquid, like liquor, sending a gush of warmth into his belly.

Jack said, "Tom, this is Gia DiLauro. Gia, my brother, Tom. But you seem to have figured that out already."

She extended her hand. Her skin was like silk, her touch a revelation. He sensed every nucleotide in his DNA drawing him toward her.

Gia . . . even her name was beautiful . . . soft, smooth, sensual . . .

Her azure eyes locked on his. "If Jack had told me he was an only child and you'd sat down at the other end of the bar, I'd have thought you were his long-lost brother."

Okay. She wasn't perfect. She obviously needed glasses. He and Jack looked nothing alike.

Jack shook his head. "You know, that's the second time today we've heard that. I don't get it. We couldn't be more different."

"When was the last time you saw yourselves side by side? Before the night's over, go into the men's room and look at yourselves in the mirror."

Tom figured he'd pass on that.

8

They'd moved to their table, a half banquet in a rear corner with a good view of the stage. The backrests were done in alternating sections of black and white; their table sported pieces of blond and brown wood done up in an art deco-ish pattern.

Tom looked around. Only half the tables were occupied. His brother's reservation had been redundant.

Canned music—nondescript blues—was playing too loud. Tom nursed his second vodka while they waited for their appetizers. He'd had a couple of pops at the hotel bar before coming over and so he could take it easy now. Didn't want to get sloppy in front of this woman.

"Where's this band you came to see?" he said.

Jack shrugged. "It's blasphemy for a blues band to start on time."

Tom hoped they never came on. He wanted to talk to Gia, learn all about her. Something he couldn't do if the band really cranked up.

"Do you like blues?" Gia said.

"I like all kinds of music."

Her eyebrows rose. "Really? How about opera?"

"Love it. *Tristan and Isolde* is my favorite."

Not necessarily true. He used to hate opera, but part of the politics of his judgeship included attending an endless line of functions and fund-raisers. Too many of them included nights at the opera, or the ballet, or at an art museum. Boring as all hell, but his wives, all three, had loved the affairs, loved mingling with Philadelphia's *haut monde.* Those were the times they appreciated being the wife of a judge.

Along the way, mostly through osmosis, Tom had managed to become an esthete manqué, absorbing enough culture to blow highbrow smoke when the situation called for it.

As Gia's eyes lit, he sensed this might be one of those situations.

"I love that one too," she said. "*The Merry Widow* is another of my favorites. It's at the Met now." She cocked her head at Jack. "But try getting your brother to go. He hates opera."

"Don't listen to her," Jack said. "I like opera just fine . . . it's just the singing and all the gesturing I don't like. Lose those and do it in English and I could be a major fan."

Gia laughed and leaned against him. "Stop it."

Jack turned to him. "Gia's an artist—she sees things in opera and ballet that I can't."

"That's because you don't lend yourself to the experience," Gia said.

"Artist?" Tom said. "Have you had a show?"

Still smiling, she shook her head. "I hope to someday, but it's commercial art that pays my bills—advertising, book covers, that sort of thing. Between assignments I'm working on a series of fine-art oils for an eventual show."

Time to score some points, Tom thought as he nodded.

"Speaking of fine art, Gia, may I say that you are a vision straight out of a Botticelli."

Her cheeks colored. "What a sweet thing to say."

He didn't mention that he was trying to picture her posed as Botticelli's Venus.

"Botticelli . . ." Jack said, snapping his fingers and looking perplexed. "Botticelli . . . isn't that the tropical plant place down on Sixth?"

"Ignore him," Gia said with a laugh. "He loves to play the philistine."

"Are you sure he's playing?"

Her fingers wrapped around Jack's hand. "I'm sure."

Tom repressed an insane urge to grab those intertwined hands and yank them apart. Gia should be holding *his* hand.

He took a sip of his vodka and forced himself to lean back.

What was the matter with him? Why was he so . . . so smitten with this woman? Yes, that was what he was: smitten. He'd been under her spell since the instant he'd laid eyes on her. Why?

Maybe it was genetic. Jack was obviously smitten too. Maybe Gia emitted a pheromone that interacted with the genes they shared.

She added, "But he really does *not* like opera."

"Or ballet," Jack said.

Gia nodded. "Right. Hates ballet."

Jack said, "Hold on now. I don't know about hate. Don't I go to *The Nutcracker* with you and Vicks every year?"

"And every year you doze off during the first act."

He shrugged. "It's always the same story. I know how it ends."

Gia looked at Tom. "And to be honest, your brother's not too crazy about modern art either."

"I like lots of modern art. I just don't like linoleum patterns and drop cloths passing as art. Who's that guy who does all those big splatters?"

"You don't mean Jackson Pollock?" Tom said, trying to worm his way back in.

"That's the one. Pollock. Gia can paint rings around him."

Gia gave Jack an appraising look, then turned to Tom. "I take that back. He *is* a philistine."

And then the two of them leaned together and laughed. The sound was acid, etching the chambers of Tom's heart.

The way these two looked at each other, laughed with each other, and seemed to communicate on their own private wavelength filled Tom with a boundless longing. He'd never had that sort of easy intimacy with a woman—no, not just intimacy . . . *friendship*. He'd never thought it mattered, never cared enough to miss it. But seeing his brother so bonded to a woman like Gia, sharing something precious, timeless, and so uniquely theirs . . . it awakened strange feelings within him . . . strange because he'd never experienced them, never known they existed, wasn't even sure what they were.

One feeling he did recognize: envy.

He wanted that for himself. He couldn't remember any woman ever looking at him the way Gia looked at Jack. But he didn't want just any woman to look at him that way, he wanted Gia.

The waiter arrived then with the appetizers. Tom had ordered the crawdad soup—crayfish in a thick brown broth he couldn't identify.

Delicious.

"A delightful decoction," he said. "Anyone wish to partake?"

Gia's eyebrows rose. "Decoction? Really?"

He'd used the term loosely and she'd caught him. Obviously she knew her way around a kitchen.

Before he could backtrack, the house lights went down and a voice announced Jesse Roy Bighead Dubois and his band. As the musicians filed onstage and picked up their instruments, a tall black man took the microphone and introduced himself.

The singer said, "Our first song is dedicated to a fellow in the audience. No, wait. Not just dedicated—*about*. I wrote it for him and about him. I won't point him out because his deal is slipping through the cracks. He's a ghost, my friends. You don't see him unless he wants you to. But he's out there now, among you. The song's called the 'R-J Blues.' The music comes from Elmore James, but the words are mine. This one's for you, Jack."

A piece of cajun shrimp stopped halfway to Tom's mouth.

Jack?

He looked across the table and knew immediately from his brother's tense posture and uncomfortable expression that he was the Jack Bighead was talking about.

Jack . . . a ghost who slips through the cracks? This was going to be interesting.

Bighead gave his band the count and then they ripped into an up-tempo blues. Tom immediately recognized the wailing slide riff of Elmore James's version of "Dust My Broom."

Then Bighead started to sing.

I wake up ev'ry mornin, feelin troubled all the time
You know I wake up ev'ry mornin, feelin troubled
* all the time*
Gotta find me a repairman, who can fix my
* worried mind*

Goin down the corner, find this guy I heard about
Gonna drop a dime on Ma Bell, call this guy I
* heard about*
Gonna tell this guy my problem, see if he can help
* me out*

Well I give him all my money, every cent and that's
* all right*
Yeah, the repairman took my money, every cent but
* that's all right*
He went and fixed that problem, and now I sleep so
* good at night*

Don't go messin' with this fella, or you'll find a
* world o' hurt*
You mess with the repairman, you could find a world
* o' hurt*

You may think you're havin' dinner, but you'll get
*   yo' just desserts.*

This guy might be an angel, but he could be the de-
*   vil too*
Yeah, Jack might be an angel, or he could be the de-
*   vil too*
Only thing I know is, you don't want him mad at you.

Tom sat mesmerized as the song closed with a slide guitar solo and the sparse audience gave up an appreciative round of applause. Was that about his kid brother?

And then he saw Gia lean close to Jack's ear. Tom caught her whisper.

"I don't know what you did for that man and I don't want to, but to have that kind of effect on a life, to make someone want to sing about you . . . that must be indescribable. I can see why you keep going back for more."

And then it all came together.

Dad's remark about calling on Jack if he needed someone to watch his back . . . then that character Joey this morning asking Tom if he could "hack" what Jack hacked . . . and now this blues singer talking about a ghost named Jack who slips through the cracks, and singing about a "repairman" named Jack . . .

Somewhere along the line Dad had come up with the idea that Jack was a repairman . . . an appliance repairman. But the "R-J Blues" was about someone who fixed other things.

R-J . . . Repairman Jack? Was that what it stood for?

Had to be. Little brother was some sort of urban mercenary.

Taking it further, Tom realized that might explain why Jack had needed him to claim Dad's body. It wasn't that he hadn't *wanted* to claim it—he *couldn't*. Because he was probably living under a false identity.

Ho-lee shit.

FRIDAY

1

"Well," Tom said as they walked away from the grave, "that's it then. Still hard to believe he's gone."

Jack only nodded. He felt drained, emotionally and physically spent.

He was now an orphan. That had struck him like a blow as he'd watched his father laid to rest beside his mother.

Gia clung to his arm, wiping away tears for a man she'd never met. Vicky held her mother's hand, cheery but bewildered.

Everyone else had left. Tom's current wife, Terry, a shapely brunette about ten years his junior, had fled the chill to wait in their car.

During the past twenty-four hours Jack had encountered a dizzying array of new names and faces. The parade of mourners telling him how sorry they were, what a terrible tragedy it was, how his dad would be missed. He'd met his sister's kids and had almost lost it when he saw how closely Lizzie resembled Kate when she was a teen. Like going back in time.

Tom's two ex-wives—the oft-referred-to Skanks from Hell—showed up. Their splits from Tom apparently hadn't lessened their affection for his father. Tom's two sons from his first marriage and the daughter from his second had come along. Jack still wasn't sure what name went with what face. Not that it mattered. Small chance he'd see any of them again.

As they reached the curb at the bottom of the slope, a white Lincoln Navigator raced up and screeched to a halt.

Four young black men jumped out, all dressed in snappy-looking suits.

The tallest of the four, who'd emerged from the front passenger seat, looked at Jack and said, "Are we too late? Did we miss it?" His quick, dark eyes shifted between Jack and Tom. "You guys Tom's boys?"

Jack nodded. "Uh-huh. And you gentlemen are . . . ?"

He stepped forward and extended his hand. "Ty Jameson."

He quickly introduced his three companions. The names blurred through Jack's brain.

"We're really sorry about your father. An awful fu—"—a quick glance at Gia and Vicky—"an awful, awful thing to happen to anyone, but your father . . ." Was that a catch in his voice? "He was one of the good ones. We would have been here sooner but we only heard this morning."

Tom cleared his throat. "What's your connection to my father?"

Our father, Jack thought.

"He taught us computer programming back when we were in middle school." He checked with his companions. "About fourteen-fifteen years ago, am I right?"

They all nodded.

Jack tossed Tom a questioning look.

He shrugged. "News to me."

"We belonged to a Boys Club in Camden where he used to volunteer. He donated two PCs—used but still in great shape—and every Wednesday afternoon after school he'd be there to teach the rudiments of BASIC to anyone who was interested. We were interested."

The three others nodded. One of them said, "Word. Changed our lives."

Jack remembered Dad's fascination with the home computer, remembered the time he'd bought and assembled an Apple I—back in the antediluvian days when data was stored on cassette tapes.

Ty nodded. "He infected us with the bug. We joined the

computer club in high school, took programming courses there and in CCC. Finally we decided we didn't need degrees to do what we wanted, so we dropped out and started our own Web design company."

Jack nodded toward the big, spotless SUV behind them. "Looks like you're doing okay."

He grinned. "More than okay. We flush." The smile faltered. "Everything I have I owe your dad. Did more for me than my own father ever did. I tried to get in touch with him last year to, you know, thank him and let him know how he'd changed our lives, but he'd moved away." Ty swiped at a tear starting to roll down his left cheek. "And now he's gone, and I can't tell him. He'll never know."

Ty's voice choked off. Jack heard Gia sob, and he wanted to say something but couldn't speak past the baseball-size lump in his throat.

Ty recovered first. He pointed up the hill toward the gravesite.

"We want to go up and pay our respects, but first . . ."

He reached into a pocket and came up with a small gold case. He handed business cards to Jack and Tom.

"Either of you ever need anything a computer can do— anything—you just give us a call."

All four again shook hands with Jack and Tom, then trooped up the slope.

Jack watched them, trying to get a handle on this stunning revelation. Never in a million years would he have guessed . . .

"Can you believe that?" Tom said.

"I'd like to. I want to."

"No, I mean dear old Dad, Mr. Conservative, charter subscriber to the *Limbaugh Letter,* doing something like that."

During his Florida trip, Jack had realized that his father's conservatism was neither political nor ideological.

"Dad was mostly a traditionalist. You know, this is the

way we've always done it, so this is the way we should go on doing it. But he was never racist."

"Hey, he retired because of the company's affirmative action policy."

"Yeah. He told me about that. Called it 'profiling.'"

During Jack's last night in Florida he and his father had had a long, rambling, scotch-fueled talk about all sorts of things. Some of it touched on his career as an accountant.

"But that's only half the story. Do you know the hell he caught back in sixty-one for hiring a black guy for his department—the angry calls he got from his fellow employees, calling him a commie and a nigger lover?"

Tom shook his head, his expression confused, surprised. "No, I—"

"He told me he wanted to hire this particular guy because, of all the applicants, he was the best qualified. Dad didn't care what color he was, he wanted the best. So he hired him. The result? The fast track Dad had been on suddenly slowed. That hire cost him promotions and position. I won't say he didn't care, because I sensed he was still a little bitter about it. Then in the nineties things exploded when he was directed to hire a black guy over a white guy. Dad refused because this time the white guy was better qualified. He still wanted the best guy. Dad hadn't changed, but the world had. The former commie nigger-lover was now a right-wing racist bigot. He couldn't take it, and refused to be part of a system that put ability second, so he opted out."

Tom looked hurt, but his tone was angry. "How come he never told me any of this?"

Jack shrugged. He had no answer.

He put his arm around Gia's shoulders and they looked back at the four young men standing around his father's grave with bowed heads and folded hands.

Gia whispered, "I guess that's proof the good a man does isn't always interred with his bones."

Jack, not trusting himself to speak, could only nod.

2

When they reached the cars Tom signaled his wife to roll
down the window of their Lexus.

"Terry, would you mind driving Gia and Vicky to the
restaurant? You can follow us. Jack and I need to talk."

Gia looked at Jack. He shrugged and nodded. This was
news to him.

He held the doors for them—Gia in the front, Vicky in
the back—then led Tom to his Crown Vic.

"I've been trying to get you alone for two days now,
Jack," he said as he slipped into the passenger seat.

"Yeah?"

"Need to talk to you about something."

"Like?"

"I need your help."

Jack did not know if he wanted to hear this. Hell, he
was pretty damn sure he didn't.

"What kind of help?"

"I'm in trouble. I've screwed up my life, Jack. I mean I
could give a course in screwing up a life."

"In what way?"

"Every way imaginable. First off, I am, for all intents and
purposes, broke. The Skanks have been sucking me dry for
years. And you've met Terry. See the way she dresses?
She's never seen a pair of shoes she didn't love. Doesn't believe in sales, either. Only shops boutiques. Three wives . . .
can you believe I've been married three times? The triumph
of stupidity over experience. And whatever's left behind
after they're through with me goes for legal expenses."

The last two words startled Jack.

"Legal expenses? But you're a lawyer . . . a judge."

"I'm a judge in trouble. Big trouble. The Philadelphia DA is after my ass, but he's got to wait in line, because the state attorney general and the feds, not to mention the state attorney ethics commission, all want a piece of me too. At the very best, I'm looking at disrobement, disbarment, huge fines. If I had some hope, any hope of getting off with only that, I'd be a much happier man. But it appears I won't be that lucky. Things aren't going my way. I'm looking at jail time, Jack."

Dumbfounded, Jack could only stare at his brother. Tom? In the joint?

Finally he found his voice. "Why?"

A harsh, forced laugh. "*Why?* I can look back now and say hubris and poor impulse control. But back when I was at the top of my game—what I *thought* was the top of my game—it was all just a big puppet show and I was one of the string pullers. As for *what* . . . you want a list? Got an hour? How about kickbacks and influence peddling? How about indictment for judicial malfeasance and conspiracy?"

"Jesus, Tom."

"I did some shady things when I was in private practice, but it was the stuff most attorneys do. Padding the billable hours was a biggie. Double, triple, even quadruple billing was another. If I had to visit clients, I'd try to set up two or three meetings in the same area on the same day. My clock started running when I started the car, and I'd not only bill each client separately for the same travel time, but along the way I'd be talking to still another on my cell phone. Hell, I sometimes billed twenty-plus hours for an eight-hour workday. And on the side I was playing fast and loose with trust accounts. Had some close calls, but never got caught."

Jack wondered why Tom was telling him all this. Had

to have a reason. If he wanted a loan, why didn't he just come out and ask for it?

"The judgeship did me in. Being appointed for life wasn't a good thing for me—at all. If I'd had arrogance and hubris before, I now became positively regal. My biggest risks were errors in rulings, which could be changed by an appellate court; but otherwise I pretty much ruled the roost. I was the lord of my courtroom, a king. In reality I was a petty satrap with a big head.

"I did the usual time-honored gray-zone stuff—you know, using marshals to pick up my dry cleaning, taking trips on city money, beguiling attractive lady lawyers or clerks. And then of course I engaged in the time-honored judicial practice of 'leaning.' It's very easy to shade rulings. I leaned toward my old cronies, and against my old rivals. But I really stepped over the line when I started accepting gifts from parties related to cases I was involved with, and then shading rulings their way."

My brother the crooked judge . . . jeez.

Part of Jack wanted to shut this off now, but another part, the part in everyone that slows down when passing a car wreck, wanted more.

"Bribes?"

"If you're talking envelopes stuffed with cash, no. At least not at first. No, what I'd get was, say, an all-expense trip for me and the current skank to Bermuda or Grand Cayman or San Juan where I'd collect a fat speaker's fee to address some convention. All done through third and fourth parties, all very circumspect, all ethically questionable but almost impossible to prove.

"Trouble started after my second divorce when I had not one but *two* skanks with siphons in my jugulars. With alimony and child support payments up the ass, I had to do something. So I started accepting cash. Got to the point where I might as well have had a 'For Sale' sign on the door to my chambers. 'The Finest Judge Money Can Buy!' "

Jack was shaking his head. "Sounds like you were asking for it."

"I was. I was caught in this spiral but I didn't see it. I was into that sovereign mind-set of being a judge, of having the power to decide the fates of people and companies . . . heady stuff."

Jack said, "Where do the feds come in?"

Tom grimaced. "A tragedy of errors, that. It all goes back to certain trust fund conservancies I was involved with."

"Want to run that by me in English?"

"When there's a large settlement, say from a medical malpractice case where a birth is botched and the kid's going to need special care for the rest of his life, the money—often millions, sometimes tens of millions—is put into a trust fund which is overseen by a conservator. The conservator is an attorney appointed by the judge in the case. In a number of cases that judge was *moi*. A conservancy is like an annuity. The conservator has legal duties and he's paid out of the fund for the hours he bills. If he works it right, he can bill a lot of hours."

"Skim off a sick kid's funds?"

"It's all perfectly legal. But I got to thinking, why should I drop these valuable conservancy plums without getting something back? So I made arrangements: You want a conservancy, you cut me in."

"Jesus, Tom."

"Yeah, I know. Risky."

"I wasn't talking about the risk."

Tom waved him off. "Everybody does it."

"Obviously not, or you wouldn't be in trouble."

"I'm only in trouble because I was sold out. That was partially my fault for appointing a jerk named Marty Bieber to a particularly juicy fund. You've got to have a little subtlety in these matters, and it turned out Bieber had none. Not only did he overbill outrageously—enough to start the kid's parents smelling a rat—but he was also gambling with the funds. And losing. A complaint to the local attorney ethics committee turned up shortages. To partially save his ass, he rolled over and pointed a finger at me."

Jack shook his head. This was so scummy it was scary, this was . . . he didn't have the words . . .

"Okay. But that's all local stuff. I still don't see how the feds got involved."

"Since the damage had happened in a Philly hospital, it was tried there. But the kid's parents lived in Jersey, in Camden. Bieber's office was in Camden but he was licensed in both states, so he seemed like a good choice. Unfortunately the tribute he was paying me crossed state lines and the feds used that as an excuse to horn in."

Tom slammed a fist against his thigh.

"Fucking feds! If I'd stayed local, I might have been able to work something out. You know, use some connections here, spread some cash there. But once the feds got involved and started a taxonomy of my infractions, it was like raising the Yellow Jack over my career. It was as if I'd developed an advanced case of leprosy. Nobody returned my calls, everybody was always busy when I wanted a meeting. Hell, I couldn't even get people to make eye contact!"

He glanced at Jack with a hunted look in his eyes.

"I'm cooked, bro. I've been released on my own recognizance because I'm a member of the club and because I have such 'strong ties to the community.' Ha! If they only knew!"

"Why are you telling me all this?"

Instead of answering, Tom pointed to the left. "Turn here."

"But the restaurant's—"

"I just want to swing by the old neighborhood."

Not a bad idea. Jack complied. He kept an eye on the

rearview mirror to make sure Terry was following. He caught the puzzled look on Gia's face.

A wave of nostalgia swept over him as he turned the corner by Mr. Canelli's old house. Jack had cut many of the lawns in the old neighborhood, but not Mr. Canelli's. He did his own. Cutting didn't describe what the old guy did: more like manicuring.

But old Canelli was gone now. Just like Dad.

Jack slowed as they passed the three-bedroom ranch in which he, Kate, and Tom had grown up. He remembered it had started out with asbestos shingles, which Dad had later replaced with vinyl siding. He was saddened to see that the new owner had torn out all the old junipers and replaced them with hydrangeas. Dumb. From fall to spring, hydrangeas were little more than bunches of brown sticks. Junipers stayed green all year round.

"Remember playing catch in the backyard with Dad?"

Jack nodded. "I remember you winging the ball hard enough to knock me down."

Tom smiled. "But you always caught it, always held on to it."

Tom was laying it on thick. Jack knew he was being set up, but was curious as to where Tom was heading.

"You said you need my help. I'm baffled as to why? What can I do?"

"Help me disappear."

Jack suppressed a groan. "That wasn't easy before nine-eleven. It's a hell of a lot harder now."

"But it can be done—if you've got enough cash."

Yeah, it could.

"You have enough?"

Jack held his breath, waiting for Tom to put the touch on him. But his brother nodded instead.

"Yeah. I think so. Enough for a new identity and a start as someone else."

"I still don't see where I come in."

"I need you to help me get it."

"All right. I'll bite: Where is it?"

"In a secret account in Bermuda."

"Whoa. Hold it right there. Bermuda? I don't have a passport."

"Neither do I. At least not anymore. But we won't need them. We'll take my boat over."

"You have a boat big enough to go to Bermuda?"

"Sure do. Listen, we wheel down to the Outer Banks where I keep the boat, then sail straight across to Bermuda. When we get there we just chug into the harbor like a fishing boat coming back from a run, and tie up. No one will bat an eye."

"How do you know all this?"

"I've done it at least half a dozen times."

"Really?"

"Sure. Nothing to it."

Yeah, right.

"How long a trip?"

"Forty hours, tops. Look, Jack, I know you're thinking two days trapped, cooped up in a floating oubliette with me will be a new definition of hell. But I'm not such a bad guy. Look, we've been apart for fifteen years, and now, with what we've gone through in the past few days . . . I mean, after all, we're the only ones left. Our old family of five has been cut down to just two: Us. Don't you think we should try to reestablish some ties?"

Jack couldn't remember ever having ties beyond blood to this stranger.

"All well and good, Tom. But there are other ways to do that, safer ways than sneaking into a foreign port."

"Jack, please. I need that money."

"I'm sure you do. But that doesn't mean you need me."

"But I do. I could get someone else to go along with me on this—I've got fishing buddies who'd sign up on a lark—but we're talking big bucks here, and all in bearer bonds. I need someone along I can trust, someone who knows how to keep his mouth shut."

"And you think that person is me."

Tom nodded. "I told you what Dad said: 'If you ever need someone to watch your back, call Jack.' Well, consider this a call for backup."

Dad . . . was he kidding?

"Not fair."

"Maybe not, but do you think he'd want you to turn your back on your brother in his hour of dire need?"

"Oh, cut me a—"

"I'm serious, Jack. I can't do it alone."

"No."

He had a child coming in mid-March. Also had people looking for any possible trace of the shits who'd gunned down Dad. That took precedence.

"We're talking four days—*four days*. Come on, Jack, you can spare me that, can't you?"

Jack said nothing as they pulled into the restaurant parking lot.

Tom leaned closer. "Maybe you can't give me an answer now, but if you could get back to me by tomorrow . . ."

"What's the rush?"

"I've only got a small window to do this." He pointed to Terry as she pulled into a neighboring spot. "And don't mention any of this at lunch."

"Terry doesn't know?"

"Not yet, and she's going to be a hard, hard sell. So let's keep this sub rosa, okay?"

Jack shrugged. "If you want."

He laid a hand on Jack's shoulder. "Promise me you'll think about this."

Jack didn't reply. Tom's remarks about Dad reverberated through his head. Would Dad have expected him to put vengeance on hold and stick by the only other surviving member of their family?

Bastard.

3

"You won't believe the harebrained idea Tom came up with," Jack said as he steered his Crown Vic north on the Jersey Turnpike.

Gia had the front passenger seat, Vicky sat behind them, lost in her Game Boy—which she called "Game Girl." Her mother's influence, no doubt.

"Harebrained? Your brother doesn't strike me as the harebrained type. As a matter of fact I think he's bright and charming."

"That's because he's giving you the full-court press."

She reddened. "Don't be silly."

"Come on, Gia. You've dazzled him. He's got a crush on you."

"You're exaggerating, Jack. We simply have certain tastes in common."

And many, many more you don't, he thought.

Jack smiled. "I wonder if he's making a play for you."

"Don't be silly. I'm pregnant with your baby." She returned his smile. "But every woman likes a little attention and flattery now and then."

Jack put on a shocked expression. "I'm not attentive?"

She patted his thigh. "Sometimes you're . . . remote."

That was a gentle way of putting it. Jack knew sometimes he became so preoccupied with a fix that he was virtually not there.

"Guilty. Hey, how did we get from the subject of Tom's crazy idea to me?"

"Okay. What's his crazy idea?"

"He wants me to go to Bermuda with him."

Gia looked at him. "When?"

"Now."

"Now? Right after the two of you just buried your father?" She shook her head. "I gather he's not talking about a vacation."

Jack wondered how much to say.

"No, he's talking about money. Apparently he's in some kind of trouble."

"What kind?"

"The legal kind."

She made a face. "Violence?"

"No. More the white-collar kind—or maybe I should say black-robed. Anyway, he needs money and he's got some stashed in Bermuda."

"Did you tell him you don't have a passport?"

"Yeah. But neither does he. Apparently it was confiscated."

Gia winced. "Ooh. Sounds like he's in big trouble. So how does he figure on getting to Bermuda without a passport?"

Jack told her about Tom's boat scheme, finishing with, "No way I'm doing that."

"You don't sound too happy about the decision."

"I'm not. He played the Dad card—said Dad would want me to help him out."

Gia shrugged. "I think you should go."

"What?" He glanced at her. "You're not supposed to drink or do drugs while you're pregnant, you know."

"I'm serious. You need a break, Jack. You've been going nonstop since Kate died. You're overdue."

"I had that week in Florida."

She squeezed his thigh. "You're not going to try to tell me that was a break."

"Well, no."

Anything but.

"Getting away will be good for you."

"With you pregnant? Forget it."

"How long is he talking about?"

"About four days, I'd guess. Maybe five. Way too long with you in your sixth month."

"I'm fine. And I'll *be* fine. Nothing's going to happen in five days. And in case anything does, I've got Doctor Eagleton just minutes away."

"But—"

"No buts. You can't use me as an excuse."

"I've got other reasons for not going."

"Such as?"

Jack didn't want to mention his plan to exact some unofficial payback, if possible.

If possible . . . a big *if*. But if the opportunity came around, Jack didn't want to be out of the country.

He did *not* want to miss out on something like that.

Gia touched his thigh again. "Jack, he's your brother. He needs your help. How can you say no?"

Jack would find a way.

4

When Jack got back home the first thing he did was call Ed Burkes at the UK Mission to the UN for an update. Jack had done a fix-it for the UK mission there a few years ago and so he'd asked Burkes for help. Ed had been shocked to hear about Jack's father. He'd promised to do anything he could to help Jack get a line on the Wrath of Allah.

But Burkes had nothing. His buddies in MI-5 were as

baffled as everybody else. None of their contacts in the Arab world had ever heard of the Wrath of Allah.

Jack slowly, grudgingly was reaching the point where he had to admit that international terrorism might be out of his league. Way out. Not that he wouldn't take on a roomful of them if given the chance. But the chance part seemed a dead end. Like chasing smoke. These Islamic nuts didn't frequent the bars and clubs where Jack's contacts hung. They weren't out and about, drinking too much, shooting their mouths off. How do you get a line on crazies who cluster in tight, insular, incestuous knots of fanaticism?

He thanked Burkes and hung up.

5

Jack loitered at the rear of the Isher Sports Shop and made small talk with Abe about the wake and funeral until the door closed behind the last customer. When he was sure they had the shop to themselves, he leaned on the scarred counter.

"Any news?"

Abe spread his hands and shook his head. "Not a thing."

Jack had asked Abe to poll his fellow gunrunners about the Tavor-2.

"Nothing?"

"What can I say? This will take time. Not like there's a directory out there. And the ones I do know aren't talking."

"Really? I'm surprised they wouldn't trust you."

"Trust shmust. Who knows anymore in this business? What if I'd been picked up and what if I'd cut a deal to rat out my competition? After nine-eleven, already we were paranoid. Now . . ."

Jack nodded. The runners took a beating from all the post-9/11 security measures—especially the truck and van searches.

Abe said, "After La Guardia, with the feds trying to trace the Arabs' weapons, we're all running scared."

"Nobody's saying *anything*?"

"Like clams they become as soon as they hear what I'm asking. Not that I expected them to yammer like yentas, but I can see the shutters close and hear the doors slam when I say the magic word."

"Tavor-two?"

"Right. 'Never heard of it' . . . 'Never carried it' . . . 'Don't know what you're talking about' . . . 'Why ask me? I run a candy store.' *Bupkis* I got. Sorry."

"It's all right. Least you tried."

"Until this cools down or something breaks, like mummies they'll be. Too scared of the feds."

That started an idea . . .

"But what if they're hit by something that scares them more?"

He decided to put in a call to Joey Castles.

6

Jack had called him and asked for a meet at this Upper West Side dive called Julio's. They'd met out front and wandered in. Typical neighborhood watering hole except for all the dead plants hanging in the front windows. What was up with that?

Joey could tell Jack was a regular by the way just about everyone crowded around him, patting his shoulders and shaking his hand and saying how sorry they were about his dad.

Joey hung off to the side, feeling like he was standing there with his dick in his hand. But not for long. Jack cut it short and said thanks but he had some business. Everyone wandered back to their places.

So now the two of them sat in a back corner. A short, ripped spic brought them a couple of Rolling Rocks. Jack introduced him as the owner.

"Anything I can do, meng," he said as he gripped Jack's hand. "Anything. You just say the word."

When he was gone Joey ran a finger through the wet ring left by his beer bottle and said, "You got something shaking, Jack?"

"Not a thing. Nada. My guy's been asking around and coming up empty."

"And your guy is . . . ?"

Jack gave him a look.

Joey smiled. This was what he liked about this guy.

"Jack the Sphinx. A *boccalone* you ain't."

"I put the word out to everyone I know on the street to call me first if they hear anything. No one's called."

"Same here."

"The key is those Tavor-twos. They weren't bought at Wal-Mart. Can only be so many in the country. We find who sold them, we can find who they sold them to."

Joey shook his head. He'd had the same thought.

"Trouble is, no one's talking."

"That's because they're not scared of us."

"So what do we do? Brace them? Put the hurt on them?"

Jack gave him another kind of look.

"Come on, Jack. I know what you're thinking: Joey's a bidonista, what's he know about rough stuff? Maybe you don't know 'cause you've never seen, but I can handle myself."

"Never crossed my mind, Joey. No, I was thinking of a bigger scare than us."

"Like?"

"Well, I know your last name isn't Castles. What I don't know is if you're connected."

Joey wondered where this was going.

"Not directly, no, and we like to keep it that way. But you can't operate, least not for very long, you don't give the outfit a piece. Pop did it; Frankie and I been doing it."

"Can you make some calls?"

"Yeah, some. But I know someone who can talk higher up the chain." Joey was liking the idea more and more. "Yeah, by the time Pop retired, the boys had made a chubby piece from him, a piece they didn't do nothing for. Got it 'cause they fucking exist and nothing else. No reason he can't look for something back. Not a lot, nothing that'll cost them anything, just some information."

"Think he'll do it?"

"Pop? He'll jump at the chance. I'll tell him to ask the boys check around and see if anyone's sold a Tavor, or even a bunch of five-fifty-six hollow-points, to a dune monkey."

"That'll do it. But the cops might already know that."

Joey shook his head. "They don't."

"You know for sure?"

"For double sure." Here was a chance to impress Jack. "Frankie and me made us a few friends in the PD over the years." He made a motion of slipping his right hand into his waistband. "You know what I'm saying. That's how I found out about the cyanide bullets. They're keeping me posted. Seeing how much me and Frankie paid them over the years, they damn well fucking better. Time those meat eaters earned it by doing something more than looking the other way."

A smile twisted Jack's lips. Just a little. Just for a second.

"You sound like a good guy to know. They telling you anything else?"

"They hear the Homeland Security people are pretty sure the shooters had inside help."

"*Pretty* sure?"

"Well, they don't know who yet, but they say someone at the airport had to be helping the fucks. First off, they came and went through an 'Employees Only' door. Second, they got away so clean, they had to have inside help."

Jack shrugged. "Maybe, maybe not. Look at me. I got out, and no one was helping me."

"Yeah, that's right. You were there. But why didn't you just—?"

"Long story. But back to our problem: Who, what, and where is Wrath of Allah?"

Joey shrugged. "Gotta be somewhere. I mean, we *know* they exist."

"But they may not be calling themselves Wrath of Allah. In real life they could be calling themselves Seventy-five Virgins Here We Come, but they use a different name when they call the media."

Joey closed his eyes and squeezed the neck of his Rock until he thought it would break.

"The slick fucks."

He relaxed his grip, opened his eyes, and stared at Jack.

"How do you stay so cool, man?"

He watched Jack's jaw muscles work.

"Cool? Who's cool? I'm so burned I want to throw something. Or break something. If the owner wasn't a friend I might be going for a twofer and toss this table through a window."

"You hide it well, man."

"Years of practice."

Joey leaned back. "So . . . what we do we find these *faccio di stronzones*?"

"We'll cross that bridge—"

"Hey, I know it's a long shot, but what say we get lucky? What we gonna do? Call nine-one-one and tell them where they're hiding? As if. Don't know about you, but I don't wanna see them sit in jail for a couple years waiting to go to court, then get traded for some hostage somewhere. Or get sprung on some technicality. Blood demands blood, Jack. Know what I'm saying?"

This scary look passed across Jack's face, then it was gone.

"Yeah. I know exactly what you're saying. I can hear my father's blood screaming."

"Okay. We find them, we waste them. Deal?"

Jack hesitated, then nodded.

They sat and sipped in silence for a moment or two, then Jack cleared his throat.

"How're you doing without Frankie?"

Joey didn't answer right away. Couldn't. How to explain? He hadn't lost a brother, he'd lost a piece of himself. He'd be less torn up if it had been the old man.

When he finally spoke, he had trouble getting the words out. His voice sounded thick.

"It's tough, Jack. Real tough. I miss him. We was always together. Maybe that's why we fought so much. Like a couple *gavones,* y'know? But the fighting never meant nothin'. When it was over it was over and we'd go grab a beer. I loved the guy, Jack, and now . . . I'm tellin' you, Jack, I'm gonna waste those fucks. I swear on Frankie's grave, I get the chance, they're dead meat. I . . ."

Joey felt his eyes filling and heard a soft sob. When he realized it came from him and that he was going to start bawling like a baby, he got up and turned away.

He managed, "Gotta go, man. Talk to you later."

And then he was heading for the door, keeping his head down so no one would see him crying.

7

Gia snuggled up against Jack as they watched the six o'-clock news on the TV in the Sutton Square sitting room. He lived for moments like this.

"Have you given any more thought to helping Tom?"

"A little."

"And?"

"I don't know."

She squeezed his arm. "Jack, if he goes to jail, how will you feel, knowing you could have helped him and didn't?"

The old saying, *Don't do the crime if you can't do the time,* came back to him, but he bit it back.

"I don't know."

She gave him a concerned look. "This isn't like you. You're usually so . . . so decisive."

He sighed. "To tell the truth, I don't feel like me. This thing has me turned inside out. Dad . . . I mean, somewhere in the back of my head was the idea that he'd always be there. Stupid, I know, especially after what happened to my mother, but—"

"Not so stupid. It's the same with my folks. If your parents are in decent health, I think we all feel that way."

"Well, anyway, he's gone." Jack snapped his fingers. "Like that. My mother died in my arms. Kate died minutes after I let the EMTs take her from me. And my father's body was still warm when I found him. Too much déjà vu. It's got me all twisted up."

"That's why you should go, Jack. It's not a long time,

but it'll get you out of this city, away from the airport, the constant reminders. A little time at sea doing next to nothing might help you get a new perspective. Maybe you'll come back right-side in."

He knew she was right, as usual. But he wanted that time away with Gia, not Tom.

He wished he felt different about Tom. He wished he had the kind of relationship Joey had described with Frankie.

But Joey no longer had his brother. And Joey had said that blood cries out for blood.

Tom was blood . . . maybe Jack owed Tom the chance.

Joey had the ball now and he'd be running with it. If the gun guys decided to talk, they'd only want to talk to someone connected. That meant Joey.

And that meant Jack would be something of a fifth wheel for a while.

He didn't like that. He preferred to do things on his own. His business was the sole-proprietor type. He never worked with anyone, didn't know if he could. And Joey . . . he didn't know Joey all that well.

But what choice did he have?

Gia had said she'd be fine for the four or five days he'd be away, and he knew she was right.

And it would be at least four-five days before word filtered down from the outfit and Joey got anything going.

And Dad would have wanted him to help his brother.

Jack sighed. Maybe it was time to call Tom.

Brother Francisco Mendes, member of the Society of Jesus, wound through the bales of fabric, the barrels of food and water and grog, the milling crowd of workers and passengers and animals until he found the *Sombra*.

He paused at the gangplank and looked her over. A black-hulled, three-masted *nao* with the typical elevated stem and forecastle. Francisco knew all about her: three-hundred and fifty tons with a seventy-five-foot keel and a twenty-five-foot beam. Very much like the galleon he had piloted with the first Armada, but much less heavily armed.

Saying a prayer that he'd be successful in his deception, he strode up the gangway.

As he stepped upon the deck he looked around for a familiar face. He spotted an older man in his forties—perhaps ten years older than he—with a stubbly beard and a mild limp moving toward him. Francisco was startled to recognize Eusebio Dominguez. He looked so different with a beard.

They'd met a week ago. Eusebio had been sent by the Vatican and was to be their man among the crew. Francisco knew nothing about him other than the fact that he had been a seaman in his younger days. As for his present circumstances, for all Francisco knew he could be a cardinal or a chimney sweep.

Francisco was glad he had not been assigned the role of a sailor. He was too slight of build to pass for one. His neat black clothes, his shaven cheeks, and long black hair better suited him to the role of navigator.

As arranged, Eusebio gave no sign of recognition. Instead, he made a show of a smirk and a surly tone as he eyed Francisco's Valencian clothing.

"What do you want?"

"To see your captain."

"Do you? And who shall I say is calling?"

"Your navigator."

The smirk turned into a grin. "You are on the wrong ship, señor. Sergio Vazquez is our navigator." He shrugged. "Of course he has been ill—"

"Señor Vazquez died in his sleep in Compano last night. I have been sent by the ship's owner to replace him."

Now the smirk disappeared. "Vazquez . . . dead?"

Nearby, two seamen paused in their labors and looked up, echoing Eusebio.

Francisco feigned losing patience. "The captain?"

"He is ashore but he will be back soon. You can wait outside his cabin."

He followed Eusebio up the steps to the aftcastle.

"Here," Eusebio said, pointing to a spot in front of the door to the officers' quarters. Then he wagged his finger. "Not inside."

"Very well."

"As soon as he gets back I will tell him you are here."

Francisco nodded and placed his belongings on the deck: a cloth sack with his clothes and personal items, a mahogany box containing his astrolabe—which he would not need until they were out of sight of the coast— and his oilcloth-wrapped portolano.

He gazed out over the main deck, bustling in the dawn. Three masts, naked now, but soon to be rigged square and lateen. But what lay belowdecks interested him more: a secret nestled among the cargo bound for the New World.

It was that secret that had brought him here.

It had to do, in a way, with King Philip, old and sick and not long for this world. Perhaps it was the humiliation of three failed attempts to invade England, the most recent just last year when the third Armada was turned back by heavy seas. Philip ruled the most powerful nation in the world, yet his heavy taxation threatened Spanish hegemony; he would be leaving his successor an empire in crisis.

Perhaps Spain's day had passed. The thought saddened Francisco. He had sailed in her navy as a younger man, and had piloted the *Santa Clarita* in the first Armada. Could it have been only a decade ago? It seemed like a lifetime.

His small galleon, the *Santa Clarita*, had escaped Drake's fireboats but had been driven north with the rest of the fleet. Francisco had guided the ship through the stormy Orkney isles north of Scotland and back to Lisbon. His ship was one of only sixty-seven out of the one hundred and thirty of the original fleet.

Despite his failings, Philip remained favored by the Vatican as a loyal member of the Catholic League in the wars against the Huguenots, and as a staunch defender of the faith against the rising Calvinist threat.

This was why the Church was maintaining the utmost discretion as it dealt with the theft of a valuable relic from its proscribed vault deep below the Vatican. The cardinals still did not know how the thief had eluded detection by the Swiss Guard and gained access to the vault, but there was no doubt about his identity: Don Carlos of Navarre, King Philip's beloved nephew.

Six weeks ago his Holiness Pope Clement VIII had summoned Father Claude Aquaviva to the Holy See. There, behind the locked doors of the innermost sanctum of the Vatican, the Father General of the Society was charged with the retrieval and disposal of the purloined relic, with no harm to Don Carlos in the process, and no connection to the Vatican. In fact, if the object's loss appeared to be an act of God rather than man, so much the better.

Francisco found it astounding that an honor of this

magnitude would be bestowed upon such a young order. A former soldier named Ignatius Loyola had founded the Society of Jesus fewer than six decades ago, but since its inception it had proved a magnet for some of the best minds in the civilized world.

That Francisco, a yet-to-be-ordained Jesuit brother, should be chosen for the mission . . . well, it seemed beyond belief.

Could it be but three weeks since Father Diego Vega, the Father General's second in command, had stepped into his quarters, closed the door, and told him what he must do?

Francisco understood that he had been chosen because of his nautical past and his interest in astronomy. And of course, because of his devotion to the Society.

His head was still spinning. He had spent the last three years in Greece studying their ancient texts on the stars, and had only recently returned. He was still recovering from the disorienting experience of seeming to lose ten days of his life because of Greece's refusal to give up the Julian calendar. Spain had been utilizing Pope Gregory's new calendar for decades.

And now this.

The world was changing too fast. Ah, but the stars . . . one could always count on the stars.

He had joined the King's Navy at a young age and learned navigation by trial and error. Before too long he was assisting the pilot, honing his skills as he sailed the length and breadth of the Mediterranean, staying mostly within sight of shore as did most navigators, but unafraid to leave the comfort of land on the horizon and strike out into open water.

Not a terrible risk in the Mediterranean. If one set sail from its African shore and held to a northerly course, soon enough one would spy Europe.

But the Atlantic . . . now that was a different matter.

The swells, the storms, the space between its shores. Not a place for the faint of heart.

Francisco remembered the first time he had piloted a galleon through the Straits of Gibraltar and into the Atlantic. The captain had wanted to test the seaworthiness of his vessel as well as Francisco's skills. They traveled west-northwest for two days, then south for one, and then the captain told him to guide them back to where they had begun.

Using his astrolabe and cross staff, Francisco piloted the ship with such accuracy that their first sight of land was the high cliffs of Gibraltar.

He would have had a future in the navy, but instead he obeyed a higher calling.

He looked now again at the main deck of the *Sombra.* Originally christened *Santa Inés,* it had served Spain until last year when the navy sold it. Francisco was no expert on naval policy, but he wondered how often a navy sold off one of its ships. Another sign of an atrophying empire? He might understand if the *Santa Inés* was old and decommissioned, but this *nao* was in excellent condition.

Even considering King Philip's financial troubles, selling it seemed unusual. So unusual that one would have to assume the buyer to be a most influential man. Like Don Carlos of Navarre, perhaps.

But why had the new owner changed the ship's name from something holy to something unquestionably dark—from a saint to a shadow? Why would anyone choose such a name for a ship?

And why would it be sailing without escort through waters infested with pirates and British privateers?

He had to wonder as to its intended purpose.

He saw a heavyset man in a white ruffled shirt and black waistcoat step aboard. He watched Eusebio make an obsequious approach and point toward him.

Francisco gave a slight bow as the man reached the aftcastle.

"Captain Gutierrez, I presume?"

He looked irritated. "Yes-yes. What is this about Vazquez? Is he really dead?"

"Quite."

"Who sent you, then?"

"Apparently the owner of *Sombra* and I share an acquaintance whose craft I have piloted on numerous occasions. He recommended me and I accepted the assignment."

A flagrant lie, and if the captain had the time to check with the owner's agent, he would expose the untruth. But Francisco knew the captain had already been delayed by Vazquez's illness. He had to put to sea today if he wanted to reach Cartagena anywhere near his expected time of arrival.

He shook his head. "Crossing the Atlantic with an unproved navigator . . ."

"Hardly unproved, sir. I learned my craft in His Majesty's navy. Where, I assume, you learned yours."

Captain Gutierrez quizzed him on the ships he had piloted, the captains he had served under. He too had been in the first Armada and was most impressed by Francisco's bringing the *Santa Clarita* safely back to port.

That satisfied him.

"Very well. We sail with the tide. You will have Vazquez's cot in the officers' quarters."

As the captain brushed past him, Francisco allowed himself a deep breath of relief.

He had succeeded. He was now *Sombra*'s navigator.

He hoped God would forgive him for what he had done to poor Vazquez, and for what he would eventually do to this crew. Father Diego had said he would receive a Plenary Indulgence from His Holiness himself after completing this mission.

Opus Dei . . . Francisco had to keep reminding himself that he was doing the Lord's work. He was removing an evil from the world, hiding it where no one would ever find it, where no one could ever steal it again.

He knew the name of the object hidden in the hold, but did not understand the nature of its evil—Father Diego had been coy on that. All he knew was that he must prevent it from reaching the New World.

SUNDAY

1

Jack stood on the dock and stared at Tom's boat. Most of the surrounding slips in this marina in Nowhere, North Carolina, were empty. But even if they'd been crammed, Tom's forty-footer, with its flag-blue hull, white superstructure, and varnished teak trim, would have stood out.

"What's wrong?" Tom said as he carried his backpack and one of the food coolers past Jack.

"I didn't know judges made this sort of money."

"We don't."

Jack watched him step onto a rubber footplate on the gunwale and hop onto the rear deck.

"Then how . . . ?"

"It's not really mine. But the owner owes me a few favors, so I get to use it pretty much whenever I want."

Jack shook his head in wonder.

It had been one long, strange car ride. Four-hundred-plus miles covered in eight-plus hours to these private docks on Wanchese harbor. Most of the time—when Tom wasn't pumping him for details about his lifestyle—they'd played blues. Tom had asked him if he was the Jack mentioned in Bighead's "R-J Blues." Jack had told him he'd have to ask the singer.

"No kidding? This thing's got to be worth a million or more."

Tom shrugged. "Maybe. It's a Hinkley T-forty but it's got some years on it."

"Who's the owner?"

"Someone you never heard of."

"Try me."

"Okay. Name's Chiram Abijah."

"You're right. Never heard of him. What's he do?"

"This and that."

Jack watched his brother's expression as he asked, "Just what kind of favors did you do for What's-his-name?"

"The kind that have me sneaking off to Bermuda."

"Such as?"

"I helped get him off the hook a few times. But he's now under federal indictment for money laundering. Can't help him with that. The good thing is the feds don't know about the boat, otherwise they would've RICO'd it along with his other stuff."

Jack hung back on the dock, still holding the other cooler and staring at the craft.

Tom spread his arms. "Kevlar hull, teak deck, and wait till you see the pilot house—everything teak, cherry, and tulipwood."

Jack backed up a step and squinted in the fading light at the large, gold-leaf script across the transom.

"*Sahbon* . . . what's that mean?"

"Means 'soap' in Hebrew. Get it? He used the boat to launder money, so he named it *Soap*. Pretty funny."

"A riot. He'll be the Robin Williams of Leavenworth."

Jack stepped aboard and put his cooler in the cockpit near the helm. He stared at all the dials and screens and readouts.

"Looks like a 747 cockpit. Not that I've ever been in one, but . . ."

"State of the art," Tom said. He looked like such a proud papa, Jack wondered if the boat might really be his. "Every telltale and navigation device you can imagine, and each backed up with another just like it. The previous owner is a very careful man."

But not quite careful enough, Jack thought. Otherwise he wouldn't be facing a vacation in a federal pen.

Jack nodded appreciatively. "Lots of navigation gizmos. Good. I like that. Wouldn't want to miss Bermuda and wind up in Africa."

Tom laughed. "This is the age of GPS, my boy. In case you don't know, that stands for Global Positioning—"

"—System. I know. So this stuff works like one of those car navigators?"

"Even better. Soon as we clear the inlet, we plug in the latitude and longitude of Bermuda's Great Sound and then we just sit back, crack a few beers, and relax."

"Just how far is Bermuda?"

"About six hundred fifty miles due east."

The figure jolted Jack.

"Six hundred—Jesus! How many miles a gallon does this thing get?"

"Maybe one."

"One? That means we need—"

"Lots of gallons. Seven hundred to be safe."

Jack looked around. "But where . . . ?"

"Don't worry. We've got plenty. Good old Chiram more than doubled *Sahbon*'s range by sticking extra tanks everywhere—under the bunks, under the dinette, in every available open space, all with a state-of-the-art manifold system to feed it to the engines. We'll be riding low and slow at first, but we'll do better as the tanks empty."

"What about storms?"

"We're past hurricane season and the seven-day forecast is clear and calm all the way."

"And you say you've done this before?"

"Loads of times. Piece of cake. With this kind of equipment the boat literally drives itself."

"Awful long way to go in a little boat."

Tom bristled. "First off, it's not 'little.' And second, if you think Bermuda's far for the *Sahbon*, consider this: Every year people race to Bermuda in sailboats from places like Halifax and Newport."

Another shock. "Sailboats?"

"Sailboats."

"Why?"

"Because."

Jack shrugged. "Good a reason as any, I guess." He locked his gaze on his brother. "You're sure you know what you're doing?"

"Of course. Why do you keep asking me?"

"Because I'm leaving there"—he double-jerked his thumb over his shoulder at land—"and heading there"— he pointed to the water—"so I'd like to be—"

Tom snapped his fingers. "Yul Brynner, *The Magnificent Seven.* Right?"

Jack experienced a few seconds of disorientation, then realized what Tom was talking about. One of the few neutral topics of discussion on the drive down had been movies. Tom seemed to love them as much as Jack.

"Yeah, right," he said. "Talking to the traveling salesman. Good pickup."

Jack was impressed. Might have been more impressed if he weren't facing the prospect of six-hundred-plus miles across open sea on a ship belonging to an indicted money launderer.

I'll soon be in the middle of the goddamn Atlantic Ocean, in the dark, heading for the Bermuda Triangle, with Tom as my skipper.

Now there was a comforting thought.

At least the boat wasn't named *The Minnow.*

2

Jack sat on a deck chair and kept his back to the coastline— so he wouldn't have to see the lights disappear—while Tom manned the helm. Ahead, only water . . . a limitless expanse of black, gently rolling waves.

It had been full dark by the time they'd chugged away

from the docks, heading south into Pimlico Sound. After maybe eight or nine miles—or should he start thinking in leagues now?—they'd passed under a highway arching over a gap called the Oregon Inlet, and then they were out to sea.

Am I having fun yet? Jack thought. Answer: no.

The breeze felt cool but Jack was comfortable in his jeans, flannel shirt, and hoodie. Crying seagulls swooped and glided between the boat and the starlit sky.

Half of Jack had wanted to wait for tomorrow and get a fresh start first thing in the morning; the idea of cruising through the dark sent ripples through his gut, but there was no way around it: They were going to have to spend a night or two at sea no matter what time they left.

The other half wanted to get this whole deal over with, reminding him that the sooner they got going, the sooner they'd be back.

Tom came aft to the cooler and pulled out a Bud Light. Jack grimaced. Good movie sense, no beer sense. Maybe all the vodka he drank had killed off his taste buds.

"Want one?"

Jack shook his head. He'd stocked his cooler with Yuengling.

"Maybe later."

Tom stepped below. He returned a few seconds later with a folded piece of paper, pulled up a chair, and settled beside Jack.

"Ever see a treasure map?"

"No." Jack pointed to the helm. "I don't mean to be picky, but shouldn't someone be driving the boat?"

"Like I told you, this thing pilots itself. It knows where Bermuda is and knows it's supposed to go there. And there's not another boat around, so relax."

Yes, Jack knew what Tom had told him, but he still didn't like it.

He unfolded the sheet and handed it to Jack.

"Take a gander."

The sheet was actually four Xeroxed pages taped together into a large rectangle. A compass rose indicated that north was toward the top of the sheet. Right of center was a wedge-shaped landmass with a northward-pointing nipple. A line ran on a diagonal to a star surrounded by wiggly lines. The star had been labeled *Sombra*. The number of miles—eight and a half—had been written in ornate script along the line. Readings in minutes and degrees that Jack assumed to be latitudes had been placed above the nipple and the star.

Ornate handwritten Spanish filled the lower right corner. Jack's Spanish wasn't up to a translation.

"'Splain to me."

"Okay, Ricky."

Tom had spotted Ricky Ricardo. But that was an easy one.

"Translation?"

Tom closed his eyes and recited. " *The resting place of the Sombra and the Lilitongue of Gefreda, in the depths near the Isle of Devils, this Twenty-eighth day of March, Year of Our Lord Fifteen-ninety-eight.'* And then it's signed by Francisco Mendes, Society of Jesus."

Fifteen ninety-eight . . .

"This is over four hundred years old?"

Tom nodded. "The original is. It's parchment and barely holding together as it is. I wasn't about to take it out on the Atlantic."

"What's *'Sombra'*? And what the hell is the Lilitongue of Gefreda?"

Tom held up a hand. "Let me start at the beginning. When I was in private practice I joined a firm and inherited this client from one of the partners who was retiring due to ill health. The client's name was Allan Wenzel, a sweet old guy who was a devoted antiquities collector—especially maps." He tapped the sheets in Jack's hand. "This was one of his favorites. He told me it'd been found in the ruins of a Spanish monastery and had languished in various antique shops for years before he discovered it."

"How did he know he wasn't buying a Brooklyn Bridge?"

"He had the parchment dated and it's from the late sixteenth century. The details—the distance and the precise latitude reading—point to someone who was on the spot and knew what he was talking about."

"But who *is* that someone?"

Tom pointed to the signature on the lower right sheet. "This Jesuit named Mendes, I'd guess. Wenzel's guess was that he must have been a passenger."

"On what?"

"The *Sombra*—a Spanish cargo ship."

Jack couldn't help laughing. "Don't tell me: It's a treasure ship laden with gold and jewels."

Tom shrugged. "Could be."

"Okay. I'll bite: Where's this Isle of Devils?"

"It's the old name for Bermuda before she was settled."

He and Tom were headed for the Isle of Devils. Why did that set off a warning bell?

Tom was pointing to the map again, this time at the tip of the nipple.

"That latitude crosses the northern tip of St. George's—Bermuda's northernmost island. The line runs three-oh-eight degrees northwest and intersects the latitude of the map's star right here."

"Why no longitude?"

"Longitude was iffy in those days. They were pretty good at telling how far north or south they were, but the science of east-west location hadn't been nailed down yet. But longitude isn't necessary here. Run eight-point-five miles from the tip of St. George's to this latitude and you'll find the *Sombra*."

"If there ever was such a ship."

"Oh, there was. I did some research: *Sombra* was making a run to Cartagena."

"So how'd it end up in Bermuda?"

Tom shrugged. "No one knows. She left Cadiz on March sixth, 1598, and that was the last anyone ever saw or heard of her. Maybe a storm blew her off course, maybe she caught fire, maybe an onboard emergency forced her to seek land. But whatever the reason, the *Sombra* hit the northern reef—those wavy lines around the star indicate reefs—and went down, probably like the proverbial stone."

"Why do you say that?"

"Her class of ship had a deep draw—six feet. The reef out there is about three feet deep. If the *Sombra* was making decent speed, she probably traded damage with the reef: carving a path through the coral as the reef tore her open. She broke up and sank, and that was the end of her."

Jack waved the sheet. "I don't get the point."

"Simple: Someday I'm going to find her."

"If she hasn't already been found."

Tom shook his head. "The *Sombra* is not on any map of Bermuda wrecks, and believe me I've checked them all."

"So you've got a map of a wreck that isn't there."

"No, I've got a map of a wreck that no one else knows exists."

"How can you be so sure?" Jack tapped the big sheet. "The map maker knew. And if there were any survivors, wouldn't they talk up the wreck?"

"To whom?"

"I don't know—the Bermuda government?"

"The island wasn't inhabited at the time. The Brits didn't colonize it until 1612, and even then it was considered part of the Virginia colony."

Jack was confused. "Then how . . . ?"

Tom smiled. "How did the map wind up in a Spanish monastery? Good question. That's what makes the *Sombra* so interesting. Someone drew the map, then hid it away."

"Doesn't make sense."

"Does if the *Sombra* went down with something valuable—very valuable—that you someday wanted to go back and retrieve. And here's another little tidbit: *Sombra* means *shadow*. Isn't that cool?"

So cool it gave Jack a chill.

"Did you find a manifest or anything like that?"

Tom rose and went to the cooler. "Want one while I'm up?"

"I'll take a Yuengling."

Tom returned and handed him a green bottle.

"No . . . no manifest."

Jack sipped and considered how little sense this made.

"Without a manifest, what makes you think the wreck holds anything of value?"

"Because of another ship of the same class named *San Pedro* that went down two years before the *Sombra*. It was discovered back in the fifties and yielded gold bars, emerald-encrusted jewelry, and a couple thousand silver coins."

"Which must have kicked off a massive treasure hunt."

"It did. The gold rush turned up three hundred fifty different wrecks. And those are just the documented ones."

"But not much treasure, I'll bet."

Tom shook his head. "Not a whole hell of a lot. Most were just rotting wood."

Jack sighed. He didn't get this.

"What makes you think you'll find any more than that?"

"Wenzel. He did a lot of research and learned that the *Sombra* was carrying a very special cargo—the Lili-tongue of Gefreda that Mendes mentioned."

"Which is?"

Tom's brow furrowed. "He didn't know, and couldn't find out. All his research yielded only a few veiled references. But apparently it was considered something of great value."

"Just what *is* a Lilitongue?"

"Haven't the foggiest. I Googled it and came up empty."

"Think it's shaped like someone's tongue?"

Tom made a face. "The word 'tongue' has a load of

meanings besides that incessantly wagging muscle in your mouth. It can be anything from a spit of land to the pin on a belt buckle to the clapper inside a bell to the pole that runs between the horses on a stagecoach."

"So which is it?"

"I have no idea."

"And Gefreda?"

"Same thing. I assume it's either the name of the maker or the town where it was made. But I've got my own theory about the Lilitongue of Gefreda. I think it's some sort of jewel, or a unique piece of jewelry, and I'll bet it's worth a fortune."

Yeah, right, Jack thought. And I'm Captain Hook.

A lost jewel. Sheesh. Had Tom really bought into this?

The reefs Tom had mentioned, however, were apparently real, and they worried him.

"Three hundred and fifty sunken ships. Maybe those stories about the Bermuda Triangle are true."

"Don't tell me you believe any of that balderdash."

Jack had come to believe a lot of things he'd once considered "balderdash." He didn't want to add Bermuda Triangle lore to that list. At least not while he was sailing through it.

"Well . . . easier to believe in than the Lilly Lips of Gandolfini."

"The Lilitongue of Gefreda. And forget the Bermuda Triangle. No one can even agree as to where the 'triangle' is supposed to be. But the wrecks are real. All three hundred and fifty of them have been mapped, but not one of them is called *Sombra*. And not one location matches the location on my map."

"So what's that tell you?"

"That it's waiting to be discovered!"

Jack shook his head. "Tells *me* it's probably not there. Or it was there once and the tides carried it off."

Jack refolded the sheet and tapped it against his thigh.

"I don't get it, Tom. This treasure map thing ... where's it going?"

"Nowhere at the moment. But someday I'm going to dive that wreck and find the Lilitongue of Gefreda."

"When? I thought you were going to disappear."

He shrugged. "Maybe someday I'll sneak back."

Yeah, right.

"Speaking of disappearing, it's no easy thing these days. You'll need help."

"Like who?"

"Me. I can put you in touch with folks who can fit you for a new identity."

Tom looked touched. Maybe even a tad guilty.

"You'd do that for me?"

"Yeah," he said, but knew he was really doing it for Dad.

Añaza Harbor—Tenerife
March 14, 1598

Brother Francisco Mendes smelled the rot, heard the scuttling of the rats as he picked his way through the oaken beams, braces, and knees of the *Sombra*'s midship cargo hold. Had this been a galleon, the hold would have been crowded with rows of cannon and bins of shot and powder. Not so an unarmed merchant *nao*.

Francisco had suspected that the ship was running light, and indeed it was. As much as he had wanted to, no opportunity to inspect the hold had presented itself until now.

He had guided the *Sombra* along the first leg of the established merchant route: out from Cadiz into the Atlantic, past Gibraltar, then hugging the African coast, keeping land always in sight. The planned route led south to Cape Verde, where they would turn due west and head for the Caribbean.

But Francisco had seen to it that Captain Gutierrez fell sick as they approached the Canary Islands. The first mate, a wisp of a man named Adolpho Torres, had argued for a return to Cadiz but the captain had forbidden it. A matter of pride.

Francisco had guided the *Sombra* to Añaza Harbor on Tenerife where they had anchored and had the captain taken ashore for treatment.

And now, here in the hold, his suspicions were confirmed. *Sombra* was indeed running light. He'd found bolts of fabric, worked iron, samples from many of Spain's manufacturing sectors . . . but only samples.

Why? Merchant ships unfailingly set sail with their holds packed floor to ceiling, leaving no space, no matter how small, empty. That was why their crews usually slept on the deck. They slept on the *Sombra*'s deck too. Not because of lack of space below, but by captain's orders.

Yet to Francisco even this half-empty hold seemed too crowded, the air too thick. He felt his throat closing.

He forced himself forward. He had a description of the relic—or rather its container—but so far had had no luck finding it. He wanted to locate it before the ship got under way again. Moving belowdecks with a lamp held high was difficult enough on a docked ship. But once at sea the pitching and rolling might cause him to drop the lamp. The greatest threat to a ship—greater even than running into one of England's race-built galleons—was fire. Once they put to sea again he would need another pair of hands to help him. Those would be Eusebio's, but Francisco could not risk anyone learning of their connection. Not yet, at least.

Eusebio had been conducting his own clandestine searches, taking turns with Francisco while the ship was in port. But it would not be there much longer.

His search so far—nearly an hour—had yielded nothing. Could the cardinal have been wrong? Was the relic on another ship, perhaps?

But then, as he lifted a bolt of dark blue fabric, he spied a small chest tucked into the forward port corner. It perfectly fit the description: small, almost square, with teak sides and brass fittings.

The Lilitongue of Gefreda . . . what was it? What was its dark power?

Better not to know.

And now, God forgive him, he must take the next steps in the plan.

"Señor Mendes?"

Francisco started at the sound of his name and dropped the fabric. He turned and found one of the crew hanging from the rope ladder to the deck.

"Yes? What is it?"

"Señor—I mean, Captain Torres wishes to see you immediately."

"Captain Torres?"

"I am afraid so, señor."

Eusebio had told him that the crew did not like the first mate. But from the sound of it, he was now in charge. Francisco hoped that Captain Gutierrez had not died. He had grown to like the man during the short time he had known him. He had intended to give the captain only enough poison to make him sick. He prayed he had not miscalculated the dose.

With uncertainty gnawing at his viscera, Francisco climbed the ladder and headed for the officers' quarters.

He found Torres standing in the middle of the captain's cabin. Everything about the man was thin: thin physique, thin lips, thin face, thin hair.

"I was informed that you were in the hold. What were you doing down here?"

"Simply checking the cargo to make sure none of it has shifted."

"Such is not the navigator's concern."

"You are correct, sir. But since navigation is dependent on the helm, and since shifting affects the helm, and since my services are hardly needed while at anchor, I thought I might take a look. I must say, I am puzzled."

"Why is that?"

"There is so little cargo."

Torres smiled. "I said as much to Captain Gutierrez, and he told me the holds will be bursting at the seams on the trip home."

Francisco could imagine only one reason for that: Someone was paying mightily for the relic.

How could that little chest hold something of such value?

Torres sniffed. "But be that as it may, the captain is too sick to continue and has relinquished command to me."

"Then he is alive?"

Torres nodded. "Just barely. He almost died, but now he appears to be recovering. But it will be at least a week before he is on his feet. He wished me to complete the voyage."

Francisco breathed a sigh of relief. Gutierrez, at least, would be spared.

"I will aid you in any way that I can, Captain. In fact, I know a route that will help us make up much of the time we have lost here in port."

Torres's eyebrows rose. "Oh?"

"Yes. Instead of waiting until Cape Verde to begin our westward tack, we head west from here."

"But we're too far north. That will land us in the English colonies."

"Yes, if we hold too long to a westward course. But two hundred leagues before we reach land we will find a swift, southward flowing current that we can ride all the way to the Caribbean Sea."

Torres frowned. "I have never heard of such a current."

"I have—from sailors who had to sail that route to escape the English. But more than the current, the winds have a southerly flow there. We will be riding the current and running before the wind. We will have an excellent chance of making up the days we have lost here. We might even arrive in Cartagena on schedule."

"No." Torres shook his head. "I cannot risk it. Better to be late than not reach port at all."

"But—"

He raised a hand. "Enough. I have spoken. I will hear no more of this."

Francisco swallowed his anger and forced a smile. "You are the captain of this vessel. I will do as you command."

"Excellent, Mendes."

"And now, in celebration, may I pour you a little of the captain's sherry?"

Torres glanced around. "I'm not sure I should—"

"You *are* the captain, are you not?"

Before Torres could protest again, Francisco had the captain's Murano glass decanter in hand and was filling a goblet for Torres. He put a few drops for himself into a second goblet, then handed the first to the captain.

"To the success of our voyage."

As Torres quaffed, Francisco tilted his glass but did not drink.

"Why so little for you? You do not care for spirits?"

"Oh, I care for them very much. A little too much, perhaps."

Torres laughed. "All the more for the rest of us!"

Francisco smiled. "Indeed you are right. Here, let me pour you a little more."

Francisco nodded as he watched Torres drain his second glass.

Soon . . . very soon they would begin their westward tack. And their destination would not be the Caribbean, but a place known to the seafaring world as the Isle of Devils.

Once there he prayed he had the courage to perform the duty he had been charged with.

MONDAY

Jack awoke in the dark not knowing where he was or why the room was rocking or where the hell that awful noise reverberating through his skull was coming from.

He hit his head as he sat up.

"What the—?"

And then he realized where he was.

Tom's boat.

Okay. That explained everything but the noise . . . a booming moan . . . like a foghorn . . .

Or another ship!

Jack lurched to his feet, trying to remember where the steps up to the deck were . . . left or right? He guessed left, found them, and started up.

What was he worried about? He and Tom had split the nighttime steering chores into two six-hour shifts. Jack had taken the first. Talk about boring—the boat drove itself, leaving him nothing to do but make sure none of the equipment failed. He'd caught himself dozing off a couple of times.

Finally his six hours—seeming like twelve or more—were up. He'd yanked Tom out of his bunk and sent him topside.

Tom would be up there now. Even if he'd dozed off at some point, that horn would have awakened him.

Jack reached the deck. At last—light. Not much. The cockpit's instruments and running lights didn't cast much of a glow, but enough to see what was what.

The first thing Jack noticed was the unmanned helm.

He did a slow turn, checking the deck chairs, expecting to find Tom slumped in one, but they were empty.

Jack was the only one here.

His gut tightened. Where was Tom? Had he fallen over—

Another booming honk—louder than ever—shook the boat. Jack turned toward the bow

"Oh, shit!"

Ahead and to his left—port, north, whatever—a looming supertanker, a mile long if it was a foot, lit up like some bioluminescent behemoth, plowed through the black water on a collision course. Obviously the *Sahbon* had shown up on the tanker's radar or whatever it was ships used to detect each other, and it was sending out a warning that Jack read loud and clear:

Yo, pip-squeak! No way I can stop or turn, so it's up to you.

The tanker's prow plowed along less than a hundred yards ahead at eleven o'clock, with the *Sahbon* aimed like an arrow across its path.

Jack had a flash vision of the collision, the *Sahbon* reduced to kindling while the tanker barely noticed the impact—a fly glancing off an elephant's thigh.

Panic hurled Jack to the cockpit, where he grabbed the wheel and—

Which way to turn? Left? Right?

He chose left. Or port. Whatever. If he couldn't completely avoid contact with the tanker, at least he might escape with a glancing blow. He spun the wheel as fast and as far as it would go. Holding on as the deck tilted under him, he found the throttle and hauled back on it, reducing the power but not fully cutting it—no power would mean no control.

The *Sahbon* was slow to respond, but it came around. It would miss the prow, but a long, long span of reinforced steel remained to be dealt with.

Just then the *Sahbon* hit the tanker's bow wave square on, lifting the front half of the hull clear of the water as it came over the top. The boat angled downward, plowing deep into the water behind the wave and killing most of its momentum.

Jack yanked the throttle back to idle and looked at the knobby expanse of riveted steel sliding by.

Close . . . too goddamn close.

Above he saw half a dozen figures backlit by the wash from the tanker's superstructure lights, standing along the rail, looking at him. One of them gave him the single-digit salute.

Jack waved. We deserve that, he thought.

No, wait . . . not *we* . . .

A noise behind him. He turned to see a bleary-eyed Tom emerging from below.

"I just got tossed out of my bunk. What the fuck's going on, Jack? What are you *doing* up here?"

Jack wanted to kill him—flatten his nose, knock out a few teeth, and toss him overboard—but he limited himself to grabbing Tom by the scruff of the neck and yanking him around to face the tanker.

"Avoiding a collision with *that!*"

He felt Tom stiffen in his grasp, then go slack.

"Jesus, God!" He looked at Jack, his face a mask of shock. "What . . . how . . . ?"

"*How?*" Jack shook him by the neck. "You sack out on your shift—worse than sack out, you left the helm unattended—and you have the goddamn nerve to ask me *how?*"

"Hey, fuck you, Jack!" Tom said, regaining some of his bluster. "You don't know shit about any of this. I'm the one who's made this trip before. I'm the one—"

"You're the one who was supposed to be up here, watching the store. That was our deal."

"Screw the deal. I've made this trip on my own *lots* of times. I always sack out while she's running at night. You know what the chances are of *seeing* another boat let alone crossing paths with one? Astronomical!"

"Well, so far in my experience we're one for one. One hundred percent. But I don't care how many trips you slept through the night before. On this trip we agreed—"

"Would you forget about that? You're like an old—"

Jack punched him. Once. In the gut. Then he headed below. He turned at the top of the stairway. Tom was bent almost double, one hand clutching the gunwale, the other pressed against his stomach.

"Here's a new deal: You set so much as one foot downstairs before sunup and you're shark food."

He slammed the door behind him.

The Isle of Devils
March 28, 1598

The sun was rising behind him and the Isle of Devils lay directly ahead, but Brother Francisco took no pride in his navigational expertise. Instead he looked down at the crew, scattered like jackstraws across the *Sombra*'s main deck, and wept.

Fifty-seven seamen, most dead, and the few figures still writhing below were sick unto death. Fifty-seven souls on their way or soon to be on their way to their Creator.

All his doing.

But not his idea.

Francisco gazed heavenward. Was this truly God's will? He knew the Lord spoke to the world through the Holy Father, but so many deaths . . . what was so terrible about the relic below that warranted so many deaths to hide it from the world?

He looked back at the deck. Eusebio moved among the

littered forms, adjusting the rigging on the foremast. The *Sombra* was using only two sails to keep her under way— the small rectangular canvas set low on the foremast, and the lateen sail on the aftcastle. With a crew of but two, they dared not raise more canvas.

Francisco wiped away his tears and motioned to Eusebio to take the helm. He gave up the wheel and headed below to the midship cargo hold to check the relic.

He found it where he and Eusebio had left it, wrapped in anchor chain and fixed to the forward bulkhead. He didn't know why he needed to see it again. Perhaps simple curiosity. He was glad that the chest was locked, otherwise he feared the urge to peek inside and see what was worth so many lives might have been more than he could have resisted.

The links of heavy chain were still wrapped around the little chest and secured with padlocks. This hadn't been in the original plan, but a squall on their third day out from Tenerife had worried him about the possibility of the ship going down before he'd guided it to its destination. So he and Eusebio had weighted it to assure that if the *Sombra* did go down, the relic would go down with it. And stay down, never to wash up on any shores.

Assured that it was secured, he climbed back to the main deck and reclaimed the helm.

His instructions were to bring the ship through the reefs to the shore of the Isle of Devils, carry the relic inland, and there bury it deep in the earth.

Despite the use of only two sails, the *Sombra* was making good time in the cool, strong wind from the northeast. Francisco wished it weren't quite so strong. It had raised a chop that would make it more difficult to navigate the Isle of Devils' notorious reefs. The lateen gave them more maneuverability than a square sail, and passages existed, he was sure of that. Finding them under any conditions could be difficult. But with all these whitecaps . . .

He tapped Eusebio on the shoulder.

"Is the longboat ready?"

The older man nodded and pointed. "Food, water, sail, and all our belongings—ready and waiting."

"Excellent. Why don't you—"

Francisco pitched forward against the wheel and Eusebio was hurled against a railing as the ship bottomed against a reef. But it didn't stop. Propelled by the stiff wind it shuddered forward amid a deafening cacophony of grinding coral and splintering, smashing wood.

"She's breaking up!" Eusebio cried.

Francisco pointed to the cargo hatch in the deck below. "The relic! We have to free it!"

The deck shook beneath their feet as they staggered toward the hatch. The *Sombra* shook as if in an attack of ague but continued to plow ahead, though more slowly now.

Eusebio knelt and peered into the hold, then looked up at Francisco.

"It's half full already!"

Panic squeezed Francisco's throat. "To the boat!"

With the deck tilting under them—listing to port as the bow sank and the stern rose—they undid the longboat's securing lashes and climbed in. Moments later they floated off the sinking deck. Eusebio rowed them away from the roiling water as the *Sombra* rolled onto its side and sank beneath the waves.

Francisco had been shocked at how fast it was going down, but then he saw the gaping rent where the keel had been.

Soon all that remained were a few loose timbers and the floating bodies of the crew. He made the sign of the cross and recited the Litany for the Dying—for them and for himself.

Then he thanked God for inspiring him to weight the chest. It wouldn't be buried on the Isle of Devils as planned, but even so, it would never again be seen by the eyes of man.

The water within the reef was calmer than beyond. He

unpacked his astrolabe and made as accurate a measurement as possible on the rocking craft.

That done, the next task was to sail to the Isle, find a landmark, and measure the distance and degrees from there to this spot.

After that, he and Eusebio would anchor off the reef and search the horizon for the two lateens of the Vatican caravel that had been following a day behind the *Sombra.*

TUESDAY

1

Land ho.

Bermuda's brightly colored, beckoning shores lay ahead. Beyond the pastel splotches of houses with glaringly bright roofs, Jack couldn't make out much in the way of detail. Everything he'd read said it was a beautiful, cultured, *civilized* place.

Great.

But Jack wouldn't have cared if it was a barren lump of rock, or the relocation of Sodom and Gomorra. It was land. He'd started to believe he might never see land again.

After the supertanker incident, the remainder of the trip had proved unremarkable.

Jack had climbed from belowdecks the following morning to find Tom sipping a beer and acting as if nothing had happened—no near collision, no punch. No apology for dereliction of duty, no mention of the punch. Everything copacetic.

So Jack adopted the same attitude: The night before hadn't happened.

Not a bad approach, considering how they were looking at another day or so cooped up together on the *Sahbon*.

The truce allowed them to talk civilly. They got along. They stuck to neutral subjects like sports and movies; they watched videotapes—*Dazed and Confused* twice at Tom's insistence—and studiously avoided the landmine of worldview.

Jack didn't get Tom. He was unquestionably bright, clever—perhaps a little too clever—and could be charming when it suited him. He'd make a good acquaintance or card-playing buddy as long as you first made sure the deck wasn't marked. But a friend? Jack wondered if Tom had any friends. True friends . . . people who knew all about him, people he could call on when in need, and who could in turn depend on him to come running when they needed him.

Look at who's wondering about friends.

Jack could think of only three people in the world he could call friend: Gia, Abe, and Julio.

Three was enough. More than enough. A friend was a commitment. Friends took time and nurturing. And you had to give them your trust. That was the big stumbling block for Jack: You had to let a friend know you. Jack realized he had limitations in that department. He didn't want to be known. The fewer people who knew how he made his living, the better.

Gia, Abe, and Julio. They knew. They were enough.

But Tom? Who did Tom count as a friend? Who called Tom friend? Jack couldn't imagine it.

And that was sad to say about your only living kin.

"Okay." Tom clapped his hands. "Time to get out the fishing rods."

"Fishing? No way. My feet need dry land under them again ASAP."

"You kidding?" Tom laughed. "Fishing? I can't stand fishing. Rather watch paint dry. The rods are our camouflage. We're going to sneak in in plain sight, and then we're going to hide in plain sight."

"Just as long as we don't end up like the *Sombra.*"

"Not to worry. We've got all sorts of advantages they didn't: like charts and channel markers and depth finders."

Jack tried to squeeze some assurance from that, but came up dry.

"All of which you know how to use, right?"

"Of course. I'm not exactly what you'd call an old salt,

but I do know a few things. The channel markers are the easiest. Just remember the three *R*'s: red-right-return."

"Meaning?"

"Always keep the red channel markers on your starboard side when returning to port."

Jack nodded. Sounded straightforward enough. He didn't see how Tom could screw that up. Even he could handle that.

Jack scanned the water. The sky was a clear blue dome, the midday sun glinted on the gentle waves. The breeze ruffled his hair. He guesstimated the air temp in the mid-sixties.

And straight ahead, taking up a good chunk of horizon, lay the islands of Bermuda. *Islands.* Jack had been studying the maps and a tourist guide. He'd always thought of Bermuda as a single island but had learned it was a group—five major and a horde of small ones.

More accurately, Bermuda was the remnant of the rim of a giant, ancient, long-dead, undersea volcano ringed with coral reefs. It ate up a fair number of degrees of their horizon now. Not a desert island—anything but. Its surface undulated with green, pastel-studded hills.

Directly around them lay dark blue water; but not far ahead it changed to a pattern of turquoise interlaced with thick, dark threads: sand and coral.

The maps placed the western reefs about six miles from shore. The *Sahbon* looked to be about that distance right now.

"Where are the reefs?"

Tom jutted his chin forward. "Dead ahead. Just under the surface . . . waiting. Five miles deep out here, three feet or so in there where you see those little breakers— that's the only giveaway. Helps you understand why there's three hundred fifty wrecks around here. I mean, imagine coming through these waters at night, or during a storm." He shook his head. "No thanks."

Jack stared at the water. If Tom hadn't pointed it out, he wouldn't have had a hint that a reef lurked below the surface.

"Thar she blows."

Jack swiveled, searching the water. "What?"

Tom pointed to the left. "Our first channel marker."

Jack spotted a red triangle fixed to the top of a flimsy pole. He searched and found another a few hundred yards beyond it.

Red-right-return . . . all right.

"Let's get those fishing rods in their holders. We need to look like locals."

2

On the way in Tom hooked up with two other sport fishers. They all exchanged friendly waves and three boats cruised into Bermuda's Great Sound as if they all belonged there.

The five major islands are arranged in a rough, irregular, fishhook shape with the convexity of the hook facing west, its barb pointing north. The Great Sound occupies the space inside the hook.

Jack had followed their progress through the reefs on the tide chart. Once they reached the sound he refolded the map and stowed it. No reefs here. This was the deep caldera of the ancient volcano.

A little ways into the sound Tom veered west toward the bulkheaded shoreline. He pointed to a squat box of a building on their right.

"There's the island prison."

"Swell," Jack said. "Let's hope this is as close as we ever get to it."

He noticed Tom's attention was fixed more on the houses lining the shore than on the water. Pastels, especially turquoise and coral pink, seemed to be the local favorites—but only their walls. The roofs were a uniformly dazzling white.

Tom must have noticed his interest.

"The white roofs are traditional but not just decorative. See those slanted ridges? Rainwater runs along them and down into a cistern below each house. Not much rainfall here, so every drop is precious. This island is called Somerset Parish, by the way. Bermuda is divided up into parishes. Don't ask me to explain. I don't know."

Jack watched Tom's attention drift back to the shoreline.

"What're you looking for?"

"An empty dock."

"Lots of them along here."

"Maybe I should have said, An empty dock belonging to an empty house flanked by a couple of other empty houses."

"Sounds like a tall order."

"In season, yeah. But this is off-season. People who have second homes here are elsewhere, and even native Bermudians tend to leave the islands for shopping sprees in the U.S. All we—" He pointed to an orange-sherbet house. "There. That looks like a possibility."

Tom cut the engine to near idle and drifted toward the dock jutting from the bulkhead in front of the brightly colored two-story house. A sign on the dock proclaimed THE BERESFORD'S. Jack shook his head. The world seemed full of superfluous apostrophes. He didn't know why they irritated him. Lots more serious problems around.

Focusing on the house he noticed the corrugated steel storm shutters rolled down over all the windows. Definitely looked like someone was away for a while.

A twenty-foot speedboat, partially sealed in some

bright blue material and suspended from a pair of davits, took up half the yard.

Jack said, "It's got a boat . . ."

"Yes, but notice that the outboard engine has been removed, and the open area is sealed in shrink-wrap tarp. Definitely winterized. I can't see these folks coming back till spring."

Jack checked right and left. The neighboring houses looked equally deserted.

"So what's the plan? Tie up like we belong here?"

Tom smiled. "Exactly. Like I said: Hide in plain sight."

He turned the *Sahbon* so that its stern faced the bulkhead, then tried to maneuver it into the dock. The wind and current did their best to frustrate his attempts.

After the third failure Jack said, "Wouldn't it be a lot easier to go in nose first?"

Tom nodded. "Damn straight, but I don't want the transom visible to everyone who cruises by."

On the fourth try he maneuvered the stern close enough to the dock for Jack to jump to it with a rope. While he quick-tied to a piling, Tom hurried forward along the narrow port deck to the bow where he grabbed a rope and threw it to Jack. With the bow and stern tied, they were docked.

"Not pretty," Tom said, "but we made it."

Jack stepped off the dock planks onto the yard. He ground his sneakers into the sandy soil.

"Guess what?"

Tom turned to him with a worried look. "What? No surprises, please."

Jack spread his arms. "This is the first time I've set foot on foreign soil."

Tom stared at him. "You're kidding."

"Nope. You might say I'm a homebody."

A homebody without a passport. Can't get too far without one of those.

"Welcome to the rest of the world. How's it feel?"

"Pretty much like anyplace else I've been."

Why should it feel different? With no official identity, he didn't officially belong anywhere. He was a man without a country.

Not such a great position in these times.

3

After Tom had adjusted the securing ropes to his satisfaction, they hurried north along a narrow asphalt road toward the ferry stop. Jack had his new backup strapped to his ankle, and carried a small duffel with clean clothes. Tom had his backpack and nothing more.

Jack knew from the tourist guide that the Ferry Authority cut the number of runs in the off season, and the next could be the last of the day.

He hadn't been able to call Gia from the boat—Tom had insisted that absolute radio silence was necessary—but he'd take care of that as soon as they got to town.

The ferry wait was less than twenty minutes. Not much to see at first as they plowed across the open water of the Great Sound, so he sat inside on the lower deck and nursed one of the beers Tom had brought along. When the shoreline began to close in, Jack climbed to the upper deck and took in the view.

A range of dark green hills rose from the water to the south. The pastel colors and white roofs of the houses clinging to their flanks reminded him of a grassy mound studded with mushrooms. Here and there a Nelson pine or a narrow cedar jutted dark green fingers above the surrounding vegetation.

But the smaller islands, clumps of palm and pine-encrusted lava rock scattered throughout the eastern half of the sound, caught his attention. Many were too small for habitation, while others supported compact neighborhoods. But the in-between size, the ones with only a single house, captured his imagination.

What would it be like to live on one of those? Like owning your own country, or an island fortress protected on all sides by deep water. The isolation appealed to him: He, Gia, Vicky, and the baby, living apart from the world, making their own rules for their own tiny sovereign state.

An impossibility, of course. A wild, absurd fantasy. But still . . . no law against dreaming. At least not yet.

The ferry wove a path through the islands, stopping here and there among them, then veered north toward a crowded shore—Bermuda's business, entertainment, and cultural center, Hamilton.

As soon as they docked Tom led him down Front Street. It ran along the waterfront; the arcaded sidewalk sported a wide array of tony shops, but few pedestrians. Definitely the off season around here.

"Where are we going?"

"Well, the bank's closed, so that'll have to wait till tomorrow. Eventually we'll get to a place called Flanagan's, but I've got a few stops I want to make along the way."

"So do I."

Jack meant to call Gia before he did another thing.

4

Joey Castles sat in a rear-corner window booth of the Empire Diner. He watched the traffic on Tenth Avenue and marveled at the power of a phone call from the right people.

Joey used to love diners. Mainly because he used to

love breakfast. Used to be he could eat bacon and eggs or a ham-and-cheese omelet—American, never Swiss—three times a day. And the only place you could do that was a diner.

Trouble was, he hadn't been feeling very hungry since Frankie bought it. He ate maybe once a day, if that. He was losing weight. He had to pull in his belt an extra notch yesterday morning, and the way things were going, it'd be two notches soon. He'd never been fat or even chubby, but Christ, he'd be a scarecrow soon.

He and Frankie had been more than brothers. They'd been like one person. Half of him was gone. Had to get a grip or this would eat him alive.

The man across from him snapped his phone closed and smiled apologetically.

"Business. Always business."

Joey nodded. "I hear you."

This was their second meeting. The first had been in a Coney Island *merdaio* that served them tea and some mix of black bread, sour cream, and onions that had made his breath stink into the next day. That meeting had been precall, and a waste of time.

This guy was Valentin Vorobev but everyone called him Valya. He had no license to sell guns but that hadn't stopped him from supplying factions of the Russian mob in Brighton Beach for years. He'd agreed to meet with Joey, but only on his home turf. But as soon as Joey mentioned the Tavor-2, Valya had developed a sudden case of amnesia.

Joey had wanted to put a few into the *cacchio* right then and there. He didn't care who sold the guns to the Arabs—

All right, he did care. After 9/11, anybody who sold anything lethal to a fucking Arab ought to be redesigned so he could join a castrati choir. But Joey was willing to overlook that.

You made a sale. Fine. Okay. That's just doing business. I'm all for doing business. Just tell me who did the buying.

What he wanted more than life itself was the names of the shits who pulled the trigger on his brother.

He'd contacted three runners before his meet with Jack. Same old story: Nobody was talking. Nobody knew nothin'.

Then he'd called Pop. Soon as he got on the phone the old man went off on a ten-minute half-English, half-Italian rant. His folks had come over on the boat from Palermo, so he'd grown up speaking Italian at home and English on the street. Sometimes when he got upset he spoke both at once. Joey and Frankie had heard a lot of Italian growing up. Frankie had picked it up pretty good. The only thing Joey could do in Italian was curse and swear.

But he knew enough to hurt when Pop dismissed his efforts as *minchia del mare*. No fucking fair.

But Pop's attitude did a one-eighty when Joey told him Jack's idea—except he'd said it was his own. The old man got right down to making calls to people who started making calls to other people, and finally one of those calls had reached out and touched good old Valya. Which had led to this second meeting—not, it was worth noting, at a place of Valya's choosing, but Joey's.

Others had called back as well. He'd be doing a round of new meetings during the coming days. Maybe one of them . . .

"Again, I am sorry for your brother," the Russian said in a thickly accented voice. "Terrible thing to lose brother."

He had a broad face, small dark eyes, and a jarhead haircut.

"You got that right."

Joey wanted a cigarette. Bad. But you couldn't light up indoors anywhere in this fucking city no more. Normally he might just fire one up and flip the old *vaffanculo* at anyone who hassled him. But the last thing he needed now was to draw attention to this booth.

So he tried to satisfy himself with coffee.

"I thought long and hard about your sorrow and decided that I, Valya, should share with you what little I know."

Yeah, right. You got a call *telling* you to cooperate.

"That's very kind of you." Joey leaned forward. "What can you tell me?"

"Only that items you are interested in, they are easy to get, but not easy to sell."

"What's that mean?"

A big shrug. "No one wants. Or better to say, no one cares. Not well known. Everyone want other Israeli item. You know what I mean?"

Joey nodded. He knew: Uzis. Every gangbanger and *cugine* lusted for a Mac-10 or an Uzi.

"Before this happened, who has heard of this item you seek? No one, I think. I have two of them for three years now and no one even ask. Not once." Another elaborate shrug. "If I have business where I could send back, I would send these back today."

Joey felt his voice rising with his temperature. "That's it? You meet with me and that's it?"

"I do this out of respect for your sorrow. And to save you from waste time."

Joey found himself talking through his teeth.

"Ay, *puttana*! Frankie was my brother! This ain't wasted time!"

Valya held up his hands. "You do not understand. What I say is these items most probably bought not in States. If this Wrath of Allah connects to al-Qaeda, then guns most likely smuggle in."

That was what Joey had been afraid of all along. He didn't want to hear it. It meant he'd never track down the bastards.

Joey stood, threw a five on the table to cover the coffee, and walked out. No good-bye. The mamaluke didn't deserve one. Not like Joey was ever going to see him again.

He lit up as he hit the sidewalk. Then his cell rang.

"Joey?" said a voice. "It's Jack. What's up?"

"Ay, goombah. Not a lot, man. Not a whole fucking lot."

"My idea work?"

"Like a charm as far as getting people to talk. But so far I got *oogatz*."

"Afraid of that."

"Hey, it ain't over. I'm still on it. Something's bound to come through sooner or later. And when it does, you gotta number I can reach you?"

"No. Just my voice mail. But I'll be checking that and I'll keep checking in with you."

"Good enough. We'll have something soon."

I hope.

5

"Sure you don't want a cigar?"

It was the third time Tom had asked.

"All right."

"Good man. Not often you get a chance to smoke a real Havana."

While Tom had gone cigar shopping, Jack had found a liquor store where he'd bought a prepaid Bermuda calling card. He phoned Gia to let her know he hadn't been lost at sea. She'd sounded relieved. All was fine back home, and Jack had promised to call her again in the morning. Then he'd called Joey.

So now Tom and he sat on the outside deck of Flanagan's, poised over Front Street and overlooking the quiet harbor. The pub seemed authentically Irish—even had a dartboard—with dark wood, subdued lighting, and lots of regulars calling and waving to each other through the smoky air. Jack knew half a dozen places exactly like it back home. Well, not exactly. Smoky bars were now a thing of the past in New York.

The "authentic" came to a screeching halt with the Korean maître d'.

Tom had said the fish chowder was a must, so Jack had ordered that and fish and chips. He was looking forward to eating something a little more substantial—and warmer—than a sandwich.

He bit a small piece off the butt end of the cigar and fired up the tip with Tom's lighter. He'd smoked cigarettes for a few years as a teen but the allure of tobacco, especially cigars, had eluded him.

He took a deep draw and let it out slowly. Tom was watching him with an expectant look.

"Well?"

"Tastes like roofing material."

It didn't taste *that* bad, but it didn't taste good either. What was all the fuss about Cuban cigars?

Tom sputtered. "B-but it's-it's a Montecristo!"

"I think you got gypped. It's an El Shingelo."

Tom muttered, "De gustibus," then glared and fumed and puffed while Jack rested his cigar in the ashtray and hoped it would go out.

"Was Dad ever here?" Jack said.

Tom blew blue smoke and looked at him over the rim of his third vodka on the rocks.

"Bermuda? Yeah. I think it was back in your freshman year. Mom had an empty-nest thing going and so Dad brought her here. Don't you remember?"

Jack shook his head. Something about that hovered on

the edge of his memory, just out of reach. He'd done such a bang-up job of leaving his past behind for fifteen years that a lot of it had slipped away.

"Do you know if he liked it?"

Tom shrugged. "Never asked. But hey, what's not to like?"

Jack nodded. Bermuda might be one of the only areas where he and Tom were in agreement.

He was sure his folks had loved it. How could they not? Even in its cold season, with the deciduous trees standing naked here and there among the palms, it looked like paradise.

On the rare occasions when Jack had thought of Bermuda at all, he'd considered it little more than a new-lywed destination—pink-sand beaches and all the rest of the honeymoon hype. But the ride across the Great Sound had shown him a different island.

Tom signaled for another vodka. "Speaking of Dad, have you any idea of the size of his estate?"

Jack sipped his pint of Courage and shook his head. "Not a clue."

"I got a peek at his finances last summer when I helped him add a codicil to his will."

Jack pushed away a sudden vision of Tom fixing the terms so that it all went to him.

"What did he change?"

"Don't worry. You're still in it."

Jack had already punched Tom. That remark deserved a head butt. But he sat quietly.

Finally Tom said, "It was after Kate's death. A third of his estate had been slated for Kate. He'd never conceived of the possibility that she'd predecease him. He changed it so that Kate's third would be split evenly between Kevin and Lizzie—trusts and all that. He'd already set up an insurance trust to protect the benefits from the inheritance tax." He shook his head. "The old man knew finances and tax laws. Covered all his bases."

Dad's will . . . talking about it made Jack queasy. He felt ghoulish. He wanted off the subject.

"Well, he was an accountant after all."

Tom looked Jack in the eye. "How many accountants do you know who're worth three million bucks?"

Jack sat stiff and silent, stunned. "Three million? Dad? But how?"

"A major reason was Microsoft. He wasn't in on the IPO, but he got in shortly after. You know how he was about computers—way ahead of the crowd. He saw the future and bought into it. He was also one of the first home-computer day traders." Tom tapped his fist twice on the table. "Wish to hell he'd clued me in."

"Would you have listened?"

Tom's drink arrived. "Probably not. Moot point, anyway. With kids and family and living high, who had spare cash?"

"You must have a retirement account."

He nodded. "Yeah, but I left that in the care of a reputed whiz kid who royally fucked it up. Shit, if I'd wanted it to crash and burn, I could have done that myself." Tom stared into his drink. "What're you going to do with your million?"

A million . . . the number whacked him across the back of the head like a blackjack. Dad had left him a million bucks.

"I . . . I'll have to think about that. How about you?"

"By the time the estate's settled—and it'll be a while—I hope to be long gone." He gave a disgusted grunt. "Otherwise I'll be a rich jailbird. But even if I hung around I wouldn't see much of it. With two rasorial ex-wives—the Skanks from Hell are both well practiced at deficit financing—and a third who spends like the Hilton sisters, and three kids with college funds, what do you think?"

Jack had a sudden idea. "Is there any way to split my share between your kids and Kate's?"

Tom's drink stopped halfway to his lips. He stared wide eyed and open mouthed.

"You're shitting me."

"Nope. Just made up my mind."

"No, you're *out* of your fucking mind."

He couldn't accept the money. Not that it wouldn't give Gia and him a nice, fat financial cushion, but a man who doesn't exist can't inherit money.

"I have my reasons."

"What? You don't seem the superstitious type. You think it's somehow tainted because Dad was murdered?"

That had never occurred to Jack, but he decided to run with it.

"Yeah. It's blood money. I don't want it."

Tom shook his head. "Well, as much as I'd like to see the kids get an extra half a mil, it can't be done."

"Why not? You're the executor, aren't you?"

"Yeah, but I won't be around. And an executor can't change the terms of the will."

"You could hang around long enough to find a way."

"But it's not necessary. Once you claim the money you can divvy it up any way you please."

That was just the point—he couldn't claim the money.

Another idea: "Okay, have me declared dead."

"What?"

"Look, I disappeared more than seven years ago—twice that. Isn't that enough to have me declared dead?"

"But you're not."

"I am—at least as far as officialdom is concerned."

There—he'd said it. Hadn't wanted to, but there was no other way. He didn't want his inheritance moldering in some account when the other people in Dad's will could use it.

Tom grinned and slapped the tabletop. "Knew it! I *knew* it!"

"Knew what?"

"You're running around under a false identity. That's why you couldn't claim Dad's body. And—of course! You can't claim the inheritance for the same reason." He leaned forward. "What's the story? Who are you hiding from?"

"You know all you need to know, Tom. Back to the subject at hand: Can you have me declared dead?"

"But everybody at the wake and the funeral . . . they know you're alive."

"Yeah, but do they have to know I've been declared dead? Nobody knows how much they were slated to inherit in the first place. If you don't tell and I don't complain, who's going to be the wiser?"

Tom leaned back. "I don't know. It might be possible. I'll hang around long enough to look into it."

"Do that. And no funny stuff."

Tom looked offended. "You think I'd gyp Kate's kids?"

"After what you've told me? What do you think?"

"I'd never—"

"Good. Because if I ever find out you've shorted those kids, I'll hunt you down and chop off your right hand."

Tom started to laugh but it died aborning as he looked in Jack's eyes.

"You—you're kidding, right?"

Their food arrived then. Jack sniffed his fish and chips—fresh from the fryer, all hot, crisp, and greasy.

"Let's eat."

6

When the check arrived, Tom said, "You mind getting this? I mean, I could charge it, but I don't want to leave a trail to Bermuda and back."

Jack reached for his wallet. "Good thinking."

Jack didn't mind. John Tyleski didn't exist.

"How much cash did you bring?"

"I've got plastic."

"You do? How?"

Why was he acting so surprised? Tom knew he'd reserved that hotel room for him. Can't do that without a credit card.

"There are ways."

"You and I need to talk about rebirth real soon. But for now we have to find us a place to spend the night."

"Why not the boat?"

"Too far. Doesn't make sense to go all the way back to Somerset tonight, then come all the way back in the morning. Besides, lights and activity on the boat might draw attention. Better to stay here."

He was probably right.

"I saw a big pink hotel as we got off the ferry."

Tom made a face. "The Princess? Uh-uh. No can do."

"Why not?"

"That's where I honeymooned with the first Skank from Hell. No thanks." He shook his head. "I stayed at Elbow Beach my last few times here." Another head shake. "We'll find some other place. You'll have to cover the rooms."

"Figured that. And everything else, I guess."

"Not at all. We'll settle up tomorrow as soon as I withdraw my money."

"After which we head home, right? As in right away."

Tom gave a thumbs-up. "You got it. I want to get that money back and stashed in the States ASAP. And then you can show me how to disappear."

WEDNESDAY

1

Tom glanced at his watch as he paced the marble floor of the Bermuda Bank and Trust Limited, waiting for Hugh Dawkes. Nine thirty. He wanted to get back to the *Sahbon*.

He wore a wrinkled shirt and slacks—the best clothes he'd brought along—and had his backpack slung over his shoulder. The backpack probably wasn't a good touch, but its contents were too precious to leave in the truck.

The BB&T occupied a pink stucco building on the up-hill side of Reid Street in Hamilton. The idea of a pink bank had put Tom off at first, but then this was Bermuda where it was no strange thing to see businessmen— bankers included—dressed for work in a jacket, tie, short pants, and knee socks.

Dawkes appeared, a slim, silver-haired gent in dark blue jacket and matching Bermuda shorts and knee socks. Tom had made a point of dealing with the same man on every visit he'd made to BB&T. He'd also made a point of calling the Gosling Brothers' store on Front Street and having them send Dawkes a bottle of their 150-proof rum every Christmas. Never knew when you were going to need a favor.

As they shook hands and exchanged greetings, he sensed tension in Dawkes. Maybe he was having a bad day.

Tom didn't have much time so he got right to the point.

"I'll be relocating to the West Coast soon, so I'm afraid I'll have to close out my account."

Now Dawkes looked even more troubled. "I'm sorry to tell you this, sir, but at this time that will not be possible."

Tom's stomach did a flip. "Why not?"

"Your government has been in touch with the bank and . . . I . . ."

With his knees going soft under him, Tom reached for a chair.

"May I sit down?"

"Of course, sir."

"What do you mean 'my government'?"

"I'm not sure, sir. Some agency approached the bank. The president, Mr. Hickson, dealt with them. He has not seen fit to inform me of the details."

Dawkes pursed his lips and sniffed, obviously slighted.

Tom didn't give a shit about this twit's wounded feelings. The feds! The feds had been here!

"What's the bottom line here, Mr. Dawkes?"

Dawkes looked embarrassed. "Your account has been frozen, sir."

Tom leaned back and closed his eyes. This was scary. No, it was beyond scary—this was fucking terrifying. How did they find out about it? How had they connected him to BB&T?

Chiram . . . the *Sahbon*'s former owner, Chiram Abijah. Had to be him. Probably made a deal and gave up Tom.

But an even more terrifying question roiled his gut: What else did they know?

The savings account itself wasn't important. He'd deposited a thousand in it years ago simply to establish himself as a customer. He'd wanted to use a phony name, but the bank required a passport as ID for foreign depositors, and the only passport he'd had was the real thing.

Although he needed every penny he could get his hands on, he could let the thousand go. His real stash was in the back.

At least he hoped it was. Tom was almost afraid to ask. He put on a brave face, looked Dawkes in the eye, and . . .

"This is most puzzling and disconcerting, Mr. Dawkes. I'll straighten it out immediately when I get home. But at this time I'd like to visit my safety-deposit box."

Dawkes looked away and Tom's heart almost stopped. Oh, no. Oh, shit, don't tell me—

"I'm afraid that's frozen too, sir."

Jesus God. Half a million bucks! His fuck-you money. He had to get to it.

He dug in his pants pocket and found the box key.

"Just a quick visit? For old time's sake?"

Dawkes gave a sad shake of his head. "I'm afraid I couldn't do that, sir."

He held up the key. "Not even as a personal favor?"

He glanced at Tom, then looked away again. "I'm sorry, sir."

Tom wanted to throttle him. You ungrateful shit. After all that rum I sent you . . .

"But there is something I can do for you, sir . . ."

What? *What?*

". . . and that's to tell you to turn around and walk away from here and don't come back."

Dawkes's furtive look and lowered voice cut off the stream of choice epithets that leaped to Tom's lips.

"What are you telling me?"

"Simply that Mr. Hickson has instructed us to report your presence to him immediately should you show up. I am the only one here at BB and T who knows you by sight, and I will, shall we say, neglect to mention your visit. But I suggest we cut this meeting short before anyone becomes curious as to your identity."

Tom bolted from the chair and extended his hand. "Thank you, Dawkes. You're a prince."

A quick shake and he was on his way.

Shit, *shit*, SHIT! Now he was fucked—*royally* fucked. He saw no options. What could he do?

And then he thought of something. A long shot. A very long shot.

But he couldn't do it alone. He'd need Jack's help.

2

Shock blasted through Jack like an icy wave when Tom told him. Not from the news that his account was frozen, but . . .

"The feds know you're *here*?"

That meant the feds would also know that Jack was here. A crawly sensation settled on the back of his neck. They could be under surveillance right now.

They stood on Reid Street, a pair of statues among bustling shoppers and workers. Fleets of motorbikes buzzed by on the street, their dinky engines sounding like a swarm of angry hornets.

Tom shook his head. "No. The feds have no idea. Otherwise they'd have been waiting for me. Good thing we came in through the back door. But obviously they've learned about the account and think I might try to get to it."

"There's nothing you can do?"

"No. And I'm lucky the guy in there didn't report me."

"Yeah, but how do you know he won't change his mind?"

"He won't. He'd wind up on the hot seat himself for not calling his boss when I showed up." Another head shake. "Shit!"

"Well, Tom. I'm sorry about this." And he was. "But there's nothing to be done, so let's get the hell out of Dodge."

"No, wait. There is something to be done. But not about my account."

"Then what?"

"The *Sombra*."

"Oh no." Jack backed away. "No-no-no-no."

"Jack, it's a chance—my only chance right now."

"It's not a chance. It's a pipe dream. Look, I'll lend you money, help you get a new identity. I'll even—"

"Help me a different way: Help me find the *Sombra*. Help me find the Lilitongue of Gefreda."

This was crazy. What was he thinking?

"Look, Tom, even if I had time to help you—and I don't because I promised Gia I'd be back day after tomorrow—how can two men excavate a sunken ship?"

"That's exactly how most of those three hundred fifty wrecks were uncovered: by two-man teams. We're not talking the *Titanic* here. The damn ship was only seventy-five feet long. And excavating is an amazingly simple process."

"Shoveling sand? Underwater? Are you crazy?"

Tom smiled. "Underwater, yes. But no shoveling. There's a much easier, better way. You just—"

"News bulletin: I've never scuba dived. Not once."

"You're kidding."

"Never had a need to. Not a frequently called-upon skill in New York."

"I'll teach you. Nothing to it. We'll only be down about forty feet, so you can learn all you need to know in twenty minutes, tops."

"I can learn all I need to know in zero minutes because I'm not going."

"Jack, I need your help on this. I can't do it alone. You promised you'd help."

"And I will help. But not on a wild goose chase."

"The ship's there, Jack. I know it. I knew it the first time I laid eyes on the map. And if it contains anything of value, it'll make up for my frozen account."

"Let's be sensible here. This map's been around for four hundred years and no one decided to go looking for the ship before you?"

"Well, it was hidden away most of those centuries. And the few who understood it probably figured it was fake."

Smart folks, Jack thought.

"Everyone except you."

"Right. And Wenzel's research confirmed it. He had no interest in the ship; the map itself was his prize. He'd researched it thoroughly and believed whoever had made it was sincere."

"Crazy people can be sincere. Some of the most sincere people I've ever met have had their receivers off the hook."

"I won't argue that. But I've been to the spot on the map. Last time I was here I went out with a handheld GPS unit and found it. I dove it. It's a deep sand hole."

Jack couldn't hide his surprise. "If you've been there already, what do you need me for?"

"Because I couldn't find it."

"And you think *I* will?"

"*We* will. I'll bet my butt it broke apart on the reef and what's left of it is still in that hole, covered with sand. And you and I are going to excavate it."

A perking suspicion bubbled to the surface.

"Was this your plan all along, Tom?"

He looked puzzled. "What?"

"A bait and switch. Do you really have a secret account in there? Or did you make me think I was helping you run some money when all along you wanted to rope me into a sunken treasure dive?"

Tom raised a hand. "Swear to God, Jack, I absolutely do have a frozen account in that bank."

"Then why make such a big deal of the map on the trip out?"

Tom reddened. "I did *not* make a big deal. I just thought it would interest you." He looked away. "Okay . . . I suppose I was hoping to pique your interest enough to get you to dive it with me as, you know, a lagniappe. We'd split whatever we found."

Bullshit or not? Jack could no longer tell truth from fiction with this guy.

Tom looked at him again. "But we're not talking bonus anymore. We're talking desperate necessity."

"Tom . . . no."

Tom's mouth twisted. "Fine. You want to head home, go to it. But you'll be going without me."

"What?"

"And if you leave me here, I'm stuck here. The only way I'll get back to the States will be in handcuffs. I'd hope you wouldn't do that to me."

"Staying will be your choice."

"And you—how far do you think you can take the *Sahbon* without me?"

Good question. Jack didn't know if he could pilot the boat through the reefs, let alone all the way back to North Carolina. He'd learned enough on the trip out to hazard a try, but couldn't guarantee that the *Sahbon* wouldn't end up on Bermuda's shipwreck map.

And if the Bermuda coast guard or whatever they were called had to pull him off the reef, they'd want some ID, they'd want to see his passport.

Shit.

Tom's tone shifted from challenging to pleading. "Two days, Jack . . . two freaking extra days. If we haven't found anything by sundown Friday, we head home. I swear—I swear on Mom's grave."

Jack could feel himself being backed into a corner.

An old saying came to mind: No good deed shall go unpunished. Right.

Never should have come.

"You've got to take my back on this, Jack. I hate to bring up Dad again—"

"Then don't."

"—but I have to. If he were here he'd say, What's two more days in the grand scheme of things if you can help your brother out of the worst jam of his life?"

Jack knew full well the guilt trip Tom was laying on him, but that didn't make it any easier to shake off.

Yeah, Dad probably would have wanted him to help Tom get another chance.

Jack held up his hands in a surrender gesture. He knew he was going to regret this.

"Okay, okay. If Gia's cool with me gone a couple of extra days, I'll stay. But only till Friday. Not a moment longer."

Tom sagged against the bank's pink stucco wall. "Thanks, Jack. You don't know what this means to me. I'll owe you the rest of my life."

Jack didn't want Tom to owe him anything.

3

By midday they were ready to get to work.

Gia hadn't minded his being away two extra days, but she had minded the scuba part. He'd promised he'd be careful.

After that the rest of the morning had been frenzied activity, starting with hiring one of the local minivan taxis to take them to St. George's Parish. Tom had called around and found a place there that had what they needed.

The cab dropped them at a salvage company were they picked up a small pickup loaded with a diesel pump and coiled lengths of ribbed plastic hose. The rental charge went on Jack's card.

A block away they rented two scuba setups: wet suits, vests, weights, air tanks, masks, snorkels, flippers, and regulators. That charge too went on Jack's card.

Good thing he had a high limit.

The credit card company regularly offered John Tyleski a higher credit limit. And John, good consumer that he was, kept accepting.

Then came the harrowing trip in the truck from St. George's at the base of the shaft all the way around to Somerset Parish near the barb on the hook where they'd left the boat.

The accent wasn't the only thing British about Bermuda. Here too they drove on the wrong side of the road.

Tom did okay navigating the narrow, two-lane roads in the left lane, saying you adapt pretty quickly. The only time he seemed to have a problem was at the roundabouts. He started to turn right at the first. He was looking left when he should have been looking right. Jack's last-minute warning yell saved them from a head-on with a taxi.

And Gia had been worried about scuba. The reefs would be a picnic compared to the roads. It might have been off season, but they were busy. No speeding and few passing opportunities on these tight strips of asphalt, and no shortcuts—at least none known to nonnatives—on this narrow string of islands.

The ten-mile trip took almost an hour, but they'd made it.

Jack immediately started his scuba lessons off the Beresfords' dock.

Tom had told him it was easy, that they'd be down in that sand hole by midday. Piece of cake.

Sure. Piece of cake.

But he had to admit his brother was a good teacher. And Tom had been right about it not being rocket science: Breathe through the mouthpiece, inflate your vest when you want to rise, deflate it when you want to descend. Know how to clear your mask and equalize your ear pressure every three feet or so as you descend.

In less than an hour he was reasonably functional with the gear and fairly comfortable in the water.

Jack wondered why no one had ever told him about the

wonders of scuba diving. Of course, not many of his acquaintances were the scuba type, and Manhattan wasn't exactly a dive mecca. Still . . .

No number of Jacques Cousteau specials or repeat viewings of *The Deep* could convey the magic of becoming part of the sea habitat, of hanging out with the fish and the mollusks and crustaceans and all the graceful, undulating plants in their own world.

But it was more than hanging out. It was becoming one with them. To sink beneath the surface and be able to stay there, to float weightless, still, silent, watching. The peace, the serenity, the solitude . . . like nothing he'd ever experienced.

He loved it.

Then they'd boarded the *Sahbon* and Tom steered them out of the sound and toward the reefs, using his GPS doodad to guide them to the spot that supposedly contained the remains of the *Sombra*. They'd anchored over a sand hole and suited up.

"Ready?" Tom said.

With his skinny arms and legs arrayed around a big gut stretching the neoprene of his hooded wet suit to its tensile limits, he looked ridiculous. All he needed were a couple of Ping-Pong eyeballs and he'd be ready to play one of the aliens in *Killers from Space*.

"What if I said no?"

Sinking beneath the surface off the dock and jumping off a boat eight miles from shore were not quite the same. Not even close. He looked back at the roofs on the islands gleaming in the midday sun.

"Jack . . ."

"Okay, I'm ready," he said, then added, "You sure this is the place?"

Tom nodded. "*Sombra* waits below."

"If you say so. What if we see a shark?"

Tom gave a dismissive wave. "If you do, it'll be a harmless variety. Now, here's how it's going to work. See the way we're pulling on the anchor line? That's the way the current is running. We're situated over the upstream end of the sand hole. That's the way we'll work: Start upstream and slowly move downstream. Got it?"

"Sure. Instead of kicking sand in our own faces, it'll all float downstream."

"Exactly. One of us handles the hose while the other stays low and watches for artifacts—preferably of the gold and silver variety."

"And that's going to uncover the wreck?"

"I know it sounds simplistic, but that's the way it's done. The intake hose brings seawater to the pump; the pump then shoots it through the outflow hose; the stream of water from the nozzle sweeps away the bottom sand a layer at a time. It's simple but ingenious."

Jack looked around. The *Sahbon* sat alone on the glittering water. The coast of St. George's lay seven or eight miles to the south. To the north, past the outer rim of the reef, the bottom dropped off to six hundred feet, and then a couple of miles down to the base of the Bermuda rise.

He felt exposed out here.

And uncomfortable.

Clear sky, clear air, clear water, gentle breeze, glittering waves . . . where did this vague unease come from?

"Tom, what are we really doing here?"

His brother's face was a study of innocent perplexity. "I don't know how to answer that, Jack. We're starting an impromptu archaeological excavation in search of long-lost treasure in an attempt to save my ass. What other reason could there be?"

Jack couldn't think of one. But he sensed one.

"All right. Let me ask you once again: If the Bermuda coast guard or navy or whatever they use to patrol these waters stops by and asks who we are and what we're doing, what are we going to say?"

He'd posed this to Tom a number of times since this morning but had yet to receive a satisfactory answer.

"They won't. No reason they should. We're anchored well outside the reef preserve, we're nowhere near any of the protected wrecks. We're just a couple of divers."

"But just say they do a random check. We are, in a very true sense, illegal aliens. I don't want to end up in that prison."

"Will you stop worrying? You sound like a nervous old biddy."

Attention to details, anticipating potential problems before they became real . . . it had kept Jack alive and on the right side of jail bars. So far.

Tom stepped over to the pump. They'd placed the heavy, steamer-trunk-sized contraption near the transom. The hoses were in the water and ready to go. The short feeder had a weighted end that hung over the port side and drifted a couple of feet below the surface; the coils of the longer one, a fifty footer, floated on the starboard side.

A touch of the starter button brought the pump's diesel engine to sputtering life. The end of the longer hose began bubbling and snaking about as it filled with water drawn through its shorter brother.

Tom fitted his mask over his face. "See you downstairs," he said in a nasal voice.

He stuck the mouthpiece between his lips, waved, then fell backward into the water. He hit with a splash, righted himself, then grabbed the end of the hose. He motioned Jack to follow him, then kicked away toward the bottom.

Jack adjusted his own mask, then took a test breath through the mouthpiece. Everything seemed to be working, but he hesitated. He was about to jump into a hole and couldn't help but remember another hole, the one in the Everglades, the one that had no bottom . . .

Shaking it off, he seated himself on the gunwale, tank over the water and—here goes—toppled backward.

He hit the water and let himself sink. Immediately the tank and the weight belt became weightless, the clumsy, unwieldy, uncomfortable gear became lithe and supremely functional. He held his nose and popped his ears, then kicked toward the bottom, following the hose down to where Tom hovered and waited forty feet below.

This sand hole was a forty-foot-deep oblong depression in the reef, about half as wide as it was long. They'd anchored near the upstream edge, so as Jack dropped through the crystalline water, popping his ears whenever the pressure became uncomfortable, he checked out the nearby coral wall.

Something strange here.

He drifted over for a closer look. The coral looked bleached and barren—no sea grasses, no algae, no vegetation at all. No sponges or anemones, no starfish or sea urchins. A closer look showed not a single living coral polyp.

The reef was dead.

Jack had heard of coral blights that wiped out entire reefs. Maybe that was the story here. He looked around and could not find a single fish. Even in the shallow water by the dock he'd been accompanied by a wide variety of brightly colored fish. He'd been able to identify a parrotfish and an angelfish, but the rest were strangers.

Here, on this reef, however . . . no movement, no color.

In a way that made sense. The coral polyps were the bedrock of the reef ecosystem. When they died, the hangers-on went off in search of greener pastures.

But you'd think you'd see at least one fish.

Jack did a full three-sixty. Nope. Not one. Nothing alive in this sand hole except Tom and him.

He shook off the creeps crawling up his back and kicked down toward where Tom was impatiently motioning him to *come on!*

When Jack reached him, Tom signaled him to sink closer to the bottom. When Jack was down, almost prone, Tom aimed the hose at the floor. The invisible stream of water stirred up the sand, billowing it up to then drift downstream, leaving a smooth depression in the floor.

Although Tom had explained it to him, he'd needed to see it in action to appreciate the simplicity of using a stream of seawater to move undersea sand.

Holding the hose at a low angle, Tom swept it back and forth in slow arcs, removing a thin layer, then stepping forward to repeat the process along the center of the sand hole's long axis. Sort of like power washing a patio or walk, except that it exposed no clean surface, just more sand.

Wondering how far down to the bottom of the sand, Jack hovered behind, checking the newly exposed layer for anything that might be manmade. It was slow going, and on their first pass they found nothing.

So it was back to the upstream end for another try. This time, midway along the course, Jack felt a tap on his wet suit hood. He looked up to see Tom excitedly pointing at the sand.

Just ahead lay the edge of a piece of wood, rotted and crumbling but still bearing unmistakable signs that it had been milled. This was no remnant of a sunken log. This had once been a plank.

4

"We've found her!" Tom said as soon as they broke the surface.

Their air tanks had been running low so they'd ascended to a depth of fifteen feet and hovered there, clinging to the anchor rope, for a brief decompression stop to clear excess nitrogen from their bloodstreams. They hadn't been deep enough to worry much about the bends, but why take the chance?

Well, Jack thought, we found something. Surprise, surprise. Too soon to tell if it was the *Sombra*. But he kept mum. No point in raining on Tom's parade.

They removed their fins and climbed the transom ladder to the deck. They decided on a beer break before strapping on fresh tanks.

Tom seemed to be a different person. His eyes danced, his movements were full of energy, he couldn't stop grinning.

"Got to be the *Sombra*." The mask had left a red ring across his forehead and around his cheeks. "Now we know where to concentrate."

Jack gave a noncommittal nod. His thoughts kept returning below, to the sand hole.

"What's up with the coral down there?"

"Yeah, I noticed that. Looks dead. Could be a pollutant, could be a disease."

"But even then, wouldn't you expect some algae or *something* to be growing there?"

Tom shrugged. "Could be a lot of things. It's a problem all over the world. They've got this starfish in the Pacific called the crown of thorns. A bunch of them can wipe out reef after reef."

"Okay, but no fish either. I didn't see a single fish."

Another shrug, plus a grin. "Neither did I, but that should make you happy: No fish means no sharks."

Tom just didn't get it.

"Maybe I'm being oversensitive and paranoid, but consider this: For the whole time we were down, you and I were the only living things in that sand hole. Don't you think that's just a little strange?"

Jack hoped nothing more than a blight or pollution was at work here.

"Whatever," Tom said, rising and starting to strap new tanks to the vests. He appeared to be vibrating with anticipation. Or was it greed? "Let's get back down there before the sun gets too low."

5

Concentrating the water stream around the plank they'd found, they turned up more wood, all equally rotted, crumbling at the lightest touch. But no treasure chest, no coins or jewels. Just sand, sand, sand.

With their tanks getting low and the light fading, Tom pointed to the surface. They were done for the day. Jack couldn't say he was sorry. He was tired and he was bored. He realized what he liked most about diving was the sea life. None of that here. He couldn't wait to get back to the surface.

But before he did . . .

Instead of hanging on the line with Tom for a decompression stop, he propelled himself to the rim of the sand hole and glided over the crest to see how far beyond the blight had spread.

He stopped and floated, gaping. Color . . . movement . . . *life*. He felt like Dorothy opening the door to Oz:

The area all around the sand hole teemed with darting, vibrant-hued fish, waving vegetation, and pastels of living coral. The die-off appeared to be confined to their sand hole. Whatever had killed all the sea life there hadn't advanced beyond it. Since coral predators and pollutants wouldn't have stopped at the lip of the hole, that removed them from the equation.

Something confined to the hole had killed off—and

was continuing to kill off—all the sea life in its immediate vicinity.

And the only thing in the hole that wasn't anywhere else on the reef was probably the *Sombra*.

THURSDAY

1

Jack was driving Tom crazy.

He'd started yesterday as soon as they hit the surface after the second dive, yammering about how the coral die-off was limited to their sand hole, how every place else down there was teeming with life, going on and on and on about something being wrong, wrong, wrong.

He'd persisted in his inchoate ramblings during the trip back to Hamilton and all through dinner. Tom didn't think he'd ever been so happy to close a hotel room door behind him and collapse on a bed. Shutting off Jack's voice had been part of it; the vodka had contributed too. But mostly it had been the crushing fatigue. He led a sedentary life and the day's exertions had exacted their toll.

Were *still* exacting a toll. He had muscle aches in places where he hadn't known he had muscles.

Jack didn't seem to be bothered at all. They'd traded their empty air tanks for fresh this morning and he'd hefted them in and out of the truck bay as if yesterday had been just another day.

No doubt about it, little brother was strong.

And fast. Tom's belly still hurt from that punch the other night. He hadn't seen it coming, hadn't seen it happen. One second he was standing there, the next he was doubled over in pain. Even though it had hurt like hell, the scary part was that he sensed Jack had pulled the punch, hitting him just hard enough to make his point. If he'd put everything into it . . .

Best to forget about it. He'd almost got them both

killed. But who'd have believed they'd cross paths with a tanker? The odds were . . .

Never mind. He'd fucked up and deserved the punch. But admit that to Jack? Never.

Jack continued with his litany of doom this morning—like a woodchuck gnawing at his brainstem.

"I'm telling you, Tom. We need to rethink this whole thing."

"Will you give it a rest? I'm begging you, Jack, give it a rest. You're wearing me out with this shit."

Tom repressed an urge to tell him to talk about something else or not talk at all. He had to be careful. He needed Jack. He couldn't do this alone.

But he needed quiet too, so he could think. He couldn't get the bank out of his mind. Half a million bucks and he couldn't get to it!

Which made finding something in the *Sombra* crucial.

He clenched his jaw and tried to think as their pickup crawled through Paget with the rest of the traffic on South Road. He hadn't driven a manual shift in ages; what a royal pain in the ass. But at least they had wheels. No such thing as Hertz or Avis here. Bermuda didn't want tourists renting anything larger than a moped. That made the taxi drivers happy.

But that didn't prevent private rentals, and Tom had arranged a package deal for the truck and the pump.

Forget the truck, forget the traffic. The bank . . . the bank . . . what if he offered Dawkes—?

"Let's just go back to the beginning," Jack said.

Jesus Christ, he's like the paperboy in *Better Off Dead*! "Jack—"

"No, hear me out. Let's recap what you told me: This wreck we're excavating ran the Cadiz-Cartagena route, right? But instead of naming it *Santa Something*, like every other Spanish ship I've ever heard of, the owner calls it *Shadow*. Doesn't that make you wonder?"

"Wonder about what?"

"About his mind-set."

Tom sighed. "Jack, the guy, whoever he was, has been dead over four hundred years. Who cares about his mind-set? Where's this going?"

"Just bear with me. The ship is on this route between Spain and South America but is way off course when it hits the reef out there and sinks into a sand hole. Yet somebody survives who knows enough about navigation to map out the location of the hole. Why?"

"Obviously because the ship was carrying a lot of valuables and he wanted to be able to locate it later for salvage."

"Who in the sixteenth century could salvage anything from a wreck forty feet down?"

"Maybe they didn't know how deep it was."

Jack shook his head. "You're not seeing the big picture. You said Bermuda was uninhabited back then—not just uninhabited, *avoided* because of its dangerous reefs. The *Sombra*'s survivors were stranded with no hope of rescue. So I ask again: Why make a map?"

"But they *were* rescued—obviously. Otherwise how could the map end up in a monastery in Spain?"

"Right. Obviously rescued. But who picked them up? They were off the trade lanes with no radio to call for help."

"Who cares who picked them up? Who cares how the map got to Spain? The important thing is it got to me and yesterday we found proof that it isn't a fake."

"Which worries me even more."

"Why?"

I can't wait to hear this.

"What . . . what if the *Sombra* was meant to go down?"

"What? Are you—?"

"Hear me out, okay? What if the ship was scuttled because it was carrying something that someone wanted to get rid of, or hide forever in a place where no one would ever find it? The Isle of Devils would be the perfect spot:

Everybody avoids it, and I'll bet no one in those days ever conceived the possibility that it would one day be settled."

A wave of discomfort swept through Tom. Jack was blundering near the truth—at least part of it. He had to turn him in another direction.

"That's crazy."

"No, what's crazy is the dead zone in that sand hole. Something that went down with that wreck is either killing or repelling every form of life around it. Who knows what'll happen to us if we hang around it too much longer?"

Tom forced a laugh. "You mean there's something *eeevil* down there?"

"Maybe not evil, but something strange, something best left alone."

He pushed another laugh. "Sounds like a bad movie where the explorer or scientist is warned against 'delving into secrets man is not meant to know.' Give me a break."

Jack crushed his empty coffee container and tossed it onto the floor of the cab. His expression was unreadable.

"I know it sounds crazy, but things aren't always what they seem. There's more going on out there than we know."

"You mean in the sense of, 'There are more things in heaven and earth, Horatio, than are dreamt of in your philosophy'?"

"Yeah. Call me Hamlet."

This was interesting. Tom had never experienced anything paranormal, but that didn't mean it wasn't there. And now, considering what he hoped to find, he prayed it was.

But he couldn't let Jack get spooked.

"Oh, come on. You don't strike me as the kind who believes in mumbo jumbo."

"Who said anything about believing?"

Tom glanced at his brother. "What are you trying to tell me?"

"That I used to laugh off a lot of things. Now I'm very choosy about what I dismiss out of hand."

"And this is because . . . ?"

Jack stared straight ahead. "Experience is a great teacher."

"Wait-wait-wait. You're not really telling me you've seen a ghost or spoken to God or had an out-of-body experience of something like that?" He laughed. "Come to think of it, I've had a few out-of-body experiences myself, usually with the help of a lot of Grey Goose."

He expected at least a courtesy grin from Jack. Instead, the haunted look in his brother's eyes chilled him.

"What are you *saying,* Jack?"

"That things aren't always what they seem."

"Hell, you think I don't know that? Everybody knows that."

"No, I mean in the larger sense." He swept his arm at the world beyond the windshield. "Ever get the idea that this is all a set, and the real action's going on behind the scenery?"

Another chill. Had Jack really experienced something paranormal? Tom hoped so. Because if there were inexplicable occurrences out there, events and objects linked to unknown powers or forces, then maybe what he'd learned about the Lilitongue was more than a madman's delusion.

"Care to elaborate?"

Jack shook his head. "You'll think I'm crazy."

Jack didn't seem crazy, but Tom had run into clandestine nutcases before. They seem sane and anchored and sensible, and in ninety-nine percent of their lives they are. But touch the button that triggers their fragile one percent and it all comes out.

Maybe Jack was one of those. If so, did Gia know?

Gia . . . Tom had dreamed about her every night since he'd met her. He couldn't get her out of his head.

He'd been shocked to learn she was pregnant. She wasn't showing much and so he hadn't spotted it at Lucille's. But at the wake it became obvious.

So . . . Gia had Jack's bun in the oven.

Oddly enough, it didn't matter. If anything, in some perverse way it made her even more attractive.

Maybe he was kidding himself, but he felt he'd scored some points with her on the drive from New York down to the wake. He'd used the hour and a half to dazzle her with his knowledge of the arts. Mostly secondhand opinions, true, but Tom thought he'd managed to come off as witty, urbane, and cultured. If her little girl hadn't kept interrupting, he was sure he'd have mesmerized Gia. Cute kid, that Vicky, but she talked too damn much.

At first he'd wondered if she might belong to Jack, but soon learned that Vicky was a product of Gia's first marriage. Divorce: One more thing Tom and Gia had in common.

What kind of spell had she put on him?

Spell . . . there it was again: the paranormal.

He shook it off. Either way, crazy or sane, Tom needed Jack on board.

"Try me."

Another head shake. "Too complicated, too far out. Maybe someday. Let's just let it ride for now and suffice it to say we should drop this treasure hunt and go home."

"I can't give it up, Jack." The plaintive note in his voice wasn't put on. "I've got no other options."

Jack was shaking his head. "No good's gonna come of it. I've got this feeling in my gut—"

"Can't we just put all that aside and just look at the situation rationally? There isn't a reef in the world that doesn't have patches of dead coral; the sand hole we're working just happens to be one of them. Isn't that the simplest, most sensible approach? It doesn't require dark supernatural forces at work to explain it. It's just the way it is."

"Occam's razor," Jack said.

"Exactly!"

For a college dropout, Jack seemed pretty well read.

"Yeah, well, I've discovered that old Occam's razor isn't anywhere near as sharp as people think."

"One more day, Jack. That's all I'm asking. Besides, you promised two days."

Jack stayed silent awhile, then sighed. "Okay. One more day. Today and that's it. Then we pack up and leave."

"You've got a deal!"

Well, sort of. If they didn't find the Lilitongue today, maybe he'd be able to squeeze an extra day out of Jack. After all, what was Jack's alternative? Not as if he could just up and hop a plane back to the States.

Jack was trapped.

But not as trapped as Tom. Not with his Bermuda assets frozen. But . . . if he found what the map hinted was here . . .

The Lilitongue of Gefreda—whatever it was—just might save what was left of the rest of his life.

2

Yesterday's excitement at finding and starting to exhume a four-hundred-year-old wreck quickly devolved to drudgery on day two.

Jack found the routine of sifting the newly exposed

sand in the wake of Tom's water stream deadly dull. So dull that he'd all but forgotten about the lifeless coral walls around them.

They were on their second tanks and had found nothing besides scraps of rotten wood ranging in length from a finger to an arm. The ship must have shattered when it hit the reef. Centuries in salt water had done the rest: The larger remnants crumbled under the slightest pressure.

A colossal waste of time.

But Jack held up his end, hugging the bottom, digging his gloved fingers into the sand, pulling free anything he found. He spotted the corner of another board, got a grip, and pulled. A big chunk broke off. Small fragments and dustlike particles floated away downstream.

He turned it over in his hands. Just like the rest. At first he'd wondered why no worm holes, then realized that whatever had killed the coral had probably killed the worms as well. He tossed it aside and gripped the rest of the board. As he hauled it free he caught a reflection of sunlight just below it, then sand refilled the cavity.

Metal?

He tapped Tom on the leg and pointed to the spot. Tom directed the stream into the depression. Sand billowed and sprayed while Jack worked his hands deeper. More flashes of yellow reflection. Gold?

His earlier apathy vanished. Something down there . . . something more than rotted wood. Despite all his misgivings about this wreck, he couldn't deny a surge of excitement. They might be uncovering something that no human eyes had seen for centuries.

There—metal. A bright yellow band, curved across a curving surface . . . a surface that resembled carved wood . . . *lacquered* wood.

But how . . . ?

Tom had seen it too and was working the hose nozzle back, forth, and around in a seeming frenzy. Didn't take too long to realize they'd discovered a small sea chest wrapped in rusty links of heavy chain.

Tom knelt and concentrated the stream along the left end of the chest with one hand while working his free hand deeper and deeper until he found a handle. He leaned back, pulling upward while playing the hose back and forth across the surface.

As the top was revealed Jack saw that it was a camelback style chest with a convex top crossed by three brass bands. He'd seen lots of them—even owned one, though nowhere near as ornate—but had never seen one this shape: square, running maybe two feet on each side. The most startling thing about it was its cherry condition. The chain around it had wasted to a rusted skeleton of its former self. But the chest . . . no rot, no oxidation of the brass, no dulling of the lacquer finish.

And that was wrong. The rest of the *Sombra* wasn't fit for a beach bonfire, but this thing looked as if it could have fallen off a passing boat ten minutes ago.

Despite the vague dread roiling his gut, Jack leaned in to help. He didn't see that he had much choice.

He worked a hand down along the chest's opposite side, found a handle that felt like leather—strong, *unrotted* leather—and began to pull. With the stream from the hose plus their combined efforts rocking it back and forth, they managed to work the chest free.

As they knelt in the sand, holding it between them, Jack looked at Tom's face. He was grinning around his mouthpiece and his eyes were wide and bright behind the faceplate of his mask. He released the hose, letting it snake away behind him, and tugged on the rotted chain. The links fractured and fell away amid a cloud of rust flakes.

Jack lowered his gaze to the little square chest. Except for the domed top it was pretty near a perfect cube. And as pristine at its base as it was along its top.

This was all very wrong. Jack had no idea what it was

or what it held, but he sensed that everyone would be better off if they just left this thing where it was. That look in Tom's eyes, though, said that would never happen.

Another strange thing about the chest. Its weight . . . much lighter than he'd have thought. Almost weightless.

Tom motioned for them to put it down. They lowered it to the sand and released the handles. To Jack's amazement the chest began to rise. As it picked up speed in its wobbly ascent, neither of them grabbed for it. They knelt and stared like a couple of awestruck children. Before they could react it was out of reach.

Tom pushed off the bottom and kicked after it. He caught up to it halfway to the surface and tucked it under his arm. Then he continued toward the surface.

Filled with foreboding, Jack watched him go. Everything about this was wrong, wrong, wrong.

Reluctantly he shot some air into his vest and began his own ascent.

3

"Damn thing's locked," Tom said. "Not that I'm surprised, but shit!"

Jack watched his brother kneel on the rocking deck in his dripping wet suit. He hadn't bothered to remove his tank. He had the chest tilted back and was peering at the front seam of its lid.

Jack shrugged out of his BC vest and pulled off his hood. He ruffled his hair to shake out some of the water. The wind had picked up, raising some swells. Clouds were building in the west, reaching toward the sun. The weather looked ready for a change.

He didn't see a keyhole in the front of the chest, so he leaned in for a better look. He saw a curved surface, like the edge of a cylinder, divided into seven sections. Each segment sported an embossed number.

Jack let out a barking laugh. "It's a combination lock."

Tom's frown indicated he didn't think it was funny. "Combination . . . but when did combination locks first appear?"

"Not sure," Jack said, "but I know they were around before the *Sombra*'s time."

Locked . . . not necessarily a bad thing. But as much as Jack wished this thing were still buried in the sand below, he had to admit to a curiosity about its contents—and about his brother's intense interest.

"What's in it, Tom?"

Tom was turning the little number wheels.

"Shit. They run zero to ten. That means . . ."

He paused, calculating, but Jack was ahead of him.

"Ten million possibilities. But you didn't answer my question: What's in there?"

"Who knows?" He sounded annoyed now. "Gold? Jewels? The Lilitongue of Gefreda?"

"Whatever that is."

"Well, we'll never find out if we can't open it."

"I think you already know."

He looked up at Jack. "Now why would you say that?"

"Just a feeling. A very strong feeling. Time to level with me, bro. What's going on here?"

Tom looked up at him, his face a mask of frustration. "You know anything about locks? Any idea how to bypass this?"

Yeah, Jack knew about locks, knew how to pick them, but this baby was not the pickable kind.

"Yeah. Got a pry bar?"

Tom looked shocked. "No! We might damage whatever's inside!"

"Would that be a bad thing?"

"What the hell are you talking about?"

Jack pointed to the chest. "It's been underwater more than four hundred years but it looks brand new. Now lift it, Tom. Tell me how much you think it weighs."

Tom hefted it. "Twenty . . . twenty-five pounds."

"I helped you haul it over the transom. More like forty or fifty."

Tom grinned. "Gold is heavy."

"Yeah, it is. But tell me: You're the scuba diver. You're the one who gave me lessons on the rules of buoyancy and displacement. Should something that size and that weight be able to float?"

"Well, no, but—"

"No buts about it. You saw it. This thing not only floated, it shot to the surface like a balloon. Care to explain that?"

"I wish I could. I also wish I could explain why you're so suspicious. Why do you keep going on about me hiding something from you? Here's what we found. It's sitting right here between us. I'm asking your help to open it. Where's the subterfuge here?"

Good question. Tom *was* being pretty open about all this.

Jack stared at the seven wheels of the combination lock. Seven . . . ten million possibilities . . . what seven-figure number would do it? Good thing the wheels weren't coded with letters. Twenty-six to the seventh . . . he couldn't come close to calculating that.

Letters . . . numbers . . .

And then he had an idea.

"Just for the hell of it, try these. Start from the left: seven . . . five . . . six . . . wait." Jack did a quick count on his fingers. "Okay, make the fourth eight, then five . . . four . . . one."

As the last wheel turned, Jack could hear the click of the bolt from where he stood.

"Christ almighty!" Tom looked up at him with a baffled expression. "How the hell . . . ?"

"Seven wheels, seven letters in 'Gefreda.' I took a stab."

Tom grasped the lid on both sides and tilted it back. It moved easily, smoothly, without a single squeak from the rear hinges. Inside Jack saw an irregular blue dome. It took a few seconds to register that it was a piece of silk—*dry* silk.

Tom's hand moved toward it but stalled halfway there. Jack noticed a fine tremor in the fingers. Then they pushed forward and hesitated another heartbeat or two before pinching a fold of the silk and lifting it.

Jack blinked when he saw what lay beneath.

No gold, no jewels—not even close. An irregular, slightly oblong sphere, somewhat larger than a basketball, sat in the box. Looked like an ugly piece of slightly rotted fruit with a leathery, olive-hued rind.

"What the hell is that?"

"I . . . haven't a clue." Tom ran skittish fingers over the surface. "Jesus, it feels like skin."

Jack squatted next to him and gave it a feel. Cool, slightly rough to the touch. Yeah . . . like skin. Not necessarily human skin; some kind of hide?

"You think this is it?"

Tom glanced at him. "Is what?"

"That Lilitongue thing you talked about. Could this be it?"

"I don't know. I've never seen a drawing of it."

"Doesn't look like any tongue I've ever seen. It—" Jack pulled his hand away as an unsettling thought hit him. "You don't think its hide is made from tongues, do you?"

"No. It may not even be the Lilitongue." He reached his hands around it. "Help me get it out."

Jack got a grip on two sides and together they lifted the thing from the chest. At most it was only a quarter again larger than a basketball, but it was a hell of a lot heavier. As they moved it Jack squeezed it between his hands—not a hint of give.

Once it was out he could see that it had rested in a silk-lined well.

"Custom-made for it," he said.

They gently laid it on the rocking deck. Jack steadied it while Tom checked the chest, poking about, lifting it and shaking it. He pulled his diving knife from the sheath strapped to his leg and began prying at the insides. He worked the blade around the edge of the well and popped it out in one piece. Then he upended the chest and tapped its sides. Nothing dropped out.

He tossed the chest aside.

"Shit! Nothing! Not even a piece of parchment to tell us what it is!"

Jack couldn't help feeling a little sorry for him as he returned to the sphere. No treasure, just this weird-looking thing.

A thing that looked more than ever like a piece of fruit. It even had a little navel, like an orange, but thirty or so degrees above the lower pole.

"What do you think?" Jack said. "Man-made or organic?"

Tom didn't answer. He sat staring at the thing, his face a mask of disappointment. For an instant Jack thought he might cry.

"Tom? You okay?"

"Yeah." His voice was barely audible. "I heard you. Who gives a shit?"

"Take a guess."

Tom sighed. "Doesn't look man-made. I mean, it's got no seams."

Jack agreed. That hinted that it had grown somewhere. He wasn't sure he wanted to see the garden where it had been picked.

"Yeah . . . no seams." He reached over to where Tom had left his knife. "But let's see if we can make a few."

As Jack raised the blade Tom wrapped his arms around the sphere and hugged it like a mother protecting a child.

"Don't even think about it!"

"Don't you want to know what's inside?"

"Yes, but I don't want to ruin it. It could be some price-less relic, or it could have a stash of jewels inside."

"Well, you're never going to know if you don't take a peek."

"Right. But you can do that without cutting it open. Ever hear of X-ray?"

"You've got an X-ray machine?" Jack slapped the side of his face. "Wow! I knew this boat was high tech, but its own X-ray mach—"

"Put a sock in it, Jack. We're going to gas up and head back home tonight."

"We've still got some light left. Don't you want to see if there's anything else down here? Those doubloons you were talking about?"

Tom shook his head. "I think we've stayed long enough, don't you?"

Something wrong here. Jack was about to press it until he realized he'd be arguing against heading home. Home . . . he didn't want to delay his return a moment longer than absolutely necessary.

4

Tom stood watch over the afterdeck as a dockside pump filled the *Sahbon*'s tanks. He was sipping another kind of fuel: the Grey Goose he kept stashed in the pilothouse.

Instead of making the longer trip back to the sound, they'd cruised directly to St. George's where they returned the scuba gear and the pump, paying an extra fee for the time it would take a couple of men to drive out to Somerset and retrieve the truck. Then they found a marina for refueling.

Jack was ashore, buying food and ice, and calling Gia to let her know they were on their way home.

Tom took a deep sip from the coffee cup he was using as a glass. No ice aboard, so he was drinking it warm. He preferred it freezer cold, but warm vodka was better than no vodka.

Even with half a snootful he doubted he could find a way to put a positive spin on this trip situation.

Only one way to spin being locked out of his stash and learning that the feds knew more about him than he'd dreamed.

The good news—the trip's only good news—was that he was now the proud owner of the Lilitongue of Gefreda. At least he assumed that was what the ugly thing was.

He glanced toward the door to the pilothouse where they'd stowed it in its chest.

The bad news was that he had no idea what to do with it, or how to use it.

His initial elation had begun to die when he opened the chest and got a look at it. He hadn't known what to expect, but he'd never dreamed it would look like that. Despair crept in when he could find no word of explanation in the chest as to what it held or what it could do or how it could be used.

He put down his vodka and stepped below into the pilothouse. There he pulled his beat-up green canvas backpack from under his bunk. He unzipped it and searched among the banded stacks of bills. He managed a smile. Would Jack ever be pissed if he saw this pile of cash.

There. Got it.

He pulled out a Xeroxed sheet, one he hadn't shown Jack: a copy of the inscription on the band around the Mendes map. He knew it by heart, but unfolded the sheet anyway and retranslated the ornate script.

Let this be the only record of the final resting place of the Lilitongue of Gefreda, known to the dark few as a means to elude all enemies and leave them helpless. Consigned to the depths near the Isle of Devils by order of the Holy Father. May no man exhume it from its watery grave.

He didn't know who "the dark few" were. Maybe Jesuits—they dressed in black, didn't they? But "a means to elude all enemies and leave them helpless" echoed through to his soul.

Tom couldn't think of anyone who more needed to elude his enemies. He'd wanted the map the instant he saw it. And lately, as he'd felt the noose tightening around his neck, the promise of the Lilitongue had called to him.

If he'd been able to grab his stash, he'd have had no need of the thing, wouldn't even have looked for it. But the cash in his backpack wasn't going to get him far. Might be enough to help him disappear for a while, but he'd need lots more to stay invisible.

He needed a way to elude all enemies and leave them helpless.

Am I nuts?

The whole idea was crazy, wishful thinking. A fantasy.

But a part of him sensed truth there. Years ago, out of curiosity, he'd looked into it. He'd found next to nothing about the Lilitongue itself, but he'd come across veiled references to the pope himself—Clement VIII, to be exact—wanting it disposed of. That said a lot.

Maybe it said: *Don't mess with it.*

But Tom didn't think so. The pope in those times was king of the hill; he didn't need to "elude" his enemies. In fact, a great many people, especially heretics, had needed to elude him. The Spanish Inquisition was still in full swing back in 1598. When it had started in the preceding century, its main targets were Spanish Jews and Moors; but in the sixteenth century a real threat to the Church arose: Protestantism.

Could Pope Clement have assigned the Jesuit map

maker to send the Lilitongue to a watery grave because of wild-eyed Lutherans and Presbyterians?

Well, they *were* heretics. And maybe he didn't want it to fall into their hands. Because it worked.

Or he believed it worked.

But if the inscription was to be believed, Pope Clement had been pretty damn determined to be rid—permanently rid—of the Lilitongue. He sent a ship on a four-week voyage, far off the trade routes, to hide the thing where no one would ever find it. No one considered Bermuda habitable back then—no one dreamed it would *ever* be inhabited.

Tom had wondered why go to all that trouble. Why not just dump it overboard in midocean?

He'd learned the answer today when he saw the chest shoot to the surface: The Lilitongue floats. And the pope hadn't wanted it washing up on shore.

But to sink an entire ship . . . that said something.

Maybe it said the Lilitongue was what he needed to save his sorry ass. And maybe it was.

But he hadn't the faintest idea how to use it.

Tom sighed—he'd been doing a lot of sighing lately—and stuffed the sheet back into his backpack, then returned topside for his vodka.

Let's face it, he thought as he took a gulp. I'm fucked. Might as well hold the fuel hose over my head, give myself a good soaking, and light a match.

He shuddered. Couldn't see himself doing that. Although the feds and the powers-that-be in Harrisburg were planning a figurative auto-da-fé for him, he wasn't about to give them the real thing.

He took another slug of Goose.

That didn't mean he might not come to the point where he'd look for another mode of exit, though one kinder and gentler.

"I t'row it right back in de water, me."

Tom looked up and saw a young black girl, maybe fifteen or sixteen, standing on the dock, staring at him. Her hair was cornrowed and she wore baggy, cut-off shorts and a stained yellow T-shirt. The nipples of her small, budding breasts poked two little points in the fabric. She was smiling at him.

"Pardon?" he said.

"You hear me."

The homely, brown, short-haired mutt seated beside her on the dock barked. Its pug face hinted that a bulldog had sneaked into its lineage. One of its ears had a chewed look. Its pink tongue lolled as it stared at him and panted.

"I'm sorry, I wasn't paying attention."

"I say, I t'row it right back in de water, me."

Her voice was musical but didn't carry the cultured Brit tones of the typical Bermudian black; she sounded more like a Jamaican.

Tom looked at his almost empty vodka cup. "Throw what back?"

Her huge brown eyes bored into his. "Youuuu know."

Tom's mouth had gone a little dry. He took a sip to wet it.

Did she mean the Lilitongue? No. She couldn't know. There hadn't been another boat anywhere near them the whole time they were out today.

Or had there? No telling who had been around while they were underwater. But certainly no one too close—they would have heard the motor, seen the hull. And he was sure no one had been in sight when they'd brought it aboard.

So what was she talking about?

"I'm sorry, miss, but you'll need to be more specific."

Her smile faded. Her hands went to the hem of her T-shirt, gripped it, and slowly started to raise it.

Tom glanced around, nervous. He was an outsider, an illegal one to boot, and here was this local black girl, a minor, about to flash him. And not a soul in sight. She could accuse him of anything.

He licked his lips. "What on earth are you—?"

He never got to finish the sentence and she never got to exposing her breasts. Just her abdomen.

Tom looked, blinked, looked again. He felt his jaw drop, his tongue turn to sand. The cup slipped from his fingers and bounced on the deck.

The girl had a hole through her. Just to the right of her navel. Clear through her. He could see the yellow wall of the marina office shack behind her through the opening.

"T'row it back," she said, then lowered her shirt and walked away.

5

Whistling the chorus from Alice Cooper's "School's Out"—stuck in his head since the second viewing of *Dazed and Confused*—Jack arrived back at the dock with two sacks of groceries, a bag of ice, and a feeling that he'd wasted nearly a week of his life. Except for a weird, mysterious piece of junk, Tom was in the same straits now as when they'd set sail.

Despite that he was feeling pretty good. He'd talked to Gia. She and Vicks and the baby were all fine. In two days he'd be back with her.

He'd also checked his voice mail. No word yet from Joey.

In a way that was a relief. Meant he hadn't missed out on anything. His rage had receded underwater. Real-life cares seemed a world away down there. He couldn't help feeling guilty about that.

But soon he'd be home and back to the reality of the streets. Soon he'd rejoin the hunt for payback.

Back at the boat, he found Tom sweeping pieces of what looked like shattered ceramic into a pile on the deck. He looked pale, shaken.

"What happened?"

"Dropped a cup."

"You okay? You don't look so hot."

"Don't feel so hot."

"Sick?"

He shook his head and gave Jack a wan smile. "Nah. I guess I'm not used to the active lifestyle. I tend to eat more and exercise less. Maybe that's why the vodka hit me so hard."

Oh, hell, Jack thought. Am I going to have to drive all the way back to the States?

"You're drunk?"

He shook his head. "Don't feel drunk. But I think I hallucinated a little while ago."

"Yeah? What did you see?"

Another head shake. "Too weird to even talk about." He swept the fragments through a scupper and into the water, then pointed to the neatly dressed, middle-aged black man standing by the pump. "Pay the man and let's get out of here."

Jack pulled out his credit card as he approached.

"What's the damage?"

The man looked at the gauge and said, "Two thousand seven hundred and two dollars and seventy cents."

Jack laughed. "Very funny. Now give me the real number."

The man looked at him. "That is the real number, sir."

"Twenty-seven hundred bucks for gas? You've gotta be kidding!"

"Twenty-seven hundred and *two* bucks, sir. And seventy cents."

Jack looked at the meter. "Twenty-five hundred and seventy-four gallons! This thing only holds seven hundred!"

"Those are liters, sir. In gallons that would be somewhat less than seven hundred, but not much."

"Liters?"

Jack studied the sign over the diesel pump: 1.05/L.

He'd been so happy to see such a cheap price that his
brain apparently had registered only the number and assumed it was the gallon price.

He handed over his card.

"No wonder everyone around here drives mopeds."

Joey climbed the subway steps up to Madison Square
Park—which, for some reason he'd never been able to
figure, was nowhere near Madison Square Garden. He
squinted into the cold wind as he looked around. Benny
the Brit had said he'd meet him on the downtown end of
the park.

There. Perched on a bench just as promised.

Joey started toward him, praying this wasn't another
wasted trip. Despite the support of the big shots in what
was left of the families, he'd come up empty. *Bel niente.*
Then a call from Benny. He had something. Didn't know
if it would help, but meet him in the park and he'd give
Joey what he had.

So here was the park and there sat Benny.

Joey seated himself a couple of feet to Benny's left.
He was maybe ten years older than Joey, squat and fat—
a real *tappo*—wearing one of those tweedy British caps
that snapped onto the peak.

"Morning, Benny."

He started. "Oh, 'allo, guv. Gave me a bit o' a start there, you did."

Everybody knew Benny wasn't British. He grew up in Flatbush and had never been within a thousand miles of England. But for some reason the *ceffo* liked to fake an English accent. Did it so much he never stepped out of character now. Trouble was, he wasn't that good. In fact, he was freaking terrible. Picked up his accent from television—the "telly," as he liked to call it—and movies. His accent was bad even by those standards. Drove everybody bugfuck crazy, but Joey would put up with it if Benny had the goods.

"Whatta y'got for me?"

"A bit o' tape is what I got. I tapes everyone who does business wif me, and I caught meself an Arab in the act."

"Which means?"

"Which means I sold the bloke a couple o' Tavor-twos, I did."

Joey gripped the edge of the bench seat. He was sitting next to the *stronzo* who'd sold the guns that had killed Frankie. He didn't know whether to kill him or kiss him. Because if he had these guys on tape . . .

Too freaking good to be true. Joey's livelihood was built on peddling too good to be true, so he knew what that usually meant . . .

"Let me get this straight: You taped an Arab buying a pair of Tavor-twos."

" 'Sright, mate."

"So why the fuck didn't you tell me that the first I asked you about it?"

Benny leaned back, looking scared, and Joey realized he'd been pretty damn near shouting.

"Easy, mate. Don't 'ave to shout. I ain't Mutt an' Jeff. An' the reason I never said nuffin' was I didn't 'ave it then."

Joey worked at calming himself but wasn't doing such a hot job.

"Whatta you mean you didn't—?"

"'Ere now, don't get yer knickers in a twist. I only taped them yesterday. Got on the dog and bone and called you right away, I did."

"Yesterday? What the fuck good is that? Frankie was killed two weeks ago!"

"Think about it, guv: The blighters left their guns at the airport, right?"

"Yeah, so?"

"So they might be needing replacements. Not to mention the fact that he bought two 'undred hollow-points to go wif 'em. Bit much to be a coincidence, i'nit?"

Joey thought about that. Jesus, if this wasn't a freakin' coincidence, then that meant . . .

"You wouldn't happen to have that tape on you, would you?"

"Right 'ere in me sky rocket, mate."

Benny pulled a manila envelope out of his coat pocket and held it out. Joey snatched it and clutched it with both hands.

"And that's not all," Benny said. He pulled a plastic bag out of another pocket. Joey recognized a pistol magazine. "This 'ere's a li'l somethin' the blighter 'andled while 'e was shoppin'. Got 'is prints all over it, it does."

Joey took the Baggie and stared at the magazine.

Oh man, oh man, oh man. If this panned out . . .

"Got a name or something to go with these?"

"Don't get to 'ear many names in me business, mate. No credit cards neither. Strictly bangers and mash. But I fink you know that."

Yeah, Joey knew that. But it never hurt to ask.

"Thanks, Benny."

"Under normal circumstances I would 'ave told those pandies to bugger right off—I'll not be sellin' to the likes o' them—but I remembered you was lookin' for blokes of that ilk, so I made the transaction. Just for you, mate. Just for you."

Not to mention a heaping plate of "bangers and mash" to boot.

"I'll remember this, Benny. Anything I can ever do for you—"

"Just find those pandies and give 'em what fer." He hauled himself off the bench. "And now I'm off to see me trouble and strife. Left 'er in Macy's, I did. Spendin' me into the poor 'ouse, most likely."

Joey was aware of Benny moving off and taking his bad accent with him, but he didn't say good-bye. He sat in the blessed silence and stared down at the envelope.

A video of a gun-buying Arab. Great. But what was he going to do with it? How did he go about ID-ing the *figlio di puttana*? Where did he go from here?

He didn't know. Have to think on that. But he didn't let it get him down.

Finally, *something*.

7

Tom had been strangely subdued as he'd piloted the *Sahbon* along the channel through the reef. They made it to open ocean before nightfall and headed toward the dying glow on the horizon.

After entering the coordinates for Wanchese harbor and setting the autopilot, he turned to Jack.

"Want to take the first watch?"

Jack couldn't see why not.

"Sure."

"Good. Because I'm bushed. I'm going below for a little shut-eye."

So now, after a couple of hours of dividing his attention between the empty ocean ahead and the dwindling lights of Bermuda behind, Jack was bored out of his skull. On the trip out, the concerns of being a novice sailor in the middle of the ocean, inexperienced with the navigation equipment and bound for an unfamiliar—at least to him—destination, had kept him alert and attuned. Now it seemed like old hat. The *Sahbon* was heading home and he was confident he could get it there on his own.

He took a good look around to confirm that no other running lights were in sight, then descended to the pilot-house to use the head.

He found Tom sitting on his bunk holding a coffee cup and watching the TV. *Dazed and Confused* again. Didn't he ever get tired of that movie?

Look who's talking, Jack thought.

He'd seen certain favorite films dozens of times.

"Thought you were grabbing some z's."

When Tom didn't answer Jack took a closer look.

Oh, shit. Is he sloshed?

Maybe, maybe not, but those looked like tears in his eyes.

"You okay?"

He shook himself, did a quick eye wipe with his sleeve, then pointed to the screen.

"That was me, you know."

Jack looked. The Slater character—Jack didn't know the actor's name—was on the screen.

"A stoner?"

"No. I did my share, for sure, but I mean the times. The mid-seventies were my high school years. I'm looking at me and my friends. Jesus, we never knew how good we had it back then. I mean, the whole future, the whole world lay before us, ours for the taking. So I took it. And screwed it up."

He sipped from his coffee cup. Jack knew it wasn't coffee.

Tom's troubles were his own doing, yet Jack couldn't help feeling a twinge of pity.

He looked around for the sea chest, didn't see it in the cabin, so he opened the door to the bow compartment. There he found it bungeed into place near the anchor. He felt an unexplainable urge to grab it, haul it up on deck, and toss it overboard.

Instead he closed the door and turned to Tom.

"What's the real story with that thing?"

"I don't know. I'd hoped for something readily convertible into cash—like doubloons and such. But who knows? Maybe the Lilitongue's worth more."

"How do you know that's what you've got? You didn't find anything in the chest that identified it."

"Don't you worry, it's the Lilitongue. I'm sure of it." He grinned. "Besides, 'Gefreda' opened the chest, didn't it?"

He had a point. "Okay, let's just say you're right. You know, but how do you prove it? How do you sell something you can't even identify?"

Tom held up a finger. "I can find a way in Philly. We've got U of P, the Franklin Institute, plus all sorts of museums like the Mütter and the Glencairn. A gallimaufry of resources. Somebody in that city *has* to have heard about it, or at least know where to look it up."

"Maybe, but it could take you a year to find that somebody. And you'll never get to spend it if you're locked in a jail cell."

"Yeah, I'm going to have to do a lot of artful dodging. Especially since I'm not supposed to leave Philly. I got an exception made for Dad's funeral but—"

"So that's why you couldn't come right away."

"Right."

A sudden realization slammed Jack. "What about now? Where do they think you are at this moment?"

Tom took a sip of vodka. "Philly."

"Jesus, Tom! You skipped?"

"In a word, yes."

"You're a fugitive?"

"Not officially. Not until they find out I'm gone."

"Jesus, Tom!"

"Will you stop saying that?"

"I don't know what else to say. I've been thinking this trip was one colossal waste of time, but now it's worse. I'm with a guy the feds will be hunting, if they aren't already. If they catch up to you, they catch me too—"

"Always about you, hmmm?"

"Damn straight! From what you've told me, you've got nothing left to lose. I have everything."

The ramifications tied Jack's gut in a knot.

"Relax. We'll be just fine."

As Tom lapsed into morose silence, Jack popped back onto the deck to make a scan of the dark ocean. All clear.

When he returned below he found Tom refilling his cup.

"You going to be able to handle your watch?"

"Yeah, don't worry about it. I'm pacing myself. Don't want to start seeing things again."

"Like what? You said you hallucinated back on the dock. What did you see?"

"Nothing."

"Which is pretty much what you're getting out of this trip."

"Got the Lilitongue."

"Whoopee."

Tom leaned back. "Maybe I'm crazy, but I've got to tell you, I first laid eyes on that map maybe ten years ago, I . . . I can't describe it. I knew the Lilitongue was important and I knew I had to have it."

"Let me guess: You stole the map."

" 'Stole' is kind of harsh. Old Wenzel was dying and his estate was set to be divvied up equally between his three kids, none of whom had any interest in his map collection beyond its cash value. So I, um, rescued it before it disappeared into some collector's cabinet."

Jack was nodding. "I see . . . you didn't steal it, you pilfered it."

"I prefer to categorize it as an honorarium for legal work well done."

"You would."

Tom straightened and jabbed a finger toward Jack.

"Don't try that holier-than-thou shit again, because it won't work! I know your story, Jack."

"Do you."

"Damn right. You put on this supercilious, disapproving look when all the while you're as crooked as they come."

Jack blinked "What?"

"You think I'm stupid? You think I can't put two and two together?" He reached into his pocket, withdrew a wad of paper, tossed it at Jack. "How do you explain that?"

Jack snatched it from the air and uncrumpled it: his fuel receipt from the marina. Anger surged.

"You've been going through my things?"

"Didn't have to. You left it by the helm. Take a look. It's got the first name right: John. But 'Tyleski'? That's a long way from the name on your birth certificate, Jack. So here you are, ripping off some unsuspecting guy—"

"I'm not ripping off anyone."

"Really? That'd be easier to believe if your name were on the card. Don't try to bullshit a bullshitter. That's a stolen card."

Jack shook his head. "Wrong. It's mine. I get billed every month and I pay it."

Tom's eyes narrowed. "But you're not John Tyleski."

"Maybe not. But the credit card company doesn't care. And the storeowners don't care. As long as everyone gets paid for their goods and services, who cares what name is on the card?"

Tom continued his stare. "Does all this have something to do with your Repairman Jack thing?"

Jack felt as if he'd been Tasered—couldn't move, couldn't speak.

Tom grinned. "Gotcha, huh?"

Jack found his voice, but it came out a whisper. "What are you talking about?"

Tom then launched into how he'd pieced together remarks from Dad and Gia, lyrics from Bighead's song, and Jack's inability to claim Dad's body. The conclusion he'd reached was disconcertingly close to the truth.

He pointed to the receipt in Jack's hand. "That was the capper. I suspected you were some sort of urban mercenary, but when I saw you were using a false identity, I was sure." He leaned back with a smug expression. "So no more holier than thou, okay? 'Let him who is without sin cast the first stone.' Remember that one?"

"You think knowing what I am gives you a free pass?"

"I just don't want to hear any criticism from a criminal."

Jack leaned toward him. "Maybe I am a criminal. Maybe I could even be considered a career criminal. But I'm not a crook. When I say I'm going to do something, I do it. Ironclad."

Tom reddened. "And I don't?"

"From what you've told me, your word's worth less than those queer twenties you were trying to pass."

"Hey, just a fucking—"

"As a judge you took an oath to uphold the law, didn't you?"

"Yes, but—"

"But nothing. That's giving your word. I could never take that oath—too many laws I disagree with—but you did. You bound yourself to a certain code. But you broke your word. Worse, you *sold* your word."

"I didn't do anything lots of other people weren't doing—*still* doing."

"I'm not going to have to repeat what Dad used to say about if everyone was jumping off a bridge, am I?"

Tom slashed the air with a hand. "Wake up, Jack. It's the way of the world. Two sets of rules out there. One is for public consumption, for the hoi polloi. But the other set, the *real* rules, are for those who know the game and how to play it. Someone once said that all of life can be summed up by the verb *to eat*, in both the active and passive sense. I'll take active, thank you."

"Well, there's a third set: mine. And so far no one's taken a bite out of me." He sighed. "Maybe I do sound holier than thou, but Jesus, Tom . . . without your integrity, what are you? What's left?"

Tom gave a derisive snort. "Tell me what you've got *with* it? Does it buy food? Does it pay the rent? You think that guy back at the marina would've given you all that fuel for free just because you've got integrity? I don't think so."

What's the use? Jack thought. Like discussing color with a blind man.

Shaking his head, Jack made another quick trip topside. Staring at the empty ocean, he thought about that lost soul below: his brother. His brother didn't get it. He was never going to get it. Maybe because he never had it.

No. He must have had it.

Jack returned below and took the seat across from Tom.

"Let me ask you something. Are you happy with who you are?"

Tom's mouth twisted. "Happy? How could I be happy? I'm up to my lower lip in legal trouble."

"Don't dodge the question. You know what I'm talking about. Are you satisfied with yourself?"

Tom sighed. "No, I can't say I am. In my heart of hearts I know I'm an asshole."

"How'd you get there? How did it happen?"

He looked up from his cup. "I assume you'll accept that I didn't start out with the goal of being a crooked judge."

"Accepted. So how?"

"It's an incremental process. Sometimes I think law school's to blame."

Jack snorted. "Cop out."

"No, I'm serious. And I'm not saying it's not my fault. But law school teaches that the *letter* of the law is all that counts. Forget the spirit of the law—the letter, the letter, the letter. So if you find a loophole or an interpretation that lets you sidestep the spirit of the law, it's okay to exploit it. Right and wrong, just and unjust don't play into it. The only thing that matters is what's on paper."

"Okay, but even the letter of the law doesn't give you a green light on bribery."

Tom nodded. "True, true. But you don't start with bribery. You start with bending here, shading there. And as the benefits accrue, you graduate to bigger bendings and darker shadings. You get caught up in a subtly escalating process that goes on until you wake up one morning and realize you're not the man you intended to be. Not even close. In fact, you're exactly the kind of asshole you despised when you started out."

"So that's the day you start to make changes."

"Wish it were that easy. You owe people favors—it's all quid pro quo—and these people know things about you. They hold your strings, strings you can't cut. You're not quite a puppet, but pretty damn close. So you go with it. You stay on the downward spiral." He looked at Jack. "Same thing probably happened to you, right?"

That took Jack by surprise. "Me?"

"Come on, Jack. Admit it. You didn't go to New York to become a criminal. But maybe you stole a little here, sold a little weed there, did a little grifting, then bought a Saturday night special and graduated to strong-arm stuff. Now you're Repairman Jack."

Jack shook his head. "Not even close. No increments for me. When I dropped out of Rutgers and stepped onto the bus in New Brunswick, I'd made a decision to break with whoever I was and whatever future I'd been on track for. I said good-bye to a way of life I no longer felt part of. When I stepped off that bus in the Port Authority I was someone else. Didn't know who that guy was—not yet, at least—but I was sure of who I *didn't* want to be. I made a clean break, Tom. No increments. And no excuses."

Tom sighed. "Looks like I'll be doing the same thing soon: Throwing out the old me and buying a new one. You're still going to help me, right?"

Jack nodded.

Help Tom disappear? Oh, yes.

SATURDAY

1

Back again on terra firma, the first thing Tom did was plunk some change into the phone by the Wanchese dock and call home. They'd made good time coming back.

He watched the sun rise over the North Carolina pines as he listened to the rings.

Finally a voice thick with sleep answered. "Hello?"

"Terry? It's me."

Suddenly she came alive. "Tom! Oh, God! Where are you?"

Something in her tone warned him against answering that.

"In transit."

"But *where?*"

Although he already knew the answer, Tom said, "Something wrong?" Then held his breath.

"Wrong? Yes, damn it, something is very wrong! I've been visited every day by a pair of federal marshals. They know you're gone and they're watching the house. They follow me wherever I go—probably think I'm sneaking off to meet you or something. But how can I when I don't know where you are? I wasn't even sure you were still alive until just now!"

Oh, shit. Oh, hell.

Sweat oozed onto Tom's palms. He was fucked.

"Wh-why did they come by?"

"To bring you down to the federal building to ask you some questions about Bieber. I made excuses the first two times, but then they got suspicious. They know you've left town, Tom, but they don't know for how long. If you come back now, maybe . . ."

"Maybe what?"

"Maybe you can tie it in to your dad's death. You know, you just had to go see his grave or something like that."

. . . or something like that . . .

Oh, sure. That'll fly. Like a penguin.

"Come home, Tom. With your father's death—I mean, how it happened, and the national day of mourning and all—maybe you can get them to give you another chance."

Tom didn't see that happening without putting on a huge display of grief and throwing himself on the mercy of the court. And even then it was iffy.

No, he wasn't about to play the penitent bad boy for those gonifs.

Then he realized the feds probably had his line tapped. Shit! He should have thought of that. They'd probably pinpointed this pay phone already.

But he had to say something. No sense in lying about where he was . . . but he had to play dumb . . . ease into it.

He licked his lips.

"Great idea, Terry. Next time they come knocking, tell them you spoke to me. Tell them I'm like you said . . . really upset about Dad's death and hanging out at the graveyard."

"No way, Tom. I'm not lying for you. You've dug one big lousy hole for yourself, but I'm not getting in there with you."

"Come on, Terry."

"No! Look what you've done to my life! I can't go anywhere without people talking and pointing and whispering behind my back! I've tried to get together with Lisa and Susan for lunch but they both always seem to have something else to do, and they can't get off the phone fast enough. You're the one who's under indictment but *I'm* the prisoner. I'm stuck in this house because I've got nowhere I can go!"

Tom gritted his teeth at the sound of her sob.

So typical. I'm the one whose career is down the toilet,

I'm the one facing opprobrium and jail time, and she's all bent out of shape because her social life is on the rocks.

Fuck. Her.

Okay. Time to send the feds in the wrong direction.

"Terry, I'm sorry for the way things are going but I'll make them right. Just between you and me, I'm about to leave for Bermuda and—"

She gasped. "Bermuda? But that means you're . . . you're leaving the country?"

Give the virago a prize!

"Yes, but only temporarily."

"They'll hang you if they find out!"

"Don't worry. I've just got an errand to run, and when I come back, we'll be fixed up."

"What do you mean?"

"You'll see."

"But how are you getting there?"

"By boat."

"You don't have a boat!"

"I'm borrowing one."

"You can't do this! You'll only make things worse. It'll be in the papers and—"

Unable to weather another second of objurgation, he hung up. Then he leaned against the side of the booth and squeezed his eyes shut.

They'd loosed the hounds. What the *hell* was he going to do?

The feds would be sending someone to Wanchese. When they didn't find him here they'd assume he was headed across to Bermuda. Would they go so far as an air-sea search? He doubted it. But he'd bet they'd send marshals to Bermuda to nab him when he showed up at the bank.

He had to get out of here *mach schnell*. But where to?

Philly was out of the question now. Show his face and they'd toss him into their deepest dungeon.

New York . . .

Yes . . . bring the Lilitongue to New York. Probably an

even better place than Philly to learn about it, what with Columbia University, NYU, the Museum of Natural History and all.

But where to stay? He couldn't use a credit card . . .

He glanced over to where Jack was stowing the last of their gear into the coffin-sized trunk of his Crown Vic.

Jack's place . . . a safe haven. Wherever it was, a sure bet he had it listed under a phony name. Just like his credit card.

Tom had almost burst out laughing when he'd seen the name on the gas receipt. John Tyleski . . . the name from the hotel. Tom hadn't dreamed that was Jack.

Despite all the shit coming down, Tom had to smile. Little Brother was soon going to be getting one mammoth MasterCard bill.

The smile faded. The last thing Little Brother wanted was him crashing for a week or two. If asked, Jack would turn him down—no question. So he'd have to get in through the back door. There had to be a way. After all, he had an eight-hour drive to figure it out.

Yeah, like it or not, Jack was going to have a houseguest. And once he got himself inside, there he'd stay until he'd unlocked the mysteries of the Lilitongue.

Tom smiled. Call me Sheridan Whiteside.

2

Jack breathed a sigh of relief as he and Tom pulled away from Ernie's Photo ID. Ernie had taken a few photos of Tom and promised to get to work on a new identity right away.

He'd brought Tom directly to Ernie's from the Lincoln Tunnel. Ernie could work miracles, but he needed time, and the sooner Tom got started, the better.

Because as soon as Tom became someone else, he and his Lilitongue would be on their way.

It was almost four thirty and the sun was hitting the horizon somewhere beyond the high-rises.

Jack was looking forward to getting home and crashing.

Long day. Up before dawn, cooped in a car with Tom for eight hours . . . he was fragged.

Had to admit, though, that Tom had been better company on the way back than the way down. Not because Jack was getting used to him or that they'd bonded. Hardly. The simple reason was that Tom hadn't talked as much. Of course, when he had it had been about Gia, but a generally nontoxic trip.

Tom had insisted on driving the first leg. They'd switched after lunch at a no-name diner somewhere on the DelMarVa Peninsula. Tom had insisted that diners were far superior to fast-food chains. Jack's burger was okay but he really could have gone for a Whopper with cheese. Tom's beef stew had looked and smelled like hot Alpo.

Jack had had the wheel from there on.

As Jack wound through the traffic on Tenth Avenue, Tom grabbed his arm.

"Stop the car!"

Jack tensed, his eyes doing a quick 360 scan via the mirrors and windshield: nothing.

"What's wrong?"

Tom was doubled over. "Pull over! Now!"

Jack swerved right and pulled in by a fireplug. Before the car had stopped, Tom was leaning out the door. Jack heard him retching.

When he finished, he levered himself upright and sat there panting.

"Oh, God. Must be that stew. Never should have—"

Then he was hanging out the door and retching again.

"You okay?" Jack said.

Tom nodded.

"Done?"

Another nod.

As Jack put the Vic back into gear he realized with a shock that Tom had no place to stay.

"We've got to find you a hotel."

Shit. A Saturday night in Manhattan the last weekend before Christmas . . . where the hell were they going to find a room?

Tom slumped against the door.

"Jesus, Jack, I don't think I can make it."

"What do you mean?"

Jack knew what Tom meant but his mind shied from acknowledging it.

"Searching for a room." Tom groaned. "I don't think I can make today. I'll find a place tomorrow. I just need a little time to get over this."

"How much time?"

"Food poisoning doesn't last long. One night will probably do it. By tomorrow it'll be like it never happened." He winced and doubled over, then looked at Jack. "How about your place?"

Jack felt like the driver of a jackknifed semitrailer in mid-skid on an icy road, painfully, hopelessly aware that no matter what pedal he tromped or which way he yanked the wheel, the ending was a foregone conclusion.

"Tom . . ."

His voice took on a whiny tone. "Come on, Jack. Would it kill you to let me crash one night? One lousy night?"

Bastard.

3

"He'll be bunking in the TV room," Jack said.

He'd called Gia as soon as he'd unloaded the car and parked it in its garage.

Tom had carried his backpack and the Lilitongue chest up to the apartment, then slumped on the couch, leaving Jack to unload and haul the rest up to the third floor by himself.

Gia said, "You . . . with a houseguest . . ." A suppressed laugh trickled through the phone. "The hermit of the Upper West Side with overnight company. I can't believe it."

"It's not funny and I'm not a hermit."

"Is he feeling better?"

"Seems to be. At least he's not throwing up anymore. Hasn't been sick since Tenth Avenue. Perked up right after he got here."

Which only deepened Jack's suspicions. Thinking back, he remembered only hearing Tom retch. Never saw any vomit. Of course, he hadn't been exactly itching for a look at regurgitated beef stew.

Still . . . with a guy a little less honest than a wharf rat, you never knew.

Gia *tsk*ed. "Poor man."

"That's what you get for eating Alpo."

"Pardon?"

"Nothing. Look, when am I going to see you?"

A whole week away. Jack had missed her.

"Well, why don't the three of us go somewhere after

you drop off your brother? There's a German Expression-
ist exhibit at MOMA that might be fun."

The Museum of Modern Art . . . just the place he
wanted to spend his first day home from the sea.

Gia must have sensed his lack of enthusiasm.

"Give it a chance, Jack. There's no way a man who
likes *The Cabinet of Dr. Caligari*—which you insisted I
see—won't find something to like there."

Oh, right. The crazy *Caligari* set design had been created by a couple of German expressionists.

"Okay. You're on."

He hung up feeling good about tomorrow, anticipating
a much-needed Gia-Vicky fix.

The feeling did a quick fade when he walked into the
second bedroom that served as his TV room. Tom had the
convertible couch folded out into bed mode—no sheets,
just a bare mattress—and he was unpacking his bag . . .
hanging clothes in the closet.

"What are you doing?"

Tom looked up and smiled. "Just letting some of this
stuff air. It's been at sea too long. Was that Gia on the
phone?"

"Yeah. She says hi and hopes you're feeling better,
which you seem to be."

"Yeah. Amazing, isn't it. One minute you think you're
dying, and a little while later you're feeling fine."

"Amazing."

"Still feeling a little weak, though. Why don't you ask
Gia over?"

Here we go: Tom and his thing for Gia.

"I would, but what you have might be contagious."

"I'm sure it was just food poisoning."

"You never know."

Tom looked disappointed. "All right, then. Got any
vodka?"

Jack shook his head. "Only beer. Probably not a good

thing to be pouring booze into such an unsettled stomach anyway."

"Actually a beer would go a long way toward settling my stomach, I think. Could you get me one?"

Jack jerked a thumb over his shoulder. "Bottom shelf of the fridge."

Jack eyed Tom's neck as he passed. He resisted an urge to grab it with both hands and shake him like a rag doll.

He listened to the refrigerator door open and close, watched Tom return carrying two bottles of Yuengling lager. He twisted the top off one and handed it to Jack, then opened the other and held it up.

"To brotherhood."

He clinked his bottle against Jack's and drank. Jack felt like saying, *This is brotherhood?* but bit it back, choosing instead to say nothing.

For you, Dad, he thought as he took a long pull. Only for you.

He needed a beer. Had a feeling he was going to need many beers.

Tom gestured around Jack's cluttered front room. Gia once had called it "claustrophobic," and Abe proclaimed it "vertigogenic."

"I've just got to ask you about this. I mean, who's your decorator? Joe Franklin?"

"What do you mean?"

"The furniture for one thing."

Jack turned and took in his Victorian wavy-grained golden oak furniture—the gingerbread-laden secretary, the hutch, the paw-footed round oak table, the crystal-ball-and-claw-footed end tables.

"What about it?"

"Looks like stuff people used when they were listening to *Little Orphan Annie* on the radio. And speaking of Annie, is that a Daddy Warbucks lamp?"

"It is. He was a cool guy."

Tom stepped over to the inner wall and stared at the array of clocks and framed certificates.

"You're living in Gew-gawville. And look at all this: The Shadow Fan Club, the Doc Savage fan club, and Jesus, a *Shmoo* clock!" He turned to Jack and laughed. "What are you? Ninety years old?"

Jack felt no obligation to explain.

Tom stepped back into the TV room where he dropped onto the mattress and lay on his side, his head propped against his hand. He pointed to the big screen.

"Nice set. Got any movies we can watch?"

Jack was too bushed to start searching for a hotel room now. But first thing tomorrow . . . first damn thing.

SUNDAY

1

After a restless night during which his bed seemed to be rocking with the swells of an unseen ocean, Jack got up and walked into the empty front room.

He stood there for a moment and tried to convince himself that last night had been a dream—that none of last week had happened.

Then he heard the snoring from the TV room and knew he wasn't going to be that lucky.

He looked in and saw Tom sprawled on his back like a beached whale. His right arm hung over the edge of the mattress, the fingers just brushing the top of the Lili-tongue chest.

Jack had been on the phone for an hour. His first call had been to Joey who hadn't answered. Jack left a message and then got to work on the hotels. But no luck. Not one place he'd called—and he'd tried uptown and down—had a room. There had to be one somewhere in this damn city.

He needed a break. He went to the kitchen and spooned some Brown Gold into his Mr. Coffee and got a pot perking. The odor of coffee soon filled the apartment.

Jack was pouring his first cup when Tom appeared, rubbing his eyes.

"Christ, what time is it?"

Jack took one look at the wrinkled T-shirt stretched across a belly that overhung a pair of pee-stained Jockey shorts and pointed back to the TV room.

"Out, damn spot!"

Tom blinked. "What?"

"Get something on—at least on the lower half of that body."

"You're kidding, right?"

"No coffee for eyesores."

Tom stared at him a moment, then shook his head and retraced his steps to the TV room. He reemerged a moment later wearing a pair of plaid Bermudas.

"Happy now?"

"Happiness is relative. Less aesthetically offended is more like it."

Tom grabbed an empty cup, filled it, and took a long sip. No milk, no sugar.

He held up the cup. "Damn good coffee." He winked. "Give me a reference."

Jack did not want to reference that or anything else, didn't want to get started with games. But he couldn't resist.

"If you'd just toasted me with the cup and given a grin, I'd say Winston Wolf in *Pulp Fiction.* But the 'damn' means you're probably thinking of Agent Cooper in *Twin Peaks.*"

"Excellent! I'm impressed. Now how about—?"

Jack was about to cut him off when the intercom buzzer beat him to it.

Baffled as to who'd be buzzing him at this hour on a Sunday—or at any hour on any day, for that matter—Jack stepped to the wall box and pressed the button.

"Yeah?"

"Hi, Jack." Gia's voice. "Buzz us in. We've got a surprise for you."

Jack was momentarily baffled. Gia had a key. Then he realized that because he had company she didn't want to barge in unannounced.

He said, "Um, okay, sure," and hit the unlock button.

A surprise?

"Gia?" Tom looked panicked. "I've got to clean up!"

2

"Well?" Gia said, waving a hand over the laden round oak table. "What do you think?"

She wore jeans and a loose, light blue top that heightened the color of her eyes.

She and Vicky had brought bagels and cream cheese, two quiches—one bacon and shallots, the other zucchini and onion—plus a coffee ring, and even the Sunday *Times*.

Jack forced a smile. "Looks super, but you shouldn't have."

No lie. Gia's intentions were the best, but she *really* shouldn't have. This was only going to delay finding Tom a room. But then, Gia didn't know Jack was hunting for a place for Tom to stay.

"I picked out the coffee cake," Vicky said. She wore denim coveralls and had her hair pulled back into her signature French braid. "It's got sugar-coated pecans on it."

She picked one off and popped it into her mouth.

"It won't have anything on it if you keep that up," Gia said.

Vicky grinned. "I *love* sugar-coated pecans."

Tom stepped out of the TV room just then, shaved, showered, wearing slacks and a loose shirt that partially obscured his gut. He crossed the room with outstretched arms. Add a silk dressing gown and he'd be ready for a full-fledged Noel Coward vamp.

"Gia!" he said, making a beeline for her. "What a wonderful surprise! Please excuse my appearance, but I've spent the last week at sea."

She accepted a hug, then said, "You remember Vicky."

"Of course." Tom shook her hand. "A pleasure to see you again, Miss Vicky."

"Hello, Mister—"

"Oh. Don't call me 'mister.' I suppose you could call me Almost-Uncle Tom, but I'm not crazy about the sound of that." He grinned and winked at Gia. "So why don't you just call me Tom."

Vicky stared at him as if he was speaking Swahili.

"Vicky and I figured you wouldn't have any food in the house."

Tom patted Vicky on the head. "Isn't that sweet!"

Vicky said, "I picked out the coffee cake, even though I'm not allowed to drink coffee."

Tom bent toward her and spoke in a gooey voice. "Isn't that wonderful of you!"

Jack repressed a gag.

Gia said, "I never got around to asking last night: How did Jack and Tom's Big Adventure go?"

Tom let loose a deep ha-ha-ha! "Are you a movie buff too?"

"Only by osmosis." She hooked an arm around Jack's waist and leaned against him. "Can't hang around with your brother too long without picking up something."

Tom said, "Well, speaking of *something,* that's just what we found. We're just not sure what that something is."

"Really?" Gia's brow furrowed as she glanced at Jack. "Animal, vegetable, or mineral?"

Tom laughed. "We don't know!"

"Can I see it?"

A buzz of alarm surged through Jack.

"That may not be such a good idea."

Gia looked at him. "Why not?"

What was he going to say? He had no rational explanation.

"Because of what Tom said: We don't know what it is."

"Oh, come on," Tom said with a patronizing laugh.

"It's a basketball-sized lump that's been underwater for four hundred years. How harmful could it possibly be?"

Jack wished he had an answer.

Tom waved everyone toward the TV room. "Come on, let's have a look," he said, then led the way.

Jack reluctantly followed, bringing up the rear behind Gia and Vicky. Tom seemed to have taken over.

In the TV room Tom lifted the chest off the floor and onto the bed. He opened the lid and made a grandiose gesture.

"Voilà!"

Gia and Vicky were suitably unimpressed.

"Can I ask a question?" Gia said.

Tom grinned. "But of course, my dear."

"Why would you bother to bring this home? It looks like some ugly, oversized melon."

"It does, indeed, but I want to find out what it is. The quest for knowledge—what human urge is more noble?"

How about the urge to retch? Jack thought.

"Look, Mom!" Vicky was laughing and pointing at the dimple in the Lilitongue's surface. "It's got a belly button!"

"What a marvelous observation!" Tom said. "You really have an eye for detail!"

Gia said, "So now that you have it, what do you do with it?"

Jack started to say that was going to be Tom's problem, but his brother jumped in.

"Research! I'm sure we can find someone in this city who can shed some light on its identity."

It took a few seconds for the import of "in this city" to penetrate, but when it did . . .

"Whoa-whoa-whoa! What happened to Philadelphia—the Franklin Institute, the U of P . . . ?"

Tom put on a sheepish, aw-shucks grin. "I was going to discuss this with you this morning, bro, but didn't get a chance before our lovely guests arrived. I've been thinking that maybe New York has more resources with the potential of shedding light on our *objet mystérieux* here, and was going to ask if I might stay over a few days to pursue an answer."

Gia frowned. "But what about Terry? You've been away for almost a week."

"I spoke to her yesterday morning and she's perfectly fine with it. She knows how much it means to me." He looked at Jack with puppy-dog eyes. "So whatta ya say, bro? Put up with me for a few more days?"

Jack caught a look from Gia that said, You're not going to kick out your own brother, are you?

No question why Tom brought this up in front of her.

Gia and Vicky's presence, plus the certain knowledge that Dad would have wanted Jack to cut him some slack, kept him from grabbing Tom by the throat and tossing him through a window.

Bastard.

3

Jack helped Gia and Vicky clear the dishes while Tom read the paper.

"I can see it now," Jack whispered while they were in the kitchen. "I'll never get rid of him. He'll be the man who came to dinner. I've *got* to find him a hotel."

She said, "You and he are the only ones left in your family. You should find a way to get along."

Jack nodded—not because he agreed, but because he didn't want to get into a discussion about this. At least not now.

Gia was right in theory, but he saw no way the two of them would ever have much in common.

"Hey!" Tom called from the table. "*The Merry Widow* is at the Met tonight!"

"Really?" Gia gravitated toward the front room. "That's one of my favorites."

"And Noelle Roberts is playing Hanna."

"I saw her as Mimi in *La Bohéme* last year. She's wonderful."

Jack followed her in, snapping his fingers. "*La Bohéme . . . La Bohéme . . .* is that the one where somebody dies at the end?"

Gia laughed. "Someone almost always dies at the end of an opera. And you know that."

Tom slammed his hand on the table. "Let's go! Let's all go tonight!"

Listen to him, Jack thought. The feds are after him and he wants to go to the opera.

Of course, that was probably the last place they'd look for him.

"I'd love to," Gia said, "but I can't get a sitter on such short notice."

"Bring Vicky along. My treat."

Listen to Mr. Big Spender.

Gia shook her head. "No, she wouldn't like it. She's fine at the ballet where it's all music and movement, but at an opera . . . she'd be asking me every two minutes what they're saying. That wouldn't be fair to the people around us."

Jack looked at Gia. "You really want to go?"

"I'd love to see Noelle Roberts again."

"Then go. I'll take care of Vicky."

She smiled that smile. "Would you really? You don't mind?"

He knew Tom had the hots for her, but this was Gia. She wasn't a tease, didn't play games. It would be a friendly date. And she'd get to see her Noelle Roberts.

Jack put a finger to his chin and struck a pose of deep concentration.

"Hmmm . . . let's see . . . comes down to a choice between hanging out with Vicky or going through the auditory equivalent of a root canal without anesthesia . . . I'd say that's a no-brainer."

"Great!" Tom cried. "Then it's settled. I'll reserve the tickets and find a place to rent a tuxedo."

"Oh, you don't have to—"

"Oh, but I do. With such a beautiful woman on my arm, attiring myself in anything less would be not only a breach of manners, but an affront to all of nature."

Jack closed his eyes. He had to get him out of here.

4

When Jack returned from hailing Gia and Vicky a cab, he found Tom back at the table, reading the *Times*.

"Tom?" It took an effort, but he managed to keep from shouting. "The deal was you'd stay one night. What are you pulling here?"

Tom put down the paper. "Self-preservation."

"What's that supposed to mean?"

"I've been found out. Terry says federal marshals have been at the house looking for me. They know I'm gone."

Jack couldn't rein in a burst of fury.

"You've got feds on your trail? That means when they find you they find me! And if they charge me with harboring a fugitive . . ."

Jack could see his world going down in flames. The

web of secrets that cocooned his identity, his work, his whole damn life would fall apart under federal scrutiny.

"What do you mean, 'when' they find me? They won't. They won't know where to look. Terry thinks I'm on my way to Bermuda right now, not already back. They'll be chasing their tails. And as for tracking me here, they don't even know I've got a brother, let alone what city he lives in."

"But Terry knows."

He nodded. "Yeah, Terry knows a few things, but nothing of any use. If she rats me out—which she might—she'll tell them I've got a brother named Jack who lives in New York. But unless I've misread things, you're not listed anywhere under your own name, are you."

Correct.

Jack nodded.

"Thought so. That means in order to find me they've got to find you, and since you aren't findable, ipso facto, neither am I."

Jack stared at his clueless, bastard brother a long time before responding.

"You know, Tom, I've got a great idea. Let's play a game. It's called Cain and Abel. You'll be Abel . . ."

Tom laughed. "You worry too much. We're safe."

"I want you out of here. Today."

"And what? Feed me to the wolves? If I register anywhere I'll be found. Look, as soon as your pal Ernie has my new identity I'll be gone, out of your life for good. But until then, I need a hiding place. So you've got to let me stay, bro."

"Cool it with the 'bro' bit, okay? It suits you like a Kangol cap."

Tom frowned. "Kangol?"

"There—you've made my point."

"I don't know what the hell you're talking about. Just put me up till Ernie delivers. Is that asking so much?"

Jack hated this, but didn't see a way out. "Okay. But when Ernie delivers, you go."

He grinned. "Deal! Oh, one more thing. Promise me you won't mention my troubles to Gia, okay? I'd rather she didn't know."

"She already knows you've got legal problems."

Tom's face fell. "Oh hell."

"I didn't go into detail—she didn't want me to—but if she asks, I'll tell her what she wants to know. No holding back."

Jack's holding back the truth had once nearly destroyed their relationship just as it was beginning.

"Fair enough, I guess. I hope she doesn't ask. And by the way, thanks for volunteering to sit for Vicky tonight. I think Gia's going to have a really good time."

"And you? You're doing this out of the goodness of your heart, I suppose."

Tom laughed. "You ought to know me better than that by now. Just as I'm sure you know I'm crazy about your woman."

"Hardly a great intuitive leap. But I don't think of her as *my* woman. I don't think Gia is anybody's woman. She's just Gia."

"Well, she is carrying your child. Which leads to a question that's been bugging me." Tom waved his hands before him. "Now, it's not my intention to offend, but I've got to ask: What the hell does a bright, beautiful woman like Gia see in you?"

Jack had to smile. "Damned if I know."

He'd come to realize that it's often better not to probe too deeply into these things, but he'd decided that they were good together because of the way they complemented each other. Yin and yang.

Gia was strictly above ground, the product of a Catholic family in the Midwest, a believer in motherhood and apple pie. Jack lived underground, in a separate world, a mirror image of Gia's.

But somehow they'd found each other, somehow they'd bonded. And soon their child would be born.

The turmoil that prospect was causing in Jack's life had been swallowed up by his father's death. But it hadn't gone away. It remained a ticking bomb, with a timer set for March—three months away!

In order to be the child's legal father, to claim her should anything happen to Gia, Jack had to establish an above-ground identity, one that would sidestep the questions of where he'd been for the past fifteen years and why he hadn't paid a cent of taxes during all that time.

Ernie could help a guy live below the radar, but what Jack needed was out of his league.

So Abe was working on it, but progress was slow. The Holgate glacier moved at a brisker pace.

Half a year ago Jack had foreseen none of this. Hell, a year and a half ago he'd seen no hope that he and Gia would ever be together.

They'd been on the outs then—*way* out. Jack realized with a start that he and Gia most likely would still be on the outs if a mad Hindu named Kusum hadn't come to town to keep a century-and-a-half-old vow of vengeance. He'd brought them back together and they hadn't been apart since.

Tom said, "All right then, answer me this: Why aren't you two living together?"

"None of your beeswax."

Tom jabbed a finger at him. "*No, No, Nanette*, right?"

Jack didn't know what to say. He'd never seen *No, No, Nanette*. And didn't plan to.

"I'll have to take your word for it."

Time to call Ernie. Tell him he needed a rush job on Tom's new identity.

5

"Keep to the left there, Vicks. See that doorway? Head for it."

Jack hovered over Vicky's shoulder as she navigated the future noir world of *DNA Wars*. The PlayStation version had come out about six months ago. At nine she was still a bit young and inexperienced to make it through the video game on her own. Jack had fought through to the end where he'd unlocked all the secret codes, including the special gene splices. So he'd entered them for Vicky, allowing her to play in "god mode"—immortal, omnipotent, with the game's entire array of mDNA templates and weapons at her command.

He slid to the side so he could see her face, watch the images from the big TV screen reflecting in her eyes, revel in her look of fascinated concentration. She was completely into it.

Since Jack's apartment and Lincoln Center were both on the Upper West Side, and since Jack had the big TV and all the cool video games, Gia had decided it would be easier to drop Vicky here. Her Christmas break had begun, so no school tomorrow.

The black dress Gia had worn was snug around the waist, but she looked dazzling anyway. And who'd notice her swelling belly next to Tom? His dwarfed hers. The rented tux made him look like Opus the penguin on his way to an Overeaters Anonymous banquet.

So Jack and Vicky had parked themselves on the edge of the bed in the TV room—Tom's bedroom now but not for much longer. The sixty-inch screen stretched the game's pixels, but made the gameplay intensely immersive.

Before Vicky's arrival Jack had hidden the Lilitongue and its chest in the hall closet. Couldn't say why, simply didn't want Vicky in the same room with it.

Keeping her eyes glued on the screen, Vicky said, "How come Mom's going out with Tom instead of you?"

"Because I don't like opera and your mother and Tom do. This way your mother gets to see something she likes and I get not to see something I don't like."

"I think he likes Mom."

Jack had to smile. Amazing what kids pick up on.

"I believe he does."

. . . demonstrating uncharacteristic good taste.

"Then why did you let her go with him?"

"I didn't 'let' her. Your mother makes her own decisions. I trust her to make good ones, just as she trusts me. What's the point of a relationship if one person can't let the other person out of sight?"

She glanced at Jack. "What if he kisses her?"

"He won't."

Not if he knows what's good for him.

"But what if he does?"

"Then we'll have to count Mom's teeth."

"Huh?"

Jack pointed to the screen. "You stuck?"

She nodded, back in the game. "I can't fit through this door."

Jack recognized Vicky's predicament—he'd been here before.

"Switch to a smaller template."

She hit the pause button instead.

"I gotta go sprinkle."

Jack took the controller. "I'll hold the fort."

"Don't play while I'm gone."

"I'll try . . . not to . . ." Jack said in a strained voice. His hand trembled over the toggles, moving closer, then pulling away. "Won't . . . be . . . easy . . . better hurry . . ."

Vicky ran from the room.

Jack smiled. God, he loved that kid.

And soon he'd have his own.

Now there was a frightening thought. A tiny baby, fragile, helpless, totally dependent. He shuddered. Facing a raging, three-hundred-pound, knife-wielding drunk would be less intimidating.

6

-83:00

A cry from Vicky shattered Jack's reverie.

"Jack! Jack!"

The fear in her voice had him on his feet and almost to the door when she rushed in.

"What's wrong?"

"That thing!" she wailed.

He gripped her upper arms. She was trembling.

"What thing?"

"Tom's sea treasure . . . I touched it!"

Oh, shit.

"You went into the closet?"

"I . . . I wondered where it was and I peeked in and saw the box in there and I wanted to see it again so I opened it and touched it—I only put my finger in its belly button—and—"

Fear quick-crawled on clawed feet through Jack's chest.

"You touched it?"

He wanted to be angry, but at whom? Vicky or himself?

She nodded. "But only once."

"Did it hurt you?"

A quick shake of her head. "No, but it moved!"

"Moved? How—?"

"Come see!"

She pulled him toward the hall but slid behind him as they left the TV room.

"See it? See it?"

Jack's heart began to pound. Yeah, he saw it. But what the hell—?

7

-81:28

"I'm so glad we could do this," Gia said, patting the back of Tom's hand.

They sat in the rear of a cab heading uptown toward Jack's place. Tom reached across and clasped her hand between both of his.

"It was wonderful, wasn't it. And you weren't exaggerating about Noelle's voice. Magnificent. But not as magnificent as the woman I shared the evening with."

Gia slipped her hand free and laughed.

"Mah, mah, Mister Tom," she said in a Southern-belle accent, "Ah declare, how you do go on."

Tom had to smile. She was good . . . maintained a distance between them without bruising his feelings.

Why was he so damn crazy about this woman? What was it about her that made him want to be her slave? Or babble like a fool?

Christ, when he'd been sipping champagne at the intermission he'd launched into a discourse on how it's usually a mixture of chardonnay, pinot noir, and pinot meunier, and how blanc de blanc was all chardonnay—blah-blah-blah until Gia's eyes had started to glaze over. And with good reason: He'd sounded like a pedantic twit.

And the last thing he wanted to do was bore her. He felt as if his past no longer existed, as if all his life he'd been marking time until he'd met her.

Marking time . . . thoughts of his present predicament brought him down from his high. If only he'd marked time instead of wheeling and dealing and lining his pockets, he'd be free and clear today. His ass would belong to him instead of a swarm of cops.

At least Gia didn't know the depth of his troubles, and as long as that remained the case, he could pretend to be the kind of man she could admire.

He well knew that, on the surface, that didn't make sense. She was carrying the baby of a man she loved—and he could tell how much by the way she looked at Jack—even though he was a career criminal. So why should Tom think she'd be repulsed if she knew the truth about him?

Jack had nailed it on the boat: Yeah, Jack was a criminal, but he wasn't a crook. Not mere semantics there. A whole world of difference.

On another day he might have told himself that he could offer Gia the gravitas Jack lacked. But he'd finally stopped doing the Nixon thing. He *was* a crook. Not the Great String-puller, not the Master of the System, a crook, and a tawdry one at that: A guy with a FOR HIRE sign on his soul.

At first he'd regretted his transgressions only because he'd got caught. Now he wished he'd played it straight all along, so he could play straight with Gia, talk to her about his record as a judge and point to it with pride.

But Gia . . . what would this woman who had a numinous core of probity and was so naturally and effortlessly good and straight that it seeped through her skin and suffused the air around her . . . what would she think of a man with his past?

Tom knew. And he couldn't bear the thought of her looking at him like a slug.

He thought of a line from *As Good as It Gets*: "You make me want to be a better man."

Yeah. He could say that to her and mean every word. But it was too late. Way too late. Now all he could do was look at her and think how she made him wish he'd *been* a better man.

Still, he couldn't understand what she saw in Jack.

He said, "You know I never got to ask how you and Jack met."

In truth he'd asked Jack but had been blown off with "at a party."

"Strangely enough, through the UN."

"The UN? Jack?" Talk about strange bedfellows.

"Yes, he was involved with the UK mission for a while."

"No kidding? Doing what?"

"I really can't say."

Tom could tell she meant *won't* say, but didn't press.

The UK mission to the UN . . . what could they have possibly wanted from Jack?

Little brother was just chock-full of secrets and surprises.

"I hope I'm not speaking out of turn, but you and Jack . . . you don't seem to go together."

She laughed: music.

"You probably *are* out of turn, but you're pretty much on the money." She glanced at him. "Did you and Jack talk much on your trip?"

He nodded. "I'd pretty much figured out how he lives and how he makes his living, and he pretty much confirmed it."

" 'Pretty much'?"

"Well, I'm only starting to get to know my brother again, but it's not easy. He's not exactly forthcoming about himself."

Another soft laugh. "That's my Jack."

My Jack . . . Tom loathed the sound of that.

"So, given what I know, that's why I said—"

"That we don't seem to go together? On the surface we don't. I'm a vegetarian, he's an omnivore. I love the arts, he merely tolerates them. I'm a square and he's never the same shape twice. I'm a Mondrian, he's a Picasso. I'm an uptight, middle-class, law-abiding woman and he's . . . well, he's Jack. Yet despite the surface differences and divergent tastes, we agree on the big things—the things that matter. We agree on what's right and wrong, on being truthful, on value given for value received, on what's straight and what's crooked. We both believe in doing the right thing, even though we sometimes disagree on how to do it. I tend to try to tease out life's tangles. Jack tends toward Alexander's solution to the Gordian knot." Another soft laugh. "Two years ago if you'd told me I'd be partnered with this man and having his baby, I'd have laughed in your face."

"Why?"

"Because . . . I didn't know what I was looking for back then, but I was sure it wasn't him. I didn't see it at first, but Jack is a rock." She smiled. "The world flows past, but Jack doesn't move. Doesn't matter what's fashionable, what's in, what's out, what's politically correct, what's become legal, what's become illegal, Jack doesn't budge. I failed to appreciate that at first. I misunderstood him, got him all wrong, and ran from him. Said terrible, hurtful things to him. But when Vicky and I needed him, there he was, right where I'd left him. He was there for me then and he's been there for me ever since. I can always depend on Jack to do the right thing."

The right thing . . . when had Tom worried last about doing the right thing? He couldn't remember the last time the concept had made the faintest blip on his radar.

He forced a sigh. "The world's the way it is because not enough people do the right thing, wouldn't you say?"

"Hard to argue with that."

"But maybe some people have never had the right reason to do the right thing."

Gia glanced at him. "I've always figured the reason for doing the right thing is because it's the right thing."

"Do you think maybe someone who hasn't been doing the right thing could change for the right person?"

"I suppose, but then wouldn't he be doing the right thing for the wrong reason?"

"I don't get you."

"Well, the way I see it, you don't do the right thing for anyone else, you do it for yourself. Because doing anything less diminishes you."

Tom fell silent. Her words were like stab wounds. If Gia was right, if doing the wrong thing diminished you, what was left of him?

A puff of smoke in the wind . . . if that.

8

-81:25

Tom led the way up the stairs to Jack's apartment. When he reached the door and raised his hand to knock, it flew open and Vicky blew past him to leap into her mother's arms.

"Mommy! Mommy!" She sounded terrified.

"What is it?"

"Jack's mad at me!"

"What? Why?"

"I touched the treasure and it moved and now he's making me stand by the door and I heard you coming and—"

Suddenly Jack filled the doorway. His face was flushed,

his teeth bared. He jabbed his finger to within an inch of Tom's nose.

"Damn you!"

Gia said, "Jack? What on earth is—?"

His features softened as he turned toward her. "You and Vicky stay out here." Then hardened again as he swung back on Tom and grabbed the front of his shirt. "But you . . ."

"Wha—?"

Jack yanked him into the apartment and pointed across the front room.

"That should be your goddamn problem, but now it's mine too!"

Tom looked but couldn't fathom what he was talking about. Had he flipped his—?

Then he saw it. The Lilitongue, five feet off the floor, floating in the air before the open closet door.

Tom took a step toward it.

"Jesus God! Is that . . . I mean, what's holding it up?"

"Not a goddamn thing, Tom."

"But that's imposs—"

Jack grabbed his shoulder and shook him. "Obviously not! What the hell did you bring into my home?"

Tom heard Vicky's voice coming from behind.

"Isn't it neat, Mom? It's floating all by itself."

He turned and saw Vicky stepping in from the hallway.

Jack said, "Vicky, please! No closer! Gia, keep her back. I don't want either of you anywhere near this thing. I've kept Vicky back by the door since after it activated."

Vicky said, "But it's only—"

Gia had a hand over her mouth and her gaze locked on the Lilitongue. Tom would have expected wonder in those eyes, tinged maybe with some uneasiness, but instead he saw fear. Why? Granted, they were in the presence of a unique phenomenon, but there was nothing threatening about it. Why did she look so frightened as she pulled Vicky back?

"Jack's right, honey. We don't know what it is. And when something's doing what it shouldn't be able to do, something you can't explain, it's better to keep your distance until you know it won't... until you know it's safe." She hugged the child against her. "And anyway, it's late. Past your bedtime."

"But Ma-om," she whined. "There's no school tomorrow."

"Say good-bye."

Vicky made a barely audible response, then turned to go.

Gia said to Jack, "Call me later." Then to Tom, "Thank you for the opera."

He would have loved to see a smile as she said that, but her expression was tight, almost fearful.

"My pleasure, Gia. I'm sorry the evening had to end like this."

"So am I." She glanced at the Lilitongue and then back to Tom. "I hope you haven't brought more trouble into our lives."

Tom had no reply for that. He could only nod and wonder what she meant by "more" trouble. What could she be talking about?

When the door had closed behind her, Tom turned and stared at the Lilitongue. The sight of it floating in midair filled him with wonder, awe, and a strange glee.

No, it shouldn't be, and yes, it was impossible. And that meant that the paranormal hints he'd run across in research hadn't been the ravings of ancient lunatics.

The possibility that the Lilitongue just might live up to its press thrilled him. This could be his way out after all. It might prove his seemingly ineluctable fate to be, well, eluctable.

Slowly, hesitantly, he approached the thing. Its looks hadn't changed—still a misshapen, leathery, basketball-size olive with a dimple toward its lower end; no glow, no hum, no whine ... simply sitting there five feet above the floor.

Behind it, the open hall closet. Beneath it, the sea chest. Tom waved his hands over, under, and around it. Nothing. God, this was amazing. *Amazing!* This defied the laws of gravity.

"Looking for strings?" Jack said.

"Looking for *something.*"

"How about a reason for me not to break your neck?"

Tom glanced at him and backed up a step when he saw his brother's eyes. Something very scary there.

"Hey, take it easy, Jack. This is weird, I know—very, *very* weird—but not a reason to get so pissed. I mean, you act like I just dropped a cobra down your shorts."

"Maybe you have." He pointed to the Lilitongue. "I don't want this here. Get it out."

"What the hell is wrong with you? This is the find of the century—of the last four centuries! They're going to have to rewrite the laws of gravity because of this thing! It'll go down in history. *We'll* go down in history."

Jack's expression switched from anger to disgust. "Right. You'll be the most famous guy in the federal lockup. And I'll probably wind up right there beside you."

Shit. The wonder of the phenomenon had momentarily blinded him. As glorious as it would be to become an international celebrity, it wouldn't nullify the malfeasance charges. All it would accomplish was to transmit his obloquy nationwide. Maybe even worldwide.

Jack said, "I want it gone, Tom."

"Okay, then, I'll put it back in the chest, lock it, and that will be that."

Jack's expression remained fierce. "Be my guest."

Tom reached for the Lilitongue, then hesitated, his fingers only inches from its surface. What would it feel like now that it had been awakened? Would he feel a vibration? Or even more disturbing . . . a pulse?

He forced his hands forward and touched it lightly with his fingertips. No vibration, no throb . . . but it sent a peculiar feeling through him, a hint of instinctive revulsion that quickly passed.

And damn if it didn't feel warm. Almost like . . . skin temperature.

He pressed his palms against it, got a grip, and pushed down, aiming for the sea chest.

The Lilitongue didn't budge.

He pushed harder, grunting with the effort, but it was like trying to move a house.

Tom looked at Jack. "Give me a hand here."

"Okay, but it's not going to do any good."

Together they pushed. Tom could see Jack's face crimsoning with the strain—mirroring his own, no doubt—but together they achieved no more than Tom had alone.

"It won't budge," Jack said. "Trust me, it won't move up, down, or sideways. It's fixed in space. The proverbial immovable object."

"Then we'll need an irresistible force."

"How about your stupidity?"

"Hey—"

"You weaseled it in here and now I'm stuck with it."

"There has to be a way."

"Yeah?" Jack reached down behind the couch and came up with an aluminum bat. "Try this."

Tom took it and hefted it. Heavier than he expected.

"So you still play baseball?"

"It's a versatile item." Jack pointed to the Lilitongue. "Go ahead. Take a swing."

"I don't want to damage it."

"You won't. Trust me. Take a big swing."

Something in Jack's tone set off a warning bell. So instead of a big swing, he gave the Lilitongue a light tap.

Nothing beyond a dull *thunk.*

A harder tap.

Another *thunk*, plus a metallic ring from the bat.

"Come on, Tom. Don't be such a wimp. Swing for the bleachers, big guy."

Wimp, huh?

Tom raised the bat above and behind his shoulder, then let loose, putting his arms and body behind it, giving it everything.

He heard a loud *clang* from the bat and felt a stinging vibration run through his hands and up his arms.

"Shit!" He dropped the bat and rubbed his palms as he glared at Jack. "You knew that would happen."

Jack nodded. "Yeah. Been there, done that. Hurts like hell, doesn't it."

Damn right. And the pain hadn't come from the Lilitongue. It would have been the same had Tom slammed the bat against a sidewalk.

He stared at the unmarred, unmoved, unperturbed Lilitongue.

"Tough son of a bitch, isn't it."

"I want it out of here, Tom. Out."

"And how do you suggest I do that?"

"Don't know, don't care."

"Well, I can't do anything until I know more about it, and I can't learn much on a Sunday night." He shook his head. "Maybe I should have listened to that girl on the dock."

9

-81:02

Jack felt a chill.

"What girl? What dock?"

"Remember that hallucination I told you about? That

was it. I'm not exactly sure where the real left off and the unreal began."

"Tell me."

"It was in Saint George's. When we were gassing up. I was standing on the aft deck, minding my own business, when out of the blue this girl, this local teenager, starts talking to me."

"What do you mean, 'out of the blue'?"

"I didn't see her coming. I just look up and she's there, standing half a dozen feet away on the dock."

An uneasy feeling crawled through Jack's stomach.

"What'd she say?"

"Some nonsense about throwing it back in the water, but never said what 'it' was."

The uneasy feeling had graduated to gripes.

"Did she—?"

Tom waved a hand. "Wait-wait. That's not the crazy part. Here's where I think I lost it: For no reason at all she pulls up her shirt."

"She flashed you?" Jack felt a faint tinge of relief. "I see where the hallucination comes in. Who'd want to flash you?"

Tom didn't laugh, didn't even smile. "She wasn't showing me her boobs, she was showing me her belly. And . . ." His voice trailed off.

"And?"

Tom looked away. "And she had a hole through her—clear through her."

Jack felt as if he'd been hit with a bucket of ice water. He'd seen someone with the same thing not too long ago.

"Where—where was the hole?"

Tom jammed his fingers into a spot a couple of inches to the right of his navel.

"Right about here. I tell you, Jack, it was the weirdest goddamn thing. I swore I could see right through her."

Jack felt himself swaying, and not because he was at sea. He closed his eyes.

"Did she have a dog with her?"

"Yeah. Ugliest mutt I've ever—"

In a flash Jack found himself next to Tom, grabbing his wrist and shouting.

"Why the hell didn't you tell me?"

Tom blinked at him, startled. "What's with you?"

"That was a warning, asshole!"

"From a teenage girl? Cut me a break!"

"That was no ordinary teenage girl. What did she say?"

"I told you—"

"Her exact words."

"Let go, for Christ sake. How'm I supposed to think with you grabbing me?"

Jack released Tom's wrist but didn't back off.

"I'm waiting."

"All right. She had this Jamaican accent and she said . . . let me see . . . 'I t'row it right back in de water, me.' Yeah. That was it."

"Why didn't you tell me?"

In the past sixth months four women with dogs had crossed his path—three of them old, one about his age. He'd gathered that they were all linked, but to what, he didn't know. Some had got him into trouble, others had warned him of trouble to come. He didn't know their agenda, but to a woman they all knew more about Jack's life than they should. And the last one, who'd called herself Herta, had had a tunnel through her, front to back, just like the one Tom had described in the black teenage girl—a girl with a dog.

10

Tom saw Jack's hands tighten into fists. He wasn't going to hit him again, was he?

"Damn you," he said through clenched teeth. Then his fists relaxed. "All right, here's how it's gonna play. First thing tomorrow you're up and on the phone and you're calling anybody and everybody who might have heard of this thing."

"Okay, okay. Sure. Nobody wants to find out about it more than I do."

No lie there.

Jack said, "Don't be too sure of that."

Tom tried to put a positive spin on this for himself. Sure, Jack's pissed, and he's not the kind of guy you want pissed at you, but look on the bright side: You've just engaged a willing helper in your search.

He glanced back at the Lilitongue and—

"Holy shit! Jack! It's gone!"

"What?"

Tom didn't have to say any more. Nothing but empty air where it had floated only seconds ago.

But where—?

He dropped to his knees and reached for the sea chest. He tugged at its top thinking, Please be there! Please!

He pushed back the top: empty.

No! He couldn't have gone through all this just to have it disappear on him. It wasn't fair!

"Got to be around here somewhere," Jack said. "Not like it vanished into thin air."

But it had. They searched every room, every closet, every nook and cranny—nothing.

Tom wanted to scream.

11

-80:41

"I'm too tired, Mom."

"Just a quick shower," Gia said.

She'd wanted Vicky to take a bath before going over to Jack's but Vicky had found one excuse after another to put it off until it was too late.

"I don't want to."

She pouted in the bathroom doorway, her right hand behind her, scratching at her back.

Ninety-nine-point-nine percent of the time Vicky was the sweetest child in the world. But like any child, when overtired she became whiny and uncooperative.

Gia reached into the shower stall and turned on the water. Vicky's aunts, Nellie and Grace, had installed it three or four years ago. Its modern, one-piece construction sat in stark contrast to the rest of the master bath with its walls of antediluvian tiles and age-stained grout.

Though dead for almost a year and a half now, the aunts remained the official owners of this Sutton Square townhouse. Gia knew they were dead but couldn't prove it. And so even though they'd left their entire estate to their only blood relative, little Victoria Westphalen couldn't claim it. Not yet. Not until Grace and Nellie were declared legally dead. Until then, Gia and Vicky occupied the house in a caretaker capacity.

Good thing the taxes were paid out of the estate. Gia never could have afforded them.

"Come on now. You need a little freshening up. I'll put a shower cap on you so you won't get your hair wet. Zip-zip-zip, you'll be in and out and on your way to bed."

"But Ma-om." She scratched her back again. "I want to go to bed na-ow!"

"You want to stop itching? Take a shower."

"Oh, all right."

Vicky stepped into the bathroom and pulled off her sweater. Her undershirt followed. As Vicky bent to slide off her jeans, Gia's heart tripped over a beat as she spotted a large round black mark, big as a tennis ball, on her back.

"Vicky! What is that?"

"What?"

As Vicky started to turn Gia grabbed her shoulders and held her facing away as she looked closer. The tennis-ball-sized mark sat on her upper back between her shoulder blades. Black . . . Sharpie-pen black, with lightly feathered margins. Ugly and . . . scary.

A huge melanoma? But no. Impossible. It hadn't been there this morning when Gia had helped her get dressed.

She couldn't say why this strange mark filled her with such unease. So black . . . unnaturally black.

"What is it, Mom?"

Gia heard the concern in Vicky's voice, so Gia did her best to hide her own concern.

"There's a mark on your back. Did you—?"

"Where?" Vicky twisted her head as far as it would go. "I can't see it."

Gia's hand recoiled as she reached toward it, but she overcame her hesitancy and traced the mark's outline with a finger.

"Right there."

"That's where it itches."

"Did you lean against anything?"

"No. I mean I don't think so."

Gia snatched up Vicky's sweater and undershirt. Clean. That meant it hadn't come through from the outside. But where then?

A thought stole her breath: If not from the outside, that left the inside.

Gia grabbed a washcloth, moistened it, and rubbed at the mark.

"That feels good, Mom. That's right where it itches."

"I'm glad, hon."

But she'd be so much gladder if she were making some headway. It wouldn't wipe off. She hadn't lightened it even the slightest.

She rubbed harder.

"Ouch!"

"Sorry, hon. It won't come off."

Gia had an idea. She went to the linen closet where she grabbed another washcloth and the bottle of rubbing alcohol. She splashed some on the cloth and attacked the mark again.

"Ow! That stings!"

"Just hang on there and let me see if I . . ."

Gia's unease expanded to fright as she rubbed and rubbed with no result. The alcohol did no better than plain water. She couldn't even smear it.

Finally she stopped and leaned back.

"Where on earth did you get this?"

Vicky shrugged as she turned toward her. "I don't know."

She reached around and began scratching at it again.

The itch . . . somehow related to the mark . . .

"When did you start itching?"

Vicky glanced away. "Oh, a little while ago."

Gia sensed evasion. Vicky wasn't a liar. Sure, she'd tell

a white one every so often, but her usual tactic was to evade the truth rather than negate it.

But what would make her evasive?

"All right. Do you remember where you were when you started itching?"

Vicky's eyes remained averted. She spoke in a small voice.

"Jack's place."

An awful thought struck Gia. Her mouth went dry.

"Does it have anything to do with that floating thing?"

Vicky nodded, then started to cry. "I don't know. It started right after I pushed in on its belly button and it floated into the air!"

"Oh, dear God!"

Gia leaped to her feet and rushed out into the hall.

"What's the matter, Mom?" Vicky trailed behind her. "Are you mad?"

"Yes. I mean no. I—I've got to call Jack!"

She headed for the hall phone, but she skidded to a stop and froze when she saw someone moving on the staircase.

Terror lanced through her.

Then she realized it wasn't a man. Not even human. And when she recognized it she almost wished for a real intruder.

The thing from Jack's apartment . . . coming up the stairs.

She backed away as it floated over the banister and started down the hall . . . away from her . . . into Vicky's room.

She followed it in and saw it float over the bed and come to a stop in a corner.

And there it stayed, hovering.

Gia repressed a scream and ran for the phone.

MONDAY

1

"If anything happens to Vicky, Abe—*anything*—I'm going to kill him."

Hell, something had already happened to Vicky. She had a foul-looking mark across her back. The thought of it made Jack sick.

He and Abe had assumed their customary fore and aft positions at the scarred counter in the rear of the Isher Sports Shop. He'd come here because he could no longer stand being in the same room, the same apartment, the same goddamn *block* as his brother.

"Such a remark I'd take with a grain of salt from anybody else. But seeing as it's you . . ."

Jack closed his eyes at the memory of Gia's frantic call, his headlong rush across town with Tom tagging along, and then the gut punch of seeing that mark on Vicky's back and knowing—*knowing*—it was connected to the Lilitongue. How could anyone doubt that? Especially after the damned thing had appeared in Gia's home and set up watch in Vicky's bedroom.

He'd wanted to strangle Tom then and there. Still did.

Vicky had been terrified, thinking it had followed her because it was mad at her for touching it. She'd spent the night in her mother's room. Jack had sent Tom home and had spent the night in a guest bedroom. Vicky had had a rough night but had finally dropped off to sleep. She was still asleep when he'd left this morning.

"I'm serious, Abe. He's just this far from being enrolled in the Judge Crater club."

"Another explanation for the mark is possible."

"Yeah? Give me one."

"I should give you what I don't have? All I'm saying is that *post hoc ergo propter hoc* is not a reliable path to the truth."

"In this case my gut tells me it is. There's this thing floating in midair in Vicky's bedroom. That's not natural. Then there's this big black mark that appears on Vicky's back after she touched the thing and started it floating. That's not natural either. Then it shows up in her bedroom."

"Your *guderim* also tells you this mark is dangerous?"

Jack nodded. "Oh yeah."

Exactly what danger, Jack didn't know, but a black mark . . . on Vicky . . . from a thing a girl with a dog and a hole through her belly had warned against . . . no way he'd ever find anything good about that.

He pounded his fist on the counter, just once, but hard enough to send Abe's pet parakeet fluttering toward the ceiling.

"He's got to be one of the stupidest, most clueless assholes on the planet! I could—" He cut himself off. "Sorry. Just venting."

"So vent already."

Jack knew he was in a foul mood. Lack of sleep made it worse. He'd kept waking up during the night and stealing down the hall to Vicky's bedroom to see if the Lilitongue had moved. The only movement he wanted from it was back into its chest so he could lock it up and find an upstate land-fill for its final resting place. But it didn't look like that was going to happen. Not unless it was forced back into its chest.

On one such foray he remembered talking to the damn thing: *What are you? What have you done to Vicky?* Then taking a swing at it.

His knuckles and wrist still ached from the impact.

"Tom and I spent the whole morning calling every

place we could think of that might have heard of the Lilitongue of Gefreda. From the Museum of Natural History to antique dealers and antiquarian booksellers. Nothing."

"The Museum of Natural History? You should check with Doctor Buhmann there."

"Who's he?"

"He was one of my professors at Columbia. Specializes in dead languages."

"I'm not looking for a translation, I'm looking for somebody who knows about strange, ancient artifacts."

"This Lilitongue is ancient?"

Jack shrugged. "I know it's more than four hundred years old. The jerk says—"

"The jerk?"

"My brother."

"A *shmegege* you should call him. That better fits how you describe him. A *shmegege* and a *gonif*."

"I'll have to trust you on that. Anyway, the *shmegege* says the few mentions he found about it hinted that it was really old—maybe B.C. in origin. So you see, I need an archaeology type. If he can lead me to some old book, then I may need your professor friend. But at the moment—"

"*Nu*, if this Lilitongue is one of a kind, you won't find anyone who's ever seen it, but someone may have read about it . . . especially if they specialize in translating texts of ancient languages."

Hope wanted to spark but Jack wouldn't let it. Still, Abe had suggested a direction he hadn't considered.

"Okay, maybe after we've exhausted the other avenues, I'll—"

His phone vibrated in his pocket. He pulled it out and hit the speak button. Had to be Gia.

"Jack?" Gia. Something in her tone . . .

"Something wrong?"

She sobbed. "The mark—it's bigger!"

A lead weight dropped into the pit of Jack's stomach.

"You're sure?"

"Absolutely. Last night it was between her shoulder blades, now it's touching them!" Another sob—the sound tore Jack's heart. "Jack, what's happening?"

He wished to hell he knew.

He spent a few moments trying to comfort her, assuring her that he was doing everything possible. When he hung up he relayed the latest to Abe.

"How do I get in touch with this language guy?"

"I'll see if I can arrange a meeting."

"Don't see if—do." He realized how he sounded. "Please."

Abe nodded as he picked up the phone.

"He'll remember you?"

Abe looked at him over the top of his reading glasses. "Oh, he'll remember me."

2

-69:48

"So how is Abraham doing these days?"

Peter Buhmann, Ph.D., associate conservator of languages in the division of anthropology at the American Museum of Natural History, professor emeritus at the Columbia University department of archaeology, was o-l-d. Figuring his age might require carbon dating. He looked frail, bent, pale, thin to the point of emaciation. Jack sensed something gnawing at his insides. Didn't look like he had much time left.

"Very well," Jack said.

Dr. Buhmann's office was small and cramped. The overstuffed shelves, threatening to drown them in paper if the building shook, made it seem even more claustrophobic.

"I haven't seen him since he graduated. One of my best students ever. A brilliant mind. I understand he sells sporting goods."

"Yes."

Jack figured the old guy would have a heart attack if he told him what Abe really sold.

He shook his head. "Such a waste of a good mind."

"He said you might know about the Lilitongue of Gefreda."

"Yes. He mentioned that on the phone. I haven't heard the Lilitongue mentioned in decades. So I went through my papers and found an entry in one of my notebooks." He opened a black ledgerlike book on his desk to a marked page. "I'm afraid it's not much."

"Anything you can tell me will be more than I've got."

"Very well." He put on his glasses and bent over the book. "These are notes I culled from various sources. The Lilitongue of Gefreda is mentioned as one of the Seven Infernals. I—"

"Which are?"

Infernal . . . Jack didn't like the sound of that.

"Mythical devices created in ancient times, each for a specific purpose."

"Such as?"

"Well, according to legend the Lilitongue was designed to"—he consulted his book here—"help someone 'elude all enemies and leave them helpless.' No name or purpose is known for any of the other six."

Disappointed, Jack leaned back and rubbed his eyes. He already knew that. He'd squeezed it out of his *shmegege* brother right before Gia's call.

"No mention of *how* it's supposed to do that?"

Dr. Buhmann shook his head. "None that I've ever read."

"Any picture of it anywhere?"

"None that I've ever seen." He sighed. "You must understand, the history of the Seven Infernals is shrouded in mystery. Most of the few researchers who've heard of them doubt they ever existed."

"Then why are they mentioned at all?"

A shrug. "Why are vampires mentioned? Why werewolves? Something inspired those myths, yes, but though the inspiration—say, the burial of a catatonic person in the former case, a severe manic-depressive disorder in the latter—might have been real, the folk tales that grew out of them are not."

That wasn't a folk tale floating in Vicky's bedroom.

"If I had to guess," Buhmann continued, "based on the escape fantasy offered by the Lilitongue of Gefreda, I'd say the myth was the result of wishful thinking by a persecuted culture." He frowned. "But then again . . ."

"What?"

"The Church seems to play an important part in the story."

The Jesuit Mendes . . . the map maker . . .

"The Catholic Church? The pope?"

"The Lilitongue was rumored to have been hidden away in the Vatican since the sixth century."

"Doesn't that tell you something?"

He laughed—a dry cackle. "So many strange and 'forbidden' things are rumored to be hidden in the Vatican vaults that the Church would need half of Rome to store them all!"

"Any rumor of it leaving the Vatican?"

Dr. Buhmann's eyes widened. "As a matter of fact . . ." He turned back to his notebook. "Yes. Here. It was rumored to have been stolen during the papacy of Innocent IX—who died in 1591 after only two months as pope." Another cackle. "Now, if I were a conspiracy theorist, I suppose I could make something of that."

"No mention of it after that?"

He checked his book again. "Not that I ever saw."

It all fit. The Lilitongue of Gefreda disappears from the Vatican in 1591 . . . seven years later a Jesuit—at the request of the pope, if the inscription Tom had withheld could be believed—guided it to a watery grave. And it was never heard from since because it was buried in a Bermuda sand hole.

So what? He knew no more about the thing now than when he'd stepped into Dr. Buhmann's office.

Shit.

"May I ask you a question?"

Jack was tempted to say, You just did, but held back.

"Shoot."

"Why this interest in such an arcane legend? And believe me, the Lilitongue of Gefreda is *very* arcane."

How to answer that without telling too much . . .

"Someone I know thinks he's found it."

Buhmann's eyes twinkled. "Oh, I doubt that. But if your friend wishes to bring it here to the museum, I can have the objects curator take a look at it. No one knows what the Lilitongue looks like, so it will be impossible for him to identify it, but he should be able to carbon date it for you."

Nothing Jack would like better, but . . .

"It . . . it can't be moved right now."

And Jack wasn't about to self-destruct his life by becoming publicly involved with a thing that defied the laws of gravity. At least not yet.

But if everything led to dead ends, then that was what he'd do: bring the Lilitongue to the attention of the world and let the scientific community figure it out.

"Besides, what would carbon dating tell me?"

"Well, the Lilitongue is said to be ancient, fashioned in ancient Babylon or even earlier. If you brought in an object that was, say, five or six thousand years old, you might really have something."

Jack already knew he had something. He pushed himself out of the chair.

"Well, thank you for your time, Professor. Any suggestion as to where else I can look?"

He smiled. "To learn about a mythical object, you might want to consult a mythical book. According to lore there once existed a book, a 'forbidden' tome, that supposedly catalogued the histories and workings of all seven of the Infernals, along with much other 'forbidden' knowledge. But the book is most likely as fanciful as the objects it discusses."

"When and where was this nonexistent book last heard of?"

"The fifteenth century. Supposedly it fell into the hands of the Grand Inquisitor, Tomás de Torquemada, during the initial phase of the Spanish Inquisition. He tried to destroy it—burn it, tear it apart, slash its pages—but legend says it's indestructible."

Jack felt a chill. He'd heard about this book not long ago. From a lady with a dog.

But he couldn't remember its name.

"So Torquemada buried it. But more than that, he designed and built a monastery over the spot—the Monastery of St. Thomas in Avila—where he spent his final years."

The professor's words were like a head butt: Tom had claimed the *Sombra* map had been found in a Spanish monastery.

One more piece of the puzzle.

But he still couldn't remember the book's goddamn name. He'd had a lot of distractions at the time, but now he wished he'd paid closer attention.

"Let's just say I come across this book. Would you be able to translate it for me?"

Dr. Buhmann's eyes got a faraway look. "If I could see such a thing, hold it in my hands just once before I die . . ." He shook himself. "What am I saying? Forgive an old man. I'm sure there once existed a forbidden book that was so well made that it was difficult to destroy, and thence came the legend. But should the book truly exist, and if the whispers about it are true, you won't need me to translate it."

"Why not?"

"Because the story goes that anyone who opens it sees the text in his native tongue."

"I don't get it."

"If you open it, you will see modern English. I, on the other hand, born and raised in Vienna as I was, will see German." He laughed. "Have you ever heard of anything so ridiculous?"

Yeah. He had. And he'd seen worse. A book in everybody's native tongue was a walk in the park compared to his experiences in the past year or so.

But he forced a laugh of his own. "Now that's pushing things a little too far."

Dr. Buhmann shrugged. "Nothing is 'too far' when talking about a book that doesn't exist. The sky's the limit."

"I suppose so."

He adjusted his glasses and looked at Jack. "But tell me, are you a scholar? Researcher? Student?"

"Just a repairman."

Dr. Buhmann shook his head in wonder. "I must confess I'm amazed that anyone outside the academic community has heard of the Lilitongue of Gefreda."

"I'm much more interested in this book that'll tell me about it."

The old man's expression turned grave. "I sense this means a lot to you. I won't ask why, but I must tell you: If this book exists, I doubt anyone alive has ever seen it or even knows where it is."

. . . anyone alive . . .

That gave Jack an idea. If he couldn't ask a living person, maybe he could ask a dead one.

He was willing to try anything.

3

Jack called ahead to see if Lyle and Charlie Kenton were entertaining any clients at the moment. Nope. Didn't he remember that Monday was their day of rest? No seances scheduled until midafternoon Tuesday.

So he grabbed the empty sea chest from his apartment and drove out to Menelaus Manor in Astoria. He wished he could have brought the Lilitongue along too, but since that was fixed in its spot, and since Charlie couldn't leave his house, the chest would have to do.

He parked in front of the attached garage. Hadn't been back since the summer. With its dark stone walls and vaguely colonial design, the house could look menacing at night. But in the wan light from an overcast sky, it looked merely old.

Lyle met him at the door and, after making nice-nice with the handshake and small talk and why-don't-you-ever-come-to-visit preliminaries, they settled in the high-ceilinged channeling room on the first floor.

The array of spiritualist and New Age junk displayed around the room among the statues of everything from Christian saints to Hindu gods brought back memories, not all of them pleasant. The heavy drapes, usually drawn tight, had been pulled back to let in some light.

Lyle, tall, lean, black, maybe thirty, wore his hair in long, tight dreads. He was dressed in jeans and a V-neck sweater. He led Jack to the large round oak table at the far end. Lyle seated himself at the twelve-o'clock spot, directly in front of a chalk-smeared blackboard; Jack took the three-o'clock position.

Letters began to form in the chalk dust on the board, one at a time, as if written by an invisible finger.

Yo Jack

"Hi, Charlie."

The skeptic in Jack reflexively recoiled at the idea of communicating with a dead man—after all, Lyle had been an expert at faking that very thing—but his experiences in Menelaus Manor this past summer had opened his eyes. And now Lyle seemed used to, even comfortable with, being in touch with his dead brother.

He seemed to be listening, then he said, "He wants to know why you brought that chest."

"Well, my brother Tom and I—"

"—found it in a shipwreck off Bermuda. He knows. He wants to know why you brought it here."

"I need to know something, anything about what was in it. It's called—"

"—the Lilitongue of Gefreda."

"Right." This was good—very good. Looked like he was finally going to get some answers. "I need to know what it does—if anything."

Lyle didn't answer. Jack couldn't tell if he was waiting or listening. Finally . . .

"Charlie doesn't know. He says it comes from a different place and age when the rules were different."

Oh, shit. "The Otherness?"

"He doesn't know. He can't be sure."

"Can he at least tell me if it's harmful?"

"He says that's relative. If you want to escape your troubles, it will help you do that. But in a case like Vicky's, it's harmful."

Jack stiffened. "You know about Vicky?"

Lyle nodded. "Charlie does."

"Harmful how?"

"She'll be taken away from everyone she knows and loves, and will never return."

Jack felt his gut freeze.

"Taken where?"

"Charlie doesn't know."

"Is that what's going to happen to her?"

Charlie could see the future at times—at least he thought he could.

"She'd have to be here in person for him to tell you that, but even then . . . this Lilitongue is so unique, so alien . . . he's not sure he'd know."

Vicky . . . oh, God, Vicky . . . what am I going to do?

Giving in to a sudden, irresistible urge to move, he sprang to his feet and paced the room. The air felt thick, he couldn't seem to draw enough of it into his lungs, his fingertips tingled. He'd never felt it before but he had a pretty good idea what was happening.

Panic.

"Goddamn it, Charlie, there's gotta be something I can do!"

"There is," Lyle said. "Find *The Compendium of Srem.*"

Jack halted his pacing. "I've heard of that."

That was the book Herta had told him about, the one Dr. Buhmann had alluded to. But Herta hadn't been talking about the Lilitongue of Gefreda.

The Compendium of Srem . . .

"That's got the answers?"

"Charlie doesn't know. He can't pierce its covers."

Then what good is he? Jack wanted to say, but bit it back.

"Well, maybe *I* can. Just tell me where the damn thing is and—"

"Charlie says you already know. In fact, you've seen it."

Jack stared at Lyle, blinking in confusion. What the—?

And then he realized what Charlie meant.

4

"Are you sure you know where you're going?" Tom said.

Jack ground his teeth, thinking about what a jerk he'd been. But then, he hadn't heard the whole story until it was too late. If Tom had told him about the Lilitongue's supposedly magical powers, if he'd told him about the girl and the dog, Jack wouldn't have allowed Vicky within ten miles of that thing.

He glanced at his brother the *shmegege* and thought about a quick chop to his Adam's apple—not hard enough to crush his larynx, just enough to shut him up. But knowing how that mark was growing larger on Vicky's back, he wasn't sure he could pull the punch.

"Not exactly. So can the chatter and let me think."

On either side of the two-lane blacktop, evergreens stood tall among the bare branches of their deciduous neighbors. The dull, overcast sky threatened snow. He hoped it held off—prayed it held off. The last thing he needed was to get stuck with the *shmegege* in the mountains of upstate New York during a blizzard. Talk about a nightmare.

Jack had been to this area twice last month. But both times at night—once with a passenger who knew the way, and the other following someone—so he was feeling his way.

"I'm still not clear on this: We've come out to the middle of nowhere to sneak into a house you might not be able to find so that we can search for a book that might or might not be there?"

"I have it on good authority that it exists, and that it belongs to the owner of this place we're looking for."

Jack hadn't wanted to bring the *shmegege* along, but he didn't know if he'd need an extra pair of hands at the cabin—if he could find it. He'd told him about his meeting with Dr. Buhmann, but not about Charlie. He didn't want to have to explain his connection to the disgraced Luther Brady either.

Jack rounded a curve then and slowed his Crown Vic.

"What's wrong?"

"This looks familiar."

He eased ahead until he saw the uphill gravel driveway. On impulse he pulled in and climbed the grade.

"This the place?"

"No, but if it's the place I think it is, then we're almost there."

Halfway up the driveway he looked for traces of the explosion that had ripped a man apart last month, but found none. A cleanup squad—whether human or the carnivores among the local fauna, he couldn't say—had come through and left no trace.

As the house hove into view he slammed on the brakes. The tires skidded on the gravel.

"Oh, shit."

"Wow," Tom said, craning his neck for a better look through the windshield. "Somebody sure had their fun with this place."

Not exactly the traditional idea of fun: The front door stood open, its off-kilter storm door swayed back and forth, and someone had smashed every window in sight.

Tom snorted. "Vandals. The jerk who built the place probably thought he'd leave their kind behind when he came up here. But they're everywhere."

Jack hoped the destruction was due to garden-variety vandalism. Not a hell of a lot to do in these parts: Add drugs or booze to boredom and just about anything could happen. If that had been the case, fine. But he feared the destruction might have been motivated by something else.

Seized with a sudden urgency to find Brady's cabin, Jack put the Vic in reverse and started turning it around. Took him four moves before he could nose back into the driveway again.

"Jesus, what are you doing driving a tank like this? It's a cop car. Or a retirement-village car. And you're neither."

Jack could have told the *shmegege* that this black Crown Victoria was the exact match—right down to the license plates—of a car belonging to a big shot in the outfit's Brooklyn wing. But then he'd have to go into a long explanation of why he'd want something like this.

He turned back onto the blacktop and continued west. Now he had an idea of where he was going. He just hoped that Brady's cabin hadn't suffered the same fate.

A few miles farther on he found a similar driveway and turned into it. The rear wheels kicked up gravel as he spurred the car uphill. Hurrying wouldn't change things—if damage had been done, it was done.

When he saw the place he slowed to a stop.

"Shit!" He pounded on the steering wheel. "Shit! Shit! Shit!"

Only charred timbers remained of the north wall of Brady's woodsy A-frame. The rest of the house looked almost as bad—not an intact pane in sight.

Jack jumped out and hurried across the dead grass to the smashed front door. Tom tailed him.

The inside was consistent with the outside, maybe worse. Looked like someone had taken an ax to everything before starting the fire. Splintered furniture—some of it used as kindling, maybe—smashed framed photos, slashed paintings, books reduced to confetti. Rain washing in through the ruined roof had added to the damage.

But Jack didn't care about this—his interest lay below. He knew a trapdoor lay somewhere near the center of the main room, but he couldn't see where.

He dropped to his hands and knees and began searching the knotty pine planks.

He heard Tom say, "What are you doing?"

"Looking for the edge of a trapdoor."

"What makes you think there's a trapdoor?"

"I just do. Help me look."

He couldn't tell Tom that he'd been peeking through one of these windows when Luther Brady had swung up a section of the floor and disappeared below . . . carrying a book . . . a large, old-looking book.

Jack was counting on that being the *Compendium*. Herta had told him Brady had it. And Charlie had said Jack had seen it. If they were right, this had to be the place.

Tom walked around in a wavering circle.

"I don't see anything."

Neither did Jack. But he knew it was here. He tried to remember if the trapdoor's opening edge had been irregular. If so, he wouldn't find an obvious seam cutting across the boards. He stretched himself flat for an ant's-eye view.

There—a tiny depression running along one of the planks. He rose to his knees and ran his finger along the edge. Yeah, definitely a space here.

Jack pictured Brady lifting the door. It had opened toward the rear of the house. He searched for a ring embedded in a plank. Had to be one. Brady couldn't have lifted it without—

One of the knots two planks away looked different. He touched it and noticed it didn't feel like wood. He worked his thumbnail along its edge and up popped a metal ring, painted to look like wood. Jack hauled back on it and a section of the floor angled upward.

"Jesus!" he heard Tom say. "How did you know?"

He ignored the question as he threw the trapdoor back. A wooden stairway led below.

Jack started down. "Wait here."

"No problem."

5

-65:26

At the bottom Jack found himself in a dark, tiny cube of a room, maybe eight by eight. Daylight through the door above provided faint illumination. Probably should have gone back to the car for the flashlight, but hadn't wanted to waste the time. The enlarging of Vicky's mark had filled him with a desperate urgency.

He looked around. Shelves lined the space, stacked with envelopes and magazines and books of all sizes. The one he'd seen had been large, somewhere between sixteen and twenty inches on a side.

He stepped to the nearest shelf and began pulling things off it. They felt soggy—water must have seeped through and worked its way down here. He caught sight of photos in the magazines as he tossed them on the floor— naked boys. No surprise there.

He worked his way along the shelves until he came to a steel cabinet, like a fuse box. He tugged on the handle. Locked.

Well, he'd fix that.

Jack pulled his Spyderco folder from his back pocket and snapped out the blade. He worked it along the edge, wiggling and pushing until he had a third of the blade inside, just above the lock. Then he leaned against the knife, prying . . . prying . . .

The door popped open.

Blessed be the man who invented tempered steel.

Jack pulled open the door and squinted into its dim interior. Only one thing inside: a book—big like the one he'd seen Brady bring down here. Had to be the same.

But was it *the* book?

Jack pulled it out and hefted it. Heavy. The covers and spine seemed to be made of stamped metal. He stepped to the center of the space and held it in the shaft of light under the trapdoor.

Markings embossed on the cover . . . he squinted at them . . . looked like random squiggles at first, then they swam into focus . . . words . . . in English . . .

Was this what the prof had talked about . . . the text changing to the reader's native language?

Compendium ran across the upper half in large serif letters; and below it, half size: *Srem*.

Jack felt his throat constrict. He'd found it. Goddamn it, he'd found it. But was it what he needed?

He pounded up the steps to the main floor where he found Tom standing by the rear wall with a shocked look on his face.

"Got it!"

Tom didn't seem to hear. He clutched a couple of torn, water-stained eight-by-ten photos. He held one up and looked at Jack.

"Here's a picture of some guy with Oprah." He held up the other. "And here's the same guy with President Clinton. I know I've seen him before but I just can't place him."

Might as well tell him, Jack thought. Sooner or later it'll come to him.

"That's Luther Brady."

Tom's eyes widened. "*The* Luther Brady? The Dormentalist? The pedophile?"

"The same. Look—"

"The indicted-for-murder Luther Brady?"

"Yes."

And you're talking to the guy who put him there.

"This must be his place!" Tom pointed to the open trapdoor. "How did you know about that?"

"I know about a lot of things." Jack jerked his thumb toward the front door. "We're getting out of here. And you're driving."

6

-65:14

With Tom ensconced behind the wheel and winding the car back toward Route 84, Jack hunched forward in the passenger seat with *The Compendium of Srem* balanced on his knees. This being the shortest day of the year, the sun had already set, so he switched on the courtesy light.

Took him only a few pages to realize this was the oddest book he'd ever seen. Not simply the metal covers with their unusual hinges, and not the curlicue handwriting, but the pages themselves. The page paper—if it was paper at all—felt thinner than onionskin, but was completely opaque. He'd figured that if the book was half as old as it was supposed to be he'd find some damage. But no. Not a tear, not a wrinkle, not a single dog ear.

And who or what was *Srem*? If he was the guy who'd put this thing together, he at least could have had the decency to include an index or table of contents.

Jack flipped through the unnumbered, single-ply-tissue pages—lots of illustrations, many in color—hoping to catch a glimpse of the Lilitongue. He went through twice, stopping on the second run and backtracking toward the rear when he thought he saw movement in one of the illustrations.

Couldn't be. Just a trompe l'oeil of the flipping pages, like the little animations he'd drawn in the corners of his loose-leaf sheets back in grammar school when he was bored and—

Christ!

He froze and gaped at a page with an illustration that moved.

More than simply moving: an animated globe spinning in a void. He recognized it as Earth by the layout of the continents. He also recognized the crisscrossing lines connecting the dots on its surface.

He'd seen that pattern on an oversized globe hidden away in Luther Brady's office.

And he'd seen the same pattern cut into the back flesh of two of the women with dogs.

He ran his fingers over the animation. It felt no different from the rest of the page—not a ripple, not the slightest vibration, not even a tingle.

"E pur si muove," he whispered.

Tom said, "What?"

"Nothing."

"Find anything yet?"

"Oh, yeah. But not what we're looking for."

Jack tore himself away from the animation and began to plow through the *Compendium* one page at a time. He'd never learned to speed read, but he could scan text at a decent pace. He set three key words as targets: *Lilitongue, Gefreda,* and *infernal.*

About a quarter of the way through he came upon an otherwise blank page that announced:

THE
SEVEN
INFERNALS

Jack fanned through drawings of oddly shaped contraptions, each with a disturbingly organic look to its design. None of the first six even vaguely resembled the object floating in his apartment.

He hesitated to turn the last page. If it didn't show the Lilitongue . . . if Charlie had been wrong . . .

Jack took a breath, flipped the page, and exhaled in a rush when he saw the sketch of an irregular sphere with a dimple near its lower pole.

"Got it!"

Tom leaned away from the wheel and craned his neck to see. "You found it? What's it say?"

Jack pushed him back. "Watch the road. I'll read it to you."

" *'The seventh and final Infernal is the Escapement Infernal. Known as the Lilitongue, fashioned by the wizard Gefreda during the final century of the First Age.'* "

"Wizard?" Tom said. "We're talking about wizards? What is this, Dungeons and Dragons? And what the hell's the First Age?"

"Haven't a clue. But maybe we'll find out if you can shut up for two minutes and let me finish."

"Okay, okay. Go ahead."

" *'In that time Gefreda became encircled in his castle by his enemies with no hope of escape. And so he created the Lilitongue and was never again seen, by neither friend nor enemy.*

" *'For that man vexed upon all sides, who would wish to elude his enemies and leave them helpless, yet has not the courage or mayhap the means to exercise the ultimate option, that man has but to depress the Lilitongue's dimple and he will acquire the Stain.*

" *'After the appearance of the Stain, he who is marked shall have eighty-three hours to organize his affairs. Throughout that time the Stain shall spread, gradually encircling his body. When the two ends are united, completing a circuit of his flesh, he shall be removed from his troubles and transported to a faraway place, forever beyond his enemies' reach. He must bid farewell to those*

*people and all things he holds dear, for such shall forever
remain beyond the reach of the Stained.*

" *'Mark you well before depressing the dimple of the
Lilitongue: Once acquired, the Stain may not be shed—
not by cleansing, not even by flaying the Stained skin. Nor
may it be given to another.*

" *'When its task is complete, the Lilitongue shall return
to its place of fashioning.'* "

The text stopped above an infinity symbol two inches
from the bottom of the page.

Jack flipped and found blank white space. The oppos-
ing sheet sported a picture of a double-bladed sword.

Where's the rest of it?

He pushed the book flat, looking for signs that a page
had been torn out, but found no trace.

"That's it?" Tom said.

Jack nodded, then lowered the book and stared through
the window.

Tom groaned. "Damn!"

Jack couldn't tell if Tom was bemoaning Vicky's fate
or cursing the fact that she'd usurped his means of escape.

He reread the piece, searching for a loophole, a way
out for Vicky, but . . .

*Once acquired, the Stain may not be shed—not by
cleansing, not even by flaying the Stained skin. Nor may
it be given to another.*

He could see only one way to interpret that: Vicky was
in deep, irreversible danger.

Tom said, "I heard something about a 'faraway place.'
Where do you think that means?"

"Someplace you don't come back from."

The Otherness maybe. He and Dad had had a brush
with some of its inhabitants in Florida. The thought of
Vicky in a place like that . . . unbearable.

Eighty-three hours . . . why that number? Sounded like
a prime, but so what?

He did a quick calculation: Vicky had activated the

Lilitongue around nine P.M. last night. It was now going on three. That left roughly sixty-five hours before she was "transported to a faraway place."

He wanted to be sick.

Tom said, "Maybe the book's wrong."

Jack shook his head. "Cool it with the wishful thinking. You saw the mark on Vicky's back. This morning it was bigger. It's stretching out to encircle her, just like the *Compendium* said."

"Shit. I feel so awful about this."

"You should." Jack wanted more than ever to strangle him. "You damn well should."

"Hey—"

"Shut up, Tom. Just shut the fuck up. I need to think."

Did he ever. How was he going to break this to Gia?

7

-62:04

"What's wrong, Mom?"

Gia tried to hold back the tears as she looked at Vicky. She'd let a single sob escape. She had to stifle the second. She sensed that if she let it push through, it would burst the dam and she wouldn't be able to stop.

Jack sat to her right on the couch, his arm around her back. Vicky stood to her left. Tom had secluded himself in the kitchen. A single reading lamp on the side table lit the old dark book-lined shelves of the Sutton Square house.

"It's okay, honey." She prayed her voice wouldn't shatter. "I'm just very sad."

"Why? Is it the book?"

"Yes, honey."

She slipped her arms around her child and squeezed her.
"Is it a sad book?"

"Very sad."

The *Compendium* lay on her lap. Gia stared at the illustration of the Lilitongue, hating it. Then, through tear-blurred eyes, she read the text for the fourth time, searching for a shred of hope.

Part of her balked at the possibility that anything so outrageously fanciful could be true. It was the stuff of Harry Potter novels.

But another part of her called up a vision of that black mark—the *Stain*—stretching across her daughter's back and she knew it was true.

Gia felt her world crumbling around her. She couldn't lose her little girl! It wasn't going to happen—it *couldn't* happen! Not Vicky! Please not Vicky! Take me instead!

"There's got to be a way out, Jack."

His arm tightened around her. "I agree. Has to be. We've just got to find it in time." He reached for the book. "Tomorrow I'm going to take this—"

She clutched his arm. "Take it where?"

"To Abe's professor friend. I already called him but he's gone for the day. But I'll show this to him. Maybe he'll be able to tease something out of the text that we don't see."

"And what if he can't?"

"Then we go public with the *Compendium* and the Lilitongue. Haul the world's best minds here and see what they come up with."

"But you won't be able to find this professor till tomorrow, right?"

Jack frowned. "I'm still working on tracking him down tonight. Abe had only his office number. The museum won't give me his home number."

"Okay, you go looking, but leave the book with me."

"Why?"

"To save time." Dear God, so little left. "Have you been through the whole book?"

"No. Look at the size of it. Must be a thousand pages."

"That's my point. While you're out looking for this professor, I'll comb through every single page. There may be more about the Lilitongue hidden inside. And that way, when we bring this professor in, we'll know where to direct his attention."

Jack chewed his upper lip for a second or two, then shook his head.

"We'll both do it—tag-team style. You do an hour, then I'll do one. That way we won't go blind."

"But what about Abe's professor?"

"Who better to track down his home address than Abe? I'll put him on it."

Relief flooded through Gia. She didn't want to be alone here with Vicky, this ancient book, and the Stain.

8

-61:49

Tom sat alone at Gia's kitchen table, sipping a Killian's Irish Red he'd found in the refrigerator and feeling down.

Had somebody put a curse on him? Sure as hell seemed that way. Everything he touched turned to shit.

The feds were looking for him and he faced ruination and jail time if they found him.

If they found him? How about *when* they found him?

His stash had been discovered and frozen.

His last chance—the weird artifact he'd tracked down and hauled from the bottom of the ocean—had turned out a bust. Worse than a bust: It had put a little girl——Gia's little girl, of all people——in jeopardy.

Could things get any worse?

He couldn't see how. But things could *be* worse.

He tried to avoid the thought, felt ashamed that it even occurred to him, but his only luck lately had been Vicky touching the dimple on the Lilitongue instead of him.

Christ, he hated himself for the relief he felt.

Yes, he'd been the one looking to "elude all enemies," but not the way the Lilitongue was going about it. Whisked away to some undefined place from whence he could never return? No, thank you.

He shivered. He'd rather take his chances with the feds.

But of all people to be stuck with that creepy-looking mark, why Vicky? Why couldn't it have been Jack?

How low was that?

Sometimes I disgust even myself.

He heard a noise in the hallway and looked up to see Jack walking his way, a key ring in his hand.

Tom said, "Everything okay?" and immediately regretted it. What a stupid thing to ask.

Jack glared at him. "You're kidding, right?"

"It just popped out. How's she doing?"

"Terrible." He snapped a key off the ring and handed it to him. "I'm staying. You're not. This'll let you in."

"I want to help, Jack. I can——"

"You can do us all a favor by leaving." He stood aside to clear the door. "Walk up to the corner and catch a cab."

The scorn in Jack's clipped tone burned like acid. His impulse was to protest but he thought better of it. If Gia felt the same, he was better off gone.

Tom grabbed his jacket from a chair and shrugged into it as he slipped past Jack and headed down the hall. Passing the sitting room he saw Gia sitting in a pool of light, rocking Vicky on her lap.

He stopped. "I'm sorry, Gia. I had no idea . . . I never dreamed . . ."

His voice died as she looked up at him with haunted, red-rimmed eyes. He waited for her to say something, to scream curses at him, but she said nothing. He wished she would. The hurt and fear and the how-could-you? look in her eyes cut deeper than any words.

She'd lose her daughter in sixty-some hours and she blamed him.

Not fair.

"Let's go," Jack said from close behind.

Tom expected a shove toward the door. Thankful it didn't come, he began moving on his own.

And then he was on the sidewalk. He arrived there standing, under his own power, but he felt as if he'd been given the old heave-ho and landed with his face in the dirt.

The door clicked behind him and Tom was alone.

His breath steamed in the air as he looked around at all the lighted windows in the high-rises. Surrounded by millions of people and yet alone.

More alone than he'd ever been, and feeling it.

He couldn't remember ever being all that connected to anyone, at any time, but at least he'd had people he could *act* connected to. Now . . .

The Skanks? He'd burned those bridges long ago. His kids? Barely knew them. Terry? She didn't want him around—he was an embarrassment, a pariah to old acquaintances and colleagues. Even the solace of immersing himself in work was now denied him.

Perhaps subconsciously he'd considered his family something to fall back on—theoretically, at least—if worse came to worst. Now . . . ?

At this time last year he would have had Kate and Dad to lean on. Both gone now. He'd never considered Jack a possibility, because no one knew anything about him. But even Jack, his only surviving sib, wanted nothing to do with him.

Was this what the philosophers called *angst*?

He started walking up toward Sutton Place.

Not fair. None of it.

Sure, he'd recovered the Lilitongue and brought it to Jack's place, but he hadn't meant to hurt anyone. Maybe he shouldn't have shown it to Gia and Vicky. That probably had piqued the kid's curiosity, but Jack was at fault here too. Sure, he'd stowed the sea chest out of sight, but he should have found a better hiding place.

And Vicky—what about her? If she'd minded her own business instead of poking around other people's things . . .

Ah, what's the use?

He reached Sutton Place and found a cab, gave the driver Jack's address, then slumped in the seat.

When had he last felt this low? He needed a little pick-me-up. No, he needed a *big* pick-me-up.

He checked the driver's ID card: a scowling black face over a name that began with Kamal.

Tom leaned forward. "My nose has this bad itch. You know where I can get something for it?"

The cabby glanced over his shoulder, then looked ahead.

"You are a cop?" he said in heavily accented English. From Guyana, maybe?

"No, I'm anything but. Just a guy from out of town with a problem nose. Can you help me out?"

"I take you to someone. But you better be no cop."

Instead of turning west, Kamal headed uptown. The numbers on the cross streets progressed from double to triple digits, and the neighborhoods became rundown.

Kamal made a quick left and pulled to the curb near a bodega. A tall black man in an oversized, thickly padded Giants Starter jacket stepped out of the doorway and sauntered over.

"'Sup?"

This looked pretty straightforward, but Tom had seen enough hapless would-be customers hauled in via police sting operations. He decided to play it cute.

"I'm looking for my girlfriend," Tom said.

The guy looked surprised. "Are you now?" He leaned

over and glanced toward the front seat. "You know this one, Kamal?" His accent matched the driver's.

"Just met him."

The guy looked at Tom. "Girlfriend, yes? What her name? Angel, maybe? Or Roxanne, huh?"

The guy was playing along and seemed to be enjoying it.

"No, Snow White. She's a bit of a flake."

He nodded and smiled. A missing front tooth made him look like Leon Spinks. "I see her around. How much you pay to find her?"

Tom had the money ready. He'd considered using some of his bogus twenties but decided this might not be a guy you wanted mad at you.

He handed fifty bucks out the window.

"That should do for now."

With a single quick move the guy removed the money from Tom's hand and shoved it into a pocket.

"What else you want? We got alphabet soup—A, X, MJ from TJ—and we got baseball, purple rain, roofies, and Georgia Home Boy."

Tom smiled and said, "Thanks, but I'm very faithful to my girlfriend."

The guy straightened. "Okay. Leave your window open and wait here."

He said something into a walkie-talkie as he sauntered back to the bodega. A few minutes later a kid who couldn't have been more than ten ran up to the cab, tossed a little envelope through the window, and kept on moving.

Without being asked, Kamal put the cab in gear and took off.

Tom found the packet on the floor, picked it up, and stared at it. He'd had a coke problem for a while. When he'd realized where it was taking him he'd weaned himself off. He hadn't partaken for almost five years now.

But he needed a boost tonight. Needed one in a big, big way.

9

Gia glanced at the clock: almost eleven thirty.

Jack had dozed off while awaiting his turn at the *Compendium*. She'd gone upstairs to check on Vicky, asleep in Gia's bed, and then forced herself to peek into Vicky's bedroom in the hope the Lilitongue had decided to move on. It hadn't. It hung there in the air like . . . like nothing she'd ever seen or imagined.

After that she moved herself and the *Compendium* to the kitchen so as not to disturb Jack. Her mind screamed for sleep and her eyes burned like coals, but she couldn't stop. And she didn't want anyone else to take over, couldn't let go of this book until she'd read every word.

So far the words offered no hope. They did, however, depict a world rife with wonders and horrors. People and objects and devices with strange powers and obscure purposes. If even a small fraction of what the *Compendium* described was true, then life on Earth, existence itself, was far stranger than she ever could have imagined.

But nowhere, at least so far, had she found another mention of the Lilitongue of Gefreda. She was losing—

No. She wouldn't give up hope.

She turned the page and found a heading: *Remedies*.

Probably just a lot of folk medicine—herbal potions and poultices and the like. A long section. Her impulse was to skip over it, but she'd promised herself to read every word, so that was what she'd do.

As she skimmed through the pages she found lotions to

cure everything from scales to boils, elixirs to heal everything from diarrhea to blindness, solutions to—

The words *Stealing the Stain* leaped out at her.

Gia closed her eyes before reading further. Please, God, let it be about the Lilitongue stain—not wine stains or bloodstains, but *the* Stain.

Then she did a quick scan of the text and gasped when she spotted "Lilitongue of Gefreda." This was it!

But hadn't the Lilitongue text—she knew it by heart now—said that *once acquired, the Stain may not be shed—not by cleansing, not even by flaying the Stained skin. Nor may it be given to another.*

Then how . . . ?

Never mind the contradiction. Learn what it says.

She found a list of ingredients—things like sodium bicarbonate and tartaric acid and juice of the seeds of the vanilla planifolia orchid, among others. Where on earth was she going to find—?

Wait. She had some of them right here in the kitchen.

She hopped up and darted to the cabinet with her baking ingredients. She spun the lazy Susan until she spotted her box of baking soda. The label said "sodium bicarbonate."

Yes! Such a common item . . . but maybe not so common back when the *Compendium* was written.

Another spin and she found her bottle of vanilla extract. She hurried to the computer and Googled vanilla extract:

Vanilla Beans are the long, greenish-yellow seedpods of the tropical orchid plant, Vanilla planifolia. Before the plant flowers, the pods are picked, unripe, and cured until they're dark brown. The process takes up to six months. To obtain Pure Vanilla Extract, cured Vanilla Beans are steeped in alcohol. According to law, Pure Vanilla Extract must be 35 percent alcohol by volume.

Alcohol . . . the recipe or whatever it was didn't mention alcohol. But if she boiled that off she'd be left with juice of the seeds of the vanilla planifolia orchid—probably pretty hard to come by in the old days.

Going back and forth between the *Compendium* and the lazy Susan Gia discovered she had five of the eleven ingredients. But she didn't have a clue as to where to find crushed monkshood petals and dried red fly agaric. From what she learned through the Internet, she figured she could probably find the missing ingredients in some of the more esoteric ethnic herb shops downtown. She knew of one in Chinatown that sold the weirdest things.

She read further. The instructions were easy: Mix up the solution, wet your hand with it, then lay your hand palm down on the Stain and wish—yes, *wish* for it to leave the Stained.

Sounded like voodoo. And seemed too simple. But no downside to trying.

Then she read the final paragraph. There would be a price to pay.

Gia folded her arms on the book, lowered her head, and sobbed.

TUESDAY

1

Gia found the little shop she sought on Bayard Street. It had a name but it was written in Chinese. She didn't care what it was called. The important thing was that it was open.

Thank God.

A little after midnight Jack had awakened and taken over perusing the *Compendium*. Gia showed him where she'd left off—just beyond the *Remedies* section—and he'd picked up from there. She hadn't mentioned the "Stain Removal."

They'd alternated two-hour shifts through the night. Jack managed to doze between his but Gia found sleep impossible. She'd discovered what might—*might*—be a way out for Vicky. She prayed it would work. If it did, she'd deal with the price afterward.

She'd watched the clock all night, watched the sky through the window, waiting for dawn. Around seven thirty she'd left Jack dozing and slipped out, hailed a cab, and rode it to Chinatown.

As she stepped through the door of the tiny shop she half expected the proprietor to be elderly with a wispy white beard and dressed like a mandarin. Instead she found a gaunt young man, maybe thirty, dressed in a black T-shirt and black jeans.

She handed him the list of ingredients. He studied it, then frowned and pointed to the third item: crushed monks-hood petals.

"This poison."

Poison? Oh, no.

"It . . . it can't be."

"Yes. Kill you dead you eat. Rub on skin, okay, but not for eat."

That was a relief. Sort of.

"I understand. This will be used on skin. What about the rest? Have you got the rest?"

He nodded. "Yes. Not lot, but some."

"Some will do just fine."

He squinted at her. "This very strange list. What you use for?"

"An experiment. A successful one, I hope."

A few minutes later she was hurrying up to Canal Street to find a cab.

2

-46:51

She found Jack bent over the *Compendium*. He looked up as Gia entered the kitchen. His eyes were red and bleary. She was sure hers were no better.

"Where've you been, Gi? I've been worried about you."

She tried to keep her expression neutral. She didn't want to give anything away.

"I left you a note."

"Yeah: 'Went out for some things. Be back soon.' What things?"

"Ingredients."

"For?"

She pointed to the *Compendium*. "Something I saw in there. A recipe for a stain remover."

His eyes widened as he began leafing back through the pages. "Where? Where?"

"Somewhere near the middle," she said, then quickly added, "Don't bother. I wrote down all the ingredients."

"But didn't the book say it can't be removed, even if you cut away the skin?"

"No. It said it may not be 'shed.' There's a difference between shedding and having it removed by someone else."

"Sounds like a lot of parsing, but . . ."

"But what have we got to lose?"

He nodded. "Right."

Gia hoped that would be enough, that he wouldn't go back to search for the page.

She found a saucepan, emptied the bottle of vanilla extract into it, and turned on the gas. While that was heating she laid out the other ten ingredients.

She consulted her notes—many times; she could barely think—and measured the proper proportions of the other ingredients. She noticed her hands trembling.

When the vanilla extract came to a boil, she took it off to let it cool. Then she began blending the rest in a stainless steel mixing bowl.

Five minutes later she added the vanilla and the proper amount of water, then began heating it all to a boil.

"I just . . ." Jack began. "I just don't want you to get your hopes up."

She glanced at him. "You mean *our* hopes?"

He nodded. "Yeah. Our hopes."

"Don't worry. Really, how could I feel any worse? I'm simply trying something. I'm ready to try anything."

But her hopes were sky high. The remedy had mentioned the Lilitongue by name. She only prayed she hadn't messed up the proportions, and that the vanilla "juice" she'd concocted was the right one called for.

Once she'd brought the mix to a boil—it measured about a cup—she removed it from the heat and poured it into a saucepan to speed its cooling. She looked at the steaming brown liquid and thought, I'm crazy. This isn't going to work.

But she had to try. Especially since she couldn't see a downside.

Except for the monkshood. She'd Googled that while waiting for the mix to boil. What the Chinese man had told her was true: poison if taken internally but long used topically for pain relief.

Under no other circumstance could she imagine applying a poisonous mixture to Vicky's back . . .

Gia climbed to her second-floor bedroom and stood in the doorway. Her eyes filled with tears as she watched her sleeping child. She looked at the clock radio on the nightstand.

Thirty-six hours gone. That left just under two days.

My God, my God, my God, how am I going to live if she's taken away from me?

She stretched out beside Vicky and wrapped her arms around her. If the solution didn't work, maybe when the time came, if Gia held her tight enough, Vicky wouldn't, couldn't be taken away.

The pressure must have awakened Vicky because she started and twisted around.

"Mom! You're crushing me!"

"Sorry, honey. Come on downstairs. I've got something I want to try on that mark on your back . . . see if we can wash it away."

Vicky hopped out of bed and headed for the door.

"Really? Okay! Let's do it now! I hate that mark! It's ugly and I don't want it on me."

Gia clutched the banister railing for support as she followed Vicky's bounding descent.

Please let this work, God. *Please.*

When Vicky saw Jack she squealed and leaped into his arms with the abandon of a child who had no fear of being dropped. Not by Jack, anyway. Not with their history.

They'd bonded, those two, and nothing would tear them apart. Nothing except . . .

Jack squeezed her and laughed, but his expression as he looked at Gia over Vicky's shoulder revealed his desperation. She saw him blinking back tears.

"Okay, Vicks," he said. "Your mom's going to try something on your back to see if we can get rid of that Stain."

He set her on one of the kitchen chairs and lifted the back of her pajama top. Gia suppressed a gasp. The Stain . . . it now spanned almost the entire width of her narrow little back.

She stepped to the counter where she'd put the solution to cool and tested the temperature. Most of the heat had dissipated, leaving a mildly warm liquid. Gia pressed her palm into the saucepan. Once she had a thick coating, she turned and smeared the solution onto the Stain.

And now . . . the final prescribed ingredient: As she rubbed she had to make a wish. Not just any wish. The book had been very specific, going so far as to dictate the exact terms of the wish.

She felt almost silly. A wish . . . she'd been wishing the Stain away since her first sight of it. Of course she hadn't had the recipe until now. The *Compendium* said the solution plus a specific wish would do it.

A simple wish . . .

Yet she hesitated. She hated herself for faltering, but couldn't help it. This wish, if answered, would change so many things . . . would change everything . . .

And yet, how could she deny Vicky her safety?

So Gia closed her eyes and made the wish . . .

. . . and prayed . . .

. . . and hoped . . .

. . . and—

She felt her palm grow warm, hot.

"Ow, Mom! That hurts!"

"Jesus Christ!"

Jack's voice. She opened her eyes and looked at Vicky's back.

She'd smeared the solution over the middle of the Stain, planning to coat it to its borders and beyond. But that wouldn't be necessary.

With her heart bursting Gia watched the edges of the Stain retreat, fading as they drew back toward Vicky's spine.

Could it be? She ached to believe it but couldn't help thinking that her mind was conspiring with her eyes to let her see what she most desperately wanted.

"It's gone!" Jack whispered.

And it was. Not just her imagination or wishful thinking—he saw it too. Without a trace. Except for a smear of brown liquid, Vicky's back was clear.

Gia wrapped her arms around Vicky and began to sob.

It worked! It worked!

That clear little back was worth anything—even the burning itching sensation that had just begun on her own.

3

-45:42

Tom awoke and stretched. He felt crummy. A little nausea, a thick tongue, burning nostrils. Now he remembered why he'd kicked that habit.

Still, last night's little toot had got him through his bad case of the downs. Didn't make today look any better, though.

He checked the clock: after ten. He hadn't heard from Jack. Not that he expected to, but he was eager to learn what he and Gia had found during their all-nighter.

He forced himself upright, waited for the room to stop wobbling, then checked out the bedside phone. Three speed-dial buttons. He pressed number one.

Someone picked up after three rings. Jack.

"Hey, it's Tom. Any luck last night?"

"Yeah. Lucky for you. You had your sorry ass yanked out of the fire."

"You mean—?"

"Yeah. Gia found something in the book that erased Vicky's Stain."

"Oh, thank God! That's wonderful news!"

And he meant it. Now he might work his way back into Gia's good graces. And of course it was a relief that her little girl was out of danger.

"For you too," Jack said. "You get to live a little longer."

"What's that supposed to mean?"

"Never mind. Just count yourself lucky."

And then Tom was holding a dead phone. Jack had hung up on him. Must be still pissed at him.

Who cared?

Tom did a quick wash-up, dressed, then headed for the street. He caught a cab on Columbus Avenue and told the driver to take him to Eight Sutton Square.

4

-45:11

"Jack! Jack!"

Jack looked up from the *Compendium* as a wide-eyed Vicky rushed into the kitchen.

"What's up, Vicks?"

"That thing! That weird thing! It's gone! It's not in my room anymore!"

Jack was surprised, but then realized it made sense. Vicky no longer carried the Stain, so the Lilitongue would no longer be hovering around her.

"No kidding? Let's go see."

Gia was in the shower, so Jack followed Vicky upstairs to her bedroom and, sure enough, no Lilitongue hanging in the corner.

Jack let out a breath. Here was confirmation that the damned thing's connection to Vicky had been broken.

"This is great, Vicky."

She looked up at him with concern in her big blue eyes. "Is it gone for good? It won't be back?"

"Not if I have anything to say about it."

"Good. I felt like it was watching me. It was scary."

More than you know, Vicks, he thought. More than I hope you'll ever know.

When Jack stepped out into the hall she stayed close behind him—still didn't want to be alone in her room, he guessed.

She ran downstairs while he stopped at the phone in the hall and called home. He wanted to ask Tom if the Lilitongue had returned to its chest, but no one picked up.

As he passed the bathroom he heard Gia sobbing in the shower. His throat tightened. Jack had felt like sobbing himself when he'd seen Vicky's clear back. He'd been worried sick about her, but he couldn't have been as terrified as Gia.

He moved on, but as he passed her bedroom, something caught his eye. He backed up.

His blood turned to ice as he recognized the Lilitongue hovering in a corner. He stood in the doorway, unable to move, unable to breathe, feeling as though the world around him had come to a screeching halt.

The Lilitongue had moved . . . okay. But why here instead of back to its chest? Vicky had spent the night in

Gia's room, so that might explain it, but it should be gone. If Vicky was in the clear, why was it still hanging around?

Or was she in the clear? What if the Stain had been only temporarily removed? What if it was back?

He ran downstairs, but before heading for the kitchen he looked for Vicky. An awful thought had occurred to him: What if the Lilitongue's presence meant that the Stain had returned?

He found her reading the latest *Mutts* collection in the library.

"Hey, Vicks. Mind if I take a quick look at your back? I just want to make sure that mark is gone."

A concerned look flashed across her face. "You don't think it came back, do you?"

"Nah. Just want to make sure, is all."

"Okay."

She turned and lifted her T-shirt partway up her back. Jack dropped to his knees behind her and raised it the rest of the way. He released a sigh of relief when he saw her unmarred skin.

"Nope. Still gone."

He dropped the back of the shirt and rose to his feet.

"Good! I hope it never comes back."

"You and me both, kiddo. You and me both."

Okay. Vicky was clear. So why was the Lilitongue still here?

Jack wondered if Gia knew. No. Couldn't. She'd have said something. She was going to be upset when she found out. Maybe he could find an explanation before she finished her shower.

He raced to the kitchen and grabbed the *Compendium*. As he flipped through the pages, he heard the shower stop. Had to hurry.

He went back and forth until he found a section called *Remedies*. Could that be it?

A long section. He searched page after page until a heading stopped him: *Stealing the Stain*. That had to be it.

But something about it rang a warning bell.

He flashed through the list of odd ingredients until he came to the oddest of all.

"And last, to make the transfer complete, the taker must wish the Stain for himself. There can be no success without the wish. If successfully transferred, the Stain will appear on the taker who shall be required to wait only the hours remaining to the original Stained until escape. Have no fear of losing the Stain to the original Stained: Once lost, it may never be regained."

Jack read the passage again. And again. The tone was throwing him off . . . almost congratulatory. But he pushed through, trying to assemble the words into a shape, a thought, a message that made sense and wouldn't send him tearing upstairs screaming for Gia to tell him that it wasn't true, that she hadn't done this.

He couldn't. No doubt about it. He didn't need to see her back to know that Gia had taken—"stolen"—the Stain from Vicky and transferred it to herself.

He understood it . . . so typically Gia . . . she'd do anything to protect Vicky.

Jack leaned back and forced his numb brain to review his options. He came up with only one.

He heard Gia on the stairs. She walked in wearing jeans and a sweatshirt. Her hair was still wet. Her red, puffy eyes told the story. She hadn't been sobbing with relief in the shower—she was frightened.

As she entered the kitchen Jack rose and faced her.

"Gia, how could you?"

She burst into tears. "How could I *not*?"

Just then the doorbell rang. Jack looked past Gia, saw Vicky run to the front door and peek through the sidelight.

"It's Tom!"

She pulled open the door and let him in. He held up a white paper bag.

"Hi, everybody! I come bearing gifts!"

"What?" Vicky cried.

"Donuts!"

As Vicky cheered, Jack muttered, "Oh, shit."

5

-44:46

Well, at least the kid's glad I'm here, Tom thought as he started down the hall.

And what a hall. What a house. He hadn't been able to appreciate it that first night—not with all the turmoil. But now . . . look at the fine wood, the Persian rugs, the antique light fixtures . . . had to be worth millions. He'd got the impression that Gia was a commercial artist, making ends meet but with little left over. How did she afford this? He'd have to wheedle the story out of her.

Maybe the donuts would help. He'd had an inspiration on the way over: Arrive with goodies in hand. He considered it a truism that the surest way to a mother's heart was through her kid. Get the kid to like you and you enhance your chances twofold, maybe threefold.

So he'd asked his cabby to find a bakery or donut shop along the way. He'd stopped at a place on the East Side called Muller's. The donuts looked so good that Tom had scarfed down a cruller on the way over.

Vicky snatched the bag from his fingers and darted into the sitting room. Further on, in the kitchen at the end of the hall, Jack and Gia stood facing each other. Both looked upset.

Jack pointed to him. "Wait right there."

The words, the tone, the gesture took him aback. Who was Jack to order him about in Gia's house? But one look at Gia's puffy face and he knew something was wrong. *Still* wrong.

What had happened? He hadn't exactly expected to find a party going on, but this seemed like a wake. Only Vicky was in good spirits.

Jack turned away from him and back to Gia. They seemed to be in a serious, almost heated, discussion.

Tom edged closer.

"I can't believe you did this without telling me," Jack was saying.

"I knew you'd try to stop me."

"Damn right I would have! Now there are two people in jeopardy instead of one!"

Gia sobbed and the sound angered Tom. Jack was being rough on her. What was he so exercised about?

"I know! Don't you think I know that? But what was I to do? If I had a chance to save her, I had to take it."

"You should have come to me first!"

"I couldn't." She shook her head. "I know I should have. Don't ask me why . . . I just couldn't."

What was this about? What had she done?

Tom had come even with the sitting room. He glanced in and saw the kid sitting on the edge of a chair, kicking her legs, oblivious to everything but the TV and the sugar-coated donut she was munching.

"All right," Jack said. "Let's see it."

"No, I—"

"Please. This isn't just about you and me. There's the baby to think of."

Gia looked like she was again going to refuse to show him whatever they were talking about, but must have changed her mind. Because, without another word, she turned and raised the back of her T-shirt.

Tom gasped and felt his knees dissolve when he saw

the black band spread across her back. He had to prop himself against the door molding.

Sweet Jesus, it was almost halfway around her body!

Jack stared at it, then his head dropped. Gia pulled her shirt back down.

The light dawned for Tom.

No! A horrendous situation had become infinitely worse. He could comprehend a mother's love for her child, but weren't there limits? He'd heard of mothers throwing themselves in front of a car to save their child, but that was impulse. This had been premeditated.

Initially her daughter was going to be shunted off into the Great Unknown. Now Gia was going to be sent there instead.

It made no sense. Either way she loses her daughter, but this way she loses Jack too. Not to mention this exquisite townhouse.

"Only one thing to do then," he heard Jack say.

In one swift, smooth move he stepped to the counter, pressed his hand into a saucepan, and returned with his palm coated in some thick brown fluid. He then lifted the back of Gia's shirt and slipped his hand under. Gia reacted as if he'd splashed her with acid—her back arched, her eyes widened, and then she began to cry.

What the hell was going on here?

"Now it's settled," Jack said.

Gia turned and pounded her fists once against his chest. "No! I can't lose you! Not now!"

Jack grabbed her wrists. "You didn't really think I was going to let this happen to you, did you? You three are more important than anything else I can think of."

"Turn around! I want to see!"

Jack complied, lifting his shirt and revealing the Stain. Gia threw her arms around him and sobbed.

Stunned, awed, Tom watched the two of them. He couldn't imagine doing something like that—not even for his kids, let alone a woman. Especially the women he'd married. He could see no upside. And the downside was unthinkable.

He repressed a shudder. To be whisked away to some unknown place, never to be seen again . . . the idea of risking that—*embracing* it—for someone else was beyond him . . .

What planet were these two from?

Again those feelings of longing and envy he'd experienced in B. B. King's. Their devotion to each other . . . the way Jack hadn't hesitated, not for a heartbeat, to place himself between Gia and the Lilitongue. He'd given it no more thought than slapping a mosquito he'd spotted on her arm.

Tom shook his head. Inconceivable . . .

And then he thought of something else: Who would do that for *him?*

Vicky had Gia, and Gia had Jack. But Tom could think of no one who'd step up like that for him.

The realization staggered him.

No one . . . I've got no one.

That chill angst washed over him as it had last night. Was there one person in this world who gave a damn if he lived or died?

Surely not his brother. He glanced Jack's way and saw him glaring over Gia's quaking shoulder.

He heard Gia moan, "What did we ever do to deserve this?"

Tom knew the terrible answer: I came into your lives.

All his fault. He'd brought the Lilitongue up from the depths. He'd been the one who wanted to escape . . .

Tom felt himself wilting under Jack's stare. What did the man want?

He doesn't expect me to step up and take it from him, does he? Is he crazy?

Never happen. Not in a million years.

Even if Jack weren't here, even if Gia had no Jack in her life, Tom knew that he couldn't, simply couldn't, do what Jack had done.

He was made of different stuff. Wired differently.

He fought the burning shame. No one had the right . . . it wasn't fair to expect that.

He shook his head and turned away. No . . . too frightening . . . he can't . . . he won't . . .

He opened the door and let himself out. He stood on the front step and blinked in the wind. He pulled his jacket tightly around him. Cold out here, but warmer than inside.

Safer too. At least here Gia couldn't turn to him with a pleading look, asking him to save the father of her baby, to do the right thing.

And when he shook his head and backed away, as he most certainly would, her expression would change, and she'd look on him as a coward.

I'm *not* a coward. I've done things, *lots* of things that require balls the size of cantaloupes.

I just can't . . . do . . . this.

He felt a sadness descend on him. And something more . . . an odd feeling . . . an emotion he hadn't experienced in years.

Guilt.

But that wasn't enough, not nearly enough to make him turn and go back in there.

6

Jack forced himself to look on the bright side: The *shmegege* was gone. And Vicky hadn't heard any of this.

On the dark side, his back itched and burned. He didn't have to look to know why.

Gia tightened her python grip on him.

"Jack, Jack, Jack—what are we going to do?"

His gut roiled with fear . . . of the unknown, of being taken from everything he knew, everyone he loved.

"Keep looking for a solution."

But not much time left.

He glanced at the old Regulator clock on the kitchen wall: a couple of minutes to eleven. Less than two days.

He squeezed his eyes shut. Jesus. They'd already been through most of the *Compendium*. The odds of finding something else in there looked low to nil.

"I don't know what I'll do without you."

"Let's not write me off just yet. We don't even know if this thing will live up to its press."

She lifted her head off his chest and looked him in the eye.

"You're not serious!"

"Well, it's who knows how old. Maybe over the centuries it's had some internal breakdown and won't be able to, you know, take me away."

Jack didn't believe a word of it. And neither, apparently, did Gia. She scowled at him.

"You're kidding, right? It sits in midair and can't be moved. It leaves a mark, a Stain, just like the book says.

Oh, it's working all right. It's working just fine!" She closed her eyes as another sob shook her. "I don't want to lose you!"

Jack took hold of her upper arms and stared into her eyes.

"You won't. If we can't find a way out of this, and it takes me somewhere—I'll get back. Wherever that thing takes me, I'll find a way back to you."

"But what if it takes you somewhere else, someplace too far away . . . some *other* place you can't get back from?"

Jack knew what she meant: What if the Lilitongue transported the escapee to the Otherness? To where his life expectancy would be calibrated in nanoseconds.

Gia had her arms around him again.

"Why'd this have to happen? *Why?*"

The first words that leaped to his lips were, *Because of my goddamn brother.* But he bit them back when he realized that the recent string of incidents had not begun with Tom. It had begun with Dad's death. And a terrorist plot had preceded that.

Massacre . . . Joey hadn't returned his call . . . with all that had been happening, he'd forgotten about Joey.

"Who knows? Maybe Tom will steal the Stain from me."

She looked at him, shock on her face.

"What?"

"Only kidding."

"Didn't you read the coda to the recipe?"

Something in her tone . . .

"No. What—?"

She turned to the kitchen table. The *Compendium* was open to the Stain recipe. She ran a finger down the page and stopped.

"Read that."

Jack leaned over the book.

" '*The Stain may be taken by yet another, but none shall take it from him. The third Stained is the last Stained.*' "

Jack closed his eyes. That shut the door.

No. He wouldn't, couldn't, buy that. And he couldn't let Gia think he did.

"So they say," he said with more bravado than he felt. "This Lilitongue thing was made by a man, it can be unmade by another man. And I intend to be that man."

"Jack—"

He pressed a finger against her lips.

"Here's what we do. You finish reading the rest of the *Compendium*."

"And you?"

"I'm going to get some tools."

He went upstairs for another look at the thing and found it gone.

He knew where to find it.

7

-42:17

Jack stood in his bedroom before the floating Lilitongue and shoved a magazine into the grip of the Glock.

Why bedrooms? he wondered. Maybe because your scent was strongest there.

He pointed the Glock at the thing.

First he'd tried an ax. N-G. Did no more damage than the baseball bat. Not even a dent.

Next he'd fitted an electric drill with a diamond-tipped bit. Might as well have been trying to puncture steel with a pretzel stick. The drill whined and wailed as the tip slipped and slid all over the surface without leaving so much as a scratch.

How could something that felt like rough skin or old leather be so tough?

Well, he'd see how it stood up to his third and last tool: a bullet. Would have loved to hit it with a monster .454 Casull round from his Super Redhawk, but was afraid of killing someone with a ricochet. Hell, the slug might end up in Queens.

Instead he'd taken his Glock .40 out of storage—the highest caliber he had a suppressor for—and stuck a few hardball rounds in the magazine.

He had to admit he felt calmer knowing that Vicky and Gia and the baby were safe. He was in the stew now, but better he than they. He'd found himself in bad situations before. Not this bad, maybe, but hardly walks in the park. And somehow he'd always managed to find a way out. That was why he was still here.

But for how long?

He could almost feel the black ends of the Stain creeping toward each other, millimeter by millimeter.

He faced the Lilitongue and took a step back. He raised the pistol in a two-handed grip, positioning the muzzle about two feet from the Lilitongue. Worried that a direct, straight-on hit might bounce back at him, he aimed right of center and counted on a ricochet hitting the wall.

What he was really counting on was making a hole in the damn thing.

Although what he'd do with that hole once made was another question.

He took a breath and pulled the trigger. The pistol made a *phut!* and bucked in his hands. A wisp of powdered plaster puffed from a sudden ricochet hole in the wall on his right.

And the Lilitongue? Nada.

In a blind rage Jack dropped the pistol, picked up the ax, and started hacking at the Lilitongue like some sort of berserker.

Goddamn the thing!

If it were a person, or if it were alive and being controlled by someone, he could find a handle, have a chance. He could track down whoever it was and rearrange the guy's features and sundry other body parts until he gave it up. A person, no matter how sick or depraved, he could deal with, he could understand.

But this . . . this implacable, imperturbable, invulnerable, inexorably ticking bomb was indifferent, immune, just . . . *there*.

He swung at it until his arms gave out. Then, panting, sweating, he stopped, seething at his impotence.

His cell phone rang. His first impulse was to ignore it, but he answered and recognized Joey's voice.

"Jack? I got your message but was waiting to see if something panned out."

"And?"

"I think we got something. You free?"

Jack thought about that. Free? Hardly. Obviously Joey was looking to meet, but Jack was in anything but a meeting mood. Too much going on right here. But this had to do with Dad's killers. Joey wouldn't be calling about anything else.

"Depends. What've you got?"

"Got a face and a name and an address."

Jack hesitated and glanced at his watch. So little time left. And yet, if this led to Dad's killers . . .

Joey said, "Hey, if you're not interested . . ."

No way he could be not interested. If he had a chance to get his hands on the guys who murdered his father and settle that score before zero hour, he had to take it.

"Oh, I'm interested. When do you want to get together?"

"I've got my car. Where are you now?"

Jack didn't give out his address. He'd meet him in a busy public place.

"How about picking me up in front of the UN in twenty minutes?"

"UN? You ain't gonna tell me you're some kinda diplomat, are you?"

"It's my secret shame."

8

Right on time, Joey pulled up in a beat-up 1995 Grand Am. Jack slipped into the passenger seat. They shook hands and Joey roared off. He was wearing a navy blue windbreaker over a black T-shirt. He didn't look so hot. He'd lost weight, had bed head, and needed a shave. Looked like the kind of guy who'd own this car.

"Where's your Merce?"

The last time Jack had seen him he'd been getting into a sporty silver SLK roadster.

"Borrowed this for the day."

"Yeah? Why?"

"Got my reasons. But before we get into that, check out that envelope there."

Jack spotted a manila envelope between his seat and the center console. He pulled it out and dumped the contents onto his lap.

He saw a blurry black-and-white photo of a bearded man in a knit skullcap. Next came a Xerox of what looked like a page from a work visa file with a photo of a man identified as Hamad bin Tabbakh bin Sadanan Al-Kabeer.

Joey reached over and tapped the sheet. "You believe that fucking name?"

"A mouthful."

"I had it explained to me that 'bin' means 'son of.' So this fuck's first name is Hamad and his last name is El-Kabong, and he's the son of Tobacco who's the son of Santana, or whatever."

Under that lay a slip of paper with an address.

Jack stared at it. "Paterson, New Jersey? Really?"

"Yeah. Paterstine. Dune Monkey City."

"So why's this El-Kabong, as you put it, our most favored suspect?"

"Because I know a guy who sold him two Tavor-twos and a bunch of nine-millimeter hollow-points."

Jack felt a burner ignite in the base of his brain.

"Really. Who?"

"You know Benny?"

"The guy that always sounds like a bad imitation of Dick Van Dyke in *Mary Poppins*?"

"That's the one. He gave me a videotape and something with El-Kabong's prints on it. I had one of my men in blue run them for me. This is the guy who popped up."

The heat in Jack's brain jumped a hundred degrees.

"That's a slam dunk."

Joey sighed. "Not quite. He bought the Tavors last Thursday."

"Thursday? Shit, Joey. That's no good. He couldn't have used them at the airport."

"Yeah, but he could be replacing the ones he left there. Which means he's probably planning another massacre."

"You've got to get this to the feds."

Joey gave his head an emphatic shake. "Can't do that, man."

"Why the hell not? They've got tech and manpower we can't even dream of."

"No-no. Think about it: I go there I've got to tell them where I got this info. I can't give up Benny. He gave it to me 'cause he knows I'm stand up. I mention his name his ass lands in the joint. For a long, long time. No way I can do that to him."

"I still think—"

"Shit, Jack, you know the feds. Everything by the book. Take them weeks, months to move, if at all."

"Why wouldn't they move?"

"Looking for bigger fish. And you know them—always making deals. Who knows? They may let these guys walk."

The heat turned higher.

"So why show this to me if you're not going to do anything with it?"

Joey's expression took a grim turn. "Oh, but I am. And you damn fuck better believe that."

"Like what?"

"Like take a little trip to Paterstine and check out this sand nigger."

"And then what?"

He shrugged. "Play it by ear. My guy called the Paterstine cops and heard this Hamad's active in a small group called the Center for Islamic Charities. They said it's suspected of raising cash and funneling it to dune-nigger groups in Palestine. Like I give a shit what they do over there, but when they come over here and shoot my brother down like a dog . . ."

Jack noticed Joey's knuckles turning white as he gripped the steering wheel.

"All right. If they—"

"Look." Joey nodded toward the street ahead. "A fucking towel head. Think anyone mind if I run him down?"

Jack looked and recognized the distinctive peaked wrap of the turban.

"I would. He's not an Arab, he's a Sikh."

"Same difference."

"No—big difference. He's Indian. No relation at all to the guy we're after. He's on our side."

"Yeah? Well then he should damn well look it."

Jack had no response. Better not to say anything at all. Joey's blood was up and his rage encompassed anyone from anywhere in and around the Middle East. He was looking for someone to hurt and not too particular.

Jack knew the feeling, but he wasn't to the point where

he was planning to walk into a mosque and open up with an MP-5.

"Forget him for now and answer me this: If this Islamic Charities group ships money to terrorists, why's it still operating? The feds have shut down other operations like that."

"Because they're only *suspected*. No one's been able to nail them. And they're so small, no one's devoting time to them. But . . . what if this Islamic Charities place is really a cover for Wrath of Allah?"

Jack thought about that. Yeah. What if?

Joey added, "What all this comes down to, Jack, is I'm asking you want in."

Jack thought about that. Part of him still wanted to let the feds take it from here, but another part—the part boiling on the rear burner in his brain—screamed for blood.

As much as he wanted to spend all the time he had left with Gia and Vicky, he had to devote *some* time to this thing. If this Hamad Al-Kabeer had anything to do with Dad's death, then Jack wanted to settle with him before he went wherever he was going.

"All right. I'm in. But I want a little more than what we have."

"That's why we're headed for Paterstine."

"Now?"

"We can be at the GW in a few minutes, and after that it's into the wilds of darkest New Jersey."

"Step on it then. I don't have a lot of time."

9

They'd found Al-Kabeer's apartment house—a battered three-story brick-front building—and had driven by without stopping. Then they found the Center for Islamic Charities—a storefront space with curtained windows on a tattered commercial block—and circled it about a dozen times before parking half a block down and across the street.

"Now you know why I didn't bring the Merce."

Jack nodded. Crummy neighborhood. Not the kind of place two white guys in a high-ticket sportster would go unnoticed.

"He in there?"

Joey shrugged. "Don't know. But I figure we watch his house and he's already out, we sit there all day and get nothing. We wait here we got a chance to catch him coming or going."

"Double your pleasure, double your fun."

"Zackly."

Jack glanced at his watch. "I can give it two hours tops, Joey, then I've got to get back."

"C'mon, Jack. We're on a stakeout, only this time we're the cops. You can't bail out."

"No choice. If I had the time I'd sit here all day and night, but time is tight right now."

Wasn't that the truth.

Somewhere around the thirty-minute mark a bearded guy with a pleated kufi hat and a long gray jubba stepped out of the center and walked their way.

"Jesus," Joey said. "That our guy?"

Jack glanced back and forth between the man and the photos.

"Could be."

"Shit. The beards make all these fucks look the same."

Jack pointed to the visa photo, bull's-eyeing the mole on the right side of Hamad Al-Kabeer's nose.

"See that?" The guy was about even with them now, but even from across the street Jack could make the spot on his nose. "Tell me it's not the same."

A flat-finish 1911 .45 appeared in Joey's right hand. His left was reaching for the door handle.

"Let's get him."

"Whoa-whoa. He's just one guy. We want more."

Joey, grim-faced, waggled the pistol. "Oh, we'll get more. El-Kabong's gonna tell us everything we need to know."

Jack knew how Joey felt, and wouldn't have minded a little of that action for himself—*if* this was the right guy.

Jack popped open his door. "Just sit tight a sec. I'm going to see where he's going."

"What for?"

"You never know."

Jack hit the pavement and left the door closed but unlatched behind him. No use in drawing attention with a slam. He kept to the opposite side and far enough behind Al-Kabeer to stay beyond his peripheral vision.

He maintained his position for two and a half blocks until the Arab made a left turn and disappeared around a corner. If Jack's sense of direction was working, the guy looked like he was heading back to his apartment. Jack trotted to his corner and made a point of not looking left until he'd crossed.

He spotted Al-Kabeer standing midblock with a cell phone to his ear. Incoming or outgoing? Maybe incoming because he turned and started retracing his path.

Jack positioned himself directly behind him. Yeah, Al-Kabeer was headed back to the Center.

This sucked. This meant . . .

Jack had an idea.

As Al-Kabeer crossed the street half a block from the Center, Jack picked up speed to close on him. He saw Joey watching. He signaled to bring the car around. As soon as he saw Joey nod, he raced up behind Al-Kabeer and knocked him flat. Jack landed with both knees on his back, knocking the wind out of him.

As the Arab struggled for air, Jack grabbed his cell phone and rifled through the pockets of his long coat where he found another phone. He took that and snaked a wallet from a rear pocket—this needed to look like a mugging—then jumped up and ran for the car. Joey tromped the gas as soon as Jack hit the passenger seat and the Ponti squealed down the street.

A few quick turns and they hit the on ramp to 80 East.

"Remind me not to get you pissed at me, all right?"

"Why?"

"Shit, you move fast. That's what I call kicking ass. One second you're behind him, next second you're on top of him, third second you're in the car."

It hadn't been that fast.

"Didn't want him to see me, and definitely didn't want any of his pals coming to help."

"What'd you get?"

Jack flipped through the wallet. Found a couple of credit cards in Al-Kabeer's name, half a dozen business cards, and forty-two bucks. But Jack found the phones more interesting. The first—the one he'd been using when Jack hit him—was a standard Verizon model. The second, however . . .

"How about that? A prepaid phone."

Just like mine.

Joey glanced at it. "So?"

"No contract, no credit check, no name connected to

the number. So why's he got a regular phone plus one that leaves him anonymous."

Joey's grin would have made a shark wince. "So he can't be traced when he calls his fellow dune coons."

"We need a way to see who he's been calling on this."

"No prob."

Jack looked at him. "You've got an in?"

"Hey, Frankie and me, we used to hawk cell phone licenses. I got *tons* of connections. We'll get those numbers."

"Great. But make it fast."

Make it very fast.

"And one more thing," Jack said. "I need you to take me on a quick detour."

10

-39:51

"Wait here. I'll only be a minute."

Joey nodded and reached for the radio. As Jack walked away he recognized the unmistakable sound of Mad Dog Russo's voice on WFAN.

Joey had groused a little about swinging through Astoria, but they'd hit no backups on the Cross-Bronx or the Triboro and made decent time. Jack had the photos of Al-Kabeer in hand as he stepped up on the front porch of Menelaus Manor. He'd called Lyle from the car to make sure he wouldn't be interrupting a séance.

"Hey, Jack," Lyle said as he opened the door. "Charlie's been waiting for you. Want a beer?"

Jack's impulse was to refuse, then he figured, Why not?

A few minutes later he and a Heineken keg can entered the channeling room.

"Hello, Charlie," he said as he handed Lyle the photos. "I need a favor."

Lyle nodded as he took them. "Charlie says if it's at all in his power, you've got it."

Once again, that odd feeling rippled over his skin: I'm talking to a dead man.

"Thanks, Charlie. Take a look at that guy in the photos. His name is Hamad Al-Kabeer. Can you tell me anything about him?"

Lyle's ebony face broke into a grin. "I'll go first: He's an Arab."

Jack had to smile. "Gotta hand it to you, Lyle. Nothing gets past you."

The grin faded. "Charlie says you look strange."

"Well, I've had better days."

"No, he says he can't see you clearly." He paused, listening. "He says your edges are blurry and you seem to be . . . transparent."

Jack's gut tightened. Was it starting already? Was that how it would happen? A slow fade instead of a simple evaporation?

He looked at his hands. They looked as solid as ever. But Charlie saw the world through different eyes. Was he now seeing Jack's future?

"Long story," Jack said. "What about our Arab friend there?"

Lyle listened, then, "Charlie says he's got blood on his hands."

Jack stiffened as an electric jolt sizzled through him. "Whose?"

"You think he might be involved in your father's . . . ?"

"Possibly."

Lyle stayed silent a moment, then, "Charlie says he can't tell whose blood, just that it's not his own."

Jack sat in silence. One more nail in the coffin of Hamad Al-Kabeer. He just wished it wasn't all so damn circumstantial. He wanted something more concrete before he ripped the guy in half.

And if Al-Kabeer had been a part of it—didn't matter if he was the shooter or just a planner—tearing him up was too easy. He needed something worse than just death. But what? If Jack had the time, he knew he'd come up with something. But time was in short supply.

Time . . .

He straightened in his chair.

Lyle looked at him. "What?"

"Just had an idea."

"Care to share?"

"Not yet. Need to work out the details . . ."

Yeah. Many details.

Jack stepped out of Menelaus Manor in higher spirits than when he'd arrived, but not much. He squinted. The rooftops of the houses across the street flared with a corona effect from the lowering sun behind them.

. . . *your edges are blurry and you seem to be . . . transparent . . .*

Jack shivered in the twilight, and not because of the icy wind.

11

-39:17

A pale ghost of the nearly full moon rode the twilight as Jack stood outside Gia's front step and knocked. He wondered if there'd be a moon or even a sun where he was going. He swore that if he somehow managed to extricate himself from this mess he'd never again take this sort of everyday beauty for granted.

Gia opened the door. Her eyes widened when she saw him.

"Where have you been?"

"Here and there."

"But you were gone so long! You said you'd only be an hour!"

"I know. Things got complicated."

"I was getting worried."

"Can I spend the night?"

Gia burst into tears.

Jack said, "Is that a no?"

She grabbed him and pulled him into the foyer where they clinched.

She sobbed against his chest. "I can't lose you!"

"Well, I'm not gone yet. The lady in the size-forty dress hasn't started her song yet."

Jack didn't know if his half-formed plan had any chance of working, but if it did, she'd never sing.

At least not Jack's tune.

12

-33:22

Tom watched the guy step out of the bodega doorway and approach the cab. When he recognized Tom he flashed his Leon Spinks smile.

After last night's uptown sortie, Kamal had offered his cell number. He said Tom could call anytime, and if he was on duty—which was most of the time—he would take Tom back to the bodega.

Tom was glad he'd taken the little slip of paper. He'd dug it out of his pants pocket and made the call.

After being all but kicked out of Gia's this morning, he'd aimlessly wandered around the city. When he finally returned to the apartment he'd found the Lilitongue floating in Jack's bedroom. He'd closed the door. Couldn't stand to look at it.

He needed a lift. A big one.

"Lose your girlfriend again?" said the bodega man.

"Yeah, and it's got me down."

"Want me to find her again?"

"No, I think I need someone different tonight."

"I know all sort of girls. What kind you like?"

"Someone to lift my spirits. She changes her name all the time. Last time I saw her she was going by a name that began with E, but she might have changed it to something that begins with X."

"Ah, yes. I know such a one."

Tom held up a fifty. "Will this do?"

"Yes. That good for two."

"Two?"

That Spinks smile again. "Okay, since you are repeat customer, I give you three."

Tom hadn't been trying to haggle. He'd taken E a few times in the early nineties and had paid about fifty a tab. He'd liked the feeling, but not the emotional drop after the drug wore off.

As the man snatched the fifty he said, "You want else? We got other letters—A, MJ from TJ—and we got weather—snowflake and purple rain—and we got baseball, roofies, and Georgia Home Boy."

Pretty much the same patter as last night.

"Just the girl."

After that it was more déjà vu. A little talk into a two-way, then a jogging kid—different one from last night—tossing an envelope through the window.

Tom had swallowed one of the tabs before Kamal's cab reached the end of the block.

By the time they reached the Upper West Side Tom was cruising. Waves of warmth and relaxation washed over him. The African music on Kamal's radio that had bugged him on the uptown trip now sounded beautiful and perfect. Tiny bubbles swam in his vision, as if he were looking at the world through a glass of champagne.

Instead of going straight back to Jack's, he had Kamal drop him off near where Broadway cut across Columbus Avenue. As he moved through the milling crowd he felt wonderful. So *connected* to all these strangers, connected to the point where he wanted to climb atop a lamppost and shout out his love for all of them.

Jesus God, when was the last time he'd felt this good about the world, about *himself*?

War, poverty, crime, violence, terrorism all so far away. So was Jack's predicament. Even though he loved even Jack tonight—and really loved Gia—he couldn't get worked up about his impending "escape." The world, existence, were all too wonderful to allow anything really bad to happen.

Everything would be all right, everything would work out for the best.

WEDNESDAY

1

Jack tried to focus on the newspaper but the words didn't make sense. When he realized he'd been through the same paragraph three times without understanding it—and this was the *Post*—he slapped it down on Gia's kitchen table.

Less than a day until launch. For Gia's and Vicky's sakes he'd wanted to keep everything as normal as possible. Hadn't expected it to be easy, but it was proving impossible.

Especially after checking himself in the bathroom mirror this morning and seeing the ends of the Stain under his pecs . . . less than six inches apart.

Vicky barreled into the kitchen.

"Jack! What are we getting Mommy for Christmas?"

The question stunned him.

"Christmas?"

She rolled her big blue eyes. "It's on Friday, silly!"

"Jeez, that's right. Tomorrow's Christmas Eve."

With everything else going on, it had been drop-kicked from his consciousness.

His heart sank. He wouldn't be here for Christmas, wouldn't be able to lounge by the fire as he'd done last year and watch Vicky tear into her presents.

"We haven't even bought the Christmas tree yet!"

Jack cleared his thickening throat and slapped the side of his head.

"You're right! What were we thinking? Let's get right on it." He lowered his voice. "And while we're out we'll find Mommy a present too."

"Neat! Let's go!"

Jack shook his head as he watched her run to the hall closet. Vicky did everything at top speed. His throat clenched again. Christ, he was going to miss her as much as Gia.

His cell phone rang.

"Joey?"

"Yeah. How'd you know?"

"Psychic. What's up?"

"You know that pay-as-you-go phone you acquired yesterday?"

"Yeah? Learn anything?"

"Did I ever. All but four calls were local, mostly to the Center. The others were all to the city."

"Does that help us?"

"They were made at seven A.M. exactly two weeks ago today. Guess where to?"

Joey seemed to enjoy playing his guess-what-I-got? game, but Jack had no patience for it.

"Come on, Joey, spit it—" And then it dawned. That was the morning Wrath of Allah claimed credit for the massacre. "You're serious?"

"Deadly. ABC, NBC, CBS, and the *Times*. Four in a row, bing-bang-boom."

That clinched it. Some of the blood Charlie had seen on Hamad Al-Kabeer's hands was Dad's.

Instead of an explosion of murderous rage, Jack felt only crushing depression. His energy seemed to drain away, leaving him empty, mute, immobile.

Such a waste, such a futile, hollow waste of life. These fanatics murdering innocents in the name of their vain, puerile, cold-blooded god.

Jack realized that they weren't the only irrational, unreasonable force impinging on him. The Lilitongue was another.

But the Lilitongue was immune to physical force.

Not so the Wrath of Allah.

"Yo, Jack. You still there?"

"Yeah, Joey. Still here."

"For a minute there I thought we got cut off. So anyways I'm thinking of heading over to that place and, you know, bring along some exterminating equipment and maybe clean out a nest of cockroaches. Whatta y'say? You up for a little of that?"

If circumstances had been different, if the shadow of the Lilitongue hadn't been looming over him, Jack would have been more than up for a little of that. But now, with every moment so precious . . .

But then, his plan had no hope of working without his returning to Paterson. And if it did work, the hours spent there would be well worth it. He might remove both blots on his life with one move.

His spirits lifted.

"Yeah. I could get into playing Orkin man for a while. Let's just make sure we have the right bugs."

"We do."

"But I want some answers first."

"You ain't alone. I got lots of questions."

"Okay. You have floor plans of the place?"

"Uh, no."

"You put somebody out to watch it?"

A pause, then, "No. I'm handling this on my own."

Swell.

"That means we'll be going in blind."

"Yeah, but so what?" His tone turned defensive. "Look, Jack, you want to sit on the sidelines—"

"I'll be there. If I don't do it now . . ."

"You sound like you're on a clock."

Say what you might about Joey, but like all successful grifters he had a gift for reading people.

"You could say that. Pick me up? Same time, same place?"

Joey laughed. "And in the same rolling piece of junk. But let's make it later. I checked the paper. Sundown's four twenty-nine. So whyn't I pick you up around a quarter to four. That way it'll be getting dark when we show up."

Jack said, "Sounds like a—wait. Just thought of something. I can't very well stand in front of the UN with the tools of the trade."

"Not to worry, buddy. I'll put together a two-man toolbox. See you then."

Jack cut the connection and stared at the phone. Now he had to figure a way to tell Gia that he was going to leave her for a few of the hours they had left together.

2

-22:13

"Come on, Jack!" Vicky said in a stage whisper.

She stood in the hall with her coat already buttoned, raring to go.

"We can't leave without telling your mother."

"Telling your mother what?" Gia said, coming down the stairs.

She wore jeans and a navy blue wool sweater over a white T-shirt. She looked pale and haggard; dark circles rimmed her eyes.

She looked how Jack felt.

"We're going out to get a Christmas tree."

Gia stopped midstep and paled further. "Oh, God. Christmas."

Jack stared up at her. "Yeah, I know. Kind of slipped my mind too."

Gia chewed her upper lip a second, then said, "Vicky, would you do me a big favor and get my car keys from the guest room? I think I left them there."

Jack and Gia had spent the night there. Gia hadn't wanted to stay in the same room where the Lilitongue had been, and neither had Jack. They'd clung to each other in the dark, dozing for brief, fitful stretches.

"Sure."

Vicky hit the steps running as Gia reached the floor. She watched her daughter until she was out of sight, then moved close to Jack.

"I don't have any Christmas spirit," she whispered. "None. And I don't know if I can fake it."

"We've got to." Jack glanced up at the top of the stairway. "For her."

"I know, I know but . . ." Her lips trembled as her composure began to crumble. "I just don't think I can."

Jack gathered her into his arms. "You can. You're strong."

She sobbed. "I thought I was, but . . . I'm not. And how am I ever going to explain this to Vicky?"

Jack tried to steer her away from where she was going.

"Hey, do you think you could stir up another batch of that Stain oxyclean gunk for me?"

Gia pushed back and stared at him. "Why? What for?"

"On the chance I might find someone who'd be interested in escaping something."

"What something?"

Me, he wanted to say, but didn't.

"I'm working on it."

"Jack, I don't understand. Even if you find someone willing, it won't work. The Stain can be transferred only twice. You know that. The book—"

"I've never been one to believe everything I read. But I can't put it to the test without the gunk."

"I-I saved it."

"Really? Why?"

"I don't know. I guess because throwing it away would be like throwing hope out the window."

"Yeah . . . hope."

He was low on hope, and running out of time. But he had to give this a shot.

Gia said, "How are you going to find this person before . . . ?"

"Going on a little trip this afternoon."

"You're not leaving us, are you? There's so little time as is."

"Yeah, but if this works out we'll have tons of time."

"But how—?"

Vicky came bounding down the stairs.

"I can't find the keys, Mom."

Gia's smile looked forced. "Silly me. I must have left them in my coat pocket."

"Are we going, Jack?" Vicky said.

"Sure, if it's okay with your mother."

Gia opened the closet door. "I'm coming with you."

Vicky did her eye roll. "But Mah-om, we have to *buy* something."

"That's okay. You two can make a little side trip if you want, but there's no way I'm staying here alone." Her eyes bored into Jack's. "I want to spend every precious second I can with you."

Jack winked at Vicky. "You up for a little side trip, Vicks?"

She did her best to wink back. "Oh, yes!"

Jack swallowed past the sudden lump in his throat. How was he going to tell her that after tonight she'd never see him again?

3

Tom walked back toward Jack's place at an easy pace. He felt better now that he had some food under his belt. Barbecued spareribs and seafood salad from the buffet in a Korean eat-in deli. Only in New York.

Not much sleep last night. The E had kept him up into the early hours. He'd forced himself out of bed around one and it was after two by the time he'd showered and gone looking for someplace to eat.

What could he call the meal he'd just had? Breakfast? Brunch? A late dinner? An early supper? His clock was all screwed up.

The sight of men and women hurrying by with shopping bags full of wrapped gifts reminded him of how crummy the past few Christmases had been. Buying gifts, especially for the kids, was such a hassle. He didn't live with any of them and seldom saw them, so he never knew what to get them. Two years ago he'd given up and settled on gift certificates from Amazon. Let them buy whatever they wanted. Not like they appreciated anything he did for them anyway.

He hated to say it but he dreaded the occasions when he got saddled with all three kids at once. Little Tom and Nicole—offspring of Skank from Hell Number One— absolutely hated Donald, their half-brother via Skank from Hell Number Two, and Donald reciprocated with interest. What a nightmare.

Well, this Christmas they'd get nothing-nada-zip from Dear Old Dad. No Amazon certificate. Not even coal in their stockings.

Then what would the ungrateful little—

He turned onto Jack's block then and stopped as he saw the man himself trot down the steps of his brownstone. He wore a gray coverall under a brown leather jacket and had a backpack slung over his shoulder. He looked like a mechanic on his way to work.

Work . . .

Jack hadn't been exactly forthcoming about his work. Here was a chance to maybe get a clue as to what this repairman stuff was all about.

Wait. If what the *Compendium* said about the Lilitongue was correct, then Jack had less than a day left to him. Seemed unlikely he'd visit Gia dressed like that.

So what would be important enough to take him away from Gia at a time like this?

Good question. One Tom might have a chance to answer.

Well, why not? Not as if he had anything better to do with his time.

Jack hit the sidewalk and headed away from Tom. Toward Central Park.

Tom followed.

When Jack reached Central Park West he hailed a cab. As soon as one stopped, Tom hurried up to the curb to hail one of his own, all the while keeping an eye on Jack's. He breathed a little sigh of relief when he saw it stop at a red light two blocks down.

A cab screeched to a halt in front of him. He jumped in and said, "See that cab up there—the one with the plate that ends in seventy-two?"

"Yes," said the dark-skinned driver in a thickly accented voice. "You wish me to follow?"

"I wish."

"Then this is what I shall do."

And follow he did. Jack's cab picked up Broadway at Columbus Circle and followed that until it reached 42nd Street. It turned east. Jack got out where 42nd T-boned the

United Nations. He stayed on the curb, looking as if he was waiting for someone.

"Hold it here," Tom told the driver.

A few minutes later an old Grand Am pulled into the curb and Jack got in. Tom had a quick look at the driver and thought he looked familiar. Who—?

Then he remembered. Jack's scam artist friend from the morgue. Joey something.

"Okay," Tom said as the Grand Am bolted from the curb. "Now we follow *that* car."

4

-16:14

"Man, do you look beat," Joey said as Jack settled into the passenger seat. "Whatcha do, pull an all-nighter?"

"Feels like it."

Jack had retrieved his Crown Vic from the garage and driven Gia and Vicky downtown to a spot in the East Village—a former vacant lot now full of bundled trees. Pickings were slim this late in the game, but they'd found a decent one and tied it to the roof of the car.

Gia had stayed with the car while Jack took Vicky into an art supply store where she bought her mom a new set of pigment tubes.

Then it had been back to Sutton Square to put up the tree and decorate it. Jack had held Vicky up to place the star on top before hurrying back to his apartment.

The good news was that Tom hadn't been in.

Jack had donned a dark gray twill coverall, then pulled on his leather driving gloves and a navy blue knit watch cap; he packed up his Glock plus an extra set of jeans and a flannel shirt, then put on his flight jacket and headed down to the UN.

Joey said, "Decided to bring your own hardware after all?"

He was pointing to the backpack Jack had placed on the floor between his feet.

Along with his extra clothes he had a Tupperware container of the *Compendium* recipe. But how was he going to explain the gunk to Joey?

Simple: lie.

"Some extra clothes and—"

"Clothes? What for?"

"Bloodstains. This could get wet."

"Shit. I didn't think of that. What else you got?"

"A kind of truth serum I want to try on one of these guys."

"What for?"

"Oh, I don't know. See if they're the whole deal or if there's something bigger behind them."

"You mean see if they're the shooters or the handlers. That's cool." Joey smiled. "And if they're being handled, we work our way up the chain, right?"

"Right."

"Only thing I haven't figured out is how we make sure El-Kabong is in there."

"Easy," Jack said. "We call."

Jack used his Tracfone to call information, then he punched in the number.

An accented male voice answered on the third ring. "Center for Islamic Charities."

Jack tried to imitate his accent. "Yes, is Hamad Al-Kabeer there?"

"Who's calling?"

"He does not know me, but he was recommended as someone who would see to it that a charitable donation would find its way into the right hands."

"Who was it who recommended him?"

"I'd rather say so in person, if you understand."

"I understand. You are arriving here?"

"Yes, I will be in your area later today and thought I might stop in to see Mr. Kabeer."

"He'll be here, Mr. . . . ?"

"I prefer to introduce myself personally, if you understand."

"I understand."

"Good! Then I shall see you soon."

Jack cut the connection.

"He's there."

"Awright! Time to kick some burnoosed butt!"

5

-15:59

No one had answered the first ring, so Tom pushed Gia's doorbell again.

He was pissed. It had taken that damn stupid cabby all of five minutes to lose the Grand Am. When he'd resigned himself to the fact that he'd never catch up to Jack, Tom had told the cabby to drop him at Eight Sutton Square. The guy had known Sutton Place but had no idea of how to find Sutton Square. So Tom had had to direct him.

Idiot.

Tom wasn't sure why he'd given in to the impulse to come here. Best guess was that he wanted to smooth things over with Gia. He knew she was upset with him—she couldn't be anything else—and that was a weight on him. He had to make her understand.

He caught a flash of movement in the sidelight—Gia peeking to see who it was. She opened the door.

"Hello, Tom," she said, her tone as flat as her expression.

Well, no reason to have expected a big welcome.

"Hi, Gia. Since I was in the area I—"

"Jack's not here."

I know, he thought. That's why I am.

"That's okay. I really wanted to speak to you." He shivered in a gust of cold wind off the river. "Can I come in? Just for a minute?"

She said nothing as she stepped back and held the door open. As soon as it closed behind him, Tom turned and reached for Gia's hands.

She slipped them behind her back.

"What do you want, Tom?"

"I want to apologize for everything that's happened. I had no idea—"

"You did! That's why you went looking for it." Her eyes blazed, her words strained through clenched teeth. "Why couldn't you have left that thing where you found it?"

"If I'd known it would come to this, don't you think I would have?"

"I don't know what you would or wouldn't do!"

"Aw, Gia, you can't believe—"

Tears rimmed her eyes. "Do you have any idea what you've done to our lives? Not just Jack's but to Vicky's and mine?"

This was heading in the wrong direction.

"I know I—"

"You *know*? You don't have a clue! I told you that Jack is our rock! But some time around eight o'clock tomorrow morning he'll be gone!"

Her features hardened again as she jabbed her index finger against Tom's chest.

"Can you under*stand* that? Our rock will be *gone*. And all because of *you*!"

Each poke against his chest was like a knife thrust.

"Gia—"

"I don't think I have anything more to say to you, Tom.

I know you didn't mean for this to happen, but in the end it all comes back to you. You're responsible."

"Isn't there something I can do?"

She opened the door.

Tom walked out.

The frigid air on her front step felt balmy compared to the chill in Gia's foyer.

6

-15:35

They made good time to Paterson. When they reached the city limits Jack climbed into the backseat and opened the duffel Joey had brought. He gaped at the two sawed-off Browning 10-gauge pumps and suppressor-fitted 9mm Tokarevs. He ejected a cartridge from the shotgun and checked it: double-ought buck.

"Jeez, Joey! You planning on taking on an army?"

"Ya never know, Jack. I got the silencers figuring maybe we can do our work and get out without raising too much ruckus."

Were Abe here he'd be telling Joey there was no such thing as a silencer, only a suppressor. But Jack didn't correct him.

"The shotguns will sort of put a crimp in that."

"Yeah, well, they're for backup—in case we have to clear the room, y'know?"

Jack knew.

"Since you're right-handed, Joey—"

"How'd you know that?"

Jack had to think about that. He sized up a person's handedness without thinking. It had become instinct.

"I noticed. I'm right-handed too, so why don't we do it this way: I go in with a nine in my right and a shotgun in my left. You go in with a nine in your belt and a Browning at the ready."

Joey shook his head. "Uh-uh. I want the nine out—I don't get the answers I'm looking for real quick, I'm gonna spend a round or two on persuasion."

"Okay. But just stay cool."

Cool . . . Jack was anything but. He could feel his guts knotting. This headlong rush was not the way he did things. Had he the time—Christ, something like sixteen hours left, maybe less—he'd have spent days working up to this, knowing all the exits, watching the place all day so he'd know exactly how many people he'd find when he went through the door.

If they were stepping into an armed camp or, worse yet, a trap, where the Lilitongue was going to take him might be the least of his worries.

"I'm cool. But I hold the nine, okay?"

Jack repressed a sigh. This was Joey's show. He'd located these guys, set up everything. Jack had to play backup.

"Okay." He hoped he wouldn't regret it. "But remember, even if it gets ugly, I need one of them alive . . . just one."

"What—? Oh yeah. Your truth serum."

As they waited for the sun to set they cruised the area—with the windows cracked to let out Joey's smoke—and discussed some strategy: who'd go in first, the sequence of events as they wanted them to go down, things they'd say, questions they'd ask.

"Let me do the talking," Joey said. "At least most of it. I got things to say to these shits. I got a *lot* to say. And hey, I know you run a game now and then, but for me it's in the blood. I come from a family of talkers. We can talk our way into a gal's bed as fast as we can talk our way into a guy's bank account. I can get 'em saying what we need to know."

Jack couldn't argue. He'd done his share of persuading—lots of ways to persuade—but he'd never considered himself much of a talker.

"Okay. But don't go Fidel on me."

"Castro?"

"Yeah. I've heard that his *shorter* speeches run a couple-three hours."

Joey laughed. "Okay. No Fidel and no Crazy Joey. I'm going the divide-and-conquer route, Jack. In no time at all I'll have them pointing fingers at each other. And then we'll know our next step."

7

-15:21

Shortly after the sun dipped below the horizon, Joey turned onto the block of the Center for Islamic Charities. Jack scanned the twilit sidewalks. Not much happening. Of course, in a largely Muslim neighborhood, not too many would be worried about having fewer than two shopping days till Christmas.

Joey found a parking space near the front of the Center. Jack slipped out of his leather jacket. He pulled his watch cap low and the collar of his coveralls high, hunching his shoulders to hide as much of his face as possible.

"Pop the trunk, will you?"

As Joey complied, Jack stepped out with one of the Tokarevs in his belt and the shotgun under his jacket.

He did another sidewalk scan while Joey turned off the car, grabbed his weapons, and stepped out. Only one man in sight, down at the corner to the right. As Jack watched he stepped off the curb and walked away.

Jack held the sawed-off tight against his thigh as he dropped the leather jacket into the trunk, then stepped onto the curb. Joey came around and joined him.

"Case anything happens, the keys are under the front seat."

"Nothing's going to happen."

Joey grinned. "Lots gonna happen. Ready?"

Jack nodded. He still wished they'd had more time to plan, but this was all he had. He'd been handed a lemon, so . . .

They crossed the sidewalk, Joey going first to open the door. They stepped through as one, Jack so close on his tail they could have been Siamese twins.

Rug-draped walls, bare floor. Rickety chairs, battered desks and tables that looked like secondhand rejects. And five bearded wonders—four sitting, one standing—talking, reading, or drinking coffee from little cups. Three wore robes, two long coats, all wore headgear of some sort—kufis or skullcaps, some beaded, some open-weave knit. Not a turban in sight.

As planned, Jack and Joey split to flank the doorway. As Jack kicked it shut and pointed his sawed-off at the occupants, Joey began shouting and waving his pistol.

"All right! FBI! Everybody! Hands in the air!"

Shocked faces, wide startled eyes as three of the sitters jumped to their feet, hands in the air. The fourth stayed where he was, didn't raise his hands, and didn't look frightened.

"You are not FBI," he said.

Jack saw the bruise on his cheek and recognized him: Hamad Al-Kabeer.

An icy wave of rage washed away all doubt and some of Jack's sanity as he recognized something else.

The voice . . . here was the gloating voice he'd listened to almost every day for over a week.

We are the Wrath of Allah, fedayeen in the war against the Crusader-Jewish alliance. We have struck and we will strike again, until all the enemies of God and helpers of Satan are cleansed from the face of Allah's earth. This is but the beginning.

He felt his arms start to lift the Browning, his finger tighten on the Browning's trigger. One blast of double-ought . . . reduce his head to red mist . . .

No. Not yet. After we find out who's behind them, *then* Al-Kabeer goes.

"Not FBI?" Joey flashed his shark smile. "Really? What makes you think that?"

"You do not have the jackets or the vests. You are fakes. Get out!"

"You forgot to mention one other thing: The FBI don't carry silenced pistols." He pointed it at Hamad. "Can you guess why this is silenced?"

The pistol jumped and made a *phut!* sound. Al-Kabeer fell out of the chair, screaming as he clutched his left leg.

Jack couldn't imagine a sweeter sound.

Joey's voice went cold. "So I can do that whenever I want."

The four remaining upright began shouting in panic, waving their hands, pleading.

As much as Jack wanted to start pulling his own trigger, he forced himself to stick to the plan. But the situation could head south fast if he didn't slap the reins on Joey.

"Everyone be cool," Jack shouted, waving the shotgun at them. He lowered his voice and said, "You too, Joey."

"Yeah-yeah. Okay." He raised his voice. "Just cooperate and this will all be over real quick. Give me any lip and you'll end up like El-Kabong there."

"Down on the floor!" Jack said. "Face down, arms out."

"Yeah. Like you're praying to your candy-assed god. You do it, what, ten times a day, right? So you should know the position."

Jack thought it was more like five times a day. Or maybe six. Didn't matter. Why was he thinking about it?

He watched their hands as they stretched themselves

out on the wooden floor. Anyone who made a move toward a pocket or a waistband . . .

But everyone did as they were told. When they were all stretched out—the bleeding Al-Kabeer too—Joey nodded to Jack and made his way to the rear of the space.

Okay. Back on target: The plan had been to get everyone onto the floor immediately, then check the back rooms. Jack hadn't seen a floor plan, didn't know how deep the space was, and so he was only guessing that back rooms existed.

Only one door visible in the rear wall. Out of the corner of his eye he saw Joey go through in a crouch, his pistol ahead of him. Jack kept the shotgun moving, back and forth, holding his breath as he waited for a burst of gunfire, a scream of pain. He heard doors opening and slamming shut—one . . . two . . . three . . .

And then Joey returned carrying a pair of machine pistols.

"Well, well, well. Look what I found. A couple of Tavor-twos. Imagine that."

Jack felt a fresh surge of rage.

Joey moved toward the five prone men. "So this is Wrath of Allah. What a sorry bunch of fucks you are. If this is all Allah's got going for him, he's in deep shit." He kicked the nearest Arab in the ribs. "What was the Wrath's next target? A nursery school? An old-age home?" He kicked harder as the words strained through his clenched teeth. "Huh? Huh?"

"Please!" the man wailed. "We have done nothing!"

"Yeah?" He waved the Tavor. "Then what are these here for? Paperweights?" He stepped over to another and kicked him. "Which one of you did the shooting? Huh? Which one of you raghead fucks killed my brother?"

A man on the opposite end began a panicked wail. "We did nothing! It wasn't us!"

"Really?" Jack said. "We have your pal Hamad's phone records. We have a tape of his call to the papers to brag about his brave deed."

One of the men screamed something at Al-Kabeer in Arabic.

Al-Kabeer cried out, "That was only because no one had taken credit! We decided we would. It is a made-up name!"

Joey lifted the Tavors again. "And these are just made-up machine pistols, I guess?"

As they all started to babble at once, Joey shot another in the leg. That shut them up. Except for the moans of the wounded, all became quiet.

Joey began pacing back and forth before them.

"Here's how it's gonna go down: You're all gonna die."

More panicked wails.

"Not all," Jack said in a low voice.

Joey stopped, glanced at him, and smiled. "*All*. But one will go a little later than the others." Then he started pacing again. "Shut up, you shits! The only reason I'm telling you this is so you can feel what my brother and my friend's father felt when they saw two of you mowing everybody down . . . how they felt when the barrels pointed their way."

More wails of, "We didn't do it!"

"Shut *up*, goddamn it! Here's what you've got to look forward to. Me and my friend, we kill the five of you quick and easy. Me, I'd like to take a whole day with each of you, experimenting, seeing who takes the longest to die. Lucky for you that's just a dream. But listen up. Here's the really cool part. After you're dead I'm gonna cut off your dicks and feed them to the pigs on a certain farm I know in South Jersey."

More wails, but some sobs and tears too.

Jack cleared his throat. When Joey glanced his way he shot him a questioning look. This hadn't been in the plan.

Joey winked and said, "Stay with me. I know what I'm doing."

Jack had to trust him on that. Joey had made a very good living via his glib tongue.

He nodded but said, "Hurry it up."

Joey returned to his pacing and preaching.

"And what do you think Allah will say when you arrive in heaven without your dicks? No virgins for you. And when he finds out that your dicks have been turned into bacon, or baby-back ribs, he's gonna be pissed. He'll kick your hairy asses out of heaven and into hell. Who knows? Maybe he'll invite the pigs to take your places."

They wailed louder.

Joey's pacing repeatedly put him between Jack and their prisoners. Jack wanted to tell him that was a bad idea, but Joey was on a roll and had worked up a head of steam.

"And when your dickless bodies are found I'm gonna call the papers and tell them it was the work of the Wrath of Guido."

He laughed and turned to Jack. "Pretty good, huh? Just made that one up on the spot."

"No Fidel—remember?"

"Just let me finish." He turned back to the sobbing Arabs. "But there's a way one of you—and only one of you—can avoid this fate worse than death. And that's to identify the two shooters and tell us who's behind Wrath of Allah. Because I know there's got to be more to this than you losers."

Jack had been thinking the same thing. He so wanted those answers.

The guy on the far left rose to his knees and jabbered in Arabic as he pointed to Al-Kabeer. Al-Kabeer made no reply.

Joey put a bullet into the floor next to the speaker.

"English! None of this dune-nigger speak!"

The guy kept pointing at Al-Kabeer. "It was Hamad! It was his idea! It's all his fault!"

Al-Kabeer lifted his head and shouted a single Arabic word.

"No! I will not be silent!" The Arab turned back to Joey. "I warned him, I warned them all that this would bring the enemy to our door, but they wouldn't listen."

Back to Al-Kabeer. "Now see what you've done. You are to blame for whatever happens to us!"

"Our old friend El-Kabong, eh?" Joey said. "Now we're getting somewhere. What've you got to say for yourself?"

Slowly, painfully, Al-Kabeer began to rise.

Joey raised his pistol. "Easy . . ."

"I would speak."

Jack kept a closer eye on the rest as Al-Kabeer rose and stood awkwardly, favoring his bloody left leg.

"All right," Joey said. "What was your part in this? Who were the shooters?"

Al-Kabeer sneered. "I do not answer to you, only to Allah. I only wish there had been more than two heroes. I wish there had been dozens of them running through the whole of the airport killing everyone in sight. I wish they had killed hundreds, thousands. I wish such a fate on every infidel in this stinking manure pile of a country."

Joey took a bead on Al-Kabeer's face. "And I wish the same about you dune niggers. Consider this a start."

"One more thing," Al-Kabeer said, looking Joey straight in the eye. "May cancerous swine devour your whore of a mother and shit her out on the grave of your illegitimate brother."

Phut! Phut!

Joey's first shot went wide but the second caught Al-Kabeer in the neck. He fell backward and lay writhing and kicking as he clutched his throat.

And then a screaming bearded man stormed into the room through the rear door, firing a pistol as he ran. Joey was between Jack and the attacker. He must have caught one because he crashed back into Jack. As Joey went down Jack whipped the shotgun around and fired. A deafening boom shocked his eardrums as the double-ought blew open the newcomer's chest. Pumping a new cartridge, Jack swiveled to find the three unwounded Arabs charging him, their eyes on the Tavors that had slipped from Joey's grasp.

A shot rang out and one of the three screamed and doubled over, clutching his abdomen. Joey was down but not out. Jack's second blast tore into the remaining pair as they charged, shoulder to shoulder. He'd aimed off center so that the one on the right would take the brunt of the buck—he had plans for his buddy—but the sawed-off's short, unchoked barrel allowed too wide a pattern. Both went down.

Jack looked around. Last man standing.

Shit! This wasn't how it was supposed to be.

He knelt beside Joey. He looked like hell—white face, shallow, stuttering breaths. His bluish lips moved. Jack could barely hear him through the whine in his ears.

"Looks like I fucked up."

Yeah, he sure as hell had. But Jack didn't belabor it. The poor guy was paying the price of his rushed search.

He slipped his arms under Joey and lifted him.

"Let's get you out of here."

Jack did a quick scan as he stepped through the door and onto the sidewalk. Nobody near enough to matter. He carried Joey to the car, eased him into the passenger seat, then hurried back inside. A quick check of the Arabs yielded one survivor: Al-Kabeer, moaning and writhing as he clutched his bloody throat.

Perfect.

Jack hauled him out to the car and dumped him on the backseat.

Now he did a careful scan. Spotted a couple of people to his left approaching cautiously along the sidewalk, another to his right running down the middle of the street.

Jack pulled his Glock, turned, and fired three shots back through the open door at the Center's rear wall. That seemed to discourage the curious—two threw themselves flat and the third made a quick U-turn and booked.

Jack ran around the car, jumped behind the wheel, fished the keys from under the seat, and did some booking himself.

8

Joey didn't make it.

After racing toward Interstate 80, Jack turned just before the on ramp and cruised local streets at the speed limit. He wound through neighborhoods of clapboard two-family homes and rundown apartment houses, heading generally east, talking nonstop to Joey as he looked for a hospital, or at least one of those blue signs with the white *H*.

Finally he found one, pointing left. As he stopped at a red light, he leaned over and grabbed Joey's shoulder.

"Almost there, buddy."

Joey made no reply, but then he'd done little more than grunt now and then during the ride.

He was too badly hurt for Doc Hargus, so Jack's plan was to carry him into the first ER he found and give a story about finding him on the street. As soon as Joey was under medical care, Jack would disappear.

But Joey looked awfully still right now.

He shook him. "Joey?"

"We fucked up, Jack," he said in a voice like a mouse scratching a wall.

Yeah, we did.

"It's okay, Joey."

Jack saw his lips moving and leaned closer to hear.

"Ain't okay, Jack. We didn't get them."

"We did. The only survivor is in the backseat."

"No. I been *stunad*. It wasn't them."

Jack felt his gut go cold.

"What're you saying?"

"It's bigger than them. Something else going on."

"How can you know that? What makes you think—?"

"You know stuff when you're dead."

And then he fell silent.

Jack shook him again.

"Joey?"

Joey slumped further in his seat, then slid off. His head banged the dashboard.

"Oh, shit!"

Jack rotated Joey's face toward him. His skin felt cold. And even in this faint light the slack features and staring eyes left no doubt. Now old Frank Castellano had no sons.

"Aw, Joey," Jack said. "Dammit, I knew this was a bad idea."

An aching, stifling melancholy enveloped him. Such a waste . . . the airport, the Arabs, Joey . . . senseless. The futility of it all hammered at him, and he felt himself bend beneath the blows.

If only circumstances had been different . . . with just a little more time he could have reined Joey in and come up with a good plan. But there'd been *no* time. Because of the Lilitongue. And the Lilitongue was here because Tom had tricked him into looking for it, had pulled it from its resting place, had brought it into Jack's home.

Joey's death . . . one more thing to park on his brother. That and—

Al-Kabeer! Christ, had he kicked too?

Jack leaned over the back rest and poked Allah's courageous warrior. He stirred and moaned.

A horn blared behind him. He looked up and saw the light had changed. He ditched the left turn and kept heading east.

Eventually he came to a river. He didn't know its name. The Hackensack? The Passaic? Wasn't sure what town or even what county he was in. To the south he could see a highway arching high over the water. Probably Route 80.

With his lights out he eased down to the littered bank

and bounced through the thick underbrush until he found a clear spot under the span. He parked, turned off the engine, and sat.

Here it was: the do-or-die moment. Somehow he had to smooth-talk the murdering oxygen waster in the backseat into wanting the Stain, into taking the Stain.

If that was possible.

Worry about that later. First he had to snow Al-Kabeer. He wished he had Joey's gift. Joey would have had people lined up and *paying* for a chance to grab the Stain for themselves.

Jack took a breath, let it out, then pulled the backpack from under Joey's limp legs. He got out and opened the rear door. The overhead courtesy light revealed a very bloody Al-Kabeer curled into the fetal position, clutching his bleeding throat.

Besides calling the papers, he wondered, what was your part in this? He wanted to scream it, but held back. What were you? Were you the man who shot my father with lead and cyanide? Or were you a planner? Or maybe a money man?

Al-Kabeer groaned in a hoarse voice, "Take me to a hospital."

Fat chance.

Jack noticed the blood flecking his lips and dribbling onto his beard. Not much time left. Better move this along.

Jack kept his voice soft, sympathetic, almost friendly. Not easy.

"All in good time, my friend."

"*Allaabu Akbar.*"

"If you say so. Listen, Hamad. Here's the situation: The doctors may be able to save you, but even if they do, what then? You're still going to be hurting for days. And after that you're going to have to answer all sorts of questions, and if you haven't got good answers, you're going to land in the pokey."

He looked up at Jack, a plea in his eyes. "You won't . . . you won't sever my manhood and feed it to a pig? Please, no."

"I won't." Truth. Jack wanted no part of that. It had been Joey's riff, to put a little fear of Allah in them. At least Jack assumed it was. "But that other man—"

"No! Please!"

"He's not here now. But if he comes back I may not be able to stop him."

Hamad closed his eyes and whispered, *"Allaabu Akbar."*

Jack unzipped the backpack and removed the Tupperware container. Then he unbuttoned his coverall and slipped out down to his waist. An icy gust clawed his back.

Christ, it was cold. Another reason to hurry this along.

"But there is a way for you to escape—not just him, but also escape your pain, and escape the police and the federal agents who will be hounding you."

He pointed to the black band all but encircling his chest. The ends of the Stain were less than two inches apart. He tried not to think about that.

"See this, Hamad? This is the mark of Allah—"

"Allaabu Akbar."

"—and it has special powers. It will help you escape all enemies. Forever."

Jack opened the container and grabbed one of Hamad's bloody hands. He dipped it into the Stain remover, then pressed the dripping fingers against the blackened band on his chest. The hand felt cold.

"All you've got to do now is wish, Hamad. Wish to take the Mark of Allah for yourself."

His voice was a scrape, a rustle. "You are not of Islam."

"I'm a secret special agent of Islam. Undercover. I pretend to be an infidel, but I'm really on Allah's side."

"No . . ."

"It's true. The Mark of Allah was given to me many years ago by the Ayatollah Khomeini himself, to save me in an hour of direst need, and now I'm giving it to you. All you have to do is wish for it, Hamad. You want to be safe from your enemies, don't you. Sure you do. This is guaranteed to work. Trust me on this, Hamad. I'm telling you the truth. All you need do is wish."

Al-Kabeer squinted up at him, as if trying to focus.

"This is true?"

"The truest. Go ahead. Wish. You have nothing to lose and everything to gain. Just say it: I wish the mark for myself."

The Arab coughed, spraying Jack with blood. He swallowed, then whispered, "I wish the mark for myself."

Jack closed his eyes, took a breath, then looked down at his chest.

No change. The Stain was still there.

Shit.

"Try it again, Hamad. Maybe you didn't wish hard e—"

Jack sensed a sudden loss of muscle tone in the hand. It had been slack all along, but this was different.

"Hamad?" He shook him. "Come on, Hamad. Stay with me. Don't crap out on me now."

Jack grabbed his beard and lifted his head.

Dead dark eyes stared back at him.

"No!" Jack shook him. Hamad moved like an over-sized rag doll. "No-no-no!"

He threw him back, jumped up, and kicked the Grand Am's fender.

"Goddamn it to hell! *Shit!*"

He kicked the Grand Am again, then stumbled around in a circle wanting to scream his anger and frustration at the night. This had been his last chance. The book was right. He was stuck with the Stain.

He felt as if fate—or something—was plotting against him. Was this all part of a plan? He tried to repress the paranoia that this whole situation was a setup. His father's death, Tom's intrusion into his life, the Lilitongue, the Stain . . . had they all been part of some elaborate plan to take him out of the picture?

Was the Otherness after him?

If not, then who? Or what?

He finished his war dance of kicking the car, kicking stones, kicking at the underbrush, then stood panting, his breath streaming in the cold air. He was bare to the waist but didn't care. Being cold was the least of his worries.

What now? What was he going to do with Joey?

And how was he going to get home? Couldn't drive—after the Center shootout every cop in North Jersey would be on the lookout for an old Grand Am. Especially at the bridges and tunnels. Sure as hell couldn't walk. Couldn't even hitchhike—sure way to get stopped and asked a lot of questions he couldn't answer.

He *had* to get home. Every minute here was a minute subtracted from his time with Gia and Vicky.

Have to do what he'd done at La Guardia: Call Abe.

He looked up at the rumbling roadway overhead. But first he'd have to find out where he was.

He stripped off the bloody coverall and replaced it with the flannel shirt and jeans. He popped the trunk, removed his leather jacket, shrugged into it.

Then he began the steep climb up to the highway, fighting his way through the brush and a thicket of ailanthus trunks.

At the top he crouched behind the guardrail and looked around. Ten feet away he spotted a big red 80 on a blue background.

Okay. He'd figured that. Now . . . *where* on 80?

Traffic wasn't heavy so he risked standing during a gap and looking around. About a quarter mile ahead he saw a green-and-white sign for Exit 60.

Okay.

He crouched again, pulled out his Tracfone, and punched Abe's number.

"Isher Sports," said a bored voice.

"Abe, it's me and I need a ride."

"Another ride you need? What happened this time?"

"I'll explain it all when you get here."

"And this 'here' is where?"

"Jersey."

"*Gevalt!* You want I should leave civilization and venture into the hinterlands just because your car breaks down?"

With effort Jack stifled a shout and kept his voice even. "Look, Abe. I need your help and I need it now. I haven't much time left."

"Oy, you're right. Where do I find you?"

"Go over the GW and get on Route Eighty west. When you come to exit sixty, take it and wait for me near the bottom of the ramp.

"Eighty, sixty, got it. How long this should take?"

"Thirty minutes to an hour. All depends on traffic. Call me when you hit the highway."

"The keys I'm grabbing as we speak."

"Thanks."

Jack cut the connection and started back down the slope toward the river. From the look of the traffic, at least here in Jersey, Abe would probably make good time. Which meant Jack had to hurry.

He had some things that needed doing before he fled the scene, as it were.

9

"I know you can't hear me, Joey, but I'm going to say this anyway."

Jack had carried Joey's body from the car and laid it gently on the ground in an open area maybe twenty feet away. Nobody finding the car could miss Joey. Jack had straightened the body, positioning it perpendicular to the river, feet toward the water.

He felt a gnawing guilt about leaving a fellow combatant here like this, but what could he do?

He folded Joey's arms across his chest in the classic casket pose

"Wish I could take you back with me. You know I would if I could, but it's not in the cards. So I'm leaving you here with as much dignity as I can. You always liked to look good, and this way you'll look good in the crime scene photos. Almost classy."

Except for the bloodstains, of course.

"I have to leave you here but you won't be alone for long. Don't worry about becoming a buffet for whatever animals are around. None of them will have a chance to get near you, let alone chew on you. I'll see to that."

He adjusted Joey's bloody jacket, straightened his pant legs so that the cuffs reached his ankles, then squatted next to him.

"You weren't a model citizen, Joey, but you were a good guy. The marks couldn't believe a word you said but you were always square with your friends. Brave too, risking everything to do right by your brother. You have my respect. If you hadn't been standing between me and the shooter, our places might be reversed right now."

An unbidden thought: And if you'd planned this better and been more careful searching the back rooms, we'd both be having a drink at Julio's right now. Jack pushed it away.

"I need just one thing from you."

He reached into Joey's jacket pocket and removed his butane lighter, then he rose to his feet.

"Someone will be coming for you soon."

He walked back to the Grand Am and picked up his coverall from where he'd dropped it. He used his knife to cut a three-foot strip from the leg, then tossed the rest into the car. He opened the gas tank door, unscrewed the cap, and snaked the cloth down as far as it would go. Then he pulled it out, reversed it, and snaked the other end inside. He left three or four inches of gas-soaked twill hanging from the port.

Firing the car would serve two purposes. First—destroy a lot of evidence. Jack hadn't taken his gloves off since he'd left his apartment, so he wasn't worried about prints. But trace evidence was tricky. Couldn't hurt to incinerate it.

The second was to bring the cops running so they could find Joey's body before any dogs got to it. No way Joey wouldn't be tied to the attack on the Center—Jack could already see the *Post*'s MUSLIM MASSACRE! headline—but this way his body would be returned to his family intact.

He felt his phone vibrate in his pocket: Abe.

"I'm at exit sixty-seven."

"How's the traffic?"

"I'm doing sixty-five."

"Okay. Bottom of the sixty off ramp."

"You should look for the usual vehicle."

That meant Abe's van.

"Will do. See you soon."

Jack grabbed his backpack, then pulled Joey's lighter from a pocket. He flicked it and touched the flame to the free end of the coverall strip. As fire danced up its length and into the port, Jack trotted for the incline to the highway. He was about halfway up when the tank blew. He didn't look back. He reached the top and, keeping low, followed the guardrail toward the exit ramp.

10

-13:14

"Keep an eye on them for me?"

Abe shook his head. "I can't—I *won't* believe this is happening. A joke you're pulling, right? You should be honest with your old friend who's known you since you were a *yungatsh* and tell him that you've made all this up. Listen to that old friend tell you that if this should be a joke then it's a terrible one and he'll never speak to you again."

They sat in Abe's van where he'd double-parked outside Jack's place. After a couple of fitful, abortive attempts at their usual banter, talk had died. Jack found the silence awkward. He and Abe always had something to say to each other.

"No joke, Abe."

"Must be. Has to be. A world without Repairman Jack? Feh!"

How many years since Abe had given him that name? Jack didn't bother counting. Whatever the number, it wasn't enough.

"But you will look after my ladies while I'm gone, right?"

"While you're gone—that I like. It means you're coming back."

"Count on it."

"I will. I won't sit shiva then."

Although he didn't know where he'd be going, even if it was to an alternate reality, Jack had this unreasonable conviction that he'd be able to find his way home. Of course if the Lilitongue dumped him in outer space, that would be a different story: He'd be a flash-frozen fleshsicle in a heartbeat.

"As for watching over Gia and Vicky, I'll do what I can while you're away. But the type of woman who wants or needs watching over, Gia isn't."

"I know. She's a self-starter and self-sufficient, but she isn't quite as tough as she thinks or likes people to think. So look in on them for me, okay?"

"Of course. But who's going to look in on me? Who's going to *tshepe* me about my diet and my waistline while at the very same time bringing me Krispy Kremes? Who am I going to eat breakfast with? Who's going to worry about me . . . ?"

Abe's voice trailed off.

Jack heard a sniff and turned toward him. The glow from a street lamp reflected off the moisture puddled on his lower eyelids.

"Abe?"

"*Nu*, this is why you were always *utzing* me to worry about my heart? This is why you said I should take better care of it? Just so you could break it?"

The words choked off.

Jack felt his own throat constrict. This man had helped him become what he was. It tore Jack up to see Abe this way. He grabbed a pudgy hand and squeezed.

"I'll be back. I promise."

Abe shook his head and spoke, his voice thick. "So you say, but I have a feeling this is something even Repairman Jack can't fix."

Jack didn't admit that he had the same feeling.

Abe let out a shaky sigh.

"So, you want I should drop you off at Gia's?"

"Thanks, no. I've got a little something I have to take care of here first." He squeezed Abe's hand again. "See you soon. And work on that waistline while I'm gone."

"Who can eat?"

Feeling like he'd just cut off an arm, Jack grabbed his backpack and jumped out. He slammed the door and slapped the side panel. The truck lurched into motion. He watched it move off and disappear around a corner.

Jack turned and headed up the steps.

11

-13:06

The sound of the door roused Tom from semislumber. He'd been slumped before the TV, watching the end of the six o'clock news on some local channel and just beginning to nod off when a reporter broke in and started yammering about a bunch of Islamics blown away in New Jersey—as if anyone gave a damn.

Jack walked in with a backpack over one shoulder. He looked like Tom felt.

Tom rose and stepped into the front room.

"Hey, bro. Anything new on the Lilitongue front?"

Jack shook his head and stared at him. "I haven't been able to turn up a thing. As you can see . . ."

He undid a few buttons on his plaid shirt and spread the edges. Tom repressed a gasp when he saw how close the Stain's edges had grown.

"Oh, shit."

"How about you, *bro*?" Jack said, putting an edge on the

word as he redid the buttons. "Been pounding the pavement and scouring the Internet to see how you might undo this?"

Tom knew he hadn't done shit. But then, what could he do? What could anyone do against a faceless, mindless . . . *thing*?

He pointed to the closed door to Jack's bedroom. "It's still in there. Hasn't budged." He spread his hands. "I'm as helpless as everybody else."

After a long stare Jack said, "Want to make yourself useful?"

"Sure. Anything."

"Then follow me."

First stop was the kitchen where Jack pulled a pistol and a Tupperware container from the backpack and laid them on the counter.

Tom pointed to the container. "Is that the—?"

"Stain remover? Yeah."

Feeling his brother's eyes boring into him, Tom kept his head down. Jack knew neither Tom nor anyone else could trade places with him. So why the look?

Besides, Jack was where he was by choice.

Or was he? Maybe he'd seen no choice, been unable to imagine any other course of action when the Stain moved to Gia. Just as Gia had had no choice when she'd learned she could remove the Stain from her daughter.

And Vicky had acquired the Stain because he'd brought the Lilitongue into her world.

He heard Gia's voice . . .

Why couldn't you have left that thing where you found it?

All his fault . . .

He wished he could undo it all, but what was done was done. And he'd been relieved to hear that the Stain could be taken only twice. If not, Jack would think it only right that Tom complete the circle.

Not fair. No one had the right to ask that of him or anybody else.

Jack handed him the empty backpack and a flashlight and said, "Follow me."

Tom did—straight to the closet next to the bathroom.

Taking orders, following a few feet behind . . . somewhere along the way he'd become Little Brother and Jack Big Brother. How had that happened?

When Jack opened the door a faint odor of cedar wafted out. He watched Jack kneel on the closet floor and pop a piece of molding loose from the base of its left side wall. He slid this back along the floor, then pulled on the cedar plank directly above it. When this came free he slid it back beside the molding.

"Shine that light in here."

Tom aimed the flashlight over Jack's shoulder and into the opening. He saw insulated pipes—most likely to the bathroom—but what strange insulation. It looked . . . decorated. Each pipe was festooned with little cardboard squares.

What the . . . ?

He watched Jack reach in and start plucking them from the pipes like a man picking fruit from a tree. When he'd gathered a fistful he backhanded them to Tom.

"Stick these in the front compartment of the pack."

Tom inspected them first. The paper squares had round Mylar windows front and back. And inside the windows—

Tom repressed a gasp. Coins. *Gold* coins.

He squinted at the top one. A new-looking 1925 twenty-dollar gold eagle. Next, a bright twenty-dollar Liberty head from 1907. And then a 1901 ten-dollar gold piece.

"Hey, the light," Jack said.

"Oh, yeah."

He'd been so distracted he'd let the beam drift.

Jack handed back more. Tom dropped the first batch into the pack and took the next. He knew nothing about coins but all these were old and gold and beautiful.

"Jack, are these things worth what I think they are?"

"Probably more. I've made a point of buying only top-grade stuff—MS-sixty-one or better."

"I didn't know you were a collector."

"I'm not. I'm an investor."

"But how much—?"

Jack handed back another batch.

"Are they worth? More than I paid for them, but that's all I can tell you. I don't keep a list and I don't keep up on values."

More rare coins flowing from the closet. The total value must have passed six figures already.

"How many do you have?"

Another handful came back.

"Don't really know. Like I said, I don't keep a list."

"But isn't it dangerous keeping it here in your apartment?"

"Fire's my big worry. But it's worth the risk. This way I can always get to them. Unlike your Bermuda safe-deposit box."

"Touché."

After handing back a total of a hundred or more coins, Jack said, "Okay, that's it for the numismatics. Bullion next. Put them in the rear section."

"What are you going to do with all this?"

Did he think he could take it with him?

"Giving it to Gia and Vicky. They'll need it."

"That's hard to believe, considering where she lives."

"That townhouse isn't hers. It belongs to Vicky's aunts. But they've gone away and aren't coming back. When they're finally declared dead—the waiting period's got about five and a half years to go, I believe—the place will go to Vicky."

"Where are the aunts?"

"Long story."

He began handing back deceptively heavy little cloth

bags that clinked when Tom dropped them into the backpack.

"And these are . . . ?"

"Krugers."

"Kruggerrands?"

Tom knew about those: one ounce of gold each. But each little bag must have held about twenty or so, and Jack was handing him bag after bag. With gold hovering around four hundred dollars an ounce . . .

Jesus God . . . Jack was a wealthy man.

Tom looked into the almost full backpack. With this kind of money he could disappear and stay gone. But that would be stealing from Gia. No . . . couldn't.

Finally Jack's hidey-hole was empty, its contents transferred to the backpack. Tom hefted it. Had to weigh fifty, sixty pounds. And he'd bet a lot of those numismatics were worth ten times their gold weight.

"With all this money . . . why do you keep working?"

Jack backed out of the closet.

"You wouldn't understand."

"Try me."

He shook his head. "Nah. Got to head over to Gia's. And anyway, the point, as you lawyers like to say, is moot. I'm retired as of tomorrow morning, thanks to you."

Tom had to turn away from the look in his brother's eyes.

"Jack, I've got something I need to say to—"

"Sorry. No time for chitchat." He rose and took the backpack with him. "Got to get to Gia's." That look again. "Not much time left, and guess who I'd rather spend it with."

Tom watched him shrug into his leather jacket, then stuff some videocassettes into the backpack and sling it over his shoulder. He handled the weight as if it were nothing.

"Listen to me, Jack . . . I can't believe this is happening."

"Wish I could say the same."

"If you're really . . . if this really happens, I'll make sure Gia and Vicky are—"

"Are what? Taken care of? How are you going to do that?"

"I meant, I'll look out for them."

"No need. Already covered." Jack's cold gaze froze him to the spot. "And why on earth do you think Gia would want to have anything to do with the reason I'm not around?"

His words only reinforced what Gia had told him this afternoon.

He heard the words again, saw her stricken expression, felt again the jabs against his chest as if she was poking him anew right now.

Our rock will be gone. And all because of you!

No . . . no way he could approach her again. He was anathema.

"Jack, what do you want me to do?"

"Nothing, Tom. Nothing at all. I may not like where I am but I don't expect any help from you. And if by some one-in-a-million miracle you offered it, well . . . you're the last person on earth I'd accept it from."

Tom stood still and silent, reeling.

"So long, Tom. Have a nice life."

And then he was gone, the door swinging closed behind him.

Tom blinked back sudden tears. My own brother. What have I done? What have I *done*?

12

Gia pulled him inside and wrapped her arms around him. Jack eased the backpack onto the floor and returned the hug.

"You said a couple of hours. It's been four!"

He felt terrible about that.

"I know. I'm sorry. Things got complicated."

She looked up at him. "Do I want to know?"

"Most definitely not."

She tugged him down the hall. "Vicky's starving."

A leaden weight sat where his stomach had been.

"I'm not."

"Neither am I. Every few minutes I feel like running to the bathroom and vomiting. But we've got to keep up appearances, don't you think?"

"Definitely."

"I wish you hadn't promised her Amalia's. I'd have liked to make you something."

"My last meal?"

"Don't, Jack. Please don't."

"Okay, okay. It's just . . . I don't know how to handle this."

"I do." Her lower lip trembled. "I'm going to fall apart."

He held her close a moment, then, "Where's Vicks?"

"In the kitchen."

He pointed to the sitting room. "Then let's make a quick detour."

He retrieved the backpack from the hall and carried it to the sitting room couch. He set it on the end table under the reading lamp.

"I want you to take this."

Gia held back, looking uneasy. "What is it?"

He unzipped the front compartment and spread the edges.

"Take a look."

She stepped forward and took a hesitant peek. She frowned, then her head snapped back.

"Gold coins? Why?"

"They're for you."

"But aren't they your . . . ?"

"Life savings. Yeah."

She backed away. "I don't want it."

Jack had figured she'd react like this.

"Gia, I want you to have them. I need to go away knowing you and Vicky will be taken care of."

She began to fill up. "But giving me your life savings means your life is over. I can't—"

"Hey, don't look at it that way. I just need someone to look after it while I'm gone. You know . . . till I get back."

She began crying and Jack took her in his arms.

"This can't be happening, Jack. It can't."

"Maybe it's not. Maybe eight A.M. is going to come and go without anything happening and we'll all be sitting around looking at each other and feeling stupid."

"You don't believe that."

Right. He didn't.

At least not intellectually. He'd seen the wonders of the *Compendium* and knew it was no ordinary book. And so far it had been right about everything: the Stain, how it grew, how to transfer it . . . everything. So why should it be wrong about when the two ends met?

But a deeper, nonrational part of him refused to believe that he wouldn't be here with Gia and Vicky tomorrow night.

"I can hope, can't I? But just in case it does happen, I want you to have this stuff to dip into whenever you need to . . . till I come back."

He felt her shoulders quake. He had to snap her out of this. He knew she'd keep up a front for her daughter.

"Let's round up Vicky and get down to Amalia's before she starves."

Gia broke away and wiped her eyes.

"This isn't like me."

"Well, you've never been in this kind of situation before."

"Neither have you."

Not quite true. Jack had been in situations where he hadn't known whether he'd live or die. But those had been different. In those his survival depended on his actions: Make the right move, survive; make the wrong move, gone.

But this . . . he had no moves, no choices, no decision, no wiggle room. An iron straitjacket.

"Yeah, well . . . I'm a tough guy, remember?"

Not so tough that he didn't dread dinner with Vicky tonight. Because in the next hour or two he'd have to tell her he was going away.

13

-11:23

Jack was glad he didn't have to describe his feelings as he watched Vicky work on her mussels in garlic and wine sauce. He had no words for them. And he'd never be able to get them past his locked throat anyway.

Amalia's . . . an unpretentious, eons-old, storefront restaurant in Little Italy with red-and-white-checkered tablecloths over long tables for eating family style. Mama Amalia, older than the restaurant, loved Vicky and had greeted her with the usual fanfare—two-cheek air kisses and loud proclamations of what a beautiful child she was. Gia and Jack were an afterthought as she placed them all at a table near the window. No mystery why this was Vicky's favorite.

And here she was, attacking her favorite dish.

As Jack watched her work through the huge platter, pausing only for a sip of Limonata while she arranged the empty shells into an interlocking daisy chain, he couldn't help thinking of the old Squeeze song.

He sipped a glass of Valpolicella and poked at a bowl of sautéed broccoli rabe and sausage. Gia had ordered a tricolore salad and a Limonata but had touched neither.

A night out at Amalia's had always been a festive occasion for the three of them, with *mmmm*s and *aaaah*s about the delights of this or that. But for Gia and him tonight, it might have been a funeral.

Funeral . . . got to be a better word than that.

He opened his mouth, then closed it. He glanced at Gia, saw her watching him. She reached out and squeezed his hand.

Her voice was barely audible as she cocked her head toward Vicky. "Want me to—?"

He shook his head. "I need to."

He took a deep breath.

"Hey, Vicks? I need to talk to you about something."

She didn't look up from working on a mussel that hadn't completely opened.

"Uh-huh?"

"I have to go away for a while."

Now she looked up. "Where?"

"Far away."

"Yeah, but where?"

"It's a place called Shangri-La."

It was the best he could come up with. He knew she'd never seen *Lost Horizon*, and if and when she did she'd think it was a real place.

"Is that like Tralla-La?"

That threw Jack. "Tralla—?"

"You know—in that Uncle Scrooge comic book."

Didn't she forget anything? He'd given her that over a year ago.

"Something like that."

"Where's this Shalla-La at?"

Jack had to smile. Sounded like a Van Morrison song.

"Shangri-La. It's on the other side of the world. Near China."

"Wow. How come you're going there?"

"I have to visit some people."

She went to work on another mussel.

"When are you leaving?"

Now the hard part: "Tomorrow morning."

Her face tilted up, frowning. "But that's . . . tomorrow's Christmas Eve. Are you going to miss Christmas?"

He nodded. "I'm afraid so."

Her frown deepened. "Can't you go after?"

"I wish I could." He shook his head. "You don't know how much I wish I could."

"But . . . how long you gonna be gone, Jack?"

"I'm not sure."

"A long time?"

He nodded. "Maybe."

Gia sniffed and Vicky looked at her. No way she could miss her mother's red, teary eyes. She turned back to Jack with a narrowed gaze.

"Is there another woman?"

Jack let out a guffaw. He couldn't help it. He glanced at Gia and even she was smiling.

"That's why I love you, Vicks. You never fail to surprise me."

"Well, is there?"

"No. There'll never be another woman. Your mommy is it for me. Forever and ever."

She looked at Gia. "Then why're you crying, Mom?"

"Because I'm sad to see Jack go. I don't want him to, but . . . he has to."

Vicky trapped Jack with her blue gaze. Her lower lip began to tremble.

"You're coming back, aren't you, Jack? You're coming back, right?"

Time to lie.

"Of course I'm coming back."

"When?"

"The absolute soonest I can. I swear on a stack of Bibles."

She must have sensed something because she dropped her fork and began to cry.

"Please don't leave!"

"Now listen, Vicks—"

"You're not coming back! I just know it!"

Jack froze his expression to hide his surprise.

Out of the mouths of babes . . .

14

-11:08

Tom couldn't sit still.

Twenty seconds after he'd settled himself on the couch he'd be up and pacing until he perched on the edge of a chair, only to be up and moving about half a minute later. He tried watching television—no good.

Wherever he went, Gia's voice followed him.

Do you have any idea what you've done to our lives? Not just Jack's but to Vicky's and mine?

He remembered the light in her eyes, the look on her face on the way home from the opera when she'd talked about Jack being a rock in her life. And Tom wondered . . . had anyone ever looked like that when they'd spoken of him? Had he ever been a rock in anyone's life?

Who was he kidding? No need to wonder. The answer was no.

He needed something to settle his nerves.

Jack didn't seem to drink anything but beer, and that wouldn't do it. So he hunted through the kitchen cabinets until he came upon a bottle of amber liquid.

Hey. Old Pulteney eighteen-year-old single malt. He'd have preferred vodka—ideally Grey Goose or Level—but this was all right. More than all right. When it came to scotch, Jack stocked the good stuff.

Tom poured a couple of fingers' worth into a tumbler and tossed it down. After savoring the burn, he poured himself a second dose. This he drank slowly, sipping and thinking about his life and the mess he'd made of it. He ranged over possible ways to turn things around and extricate himself, but came up empty.

By the time he'd finished his second glass he knew scotch wasn't going to do the trick. Not even close.

He needed something more potent. A lot more potent.

He dug out his wallet and found Kamal's phone number. Time for another run uptown.

Before leaving he took a peek into Jack's room.

"Oh, shit."

The Lilitongue was gone.

15

"Is she asleep?" Jack said.

Gia disengaged herself from him and leaned over Vicky, curled under a blanket at the far side of the couch.

"Uh-huh. She's out."

"Okay, I'll carry her up—"

Gia laid a hand on his arm. "Let her stay with us."

Jack nodded in the semidarkness. "I'd like that."

He'd brought along a selection of movies to have something to do other than sit and count the minutes. Classics. Films they could all watch. And, for obvious reasons, no horror.

They'd let Vicky pick the first. No surprise, she chose *King Kong* because it was the colorized version.

Like most kids her age, she'd had almost no exposure to black-and-whites and didn't like them. Except for *King Kong*. She'd cried at the end of her first viewing and for days afterward went around the house repeating in a perfect imitation of Robert Armstrong's delivery, "Oh, no, it wasn't the airplanes . . . it was *beauty* killed the beast."

That had inspired Jack to hunt down a copy of Turner's colorized version. He considered himself something of a purist when it came to movies, especially ones he liked, so the idea of tinting and tinkering with a classic offended him. But mildly. The world offered a wide array of far more important issues to get crazy about.

Yet when he watched it with Vicky he'd had to admit that it was kind of nice to see a blue ocean and a green jungle. And Vicky had loved it. What could be more important than that?

"What should we watch next?"

Gia clung to him. "Why don't we just sit here."

"We can do that. But I'd rather not feel like a condemned man waiting for the executioner to knock on the door."

"It's not going to happen," Gia said. "That's the only way I can get through tonight. Just keep telling myself it's not going to happen . . . it's not going to happen . . . and maybe if I repeat it enough times, it won't."

Jack searched for something to do, something to say to ease her pain.

"Got as good a chance as anything else."

Crummy, but the best he could come up with. She snaked her arms around him and squeezed.

"Maybe if I hold on real tight it won't be able to take you."

"Now *there's* a thought."

"How do you stay so calm?"

Calm? He wanted to scream, he wanted to break things.

"Who says I'm calm?"

"Look at you. Our lives are about to be torn apart, you're about to be taken God knows where, maybe to your death. Yet you sit here watching movies. The more disordered and crazy and desperate things get, the calmer you are. Tell me how you do that, because I want some."

I do it for you, he thought.

To help Gia keep it together. He sensed she was just barely holding on, hanging by the slimmest of threads. If he kept thinking about the two ends of the Stain snailing closer and closer together, he might fall apart. And then what would happen to Gia?

"I think that somewhere down in the deepest recess of my psyche I'm convinced I'll come through this. Don't ask me why. It's not logical. And because it's not logical, my conscious mind doesn't buy it. So the films help distract me. They make it easier for me. But if they don't make it easier for you—"

"No-no. They distract me too. What else do you have?"

"Well, I brought *Citizen Kane*."

"We must have watched that four times in the last year. I'm tired of it."

Jack never tired of it—every time he watched it he found something new—but let it slide. He looked through the short stack of tapes.

"*Casablanca?*" he said and realized immediately what a bad choice that was.

"Dear God, no. That final good-bye scene . . . I can't handle that. Too close to home."

"All right then, I've got *Gone with the Wind*, *The Maltese Falcon*, and *To Kill a Mockingbird*."

"All too much like real life. I need some sort of fantasy—far, far from reality."

"How about *The Wizard of Oz*? That far enough?"

"Perfect. I could use—"

Her voice broke off as her head snapped to the right. Jack sensed it too—movement. He stiffened when he saw it. A small cry broke from Gia.

The Lilitongue had joined them in the sitting room.

If floated to a corner and hovered there. Waiting.

CHRISTMAS EVE

1

Jack started at the sound of a bell and felt Gia jump beside him.

The first thing he'd done after the Lilitongue's appearance was to angle the couch so they didn't have to look at the damned thing. He felt as if it was watching him.

They'd followed *The Wizard of Oz* with *To Kill a Mockingbird*. After that, with Vicky asleep a few feet away, they'd snuggled and tried to create a day-by-day review of the good times and bad times in their too-few years together.

Tried. Gia kept returning to their baby, saying that Jack would never see his child and the baby would never know her father.

Jack tried to lighten it up just a little by correcting her—*his* father—and insisting that the baby was going to be a boy.

And then a chime.

Gia started. "The doorbell? Who could be—?" She broke off. "Unless . . ."

Jack had the same thought. "Tom? Can't be."

"Can you think of anyone else who'd be out there at this hour? The sun's not even up."

Jack couldn't. He pushed himself upright and headed for the door.

"I'll get rid of him."

Gia followed. "Don't be too hard on him."

"Yeah, right. He's why we're in this spot."

"I know. But still . . ."

Jack pulled open the door and, sure enough, there stood Tom with a small shopping bag.

"Hello, Jack . . . Gia. I—"

"This isn't a good time, Tom."

"I know it's not. I mean, how could it be? But I just wanted to sit down with you for a couple of minutes and tell you a few things while we have a drink."

"I'm not thirsty."

"Please, Jack? Please? Just a couple of minutes?"

He felt Gia's hand against the small of his back as she spoke.

"A few minutes, Jack. We can spare him a few minutes."

A refusal sprang to his lips but he repressed it. Now, of all times, was not the time to argue. Besides, he was too tired for an argument. He'd had maybe three hours sleep in as many days.

He stepped back and opened the door.

"A few minutes. No more."

"Great. Thanks so much." He bustled inside. "Gia, could I trouble you for a couple of glasses?"

Jack said, "I told you I'm not thirsty."

He pulled a bottle of scotch from the bag and held it up.

"You don't drink this because you're thirsty. It's Old Pulteney single cask. It's thirty-seven years old, a hundred proof, and one of only three hundred twenty-four bottles. Please share some with me, Jack."

"I'll get the glasses," Gia said.

As she headed for the dining room, Jack reconsidered. Though mostly a beer drinker he had always liked Old Pulteney. And this batch had been casked before he was born. He wondered how it would taste.

And who knew when he'd ever taste scotch of any kind again?

"Okay, but just one."

"That's all I'm asking."

Gia met them in the sitting room with a pair of small crystal tumblers.

"Should I get ice?"

Tom uncorked the bottle. "Oh, no. You never dilute something this old and rare."

He poured two fingers' worth into each of the glasses and handed one to Jack.

"Prepare yourself for a treat, brother."

Jack sipped. It burned his tongue but left a wonderful aftertaste.

He had to nod his appreciation. "Good."

"Good? It's great! But can we sit down? I've got a few things I want to say."

Gia said, "I'll leave you two alone. But not for too long."

"This won't take long. I swear."

Jack hated to see Gia go. He didn't want her out of his sight during the fleeting time he had left. Another reason to resent Tom. But he put on a bland expression and dropped into a chair.

"Okay. A few minutes, but that's all."

Tom lowered himself onto the edge of a facing chair.

"That's all I want." He sipped. "But keep drinking or this will evaporate."

Jack complied. Damn, this was good.

"Look, Jack . . . I know I've been a lousy brother. Hell, I've been a lousy husband, father, and judge as well. I simply never had the opportunity to step back and see what I'd become. I was always too tied up with trying to keep all my lies straight. These past few weeks with you have opened my eyes. I look at you and see what I might have been."

Jack took another sip and cocked his head. Was he for real? This wasn't the Tom he'd come to know.

"You really believe that?"

"Nah," he said with a sharp, low laugh. "I don't mean I could be doing what you do. I mean . . . I'm not sure what I mean."

Tom took a sip and put the tumbler down on the rug next to his chair leg, then leaned forward with his hands clasped before him.

"I was sitting in your place thinking tonight how you're my closest living blood relative."

"What about your kids?"

He shrugged. "They're only half me. They're half Skank from Hell too. No, you and I came from the same place."

Jack had no idea where this was going, but he'd let him ramble for another minute or two. He gave a noncommittal shrug and drained his glass.

Tom popped out of his chair with the bottle and his own empty tumbler.

"Time for another hit."

Jack was already feeling a little buzz. But nothing wrong with that. He could handle another taste.

"Okay, but a light one."

Tom poured with a heavy hand. Three fingers this time into Jack's and his own. Then he returned to his seat.

"Isn't it strange, Jack, how you know exactly who you are, but only a chosen few in this whole city know you exist? Me? Even before all the trouble, just about everybody in Philly knew my name. But as for *who* I was, I had no idea. Never cared to look. And then in these past few weeks, when I did try to find myself—is that an overworked phrase, or what? When I did go looking, I couldn't find anyone. Nobody home."

Unable to refute that, Jack sipped his scotch instead.

"It's a sad truth, Jack, but I've realized I have no substance. I'm nothing. I'm like a hologram. A ghost. I'm barely here. My kids don't trust me—no reason they should after the way I cheated on their mothers. I'm a recidivist womanizer. Consequently the two Skanks from Hell loathe me, and current wifey number three is definitely not a fan. I'm papier mâché, Jack. If anyone tried to lean on me for support they'd fall on their ass."

Jack blinked. Was that a catch in Tom's voice? Had to be the scotch.

The room swam before him. Definitely the scotch. Not that Tom was boring, just . . . God, he was tired. Better put the glass down before he dropped it. Oh, look . . . almost empty. When did he finish it? He reached to place it on the end table but it slipped from his fingers. He watched it fall . . . in slo mo. Had to close his eyes, just for a minute . . . just for a few seconds . . .

But before he drifted off he thought he heard Tom say something about becoming the big brother again, about it being time to look out for his little brother, about doing the right thing.

But Jack figured he was imagining it. Had to be.

2

-0:28

"Gia?"

She started at the sound of her name. She'd been sitting at the kitchen table, staring at nothing, lost in a helpless, hopeless funk.

She looked up and saw Tom standing in the doorway. He had a wild look in his eyes.

"You're leaving?" she said.

He shook his head. "Not immediately, but soon. Maybe."

"I'm—"

He motioned her down the hall. "Come on back to the sitting room. I need your help with something."

Wondering what he was talking about, she followed. She gasped when she saw Jack slumped in a chair, his chin on his chest, his head lolling to the side.

"He fell *asleep?*"

"Well, yes and no. It's not what you think. Yes, I put him out, but not with my ramblings. I had a little help."

"I don't . . ." She stepped over to Jack and shook his shoulder. "Jack? Jack, wake up." He didn't stir, not the slightest. Alarmed, she turned to Tom. "What's wrong with him?"

"I knocked him out."

"What?"

He lifted the scotch bottle. "With this."

Gia felt a cold hand squeeze her heart.

"Talk sense, damn it!"

"Okay. Sorry. Here goes: I got to thinking about a lot of things tonight—how you took the Stain from Vicky and how Jack took the Stain from you, and how I couldn't imagine a single person in the world taking it from me." He sounded on the verge of tears as he shook his head. "To have somebody willing to give up their life for me— God, what would that be like?"

"Oh, there must be—"

He held up his hand. "Trust me: no one. Not after all the bridges I've burned. And I got to thinking about the way your eyes glow when you look at Jack, and the way your voice sounded when you talked about him being your rock, which I took to mean your hero. Am I right?"

Dumbstruck, Gia could only nod.

"Right. And I knew there wasn't a person alive who'd look at me or speak of me that way. I've never been any-body's hero—not even to my kids. A kid should be able to look at his dad just once in his life and say, 'That's who I want to be like.' I can't imagine one of my kids saying that. Ever. And I don't blame them. Why should they? I never gave them a reason."

Gia's confusion was giving way to fury. She clipped the words as she spoke them.

"But what's this got to do with putting Jack to sleep?"

"Well, as I was visiting my friendly neighborhood drug dealer—"

"Drugs? You?"

He shrugged. "I've been clean awhile, but the events of the last three or so days nudged me back into some old bad habits. So anyway, I'm listening to him list his wares as he's wont to do, and I hear him mention Georgia Home Boy. Now, he's mentioned this every time, but tonight, feeling the way I did, it hit me right between the eyes. That was the answer."

"Answer to what? What's Georgia—?"

"Georgia Home Boy—the acronym of which is GHB, which stands for gamma-hydroxy-butyrate or something like that. It's also called Grievous Bodily Harm, which yields the wrong acronym, but then, you can't expect the folks who use this stuff to be Einsteins. Anyway, it's one of those so-called date-rape drugs."

A flash of rage burned through Gia. "You gave Jack a date-rape drug?"

He smiled and held up the bottle. "Right in here. Odorless, colorless, and pretty much tasteless, especially in something like scotch. Mix it with alcohol—this batch is one-hundred proof—and it's good night, Nellie."

"But weren't you—?"

"Drinking it too?" He shook his head. "Just pretending. There's a wet spot next to my chair where I dumped it. Sorry about the rug."

Who cared about the rug?

"You . . . you still haven't told me why."

He put down the bottle, reached into the shopping bag, and came up with a familiar-looking container.

"You remember this, don't you?"

She nodded, her mouth dry.

Tom put the container down and stepped toward Jack.

"Okay, then let's put it to work."

Gia's legs went rubbery. She had to grab the back of the chair to stay upright.

"You can't. It won't work. The book said—"

"I know what the book said, and I'm sure it's right.

But there doesn't seem to be any intelligence behind the Lilitongue. Like it's designed to perform certain tasks, and allow certain things within certain limits. I got to thinking that if it's just a dumb infernal device, maybe I can fool it."

Gia had a sense of where this might be going but dared not acknowledge it. Hoping . . . believing . . . she'd be setting herself up for a crushing fall.

"You?"

"Well, people have been saying how much we look alike. Hell, if I was ten years younger and twenty pounds lighter—okay, forty pounds lighter—they might think we were twins. Our DNA's *got* to be similar. And I thought, maybe we're enough alike to confuse the Lilitongue . . . allow me to grab the Stain because maybe it won't recognize the difference between us."

Gia couldn't speak past the fist she'd pressed against her mouth.

Tom looked at her. "Kind of a shock, hmmm? I'm kind of shocked myself. And I'll tell you flat out I'm scared witless. So help me open his shirt before I change my mind."

Gia could only nod. Her fingers were numb, clumsy as she fumbled at the buttons. Jack was so out of it, almost comatose.

Finally she found her voice. "But why drug him like this?"

Tom snorted. "Come on. You know the answer to that. You've known him for years and I've only known the grown Jack for three weeks, but I know how he'd react. And so do you."

Gia nodded. "He wouldn't let you."

"Right. A month—hell, a week ago I'd have thought no one but an imbecile would turn down an offer like this. But knowing what I know about Jack, he'd be just that imbecile. But I can see now it's not stupidity, it's not foolishness. It's . . . it's being the rock you talked about. He'd see it as his problem and he'd solve it or find a way through it, and no way would he allow anyone, especially his no-account brother, to stand in and take the fall for him. Am I right or am I right?"

"You're right," Gia said as she finished unbuttoning the shirt. "You are so right."

What else was there to say? Tom had nailed his brother.

Together she and Tom pulled up Jack's underlying T-shirt. She gasped when she saw the edges of the Stain only millimeters apart.

"Jesus," Tom breathed. "Better hurry."

"But . . ." She couldn't help it: She was baffled. "Why?"

Tom began unbuttoning his own shirt and pulling it off.

"Well, as I said before, you were willing to take Vicky's place, Jack was willing to take yours, so I guess it's up to me to take Jack's—if I can."

Gia watched in disbelieving awe as he stood bare-chested and opened the container. He smeared the mixture on both his palms and looked at her.

"Okay. How does this work?"

"You . . ." Her voice sounded faint, miles away. "You press your hand over the Stain and wish it for your own."

He frowned. "Wish? Really? That's it?"

Gia nodded, fearing if she spoke she might break whatever spell was at work here.

Tom took a tremulous breath. "Okay. Here goes. I'm going to use both hands. A two-pronged approach, you might say."

She noticed how his hands wavered and trembled as they approached the Stain, but he kept moving them forward until his palms lay flat against Jack's skin, one on each end of the creeping black band.

"And now I wish."

Gia held her breath as Tom closed his eyes. A voice filled her head saying, *Please, God, oh please, oh please, oh, please.*

He suddenly stiffened, his arms straightening and jittering, his body shaking as if he'd grabbed a hot electric wire. His eyes snapped open as he arched his back and cried out in agony.

And then Gia noticed a mark on the back of each hand—black . . . and lengthening, stretching over Tom's trembling wrists, then up his shaking arms to his shoulders, then disappearing onto his back. She watched in horrid fascination as a black band snaked around each side of his chest to stop bare millimeters apart over his breastbone.

At last he stopped shaking. His hands pulled from Jack as he staggered back.

Gia turned from Tom to Jack, looking for the Stain. But Jack's skin was clear, unmarred.

She dropped to her knees next to him and sobbed.

Saved!

3

-0:08

When pain ceased, when he'd regained some modicum of control over his swaying, trembling body, it took all of Tom's will not to drop beside Gia and sob along with her. But with terror, not relief.

He looked down at his chest. The itching told him what he'd find, but he had to see. A low moan escaped at the sight of those black bands. At first glance they looked as if their ends were already touching, then he spotted a hairline of clear skin between them.

Since this crazy idea had gripped him, he'd known his chance of success was slim to none. But he'd figured that when his grand gesture failed, he'd rise in Gia's estimation simply for trying.

But he'd succeeded and this sent tremors of terror and triumph roiling through him. Part of him screaming in panic, and another part proud, cheering.

Gradually the feelings faded, replaced by a strange peace, a peace like nothing he had ever known.

Still no guarantee that this Lilitongue escape was going to happen. Best-case scenario was that it would be a bust and he'd end up standing here with this big brown mark encircling his body. But that would score even more points with Gia. And Jack too. They'd *owe* him.

But that wasn't what had spurred him.

"Gia," he said softly.

She looked up at him and saw in her blue eyes what he'd longed to see: Some—not all, but a good deal—of the light that shone in those eyes when she looked at Jack.

"I don't know what to say, Tom. I don't know how to thank you."

He tried to keep that stiff upper lip. "No worry about that. There's no time to thank me."

She raised her hands. "This . . . I . . . I never . . ."

She seemed at a loss for words so he helped her along.

"Never expected something like this from me? Yeah, well, that's the sad part, isn't it. Truth is, I'm more surprised than anyone. And until a few hours ago, I never expected anything like this from me either. But I got to thinking about Jack's life and mine, comparing them. I asked myself which I'd rather have led, and the answer was Jack's. And I asked myself who I'd rather be, even with the unknown fate facing Jack, and the answer was still Jack.

"But it was too late for me. Or was it? Maybe I could, in a way, still be him. So I asked myself what would Jack do."

"WWJD," Gia whispered.

"What?"

"Nothing."

"So anyway, I asked myself what he'd do if situations

were reversed—if he'd brought the Lilitongue into my life and I'd wound up with the Stain. No question, is there? He'd do the right thing. So that's what I did. I guess that makes me Repairman Tom. But I don't want you to think this is completely selfless. I get something too."

Gia gave him a questioning look.

"I get to see that look in your eyes when you look at me now. I wanted that from someone just once in my life, and I especially wanted it from you."

"Tom . . ."

"Let me finish. This has got to be the best thing I've ever done in my life. Really. When would I ever get another chance to do something this worthwhile? And this isn't such a heroic thing for me. Because strangely enough, I'm not afraid of what's going to happen here— even if it means dying. One moment I'll be here, and the next I won't. I've got to tell you, not being here won't be so bad, not after the way I've fu—I've so royally screwed up my life."

She shook her head. "What—?"

Obviously Jack hadn't told her the details.

I owe you for that one, little brother.

"Never mind. Suffice it to say I've nothing to look forward to but pain and disgrace, while Jack's got a future with you and Vicky, everything coming his way, including fatherhood. Maybe this isn't so heroic. Maybe it's a way out of having to face the consequences of how I've been wasting my life. Because I'm tired . . . so tired of living the way I do. I need a clean break. You can't imagine what kind of relief that's going to be."

He caught movement out of the corner of his eye. An oval shape. The Lilitongue. He hadn't known it was here.

And hell, it was moving toward him. He stood frozen as it came within arm's reach and then started to rise. It stopped a couple of feet over his head and hovered.

Tom felt his bladder clench, screaming to empty. Pain shot through his pelvis as he held back. He didn't want a wet stain spreading down the front of his pants to be part of Gia's last sight of him.

He saw the horror in Gia's eyes as she stared at the Lilitongue above him. No! Don't look at that. Look at *me*.

"I guess this means I don't have much time," he said, hurrying his words past a sawdust tongue. "I'm looking at it this way: Letting this thing take me away won't mean death. I'm pretty sure the guy who made the Lilitongue didn't go to all that trouble just to commit suicide. So I figure there's another kind of life where I'm going." God, he hoped he was right. "And maybe it's a better, simpler life. And maybe because I did this one right thing here, maybe I'll have it better there—I'll *be* better there."

He felt his skin begin to tingle and he ignored his bladder as it redoubled its efforts to empty.

"Think well of me, Gia. Please? I'm hoping that at least one person in this world will speak well of me after I'm gone. And tell Jack I said merry Christmas. This is his big brother's gift to him."

And then he felt the band of pigment around his chest begin to constrict, felt his skin tingle all over. The room began to fade as the tingling increased. Gia was on her feet, her mouth open. Ever so faintly he heard her scream, and then Gia and Jack and Vicky and Sutton Square and the world he knew were gone.

4

0:00

Gia couldn't hold back a scream as Tom and the Lilitongue faded from sight, leaving nothing more than a waft of cool air. She stared at the empty spot, then turned to Jack. His eyes were open, staring, but he looked disoriented.

"Jack . . . Jack, he's gone!"

5

Gia's scream had pulled him to consciousness. His vision blurred as he looked at her. She stood openmouthed, with her hands against her cheeks, like *The Scream*. Then her lips moved. He tried to hear but the words seemed garbled.

Was this how the end was going to come? Lethargy . . . cottonmouth . . . like a colossal hangover as the Lilitongue—?

Wait. Hangover . . . he'd been drinking scotch with Tom. He knew he hadn't had much sleep lately, but a couple of shots shouldn't make him feel like he'd chugged a whole bottle.

And where was Tom?

Jack looked around. No sign of him. Vicky still asleep on the couch. Gia's scream hadn't awakened her. But then, Vicky could sleep through a nuclear holocaust. Gia stood a couple of feet away, but no Tom.

And no Lilitongue.

He searched the corners but they were empty. Had it moved?

"Gia . . . where's Tom? And where's the Li—?" His thickened tongue couldn't form the word. "Where's that thing?"

Tears streamed down her face. "It's gone. And it took Tom with it."

"What?"

Straightening up on the couch, he pulled open his shirt—who'd unbuttoned it?—and looked down at his chest. The Stain—gone.

He stared at Gia again and saw her nodding.

And then she told him about Tom drugging the scotch, about Tom taking the Stain, able to because they were brothers, about him standing near the center of the room and disappearing.

She had to be talking about another Tom.

Maybe this was how you escaped with the Lilitongue: You wound up in an alternate reality that seemed the same but wasn't.

Because the Tom Jack knew would never—

Gia was talking about how Tom had said he had nothing to look forward to but pain and disgrace, while Jack had so much to live for . . .

Unbelievable . . . a mercilessly overworked word, but this was truly unbelievable. If Gia had told him that Tom had morphed into an alien from the Crab Nebula, he might have bought it before this wild tale.

But as she spoke it began to dawn on Jack that this was for real. Tom had taken his place.

"And he just disappeared?"

She nodded as tears streamed down her cheeks. "He and that thing just . . . faded away. Jack, I just saw a man vanish into thin air. I still can't believe it."

According to the *Compendium*, the Lilitongue would return to its place of origin—hopefully a hundred feet underground now—but Tom . . . where was Tom?

Gia said, "Before he went, the last thing he said was that this was his Christmas gift . . . that I should wish you a merry Christmas."

Tom? Good God, Tom . . .

Jack didn't know what to say, or how to feel.

"I can't say I'm not happy to still be here, but this wasn't the way . . . the price . . . and to be saved by Tom of all people . . ."

Gia looked at him. "I know you wanted to fix it yourself. And maybe you did."

"I was out cold."

"Yes, but I gathered from what he said that he was in more than a little trouble, that he'd done a lot of wrong. Maybe his time with you changed him, made it possible for him to decide to do this. Maybe you showed him a different way to act, to behave."

Tom, Jack thought, you never gave me a clue you had it in you. I owe you. Wherever you are, I hope you know that. Thanks, bro.

And then Gia was on Jack's lap, her arms around his neck in a stranglehold, talking through sobs.

"Thank God you're still here. I felt terrible when I saw him fade away. Then I felt this overwhelming joy when I saw you still on the couch. And then this terrible guilt for being glad it was Tom instead of you." She buried her face deeper against his shoulder. "Why did something like this have to happen? *Why?*"

Jack had no answer.

But he sensed a design here. He'd lost his father and brother—his closest surviving relatives—in less than three weeks.

But had he been the real target?

Had he been scheduled to go down at La Guardia? If he'd waited to help Dad with his bag, he'd have most likely wound up in the morgue on a neighboring gurney.

And if he'd been the Lilitongue's target, Tom had foiled that little plan at the last minute.

Why him? Why anybody?

And then Joey's dying words echoed through his head:

It wasn't them . . . it's bigger than them . . . something else going on.

What else going on?

He hoped he was just being paranoid, but he'd been warned of pain to come. Was this it? Would it stop here?

Or would . . .

He stared over Gia's shoulder at Vicky. These two precious people . . . would proximity to him put them in danger?

He closed his eyes and tightened his grip on Gia. Nothing he could do but keep close watch and take it day by day . . . day by day . . .

www.repairmanjack.com

Look for

HARBINGERS

A Repairman Jack novel
(0-765-31276-X)

by F. PAUL WILSON

**Now available in hardcover
from Tom Doherty Associates**

CPSIA information can be obtained
at www.ICGtesting.com
Printed in the USA
LVOW11s0807121017
552144LV00001B/106/P